CHASING CHARITY

Texas Fortunes — Book No. 2

CHASING CHARITY

Marcia Gruver

18915 96th ave NW

Stanwood

Warm Beach Camp

S

on 88th & Marine Drive

turn west toward

Susan Bay turn right

on 96

4th house & light green

house w/ white

Balcony

BARBOUR
PUBLISHING

ISBN 978-1-60260-206-9

All scripture quotations are taken from the King James Version of the Bible.

This book is a work of fiction. Names, characters, places, and incidents are either products of the author's imagination or used fictitiously as explained in the athor's note. Any similarity to actual people, organizations, and/or events is purely coincidental.

For more information about Marcia Gruver, please access the author's Web site at the following Internet address:
http://www.marciagruver.com

Cover Design: The DesignWorks Group, Inc.

Published by Barbour Publishing, Inc., P.O. Box 719, Uhrichsville, OH 44683, www.barbourbooks.com

Our mission is to publish and distribute inspirational products offering exceptional value and biblical encouragement to the masses.

ecpa Member of the Evangelical Christian Publishers Association

Printed in the United States of America.

Dedication

To my daughter Tracy, my inspiration and my noblest creative endeavor.

Acknowledgments

To Mr. Lee Allen Gruver and Mr. Jerry Lee Ritter for your patience, your unwavering faith, and the generous loan of your names.

To Eileen Key, who nursed this manuscript in its infancy, and Elizabeth Ludwig, who held its hand and brought it home.

To the ladies in the Humble Museum and the Octavia Fields Branch Library in Humble, Texas, for answering my endless questions.

Other books by Marcia Gruver

Texas Fortunes Series:

Diamond Duo

Humble, Texas
January 1905

A plaintive cry of *purty, purty, purty* sounded from the treetops overhead. Charity Bloom glanced up and frowned. The redbird's compliment once caused her to flush with pleasure. Now it just made her mad.

Hush, deceitful scoundrel! I don't believe you anymore. Pretty was the last thing she felt and might never feel again.

Without the sun to warm her, the threadbare fabric of Charity's dress did little to prevent the north wind from biting at her back. Only sparse, mottled beams of light fought through the canopy of pine, so the trail into town hoarded the morning chill. She pulled her shawl closer and told herself the cold was the reason for her shivers. Relieved, she reached the trailhead and took her first grateful steps into the light.

The rapscallion cardinal hopped to a lower branch and made one last attempt to convince her before she moved out of range. She ignored him and pushed his song from her mind.

It wasn't long before another voice took its place. "It's too soon, daughter," Mama had cautioned. "You'll wind up lashed to the spit and roasted. Fresh scandal's scarce around these parts. Them spiteful cats are bound to gnaw on yours 'til the hide's wore off. Folks feast on others' misery."

Charity forced the words and the shame they conjured to a dark corner and covered them with righteous determination. Humble, Texas, was home, and they wouldn't drive her away. After all, she'd done no wrong—unless love and misplaced trust were sins.

She defiantly lifted her chin, only to lower it again and sigh as Main Street came into view. Humble was indeed her home, but the landscape had changed so much over the last week she hardly knew it. Scowling, she gazed eastward to Moonshine Hill with its towering oil derrick, the culprit to blame. Strange how the unrest in Humble rivaled the recent upheaval in her life. Otherwise unrelated, both events had landed in her lap with the force of a runaway train.

Reflected sun from a row of tin roofs across the way stabbed at her eyes. She shielded them with her hand then ducked into a strip of shade along the front of the dry goods store and headed for the Lone Star Hotel. Where the crowd became as thick as Mama's grits, she raised her elbows, steeled her resolve, and surged into the multitude.

Hordes of tents spread in an ever-widening circle from the heart of town, their occupants swarming like insects. The mingled voices, all shouting to be heard, made a deafening din, and Charity resisted the urge to hold her ears until she passed. Scores of men, women, and children spilled onto the street in droves, making it hard to gain any progress. She tried to stay head-down, mind on her business, but before long the meddlesome stares and huddles of pointing, whispering people weakened her resolve along with her knees. Mama was right. She was a hardheaded girl on a foolhardy mission.

"Hush now. Here she comes."

The words filtered back from just ahead on the boardwalk. Charity glanced up in time to see Elsa Pike bury a bony elbow in her daughter's ribs. The women strolled ahead of her, Mrs. Pike tall and thin next to the decidedly round Amy Jane. The pair put Charity in mind of the number ten. Taken together, they were ten times the trouble no matter how she ciphered.

They slowed their pace and waited while Charity caught up. Why hadn't she listened to Mama?

Mrs. Pike turned with a smile as sweet as caramel corn. "Hello, Charity. What a shock to see you in town. Feeling better so soon?" Amy Jane wore a sugary smile, too—as if seconds ago they weren't crouched, feeding on her misfortune.

She fought the urge to turn tail and run but braced herself and met them head-on. "I'm feeling fine, ma'am. Thank you for asking."

Mrs. Pike took Charity's hand in her long, gloved talons. "I want you to know how awfully bad we feel for you, dear."

Charity eased her hand free. "There's no need."

Mrs. Pike clucked her tongue then lowered her voice to a whisper. "Your poor mama. I hear she took in boarders to buy material for your wedding gown."

"And what an exquisite dress!" Amy Jane added, her voice too loud. "All that fandangle and fancywork. Your mama really outdid herself."

Charity cringed. A picture swam into her mind of Mama hunched in a circle of lantern light drawing a needle through tiny sequins with work-weary hands. More than once Charity found her asleep the next morning, her face pressed to the hard kitchen table.

She could manage disgrace and every indignity heaped upon her, but the memory of Mama's fingers, blistered for naught, dealt her shame. She lowered her head. "Yes, she worked powerful hard on it."

"You looked lovely in it, too, dear, with your hair swept up, black as pitch against all that lace." Mrs. Pike wagged a bony finger in Charity's face as if she were the culprit. "Your young man should hang his head for all the trouble he's caused."

"He's not my young man." Her correction came out a whisper neither woman seemed to hear.

A brisk wind had picked up, a low moan at first and then a howl through the center of town. It whistled under the boardwalk and gusted around them, plucking at Mrs. Pike's tall, jaunty hat and Amy Jane's balloon sleeves, frills she knew Mr. Pike could ill afford.

Charity held a tender spot for Shamus Pike, her departed papa's oldest friend. How many hours of backbreaking labor had it cost the poor man to provide his two peacocks their gaudy feathers?

Mama Peacock seemed in need of extra wings as she struggled to hold her bonnet while protecting her modesty and that of her daughter from the blustery wind. "But then, men never think of such things," she said from under the flapping brim. "I'm sure Daniel never gave a thought to your mama's sacrifice."

Amy Jane stepped closer and licked her lips, eyes wide in her round, freckled face. "About the dress. . .will you be selling it? I would dearly love to have it."

Mrs. Pike whirled on the girl. "Amy Jane! How utterly crass."

"What, Mother? I didn't leave Charity at the altar. I'm sure she has no use for it now."

The wind stopped as quickly as it had come, leaving behind a palpable hush.

Charity looked over their shoulders, past the low row of buildings, to the backdrop of tall Texas pine, longing to be at home in her room.

"What on earth would you do with Charity's dress?" Mrs. Pike asked.

"Wear it, silly. Did you forget I'm getting married in three months' time?"

"It won't fit you, dear. You're quite a bit larger than she is, you know."

Charity's head jerked up at this. *Poor Amy.*

Amy Jane looked indignant. "I've starved myself, or haven't you noticed? I'll be much smaller by then. And Mrs. Bloom could let it out for me." She glanced at Charity. "Couldn't she?"

Mrs. Pike shook her head. "Amy Jane, there's not enough material on that tiny dress to cover your backside, never mind the rest of you."

Charity fought the smile tugging at her lips as she watched them spit and spar, her presence forgotten. Amused, she slipped past and continued on her way. She felt a mite guilty for walking off without saying good-bye but had no stomach for the direction the conversation had taken. Besides, a peek over her shoulder at their waving arms and lively faces told her they hadn't noticed she'd gone.

"Charity Bloom! Wait right there, sugar."

Charity groaned. She didn't have to glance to see who'd

shouted, didn't need a look to know who charged her way. *Serves me right for having a laugh at Amy Jane's expense.*

It wasn't that she minded seeing Magdalena Dane. In fact, she loved Mama's old friend. She just didn't relish an encounter with her in the middle of town.

Mother Dane lifted the hem of her stylish blue dress and sashayed into the street, to the delight of the locals gathering behind her. Oblivious to them, she picked her way across the ruts and bore down on Charity. When she reached the boardwalk and stepped up, Charity attempted to speak, but the older woman pulled her so tightly against her ample, satin-covered bosom that just to breathe was enough. "My spunky girl!" Mother Dane cried. "Imagine that, you coming out so soon. Are you all right, precious?"

"I'm fine," she said, her words muffled by yards of cloth and copious flesh. "At least I will be when you turn me loose."

Mercifully, Mother Dane eased her grip and stepped back. "Don't put on a brave front for me. Go ahead and cry if you like. You have every reason to." Her anguished eyes searched Charity's face. "I haven't called on you, dear. Please forgive me. I didn't know what to say."

Charity reached for her hand. "I understand, I really do, but Mama laid out her deck of cards on Monday."

"She did?" Mother Dane's eyes grew wide and wet. The prying cluster of busybodies across the way mumbled and shuffled when she pulled a lace handkerchief from her bodice. "Dear, sweet Bertha. I thought she wouldn't ever want to see me again, much less play cards."

"Mother Dane, you know Mama better than that. She wouldn't cast off a friendship of thirty years' standing over something like this." She winked. "Much less a game of penny candy poker."

"Stop it, now! Honey, how can you jest? I've been distraught. Grievously vexed. How's your mama taking it?" She fanned herself with her hankie. "Bertha's my touchstone. I don't know what I'd do without her."

"Yes, ma'am, she knows that. You're hers as well." *And a more unlikely pair there never was.*

"She's been on my mind every second. You both have. If there's anything I can do, anything at all. . ."

"Goodness, no, you've done enough. Sending Nash out to the house with her wages was far too generous."

The truth was, Mama nearly split a gut when Mother Dane's hired man turned up with a fistful of money for the days she'd missed, but there was no need to mention that now. "Mama plans to work off every penny, but I'm ever so grateful. Having her home the last few days has meant the world to me."

"Of course it has." Mother Dane enveloped her again. "I shrink in my boots to think my own daughter caused you such pain—and after all you've meant to each other. She always was selfish and headstrong. But you already know that, don't you?" She moved Charity to arm's length and peered at her again. "Was there any warning? Any sign Emmy and Daniel might do such a thing?"

The question brought fresh the memory Charity had struggled for days to forget. In that instant she stood again at the altar of Free Grace Church, clothed in yards of sequined lace, while Daniel Clark walked away from her.

She watched again as Emmy's lovely silhouette stepped into the aisle, took two deep breaths, and ran—not toward Charity as she expected, but out the door on Daniel's heels. That was when she knew. Given the collective gasp from the assembled guests, they knew it, too.

Her cheeks flamed at the memory, and she cast an embarrassed glance across the street.

"Emily has disgraced our family in the past, that's for sure, yet no more than we expected," Mother Dane was saying. "But this! Leave it to my Emmy to be in the right place at the right time. She always was an opportunist."

The harsh words tugged at Charity's heart. "Maybe we should give her a chance to explain."

"Don't." Mother Dane held up her satin-gloved hand. "Don't you defend her, dear. Not after what she's done. Lord knows I love my daughter, but let's be frank. She'd not extend you the same courtesy."

Charity hesitated then had to nod.

"Besides, how can she explain when she's not talking? She's holed up in her room and won't let me in. Mind you, she doesn't have a thing to tell that I don't already know. All of Humble knows her guilty little secret."

Charity shook her head, not ready to accept what the words implied. "Whatever happened, I refuse to believe she meant to do me harm."

Pain flashed in Mother Dane's eyes. "I'm afraid the days for pretense are past, dear. We know Emmy's heart best, you and I. She may be confection on the outside; inside she's a festering sore."

For the second time that morning Charity longed to cover her ears. "Please don't."

Mother Dane lifted Charity's chin with her knuckle and gazed into her eyes. "It's true, though it hurts me to say it. I prayed she might be more like you, wished with all my heart you might influence her with your goodness." She shrugged, her countenance the picture of despair. "I guess it wasn't to be. I fear my only child is bound to deal me heartache."

Charity drew the teary-eyed woman into an embrace. Over a padded blue shoulder she noticed that the interest of the locals had drawn a crowd. Now a collection of curious strangers stood alongside her friends and neighbors, and Charity grew warm under their scrutiny. She fished a handkerchief from her skirt pocket and dabbed her friend's cheeks. "There now, you just brighten up some. Emmy will be fine. You'll see."

Mother Dane drew herself up and managed a shaky smile. "There you go fretting about me in the midst of your own suffering." She squeezed Charity's hand. "You're a good girl, Charity Bloom."

Charity summoned a wry smile. "If that's so, then I need to finish my errands and get home before Mama starts to worry."

"All right, darling. You run along. Do give Bertha my love."

"I will."

"And, sugar?"

Charity sighed and turned. She'd almost made good on her escape and wanted nothing more than to flee. "Yes, ma'am?"

"Before you go, may I offer one last word of encouragement?"

"Of course."

With eyes like thunderheads, Mother Dane cast a withering

glance at the gathered snoops. "Don't let these tongue-wags get at you. They're spewing nonsense. This was all Emmy's fault. . .and Daniel's. It had nothing to do with your mama."

"Mama?" Charity closed the distance between them. "What are they saying?"

Mother Dane's chin shot up. "Never you mind. That highfalutin Eunice Clark may consider her son too good for you, but Daniel's cut from different cloth. I don't believe for a minute he feels the same."

Charity's heart sank, because she knew the truth of it. The cloth Daniel was cut from didn't fall far from his mama's bolt. Though smitten with her, Daniel had been troubled that his fiancée was the daughter of a widowed servant. It didn't help that folks believed Mama to be mad as a hatter.

"What Daniel feels doesn't concern me anymore," Charity said with a lift of one shoulder. "It's over. There's no use trying to make sense of it now. I just want it behind me if this town will allow it."

Thankfully, Mother Dane's gaze held compassion, not pity. "Are you so certain it's over, dear? Daniel could have a change of heart."

Charity's spine stiffened. "But I won't."

Tears snuffed the flicker of hope in Mother Dane's brown eyes. "It's such a tragedy, then. Daniel was a good match for you, honey. All we might've hoped for. He could've given you so much."

"Hush, now," Charity soothed. "Don't worry about me for another minute. I'll be fine."

Mother Dane wiped her eyes. "Yes, you will. You're Bertha Bloom's daughter, aren't you?"

She squared her shoulders. "I am, and glad of it. Speaking of Mama, give me a kiss and let me be on my way. I left her elbow-deep in chores."

"Now there's a dear girl. Tell Bertha to take a few more days off and to look for me come Monday. Tell her to lay out those poker cards again. I got my hands on some candy corn."

Charity smiled. "You won't make it home with any, you know."

Mother Dane sniffed. "That remains to be seen. You just tell her, you hear?"

"Yes, ma'am."

She wagged her finger. "Don't forget."

"No, ma'am, I won't."

Charity moved away, painfully aware that those around her were reluctant to disperse. She wasn't sure what they'd hoped to witness between Emmy's mama and herself, but they seemed sorely disappointed by what they saw. Charity wanted only to finish her business and get home, so she quickened her pace and headed for the first of the only two stops on her list she still planned to make. The rest of her errands could wait for a better day—sometime next year perhaps.

Stubby Morgan had taken to fetching her mail from the commissary post office at Bender's Mill. Then he left it with Sam, the hotel clerk, saving Charity a trip out to the mill. Rumor had it that Stubby went to the trouble because he was sweet on her. She didn't think it so.

Inside the new hotel, she crossed the lobby, raising an eyebrow in greeting as she passed the huge portrait of Pleasant S. Humble, the town founder. Uncle Plez, as he was known by the locals, stared down at her from his place of honor, and she would have sworn she saw one bushy brow twitch.

Sam had the mail in his hands before she reached the front desk.

Charity thanked him and stepped aside to sort it. She tried not to think about Daniel, but his face and Emmy's, too, swam in her head, making it impossible to concentrate on the letters. What they'd done was sure to hurt later. Right now she felt only anger. Which influence had Daniel finally given in to—his mama's constant braying about marrying beneath himself or Emmy's pale ringlets and haunting blue eyes?

Hang Daniel. . .and Emmy, too. They deserve each other.

"Excuse me. . ."

Charity jumped so violently she nearly took leave of her shoes, and the stack of mail flew in every direction. She whirled to find a stranger in a wide-brimmed hat beaming down from a considerable height. She pressed her empty hands to her heart. "Goodness me! You startled me out of my wits."

"I sure did, didn't I? Such a start this early in the morning can't be good for a body."

Charity struggled to settle her pounding heart. "Sir, I'm now qualified to assure you it isn't." She gazed around at the letters and mail-order catalogs scattered over the lobby then scowled up at the man.

He stepped closer and tipped his hat. "Please forgive me, ma'am."

They were the proper words and gestures, all right, but Charity reckoned he'd seem more contrite if he could straighten his grinning face.

CHAPTER 2

The handsome young man laid aside his overstuffed bag and bent to retrieve Charity's mail. He was tall and lean-muscled, the padded shoulders of his brown jacket making him seem as broad as Shamus Pike's bull. His long legs sported slim trousers, full at the top and held up by blue suspenders. Fawn-colored hair, longer than she was used to seeing, curled out from under his hat, and except for a scruffy shadow, he had no facial hair. Even inside the dimly lit hotel, she could see that his eyes were green like hers and Mama's.

Watching him bob for letters like a child on an Easter hunt, she ducked her head to smile then laughed in spite of herself. He heard and glanced up, so she leaned to help, grateful for something to do until the heat cooled in her cheeks.

When they stood up together, he still beamed like a roguish boy. Feeling silly about catching his infectious grin, she sobered and cast him a guarded look. "Have you just arrived in town, sir?"

He took off his broad, stiff-brimmed hat and held it to his chest. "Yes, ma'am, I have. Name's Buddy Pierce."

She offered her hand. "Welcome to Humble, Mr. Pierce."

His work-roughened fingers enveloped hers. "Little lady, I won't mind a bit if you call me Buddy. In fact, I'd prefer it."

Charity paused to consider. His earnest face and clear-eyed stare seemed honest, genuine, and not a bit forward. "Very well. Buddy it is. Isn't that a sobriquet?"

He released her hand. "Beg your pardon?"

"Buddy's a nickname, am I right? What's the name your mama gave you?"

He managed to frown and smile at the same time. "Never you mind about that."

She wrinkled her nose. "It's that bad, is it? Well then, welcome to Humble, *Buddy*. I'm Charity. Charity Bloom."

"I know who you are." He hooked a thumb in Sam's direction. "The clerk told me all about you."

"He did?" She shot a look at Sam, her cheeks warming again. Surely he didn't mean. . .

The little man behind the desk watched her over the top of his glasses while pretending to write in his register. Watched *over* her might be closer to the truth. Since Papa died, Sam had made a habit of keeping an eye on her and even more diligently since strangers took possession of their streets.

"Charity's an unusual name, if you don't mind my saying. Real nice, though."

His deep, rumbling voice pulled her attention to the stranger's face—and such a nice face. When had he moved so much closer?

She took a tiny step back. "Thank you. It's from the Bible."

"Is that a fact? Let's see, how does it go? 'Charity suffereth long, and is kind.' Does that describe you, Miss Bloom?"

She met his mischievous eyes and raised her brow. "Not on most days, if I'm to be honest."

His smile revealed deep dimples. "Well, Charity-from-the-Bible, I'm about to test the measure of your kindness. It seems the procurator of this fine establishment can't accommodate me, so he suggested I speak with you. Is it true your mama lets rooms on occasion?"

So that's all Sam told him.

Relieved, she took the mail from his hands and added it to her pile. "That all depends, Mr. Pierce. Have you come to Humble chasing oil?"

He cocked his head to one side, his grin widening. "What makes you ask?"

She waited to see if he was joking. He wasn't.

"Mister, throw ten stones in the air and nine will land on some money-hungry dreamer come to get rich."

He nodded and motioned toward the street. "And all those people are here because of the strike."

It was a statement, not a question, but she answered anyway. "Most everyone you see, except for the locals kept here by stubbornness or greed."

Buddy laughed, and she liked the sound of it. "Do you fall into one of those categories?"

His directness put her off balance. As casually as possible, Charity faced a nearby desk and busied herself straightening the letters so they'd fit in her drawstring bag. They were all tucked inside before she glanced over her shoulder and answered him. "I failed to mention the rest—those too poor to get out." She shrugged. "Besides, where would I go? I've lived here all my life."

She scolded herself for such boldness with a stranger. What was there about the friendly cowboy that made her tongue clatter like a snake's rattle?

He worked an envelope from under the counter with the toe of his boot, picked it up, and placed it on her stack. "To answer your question, Miss Bloom, it seems you've got me pegged. I have to say yes, I've come here looking for oil." He held up one finger. "But if it hurts my chances for a room, I'll deny ever saying it." He wriggled his brows and grinned. "I could use a hot bath and a meal."

"My goodness, of course you could. Listen to me groaning about the boom when that's what brought you to town. Not to mention holding you here with a hollow stomach and no place to lay your head. I hope you'll forgive my rudeness."

"Nothing to forgive. Besides, I owe you after the fright I gave you."

"Yes, you do," she scolded then smiled up at him. "Have you traveled far?"

He lifted his chin. "All the way from St. Louis, Missouri."

Charity stopped fidgeting with the mail and gaped. "Where they held the World's Fair?"

"Ah! The Louisiana Purchase Exposition. Quite a show."

"You were there? How wonderful! My dearest friend—that is, a girl here in town—and her mama went. They came home filling our ears. I would love to see such a thing."

He cocked his head to one side. "Is that so? I got the notion you don't like crowds."

She rolled Mama's Sears catalog and shoved it into her bag. "It's not crowds I mind, Mr. Pierce. I just don't like tripping over people in my own backyard."

He laughed. "If I promise to steer clear of your feet, can you find room in your backyard for one more wayward soul?"

The man had positively no sense for the proper amount of space to allow between them, and somehow his nearness affected her breathing. She shifted her weight away from him then tilted her head to meet his hopeful gaze. "Truthfully, we're out of the boardinghouse business, but there's a chance I might be able to help. Mama will have the final say though." She gathered her courage and blurted her brazen offer. "I have one quick stop to make at the general store; then I'll be going home. Would you care to follow along and ask her?"

Buddy dropped his hat on his head and hitched up his bag. "Yes, ma'am, I surely would."

She held up her hand. "Just one more thing. I'm afraid Mama don't take kindly to oilmen. How are you at dodging rotten eggs?"

His eyes grew wide. "Not too good, I reckon. I make for a sizable target."

Charity laughed and made for the door. "Come on. You'll be safe with me."

In front of the general store, Buddy took one look through the window at the jostling mob and said he'd wait for her outside. She left him leaning beside a barrel of brooms, one booted foot braced against the wall.

Despite impatient moans and grumbles, the beaming clerk allowed Charity to slip to the front of the line with Mama's list. She felt bad about it at first then decided there should be some recompense to the locals for the loss of peace and quiet.

Outside, Charity motioned to Buddy, and he fell into step behind her. She moved deftly through the crowd but had to stop and wait for him a time or two when his large frame and overstuffed bag caused a jam on the teeming boardwalk. She stole a few discreet glances while she waited. Buddy Pierce happened to be easy on the eyes.

"Nice little town you have here," he shouted as he drew near.

"It used to be," she said and pushed ahead of him again.

He said something else Charity didn't hear, so she just smiled and shrugged her shoulders. While they passed in front of the noisy tents, they gave up any attempt at talking.

Buzzards circled above the towering wall of trees up ahead, and Charity wondered what lay dead or dying on the forest floor. So many harsh, greedy men had come to town she knew it could as likely be a man as an animal, though the thick trees and underbrush would not easily give up the information.

Farther out away from the tents it grew quieter, and Buddy tried again. "What changed?"

"Excuse me?"

He came alongside her. "You said it used to be nice. What changed?"

"Mr. D. R. Beatty hit himself a gusher." Her mouth twisted like she'd sucked a lemon. Less than pretty, no doubt, but she couldn't help it. The sound of that man's name boiled her insides. "The multitude flocked here like Humble was the Promised Land. You've never seen the like."

"And there went your town."

"Yes, there went my town. Now our sons and brothers rub shoulders with men who'd plant a knife in your middle for a fifteen-cent bottle of booze. Two-bit saloons and gambling houses built from spit and sawmill scrap sprang up overnight. Not to mention those *other* houses set on fleecing our men of their dignity as well as their hard-earned money."

She blushed but noticed he did, too. "Forgive my candor, Mr. Pierce, but Humble used to be peaceful, filled with simple, good-hearted folk. A perfect place to live"—she glanced up and their eyes met—"if you like that sort of thing. I suppose you prefer the excitement of the big city."

Buddy flashed his teeth and winked. "There's where you're wrong. I'm a country boy at heart."

She smiled back. "A country boy with a lust for treasure?"

"Lust? No, ma'am, not me. I wouldn't turn away a blessing, but the Good Book teaches not to lay up treasure here on earth."

"Oh, you read the scriptures?"

"I try to make it a habit."

"Well, it's a good habit to have. However, I must confess that now I'm confused. Back there you said you were here because of the oil. From what I hear, striking oil brings more than a blessing. It can make a man mighty rich."

He nodded. "True enough, but I'm just a working man earning my way. I'm here to represent another fellow. A wealthy operator out of Beaumont. It's men like him who wind up with all the money."

"I see." She wasn't sure why the information made her feel better about him. His affairs were certainly none of her business.

"I'll be heading up a crew of his men that are due into Humble today."

"Today? Won't they need a place to stay, too?"

He laughed. "They're smarter than me. They had the foresight to reserve rooms."

Just ahead, Charity's mama bolted through the yard onto the dirt road, juggling a white chicken. She tripped on the hem of her faded skirt but righted herself before she went down. Long strands of salt-and-pepper hair had worked free from her disheveled bun, streaming out behind her as she ran. Feathers dotted her head and clung to her glowing face, and she was missing a shoe. A dark substance covered both feet and soaked the hem of her skirt. The distressed chicken appeared to have been dipped to the drumsticks in tar.

"Charity," she called. "Come a'runnin', baby. The chickens are loose again."

"Blast those infernal coons," Charity said and then drew up her skirts and ran.

"Raccoons?" Buddy Pierce had come alongside, his bag bouncing against his legs as he loped. "I thought she said chickens."

"The coons have learned to break into the coops. . .after the feed. There's no lock that'll keep them out."

"Really? Clever creatures."

"Indeed. Trouble is, they lack the proper manners to close the door behind them when they leave."

Charity ran past her mama then stopped and looked back.

Mama stood staring up at Mr. Pierce, the escaped chickens forgotten. "Well now, who you got here, sugar?"

Mr. Pierce held out his hand but drew it back after a quick glance at Mama's black fingers. He nodded instead. "Buddy Pierce, ma'am."

She cocked her head. "Bertha Bloom. Nice to meet you, sonny."

Charity watched her take a long, slow reckoning of Mr. Pierce. She felt a sudden affinity with whatever unfortunate creature lay in the stand of pines watching the carrion birds circle overhead, drawing nearer with every pass. She braced herself for what was bound to come out of Mama's mouth.

"Where'd you turn up this one, Charity? He's a big 'un. Right pretty, too."

Charity groaned. It was worse than she'd expected. "Mama, behave. Allow me to apologize for her, Mr. Pierce. She's become quite bold, if not brazen, in her old age."

"And rightfully so," Mama said. "Contending with body parts that drape south and wayward facial hair gives me leave to be naughty on occasion. Don't you think so, Mr. Pierce?"

Buddy's mouth worked hard at stifling a grin. "I can see your point, and that's for sure, Mrs. Bloom."

Mama leaned in as close as the chicken and her short stature would allow and presented her top lip to Mr. Pierce. "Look here, I'm sporting a 'stache to rival Teddy Roosevelt's. Pert near as impressive as the first lady's." She threw back her head and cackled in concert with the chicken.

"Oh, Mama, you're just plain scandalous. Pay her no mind, Mr. Pierce, or she'll only get worse. And where on earth is your shoe, Mama? You'll catch your death."

Buddy Pierce was paying little attention now to her mama's tomfoolery. He had focused on the hen, his hands edging in its direction, as if eager to take hold of it. "Mrs. Bloom, if I could just have a closer look at that chicken. . ."

Mama sized him up with a glance then passed him the flustered hen. "Ain't you never seen a yard bird before?"

"One or two, but none as interesting as this one. Where did you say you caught it?"

"Back yonder." She gave a toss of her head toward the rear of their place. "In the bottom."

"The bottom of what?"

Charity interpreted for him. "Out back of our property, in the low spot."

Mama nodded. "Blasted piney-woods rooters got it all dug up out there."

"Rooters?"

"Hogs, mister. Wild hogs. You might be a pleasure to look at, but you sure don't know much."

"Mama!"

Mr. Pierce continued unperturbed. "Do you own this property, Mrs. Bloom?"

Mama propped her hands on her hips, pressing gooey impressions of her fingers onto her skirt. "Why, yes, I own it. My man, Thad—God rest him—held it free and clear before we ever married. This place has been mine for nigh on to twenty-eight years."

"Do you mind if I take a look?"

She frowned. "Ain't nothin' back there 'cept swamp water and Texas gumbo. Mud," she corrected for Buddy's benefit. "Black Texas mud." She pulled back her skirt and thrust out her bare foot as evidence, squeezing her toes together until thick sludge oozed from between them.

Mr. Pierce examined her foot and nodded. "If it's where you've been chasing this chicken, then I'd sure like to see it."

She shrugged, her bony shoulders pulling even with her ears. "Young man, I can't imagine what you find so interesting about a fool chicken and an old woman dim-witted enough to chase it through a bog, but suit yourself. Anyways, you can fetch out my shoe. Follow me."

CHAPTER 3

It took Buddy Pierce ten minutes flat to see what he wanted to see down in the bog. Then he'd taken off for town like a branded cat. He was back now, having hauled two flustered men with him. Charity heard them crashing through the yaupon thicket, shouting and laughing as if they'd taken leave of their senses.

Mama watched from the rickety stoop, hands on her hips, her head bobbing like a demented bird as she followed their movements through the brush.

Charity crossed the yard to the edge of the porch and gazed up at her. "Where's your bonnet?"

Mama groped the top of her head, her eyes still trained on the bushes. "Must be in the bog."

A riotous shout gave Charity a start and pulled her gaze back to the thicket. "What will happen, Mama?"

"Cain't say, baby. Too soon to tell."

"Mr. Pierce said we got oil back there."

"That's what he said, all right."

"How can that be?" Charity's voice took on an edge. "How could oil have been there all along, and we never knew?"

"Sometimes you cain't see what you ain't looking for." Mama turned startled eyes her way. "Hush now. Here they come."

Buddy strode through the cut ahead of the other two men. All three were covered in mud. Of the lot, it would be hard to say who wore the silliest grin. One of the men, every bit as tall as Buddy but gawky and rawboned, carried several bottles of the black muck, each sealed with a cork. When Charity glanced his way, his smile widened, and he nodded a greeting. Up close, despite being awkward and thin, he was every bit as handsome as Buddy, too.

"Mrs. Bloom, where's the deed to your property?" This from the stocky, dark-haired man who balanced an odd-looking instrument on his shoulder.

Mama looked him over. "Who's asking?"

Buddy stepped forward, still beaming, and gestured to his companion. "Mrs. Bloom, this here's Mr. Lee Allen." Then he pointed at the lanky young man. "That's Jerry Ritter. These are the gentlemen I told you about."

Mama nodded at each one in turn.

Mr. Allen advanced a step so he could rest his load on the rail. He gazed up at Mama with kind blue eyes. "Ma'am, just see to it your deed is safe. There are desperate and unscrupulous men in this town. You ladies living out here alone. . .well, I wouldn't want you taken advantage of, or worse."

Mama looked at Buddy. "Is that this feller's way of saying you got good news for me?"

Buddy preened. "We can't be certain yet, but it sure looks good. Ain't that right, Lee?"

Buddy's excitement rekindled the spark in Mr. Allen, spreading a broad smile over his weathered cheeks. He nodded at Buddy then at Mama. As quick as it came, the smile disappeared. "Mrs. Bloom, is there someplace in town you all could stay?"

Charity cut around Mr. Allen and his equipment to face him squarely. "Why can't we stay right here?"

"It's ain't safe, ma'am." He answered Charity's question, but his eyes searched her mama's face.

Mama regarded Buddy with a raised brow. "When I said you could look for oil on my land, you never said nothing about us leaving. Forget it. We ain't going." She snorted. "Besides, I got nothing to fear in my own home. The Winchester my man left me warrants that."

Buddy stepped forward. "There's another reason besides the

danger." He glanced at Charity, his eyes pleading for support she couldn't give. "Mrs. Bloom, you agreed that if I saw the need, you'd allow me to bring a crew onto your place. There'll be men and equipment scattered so thick you'll be tripping over them. It'd be best if you were out of the way."

"Out of the way?" Mama's eyes blazed. "This here's our home. We got nowhere else to go."

Mr. Allen smiled again, creasing the skin around his gentle eyes. "Chances are good you'll soon afford to live wherever you choose. For now I firmly suggest you stay with family or friends. A hotel, perhaps. You can arrange a more permanent solution later."

Mama jutted her chin at Buddy. "What about you? Where will you stay?"

"Don't worry about me, ma'am. My two friends here booked rooms at the hotel. I can bunk with one of them for a few days."

Charity swallowed hard. "What about our house?" Her voice rang shrill in her ears. "Our things?"

"Pack up what you need for now; then lock it up," Buddy said. "We'll try to keep an eye on the place for you. Later on, you'll have plenty of help with moving your belongings."

Charity couldn't speak. Speaking required an intake of air, but an elephant straddled her chest.

For the last two years, after speculators drilled the first well near Jordan Gully, crooks and shysters had sniffed around their land like hounds on a hunt. Mama had taken the broom to all of them. Charity watched her now, waiting for her reaction.

She won't be pushed around by these men.

"We'll need time to pack," Mama announced. "And a ride into town. I got no horse and buggy, and it's too far to carry our things."

Buddy nodded. "I'll see to it that you get settled, ma'am."

Charity shoved past the men and rushed onto the porch. "What are you saying, Mama? We can't leave home. Where will we go?"

Mama gently pushed her aside. "Come back for us in an hour, Mr. Pierce. We'll be ready."

Not since Papa died had Charity felt so lost. In fact, the way he left was easier to bear—there one day and gone the next—but in a manner she understood. Mama had disappeared standing right in front of her.

The men tipped their hats and made for the front yard. At the corner of the house, Buddy Pierce glanced back. A puckered brow had replaced his grin, and his questioning eyes stayed on her until he disappeared behind the house.

Charity reckoned his frown was a reaction to the look on her face. Just what did her expression reveal about the goings-on inside her? She wanted to call him back and ask. Lord knew she couldn't figure it out.

She should be happy. She and mama would be better off, maybe even rich like Mother Dane and Emmy. Like Daniel. Why did that make her feel so strange?

"Rangeland," Mama said behind her. The single word made no more sense than anything else she'd said that day.

The silence that followed stood like a wall between them. When Charity could take it no longer, she glanced over her shoulder. "What'd you say, Mama?"

The stubborn little woman stood shading her eyes with one hand, staring at the oak tree behind the house as if she'd never seen it before. "You asked me what would happen. I'm answering your question. We'll buy rangeland. Acres of it, and cover it with cattle. I always wanted to raise me some beef stock." She turned without waiting for an answer and went inside.

Charity crossed to the porch rail and gazed about, seeing the tall, paint-chipped dwelling and weed-strangled plot with new eyes. In the side yard stood a row of pens where Papa had sheltered prized bloodhounds. Except for slight weathering and the need for a coat of whitewash, the pens looked the same as they had when filled with braying dogs. She could almost see Papa bent over the long basins pouring out water for squirming red pups.

She was here on the porch that day, five years ago, when Mama stepped out the back door and told her Papa was gone. He'd been swept off his feet by the current while fishing near the banks of the San Jacinto River. Mama sold the bloodhounds soon after because she couldn't afford to feed them.

Tears sprang to Charity's eyes. She'd been born in this house, lived here all her days. Just like that, her mama had agreed to walk away from everything that held them together after Papa died.

The screen door opened behind her, and the squeal of the springs set her teeth on edge.

Mama stood grim-faced in the entry. "Come inside now. There's a mess of packing to do, and we're running short on time."

An urge came over her to refuse, to scream and run headlong into the woods. Instead, she lowered her gaze to the rotting boards beneath her. "Yes, ma'am. I'll be right along."

The door closed. Charity looked at her fingers, white from gripping the weathered rail. She fought to still her trembling lips then lifted her chin and went inside.

Rustling noises drifted down the hall from her mama's cluttered bedroom. Charity found her bent over a satchel, rummaging through her clothes. The dimly lit room smelled of the pressed and dried magnolia blossoms Mama kept in her dresser drawers, but the odor had never put Charity in mind of a funeral before now.

Arms buried elbow-deep in the bag, Mama twisted around to look at her. "No time to dawdle. They'll be back directly and expect us to be ready."

"But where are we going?"

"Where do you think?" Mama averted her eyes and went back to her task. "We got no one but Magda. She'll take us in."

Charity's heart leapfrogged. "For crying in a bucket! I can't go to Mother Dane's house. Not after Emmy. . ."

"You got a better idea, let's hear it. Magda would front me the money, but there ain't no rooms left in town. Remember, that's how Mr. Pierce came to be on our place." She stood upright, her hands filled with faded undergarments. "It's amazing how the good Lord works His will, daughter. If you hadn't brought Mr. Pierce around here, I would've run him off, just like I done all the rest."

Charity groaned. Why hadn't she left Buddy Pierce right where she'd found him? "And we wouldn't be forced out into the street. I can't go to Emmy Dane's house, Mama. I won't."

This brought Mama around to glare at her with burning eyes. "Yes, you can and you will. Magda's all we got in this town. There's no place else."

Charity put her fists on her hips and planted her feet. "Then I'm staying right here."

"You cain't, daughter. You heard them men. It ain't safe."

"I'll get Sam to stay here with me."

Mama cackled. "Don't talk foolish. Sam has a hotel to run." She bent back down to grope in her bag. "I ain't aiming to deal harsh with you, baby. It's just that some things I know best. So we'll have no more arguments out of you."

Charity's legs wouldn't hold her. She sank to the side of the rumpled cot and covered her face with her hands. "Why are you doing this?" The ragged words tore at her swelling throat.

"Are you crying, daughter?" Mama hurried over and plopped beside Charity on the bed, gathering her up in skinny arms. "Don't, baby. You'll have me blubbering." Mama rocked her, patting her hair and murmuring comfort until Charity finally sat up.

"I don't want things to change again, that's all."

Mama nodded. "You've had more'n your share of unwanted change, sugar. But this is a good thing. Cain't you see that? It's an answer to prayer."

Startled, Charity looked at her. "You prayed to get rich? That's against the Good Book."

Mama raised a brow at her rebuke. "No, daughter. It ain't a sin to have money. The sin is in loving what you have more than God who gave it." She settled back and crossed her arms. "A better life is what I prayed for. If the good Lord has chosen to send me the money to buy one, then by golly, I want it."

Charity wiped her nose with the back of her hand and nodded. "So you don't have to be Mother Dane's cook anymore."

Mama sat up straight and pushed Charity to arm's length, her eyes fierce with emotion. "No, child. So you won't wind up Emmy's."

Buddy left Lee Allen and Jerry Ritter standing on the boardwalk in front of the Lone Star Hotel. They had agreed to meet there for lunch as soon as Buddy secured a rig for transporting Mrs. Bloom and her daughter into town.

Mrs. Bloom's daughter. . .

There was something about that girl. Something besides skin like fresh cream against piled-up black hair and a waist so tiny he knew he could reach his hands around it. Something besides pond-green eyes and full lips that turned up at the corners even when she frowned. He'd seen pretty girls in his time, but Charity Bloom was different, and he planned to find out why.

He sure didn't know what to make of her reaction to good fortune. He'd found oil on a lot of folks' land, but she was the first he'd ever seen scowl about it. If he didn't know better, he'd think it made her mad.

Dwelling on Charity Bloom caused him to pass right by the livery. He caught himself and laughed aloud, then backtracked and entered the stables, still chuckling as he passed through the wide doors.

"Kin I help you?" A runt of a man with rowdy gray hair stepped out of the shadows wiping dirty hands on the front of his vest. An intolerable stench filled Buddy's nostrils, growing stronger as the man approached. Buddy realized the smell of sweat, dung, and rotgut whiskey emanated from the proprietor and not from his animals.

"Yes, sir." Buddy shoved his hands deep into his pockets to keep from holding his nose. "I'm looking to hire a buggy for the afternoon. Oh, and three saddle horses that I'll need for a few weeks." In St. Louis, he had grown accustomed to the motorcar his employer provided, but it was hardly a practical conveyance for the muddy streets of Humble.

The fellow cleared his throat and spewed a brown stream in the general direction of a spittoon in the corner. Then he leaned against a splintered rail with crossed arms, looking Buddy over. "New in town, ain't you?"

"Yes, sir."

"You got kinfolk in Humble?"

"No, sir."

The old man continued to examine Buddy through narrow, beady eyes. "Anybody local who can vouch for you?"

Buddy choked back a protest. It would do him no good. "Well, let's see. I guess that'd be Mrs. Bloom and her daughter. They're the only townsfolk I've met."

The man's brows shot skyward, the pull on his eyelids widening his eyes. "Crazy Bertha?" He shook his head. "Mister, I can't give you a rig on the weight of an association with her."

"Who?" Buddy's mind scrambled to understand. "You mean Bertha Bloom? Why do you call her that?"

The old coot twisted around and fired another shot at the slimy, stained pot. "Stranger, if you have to ask, then you don't really know Bertha. But on account of you mentioning her daughter, maybe I can oblige." A leer distorted his wrinkled face. "Just how well acquainted are you with that pretty little gal?" He winked and grinned, exposing a gap in his teeth.

Buddy wanted to widen it. He stood taller and stared the man down. "How much do I owe you?"

The little man shrank under Buddy's gaze. He lowered his eyes and rubbed his stubbled chin. "Tell you what. Let's settle up when you come for the horses."

"Fine by me," Buddy said. "Get the buggy ready. I'll be back in twenty minutes."

At the hotel, Buddy found Lee and Jerry seated on benches in front of a long table laden with baskets of brown rolls and pitchers of frothy milk. The men waited their turns at huge platters piled high with sliced pot roast followed by steaming bowls of mashed potatoes and assorted vegetables. The smell of the room set off a fierce growl in the pit of Buddy's stomach.

He sidled up beside Lee on the bench, tucked a napkin into his collar, and nodded at the men. "Shovel it in fast, gentlemen. We need to get the Bloom womenfolk settled before nightfall. There's more than a few roughs in this town." He remembered the uncouth demeanor of the liveryman and scowled. "More than a few scoundrels, to boot."

Lee passed him a bowl of thick creamed corn. "Say, Buddy, what do you figure was stirring young Miss Bloom?"

Buddy's hand paused on the bowl. "You saw it, too?"

"Saw what?" Jerry asked.

Lee regarded him with one raised brow. "Son, I don't expect you took much notice of Miss Bloom's behavior. How could you? You were too distracted by her other attributes."

Jerry set down his mug with a bang. "High rickety, ain't she a huckleberry?" The flush on his young face and the wide, milk-ringed grin told Buddy more than his words.

"A huckleberry, is she?" Lee forked a serving of roast and smiled at Jerry. "Let's see now. Two days ago you used that term while referring to an oil rig. The week before, I believe a newfangled motorcar earned the same accolade. I think Miss Bloom might consider herself lumped with unflattering company. Don't you agree, Buddy?"

"I do indeed. But what can you expect from an Oklahoman?" Buddy dropped his gaze and shoved a bite of food into his mouth to keep from smiling.

Jerry sat up straighter. "By golly, I'm a Texan and you know it. Born and raised in Wichita Falls."

Buddy shrugged. "Same difference. You couldn't slip a hummingbird feather between Wichita Falls and the Oklahoma border. They may as well claim you."

Jerry drew his mug and plate closer and turned away, offering them one bony shoulder. "There ain't no call for that kind of talk."

Lee laughed aloud and pounded him on the back. "Aw, come on, Okie, don't take on so. We're just having some fun."

"Eat up, boys," Buddy said. "We don't have time for high jinks. We're burning daylight."

Across the table, a thin, balding man leaned forward and cleared his throat. "Excuse me, gentlemen. Did I hear you mention getting the Bloom women settled? Something happen out at their place?"

The three men exchanged uneasy looks. "No, sir," Buddy said. "Nothing worth talking about."

Though no one sat near them, the little man looked to his left and then his right. "Does it have something to do with the wedding?" he whispered.

"Wedding?" Buddy and his men asked together.

"The wedding that never was, I should say." The man's mouth widened at their blank stares. "You haven't heard, then?" He seemed thrilled by the fact.

Lee put down his fork. "If there's something we need to know, get on with it. Whose wedding are you referring to?"

"Why, Miss Bloom's, of course."

Troubled green eyes and a furrowed brow stole across Buddy's mind. "Miss Charity Bloom?"

"Yessir. One and the same. She was all set to marry Daniel Clark, the son of the richest man in town, don't you know. Almost done it, too. Made it all the way to the altar before things turned sour." He tried on a sad look that didn't fit. "Poor little thing, standing up there in a pretty white dress with tears in her eyes. . ." Fixing them with mournful eyes, he shook his head. "I reckon a crying bride is the most pitiful sight there is."

Jerry leaned across the table, nose to nose with the man. "What happened?"

He licked his narrow lips, all but smacking them over what would come next. "Miss Bloom's intended walked right out of the church, practically on the arm of her childhood friend, Miss Emily Dane." He raised both hands in the air. "Now there's a lollapalooza. Young Mr. Clark might've cut a fat hog when he took up with her. There's a slim chance that boy will ever tame a girl like Emmy."

Jerry's brown eyes widened in disbelief. "Are you saying some featherbrain had Miss Bloom corralled then cut her loose? Who would do a fool thing like that?"

The man shook his head. "It's a poser, all right."

Surprised and a little embarrassed for Charity, Buddy felt heat crawl up his cheeks. He stood up and threw some money on the table. "We got no more time for loose talk and speculation about other folks' business. The lady's not present to defend herself, so I suggest we hear no more."

Lee stood with Buddy, hitched up his trousers, and nodded at the man. "You have a good day, sir."

Jerry still leaned in, about to ask another question, but Buddy hooked a finger around his suspenders and drew him up. "Let's not keep our friend from his fine meal. Besides, we'd best get moving. We don't want to keep the ladies waiting."

CHAPTER 4

For Charity, the ride to Mother Dane's house felt like a walk to the gallows.

While packing the buggy, Buddy Pierce and his men were helpful but oddly subdued. It hadn't escaped her notice that Buddy never met her gaze. The other one, the tall, skinny man with eyes that matched his russet hair, stared at her for much of the evening. When told of their destination, Buddy reacted as if Mama had suggested he drive them off a cliff. They had something stuck in their craws, and that was for sure.

Charity put it aside. Her own woes had her so tightly wrapped that she had no time to ponder what might be ailing them.

Now they stood before the Danes' front door, bags in hand, to beg entry to the enemy camp. Mama had no sense for propriety, that was nothing new, but it had never stung Charity so cruelly before. Behind them, the men mumbled and shuffled their feet, overly preoccupied by something in the distance.

A loud ruckus came from inside, dominated by Mother Dane's deep, commanding rumble and punctuated by Emmy's shrill pleas. When the massive oak door began to open, it was all Charity could do not to turn and bolt. As if she read her daughter's mind, Mama tightened her grip on Charity's arm.

Mother Dane's broad smile greeted them. "Why, Bertie, bless my soul, what a pleasant but thoroughly unexpected surprise."

Her considerable girth, clad in fashionable big sleeves and full skirts, took up most of the doorway and prevented Charity from seeing around her. Forced to cast manners aside, she rose on her toes and peered over Mother Dane's shoulder.

"We need shelter, Magda," Mama said.

Mother Dane stepped aside. There would be questions later, but she'd heard all that was necessary for now. Mama needed her.

"Set those bags at the foot of the stairs, gentlemen; then hang your hats in the hall and have a seat in the parlor. I'll fetch some coffee. You all look like you could use it."

Mother Dane hadn't really asked, just issued the order. Like everyone else in Humble, the men complied without hesitation. After a tearful hug with Mama, Mother Dane hurried to the kitchen to keep her end of the bargain.

A quick, furtive check of the room told Charity that Emmy wasn't present. Whether upstairs or hiding in an adjacent room she couldn't tell, but sooner or later a confrontation would be unavoidable.

Like Cleopatra awaiting Mark Antony, Mama settled onto a plush, button-tucked divan and held court with a broad smile. The servant waiting to be served. Long graying strands streamed down each side of her face, and Charity wished she'd learn to pin up her hair.

The men sat stiffly across from Mama on the matching couch. Charity sank into a big green chair and willed it to swallow her whole.

"See? I told you, sugar," Mama said. "I knew it'd be all right. Magda wouldn't turn us away just because of Emmy and that no-account Daniel Clark."

All three men shifted their gazes to Mama, waiting to hear what she had to say next. Charity tensed, prepared to save herself from humiliation if it meant swooning at their feet.

"Here we are." Mother Dane entered the room as she always did, like an actress on cue. She approached them smiling, but a brief, nearly imperceptible frown directed at the top of the stairs told Charity that Emmy had escaped to her room.

"That was quick," Mama exclaimed.

"Already had it brewed. I'm used to making a big pot for Willem and me. When he's on the road, it's too much, but I don't know how to make it taste good otherwise." She set the tray on the low table and looked around at her guests. "Now it won't go to waste."

After seeing everyone properly served, Mother Dane lowered herself to the divan beside Charity's sprawling mama. "Now then, what's this all about, Bert?"

Mama passed Mother Dane her cup then sat forward and rubbed her hands together like a child with a secret. "You won't believe what's going on out at our place." She narrowed her eyes and jabbed her bony finger at Buddy Pierce. "That one. That boy right there has the gift, Magda. He can take one look at the ground and find treasure."

Now she had Mother Dane's rapt attention. "Treasure? Oh my, honey. Do go on."

Mama's dancing eyes returned to Buddy. "Tell her, son. Tell Magda what you found on my land."

Buddy leaned forward and smiled. With his hands clasped in front and long arms propped on his knees, he began to talk. He told about when he first caught sight of Mama's chicken, and how he realized the goo on its feathers must be oil. He explained how he rushed back into town, praying the whole way his crew had arrived with their equipment so they could do their tests.

He lit up as he talked, and Charity wondered at the source of his excitement. Was it the thrill of discovery or the joy of helping someone less fortunate that stoked a fire in his eyes?

Whatever inspired his zeal, she enjoyed watching and listening to him very much. His deep voice and dulcet tones so soothed her, drowsiness set in and she found it hard to sit upright. Snuggling deeper into the plush green upholstery, she laid her head against the overstuffed arm while Buddy's muted rumble became a nest of bees in her head.

"Charity? Wake up, dear."

She bolted straight up, swiping the back of her hand across her mouth and searching the room for Buddy and his men.

Mother Dane offered the crook of her arm to pull up on. "They're gone, honey."

"Oh my. I fell asleep."

"You sure did."

She looked back at the big chair and pictured herself lying there. "Did I do anything. . .unladylike while I slept?"

Mother Dane laughed, not out loud, but Charity knew because her bosom shook. "Child, you snored so rowdy-like you ran those nice young men plumb out of the house, and all the while your mouth was wide and drooling like a hound at suppertime. We couldn't make polite conversation for all the racket, so they left."

"Mother Dane!"

"Got quite a kick out of it, they did. Especially that good-looking one."

"Did not!"

The shaking grew violent, and Mother Dane's hearty laughter filled the room. She pulled Charity close for a hug. "Come on then, sleepyhead. Your bed is made and calling for you."

"Where's Mama?"

"Upstairs in my bed. It's more comfortable. I set up a cot in the room for me in case she needs anything. Bert was plumb tuckered out, so I promised I'd see to you. I put your things at the opposite end of the hall like always."

Just like Mother Dane. Always tending to Mama.

"Did Emmy. . . ?"

"Never graced us with her presence. She'll be down soon enough, though, or starve. I certainly won't be taking up a tray."

Charity rested her head on Mother Dane's shoulder. "Oh, it's all so awful."

"That it is, sugar, but time has a way with these things." She held Charity at arm's length. "Besides, it's not all bad news. Young Mr. Pierce said you and Bertha may come by some money."

Charity grimaced, and Mother Dane took her by the chin. "Mercy, what a face."

"I don't want those filthy oilmen's money. Mama said she didn't either. She said they come in and lease up all the land, getting rich off good-hearted people who don't know any better."

"Uh-uh, sugar. Not this time. Mr. Pierce told Bert she could drill out the oil herself and keep the money."

The words caught Charity off guard. "Mama? Drill oil? That's crazy talk. She don't know the first thing about it."

Mother Dane laughed again. "Sweetie, you're wide-eyed as a hoot owl. That young man didn't mean for Bert to do the work herself. He meant she could finance it and keep most of the profit."

Charity blinked. "Finance it? With what? It would be easier for Mama to do the drilling than to come up with that kind of money."

"Mr. Pierce is going to help her get it done. He has a plan. Something about leasing some of your land to pay for it."

All Charity could do was stare.

Mother Dane gathered her close again and patted her back. Then she turned her to face the stairs and urged her toward them. "Come now, child. I'll walk you up. I know it's a lot to take in, especially when you're still half asleep. I promise things will look better by the morning light."

"I declare, Mother Dane, I don't see how."

Alone in the big four-poster, Charity marveled that it seemed as grand as it had when she was a girl. In this very room, she and Emmy had wrestled, giggled, and whispered until the wee hours. Emmy started out in her own bed, but when the household fell silent, she would sneak down the hallway and throw herself, all gangly legs and tousled hair, into bed with Charity. In those days, they had no notions about rich or poor, fidelity or deceit.

She couldn't remember a time when Emmy wasn't a part of her life. Their mamas grew up together in East Texas. When Mama married Papa and moved to Humble, her best friend soon followed. Even after Mother Dane married into money, the two were inseparable. It took Mama eight years to conceive her only child. She liked to claim she held on to Charity until Mother Dane could meet Uncle Willem and hang up her old maid hat because the girls were meant to be reared side by side.

So they had been, and they'd loved each other since Emmy first toddled close and touched Charity's face. How could Charity bear life without her best friend?

She pictured Emmy lying in her bedroom at the end of the

hall, and her eyes flooded with tears. She almost wished the door would fly open and Emmy would sail into the room. The desire to reconcile consumed her. The pain caused by what Daniel and Emmy had done paled in comparison to the hollow ache in her heart.

I could forgive her.

The thought struck like a blow. She lay in the darkness and reeled from it.

When the next idea came, it took her breath. She could tiptoe down the hall and climb into bed beside Emmy. They would whisper and giggle tonight and save the serious talk for morning. It would be harder by the light of day, but they'd work it out. They always had.

Before she changed her mind, Charity slipped from the bed and opened the door. The polished brass banister reflected the moonlight shining from the gabled windows, providing a lighted marker along the corridor. Outside Emmy's room, she paused. Her heart pounded, but she wouldn't allow herself to go back. Turning the knob, she winced when the hinges creaked then drew a sharp breath when a rush of frigid air hit her face. Emmy's bedroom was colder than the guest room had been. Much colder. Charity shivered in her thin nightdress.

The outline of Emmy's body lay still under the quilt, so she hadn't heard the door. Charity approached the high bed, her mind awhirl with all she planned to say. She smiled in the darkness, imagining her friend's reaction, though if she couldn't stop shivering, she'd scare Emmy awake.

A stiff gust of wind lifted the curtains. *For pity's sake, no wonder. She'll have us frozen by morning.*

Charity backed away and tiptoed to the window to close it. Her hand rested on the sash when something in the garden below caught her eye. The full moon revealed a lone figure dressed in nightclothes and wrapped in a long white shawl. She stared at the fair-haired apparition in disbelief.

Crossing to the bed, she threw back the quilt. Three plump pillows mocked her. She whirled and rushed to the window, prepared to call out, but something about Emmy's lovely profile stopped her. The upturned, moonlit face held a look of longing so intense it pricked Charity's heart.

Emmy feels what I feel. Her heart is so broken she can't sleep.

She considered the trellis. She wasn't afraid of heights, but climbing the rickety framework in her nightdress seemed foolhardy. Nevertheless, she pulled the garment high and prepared to swing her leg over the windowsill just as another figure emerged from the shadows.

Emmy rushed to meet Daniel. He took her in his arms and pressed her head to his chest, her long nightdress billowing about their legs. Charity tried to turn away but couldn't. A single tear fell and splashed against the windowsill.

"I hate you, Emily Dane." She knew she whispered, but the words thundered in her head. "Oh, how I hate you."

In the moonlight, the couple seemed to merge into one, and the scene burned into Charity's eyes. Careful to be quiet, she lowered the heavy window and turned the lock. Blinded by tears, she stumbled across the room and slipped into the hall, easing the door closed behind her.

CHAPTER 5

Charity swept through the kitchen door to find her mama in front of Mother Dane's cast-iron stove. At the dawn of a new day, Cleopatra had traded her couch for an apron and skillet. Dwarfed by the huge black contraption, she looked even smaller than usual, reminding Charity of a little girl playing house.

Barefoot as usual, Mama stood like a crane, one foot propped against the opposite knee. She gazed out the window, a shaft of light bathing the side of her face, and her eyes squinted against the rising sun. Without looking, she took an egg from a basket on the sideboard and cracked it into a big yellow bowl. Lifting the bottle of milk, she poured a dollop over the eggs, never spilling a drop.

Anyone else might think the view past the checkered curtains held her fancy. By the dazed look in her eyes, Charity knew the confines of the carnation-weave wallpaper held her body, but her mind and spirit soared somewhere in the distance. Drifting off that way, among Mama's many other odd habits, had led the townsfolk to think her peculiar at best. Some even called her insane.

Charity took a deep breath and gathered her courage. "I'm leaving, Mama. I will not stay in this house another minute."

Mama glanced over her shoulder. "You hush now. And close that door. They'll hear you."

"There's no one awake to hear. Besides, I don't care." Charity swept past the threshold and did as she was told. The careful way she eased the door shut contradicted her bold statement.

The frustrating little woman chuckled and went back to her task. "There's no one awake because they were up half the night. Made quite a ruckus, they did, pounding on doors and spitting like cats."

Charity squirmed. "They weren't the only ones up all night."

Mama kept a stiff back to her, but the motion of beating the eggs set her thin frame to dancing. "Couldn't sleep, huh? Is your conscience sore, daughter? The Good Book says, 'The wicked are like the troubled sea when it cannot rest, whose waters cast up mire and dirt.' " She chuckled. "Sounds like our bog, don't it?"

Charity banged her fist on the table. "No, it doesn't. It's nothing like our bog. Mercy! You sorely vex me sometimes. When you talk like that, I go to thinking—"

Mama turned, her movements slow and deliberate. "Go on and say it."

Charity felt her stomach fill with mush. She couldn't meet those burning eyes.

"What's the matter? Lost your nerve?" Mama's work-worn fingers had gone white around the spatula. "Let me finish for you, then. You go to thinking I'm loony like this town has me pegged. Now ain't that so?"

Charity fixed her eyes on a crack in the floor. "I'm sorry, Mama. I know you're not loony. Only sometimes you act so strange."

Her long silence made Charity nervous, but Charity knew enough to stay still and wait.

"Come over here, daughter."

She dared a quick glance at Mama's face. "Ma'am?"

"Do as I say."

Eyes still downcast, Charity crossed the room. Her mama laid down the spatula and faced her. "Now then, you look me square in the eye."

Charity's head hung lower.

Mama hooked an index finger around her chin and raised her red-hot face. "Go on, take a look. Look deep in my eyes, clear past the faded skin and wrinkles. That's it. All right, tell me what you see."

She searched the soft green eyes. "What do you mean? I don't see anything."

Mama released her chin. "And there's your problem." With that she picked up her utensil and returned to the eggs.

Frustration crowded Charity's throat, making her voice come out shrill. "You're not making any sense."

The spatula went down again, and Mama wiped her hands on her apron. "Let me tell you what you missed." She raised a finger and thumped herself hard on the chest. It rang hollow in Charity's ears like the sound of a ripe melon. "Underneath this pruned-up skin, back behind these tired old eyes, I'm still just a girl. No different from you, except on the outside."

Charity shook her head. "Don't be silly. You don't have pruned-up skin or tired eyes. You're not yet fifty."

Mama placed both hands on Charity's shoulders. "It's the road I'm walking, but it don't matter none to me. Just because I've got a few years under my belt, folks expect me to act like I swallowed a bucket of starch. Well, I won't. That ain't me."

Charity knew Mama wanted some sign that she understood, but she could only stare back and nod.

"Baby, these bodies age, and there's nothing to be done about it. If we're lucky, if we don't fight it, our souls stay young forever. I won't put no face on for the world. I tried for your sake, but I cain't do it no more. It plain stifles me."

She reached around to set the skillet off the fire. "I'll tell you something else. Your papa never tried to change me. Never once made me feel crazy. But then, I reckon he was the last soul on earth willing to accept me just how I am." Her gaze jumped back to the checkered curtains, and Charity's heart pitched and dove for her feet. She suddenly knew exactly where her mama's thoughts had been when she entered the room.

She held out her hand. "That's not true. I—"

"Bertha Maye!"

Mother Dane's strident voice struck panic in Charity's heart. She spun toward the kitchen door. "I have to go, Mama. I have to leave right this minute."

"Just where do you think to go?"

"I pondered that all night. First, I'll check the hotel. If they don't have a room for us yet, I can put our names on the list."

"And then?"

"Home. I want to go back home. At least for now."

Mama put a hand on her hip and turned back to the scorched-smelling eggs. "I sure thought a daughter of mine could stand up to trouble better than this, but you go on. I won't stop you."

Mother Dane trudged into the kitchen, still wrapped in her dressing gown. "Here you two are," she announced, swiping her forehead with the back of her hand. "It's a blessing for Emmy her daddy's out of town; else we'd be planning a wake this morning." She glanced toward the skillet, sniffing the air. "You burning those eggs, Bert?"

Mama faced her. "Magda, can Nash fetch Charity into town this morning?"

"Sure thing, honey. I ain't going nowhere." Mother Dane ambled to the counter, her attention on the platter of crispy bacon. "Where's she running off to this early?"

"On a fool's errand."

Perhaps weary from her own nocturnal battle, Mother Dane didn't press. "Let me go dress and tell Nash to square the rig. That is, if I can find him. How something as bodacious big as that man disappears with such dependable regularity beats all I ever saw."

Charity eased toward the exit. "Don't trouble yourself, Mother Dane. I'm already dressed. I'll go tell him myself."

The kitchen door closed behind her, and Charity ran for the foyer, careful not to look toward the stairs. On the way, she hoisted her bag from behind the chair where she'd left it and burst onto the wide porch—straight into the arms of Buddy Pierce. They collided, and her bag jerked loose from her hands and skittered across the porch.

"Whoa, there!" he cried, pressing her against him to keep her upright. At such close proximity, his voice sounded deeper than usual and seemed to rumble from his broad chest.

"Morning, Miss Bloom. So we meet again." He squinted when he smiled, crinkling the corners of his eyes. "Not that I don't enjoy these encounters, but a simple hello would do. Unless you need a good fright to start your heart in the mornings. Have you tried coffee?"

She pulled free and peered up, raising the brim of her bonnet so she could see. "Mr. Pierce, where on earth did you come from? You simply must stop creeping up on me."

He had the starch to grin. "My sincere apologies, ma'am. I'm getting right good at it though."

She brushed at her dress and tightened the ribbon holding her hat while she fought to regain some dignity. "If you're truly sorry, you can rescue my bag from that hedge."

Buddy glanced behind him then walked to the edge of the porch and bent down. She watched him hesitate before poking in a lacy bit of cloth and closing the latch. She bit back a smile when he returned red-faced.

He held up her satchel and studied it. "Didn't I tote this inside just last night?"

"You did."

"And now you're bringing it out again?"

"Give it to me, please."

"You seem in an awful big hurry to get somewhere."

"That's because I am." She snatched the upraised bag from his hand. "In fact, I'm about to give you an opportunity to repay me for ambushing me at every turn. You may give me a ride into town."

Buddy looked at the door. "I'd be happy to, but. . ."

Charity followed his gaze. "I see. You have business inside. Very well, I'll wait for Nash." She started for the steps, but he grabbed her sleeve and hauled her around.

"Not so fast. My only business is to see that you and your mama are settled and to offer my help with moving the rest of your things."

"Is that all? In that case, you needn't worry. We're just fine."

He cast another doubtful peek at the house. "Well, if you say so. . ."

"I do." She took his arm and urged him toward the steps. "Shall we go?"

He settled his hat lower, studying her from under the brim.

"Well, yes, ma'am," he said, allowing her to lead him from the porch. "I guess so."

In the distance, a high bank of black clouds closed on the horizon, a dark swirling wall with a fluffy white top. It snuffed out the light as it inched forward, pulling a curtain over the bright, sunlit morning. Buddy wondered what more rain might do to the rutted streets of Humble. The lowland area of Southeast Texas suffered frequent flooding, but he'd heard more thunderstorms than usual had rumbled through the small town in recent weeks.

He glanced at Miss Bloom, who had remained silent for most of the ride. Quite out of character for the spirited young thing he'd first met in the hotel. He found it odd he hadn't seen that woman since, except for a glimpse on Mrs. Dane's porch.

Buddy pulled up to the crowded boardwalk in front of the Lone Star Hotel and set the brake. Hopping down, he made his way around the wagon with the mire sucking audibly at his boots. Necks craned as he helped Miss Bloom down, careful to keep her dress out of the mud. When he offered his arm, she took it, and he led her through the mob to the door of the hotel.

Inside, he intended to hang back a respectable distance to allow her to conduct business in private, but she clung to his arm and steered him straight to the counter.

"Morning, Sam." She beamed at the clerk. "I'm going to need a room for a few weeks for Mama and me."

Sam frowned. He seemed loath to be the bearer of bad news, especially to her. "I'm dreadful sorry, child. There are none to be had."

She bit her bottom lip. "Hmm, I expected as much. When do you suppose that will change?"

The little man shook his head. "Not in the foreseeable future."

"I see." Her slender fingers drumming a rhythm on the countertop, she stared at a large portrait dominating the far wall as if the mustachioed man in the frame might lend her wisdom.

The aging clerk pushed his wire-rimmed glasses higher with a palsied hand. "If you don't mind my asking, has something happened out at your place?" His anxious expression and the way he hovered near Charity reminded Buddy of a brood hen and her chick.

The pretty hatchling smoothed her fluff and released a weary-sounding breath. "It's quite complicated, really. You see, Mr. Pierce here saw black stuff on Mama's chicken and—"

Buddy took hold of her shoulders and pulled her back, upsetting her balance as well as the angle of the blue feather protruding from her straw hat. "What the lady's trying to say is"—he stared into her startled eyes, using his to flash a warning—"there are much-needed improvements going on at their house. It's not the safest place for them just now."

Sam eyed Buddy, his frown deepening. "As I recall, you're not a registered guest of the hotel, so why do I see your face in my lobby most every day of late?"

Buddy nodded. "Nothing gets past you, does it? You're right, of course. I'm not official." He grinned and held out his hand. "Name's Buddy Pierce. I guess you might say I'm a guest of a guest."

Ignoring Buddy's hand and his explanation, the man turned back to Charity. "Is there something else I can do for you, my dear?"

She stepped to the counter again, adjusting her hat and frowning at Buddy before she answered. "I understand there's a waiting list."

"Why, yes, there is."

"Can you put us on it?"

"I can, but I warn you, it's long." He pulled a ledger from under the counter and slid it toward Charity. Names filled the page from top to bottom on several sheets. "Might be weeks before we can get to you." He tilted his head toward the window. "The boom, you know."

Buddy watched Charity, waiting for her reaction. The news was sure to upset her.

"Very well." She took the pen in her gloved hand and scratched her mama's name on the last line. Following suit with the others, she added the number two and circled it then pushed the book back to the clerk and nodded. "Thank you, Sam."

The old man's gaze swept Buddy. His Adam's apple bobbed several times before he finally squeezed a question past his throat. "I don't mean to pry, little miss, but have you found adequate shelter for you and your mama until we're able to accommodate you?"

"As a matter of fact, we have. Mama will be staying at Magdalena Dane's house. I've decided on a more sensible arrangement for myself." She fixed Buddy with a determined glare. "You heard right, Mr. Pierce. I won't be going back to Mother Dane's."

Before Buddy could react, she walked away. He caught up to her near the door and offered his arm again. She took it, and he swept her through the crowd outside. At the wagon, he helped her swing up onto the seat then watched her until she began to squirm.

"What are you waiting for?" she asked, looking down at him from the rig. "Let's go."

Buddy blinked. "Fine. Where to?"

"Home." She dared him with her eyes and sat up straighter, plucking at the folds of her dress. "I'm going home, and there's nothing more to be said about it."

His mouth dropped open. He closed it fast and swallowed. "I'm sorry, you can't do that."

"Oh, but I can. I declare, Mr. Pierce, you're forgetting yourself."

Buddy hurried around the wagon, swung up beside her, and studied her angry face. "Didn't your mama tell you?"

From the look of her, it was clear she'd heard those words before. She leaned toward him, her speech slow and deliberate. "Tell me what?"

"She leased the house. To the oil company as living quarters for the roughnecks."

Thunder boomed overhead and lightning marbled the darkened sky. A quirky wind bore down on them, pushing back Charity's hat and raising tendrils of black hair to the heavens. Against the angry backdrop, she reminded Buddy of a snake-tressed Medusa.

"What did you say?" Her eyes narrowed, heightening the illusion. "Just when did she do that?"

"We worked out the deal last night, while you were. . .um. . . resting. That's why I showed up this morning. I knew you'd need a hand with your things."

Charity's gloved fingers clenched and unclenched in her lap, and her chest heaved. "That infuriating old woman. That's why she let me go so easy." She whirled on Buddy, balled fists going to her waist. "She can't do this. It's my house, too. If she can lease it without telling me, then I can unlease it. You tell that oil company the house is no longer available." She drew herself tall, obviously pleased with her stand. "That's right—the deal's off. Now take me home this instant."

Buddy shoved his hat back with his knuckles and scratched his head with his thumb. "That won't exactly be possible, ma'am."

"And why not?"

"It's too late. When I left your house this morning, twenty men were eating breakfast at the table."

Thunder sounded again, closer this time. Charity leaned toward him once more, staring hard, as if that would help his words sink in. Her big green eyes, so near he could see tiny flecks in them, flooded with tears that spilled over and down her cheeks. When she collapsed against him sobbing, Buddy couldn't decide whether to comfort her or hide her from prying eyes. He chose the latter.

Righting her hat, he pulled it low to hide her face then clucked at the horse to pull away from the boardwalk. He scrambled for the reins, fighting hard to concentrate on his driving instead of the weeping girl clinging to his side.

Buddy steered the horse down a side street that ran alongside the railroad tracks and parked the rig. Setting the brake, he pulled Charity closer and patted her shoulder while she cried. He searched his mind for comforting words but came up painfully short. "There now. It can't be all that bad."

"Yes, it is!" she wailed. "How can you say that? I'll be sleeping in the streets tonight."

He tried not to focus on how small she felt against him, how soft. "I'm right sure that won't happen."

"It has happened. I have nowhere else to go. I can't stay at Mother Dane's. I won't." Her wail became a sob, and she hid her face in her hands. "Don't ask me to explain. You wouldn't understand."

He cleared his throat. "Oh, I don't know so much about that. I might understand a lot better than you think."

Charity grew still against him. "What are you implying, sir?" When he didn't answer, she leaned to stare up at him, her face a swollen mess. "You know, don't you?"

Buddy raised his brows. "Any way I answer that question makes me a cad. If I say yes, I risk embarrassing you. If I say no, I've deceived you. Which do you prefer?"

She burrowed into his chest again. "I could just die. Oh, please don't look at me. I'm so ashamed."

"There's no need to be."

"Yes, there is. I'm a jealous, spiteful shrew."

Buddy couldn't help but smile. He was glad she couldn't see him. "I'm sure you're neither of those things."

"I am. You don't know what I've done."

He patted her on the back. "I can't imagine you doing anything wrong."

She tilted her head and peered up at him. "Last night Emmy climbed out a window to be with Daniel. I locked her out of the house. . .in her nightdress."

One look at her guilty expression should've been all the warning Buddy needed to keep a straight face, but his callous sense of humor betrayed him. He was going to laugh whatever the cost. He held her and roared until his sides ached.

When he dared to look up, he was shocked to find Charity beaming. Her nose was still red, her eyes bright with tears, but mirth lit her glowing face. By golly, the Okie was right. She was the prettiest thing he'd ever seen. Her big eyes held his for a heartbeat, and he forgot to breathe.

"You are a cad indeed, sir." Her rebuke might've stung if not for her broad smile.

He took off his hat and placed it over his heart but couldn't stifle a smile of his own. "I guess I owe you another apology."

"Well, don't you bother. Though I'm touched by your sincerity."

"Miss Bloom, I sense you doubt me."

She waved her hand. "Please, call me Charity. Now that I've bared my soul and given you a glimpse of my lower nature, I believe we can dispense with formalities."

Hat still at his chest, he bowed his head. "I would be honored."

Huge raindrops began to fall, pelting the top of Buddy's bare head. Instinctively, he held his hat over Charity.

She leaned from under the brim and peered up at the sky. "Now do you see how awful this is? I can't even get in out of the rain. There's no place for me to go."

"Wait a minute." He should have thought of it before. Or had she just inspired him? "I think maybe there is."

"But where?"

The rain came down harder, soaking them to the skin. Buddy handed her his hat and took up the reins, whirling the horse into the street. "Hang on," he shouted. "You'll find out when we get there."

CHAPTER 6

Bertha lay curled at the foot of Magdalena's green-striped divan, one finger dead center of a checker. Magda sat across from her, propped against the flower-print pillows at her back. Earlier she had raised the sash to ease the cloying stillness. Now the scent of rain wafted in on a lively breeze that pestered the curtains and flapped the shade. Though it put up a brave front, the morning sun had lost its battle with a murky sky. The shadowy corners crept so close they'd soon need to trim a lantern or abandon their game altogether.

Magda squirmed and sighed. "That's it, Bertha. You've made your move. It's my turn."

"Hold your horses. I ain't let go yet."

Another huffy exhale from across the board brought Bertha's attention to Magda's face. "You mind to stop all that blowing? You're about to scatter these checkers." She scowled and leaned away some. "Besides, you ate onions this morning, didn't you? Your breath could peel the paper from these walls."

Magda lifted her chin. "You know I like a few diced on my scrambled eggs."

"Humph! A few would mean you could still taste the eggs."

Reaching around to the side table, Magda picked up her coffee cup. "Just hush and play, would you?"

Bertha looked up as big Nash came through from the kitchen

carrying one of Magda's dining room chairs. On the way he banged it against the doorpost and bumped everything he passed.

Magda grimaced. "Land sakes, Nash. There won't be nothing left."

He glanced up and smiled as if he'd just noticed them in the room. "Maybe so, but whatever left gon' stand up straight. I fixed that wobbly leg you been fussing 'bout so long." He set the chair down and pushed it up to the table.

Bertha saw right away that the back of the chair stood four inches shy of the other five in the set. "Lookie there, Magda," she hooted. "You called it right. There's hardly nothing left."

Magda scooted forward to look. "Nash! What on earth have you done?"

He flashed another big smile and gave the chair a good shake. "See there, Miz Dane? She's steady."

Slumping against the sofa, Magda shook her head. "Never mind that fool thing. Have you seen Charity this morning?"

"No, ma'am. I ain't seen her since last evening. I would'a reckoned she'd be in the parlor with you all."

Bertha gave him a pointed stare. "Do you see her in here anywhere?"

He gazed about the room. "I don't see her in here a'tall. Is she s'posed to be?"

Magda winked at Bertha. "I thought you saw everything that happens around this place." She took another sip of her coffee. "Where've you been all this time?"

"Where've I been?" He stood taller and squared his shoulders. "Doing what I s'posed be doing, Miz Dane. Caring for old Rebel and tending chores. So unless Miss Charity come out to the barn, I wouldn't be likely to see her, now, would I?"

"Well, keep an eye out for her, you hear? She wanted a ride into town, but since the buggy never left the yard, I can't imagine how she went. I don't guess you hauled her on your shoulders?"

His grin returned. "No, ma'am."

"Did you turn Rebel out to graze?"

"No, ma'am, he's still in his stall. It's coming up a powerful blow out there. That old sky black as pitch. The pasture ain't safe for old Rebel jus' now." With that, he tipped his battered hat and backed out the way he came.

Magda sighed and settled again onto her pillows. "I just can't figure it. How did Charity leave if Nash didn't drive her, and where did she go?"

Bertha's heart lurched, but she kept her peace.

Magda cast an accusing glance. "You reckon she knows about the house?"

"She's bound to by now."

"Then where could she be, Bert? And in this storm? She's been gone an awful long time."

Bertha let go of the checker. "Hush and play. It's your turn."

Outside, what started as a heavy patter on the porch became a ruckus of hard-driving rain. Magda heaved herself up and rushed to close the window. "Honey, I think that's hail. I sure hope we don't get us a tornado."

"Me, too, but I wouldn't be surprised. A good twister's long overdue."

Magda released the tasseled shade and spun around to face her. "Charity's out in this! Aren't you the least bit worried?"

Bertha shrugged. "She'll turn up by suppertime." Magda's hard stare from across the room weighed her down, but she kept her attention on the game.

"Sometimes you're too harsh with that girl."

She looked up. "I don't go to be. Life is cruel. I want her fit to handle it."

Magda bent close to the window and took one more peek at the weather. "There's a limit to what a person can take." She turned and held up one finger in a cautionary gesture. "Mark my words–keep it up and she'll turn on you."

Bertha struggled to keep her voice even. "She already has."

"Tommyrot. That child loves you more than life. She's a good girl, to boot. Count your blessings, Bertie. Suppose you had to contend with my–"

"Emmy!"

Magda froze at Bertha's cry then followed her nod to the head of the stairs where Emmy reclined against the newel post. "Well,

well. So you decided to come out of hiding. How long you been standing there?"

The girl didn't answer. Hand in front of her face, she studied her tapered nails as though they held the answers to all of life's questions.

"Emily, I'm talking to you." Magda walked to the lower landing and stared up. "You may as well come on down. You can't eavesdrop on folks once they know you're there."

With an angry swish of her skirts, Emmy flounced down the stairs. On the bottom step, she turned a surly face to her mama. "I'm hungry. Were you planning to let me perish?"

Magda snorted. "There was no danger of that."

Sucking in her middle, Emmy looked down and wrapped her hands around her tiny waist. "Whatever do you mean? Why, look at me wasting away. I haven't eaten a bite for days."

Her mama raised an eyebrow. "Stolen provisions don't count? What about the food you've pilfered from my kitchen every night?"

"Mama, take that back! I never did."

"Emily, gnawed drumsticks don't naturally sprout from hedges, nor do lamb chops spring up in front yards. You've littered the place with your leavings. Did you think no one would notice?"

Emmy raised her chin and turned away. "Why blame me? There's no telling what's subject to spring up around this house." She flashed a pointed glance at Bertha. "Or who."

Not one to be trifled with, Magda advanced on Emmy, her voice a threatening growl. "After the shenanigans you've pulled, young lady, it would serve you best to lower that nose and act civil." She pointed. "Get over there and apologize to Bertha; then march into that kitchen and fetch yourself some food. No one will be serving you today."

Emmy dashed over and curtsied. "Sorry, Aunt Bert." Skirts rustling, she scuttled into the kitchen.

Watching her go, Bertha grinned. "Them rosebushes sure tore up that pretty face."

"Looks like she hit every one. The very idea, skulking about the windows of her own home trying to break in. She scared the dickens out of me. Served her right to meet the business end of a thorn or two."

Bertha leaned against the chaise and chuckled. "Now who's being harsh? Still, I bet it'll be quite a spell before she tries it again."

Magda grunted and picked up her cup. "It better be." Thunder shook the house as she settled on the divan to finish their game.

Bertha stole a casual glance at the window, her heart crowding her throat.

Magda moved as if to play her turn, but her hand crossed the checkerboard instead and gripped Bertha's fingers.

Startled, Bertha looked up into caring brown eyes. . .and felt her armor slide. "Oh, Magda! Where could she be?"

Emmy found a fresh loaf in the bread box and cut thick, crusty slices from the end. The corner pantry behind her yielded a jar of muscadine jelly. She scooped fat globs onto buttered bread and spread it clear to the edges. Her mouth watered before she could close the sandwich and get it to her lips. Grateful for something besides fried meat, she took a huge bite and rolled her eyes toward heaven. After pouring a tall glass of milk, she leaned against the counter and stared out the window at the storm, her thoughts turning to Daniel.

Her need for Daniel Clark rivaled her need to breathe. She wondered where he was at that moment. Did he think of her even now, yearn for her as she did for him? No one had ever made her feel the way he did. One glance from him and all was lost—her upbringing, her morals, her family. . .even her best friend.

Remembering Charity, the next bite of sandwich stuck in her throat. She gulped her milk to try to coax it down then lay the food aside. Lightning struck and thunder pealed with a crash that rattled the kitchen window. Emmy leaped away from it, and her stomach lurched. She'd heard them say Charity had gone missing, might be out somewhere in the storm.

Well, I won't think of it! I just won't!

Emmy turned from the window and picked up the sandwich

and milk. She'd finish them later, up in her room. Though she was loath to go back inside her dungeon, anything was better than spending the day with those cackling hens in the parlor.

She paused at the door. To get upstairs, she had to pass them one more time. After that, she'd hole up in her room until nightfall. Under cover of darkness, she'd sneak back down to the kitchen and pillage for more rations. After all, a girl had to keep up her strength.

CHAPTER 7

Charity clung to Buddy's steadying arm as the wagon raced up the street, spewing muddy water in its wake. The heavy rainfall had emptied the boardwalk in front of the hotel, making it easy to pull close to the door.

Buddy hauled back on the reins, took one look at the quagmire on his side, and then crawled over Charity to descend, dragging her and her bag off behind him. They ran into the lobby, laughing so hard they had to hold on to each other to stay upright, their sodden clothes leaving puddles on the polished wood floor.

From behind the desk, Sam stared with an open mouth before loudly clearing his throat. "Say, there. . .Miss Bloom. . .are you all right?"

Charity stopped giggling long enough to look over Buddy's shoulder at Sam then fell into more laughter at the astonished look on his face.

Before she could regain her composure, Buddy answered for her. "No, Sam, she's not all right. Can't you see she's soaked clean through?" He took her arm and led her to the counter. "The lady's in dire need of dry clothes. As a matter of fact, so am I." He held out his hand to Sam, his soaked sleeve dripping rivulets on the counter. "The key to Mr. Allen's room, if you please."

Sam recoiled as if Buddy's hand was a snake. "I'll do no such thing. How dare you attempt to besmirch this girl's reputation.

Sir, I won't allow it."

Buddy's earnest face relaxed into a slow grin. "Pick up your jaw, Sam. I have no lascivious notions toward our Miss Bloom." He extended his other palm. "That's why I also need Mr. Ritter's key. For myself."

He gestured at the guest book. "While you're at it, scratch Lee Allen's name from your registry and replace it with the lady's. Mr. Allen has surrendered his reservation to her, effective immediately."

Sam leaned into the counter. "On whose authority?"

Buddy's eyes twinkled, but his jaw was set. "Just the man who pays the tab. You see, the current occupants of those two rooms work for me, and I foot the bill for their housing. We'll find a corner of Mr. Ritter's room to lay another bedroll. I'll continue to pay for the other room as long as Miss Bloom needs it."

Charity whirled to face him. "Oh, Mr. Pierce, I couldn't."

He pointed at the register where Sam had drawn a line through Mr. Allen's name. "The deed is done, ma'am. Your protests won't change it."

"B-but I simply won't t-take his bed from under him and leave the three of you to one room." Yet even while she objected, she shivered so violently her words came out through chattering teeth.

Buddy smiled. "Rest easy. The three of us have bunked in closer quarters, I assure you." He nodded at Sam. "Have someone show the lady to her room while I tend to the buckboard." With that, he gave her a saucy wink, laced his thumbs behind blue suspenders, and strutted to the door.

"Buddy," Charity called after him. One glance at Sam's frowning face and she amended. "Mr. Pierce. . .I can't tell you how grateful I am."

Buddy tipped his soggy hat then turned and dashed outside.

Daniel Clark huddled in a corner of the hotel lobby among a group of men who had ducked in out of the rain. Feeling a mixture of disbelief and something else, an unsettling, uncomfortable emotion he couldn't shake, he watched the exchange between Charity and the strange man.

He'd never witnessed this Charity before—her delicate face framed by damp ringlets of coal and her wide eyes flashing, her head thrown back and her soft lips drawn in a smile full of gleaming white teeth. In all the time he'd known her, she'd never laughed so freely in his presence or clung to him weak-kneed with glee. Seeing her that way stirred something inside him that quickened his breath.

And then she was gone. Vanished from the top of the stairs, still laughing and chattering like a schoolgirl. Her absence left him as hollow as a gourd.

The fog in Daniel's head cleared enough to realize that the men crowded around him were staring, amusement dancing in their eyes. Clearing his throat, he pushed through his mockers, feigning interest in the weather past the front window. "Well, gentlemen, looks like it's beginning to clear."

Their snickers and whispers were lost on him as he hurried to the door and slipped out. Casting a glance at the offending stranger who had run into the hotel alongside Charity, he lowered the brim of his hat to block the persistent light sprinkle and hurried down the boardwalk toward home.

Charity released the bottom hook of her skirt and let the drenched fabric fall in a soggy heap at her feet. She stepped free and ran to the corner where she had tossed the wet satchel. Wrinkling her nose at the musty smell the rain had coaxed from the heavy canvas, she slid the bag over the floor then lifted it to the dressing table. Rummaging inside, she pulled out dry undergarments and her last clean dress. Shivers shook her from the draft blowing in around the window frame and under the door, and her teeth chattered until she could hear them.

There were clean towels and soap beside the basin of hot water Sam had sent upstairs. She freshened up and dressed as fast as she could. The water warmed her some, but her teeth still rattled. Jerking the blanket from the bed, she draped the soft folds over her shoulders.

The boar-bristle brush in her bag came from Mama's vanity set, an expensive gift she'd received as a girl in Jefferson and brought with her to Humble. Charity ran it through her hair, feeling guilty for having taken so precious an item without permission.

With her curls pinned up, the mirror over the basin reflected the image of her old self. So why didn't she feel like herself?

Charity leaned to study her face, so clean her nose reflected the light coming in under the shade. A fire she couldn't name lit her eyes from within and colored her burning cheeks. She put a hand to her trembling mouth to quench the smile she saw there and pushed the truth from her mind.

She turned from the mirror to look around, and her heart swelled in gratitude to Buddy. The room was small but cozy. From the blanket that covered her to the crisp sheets, the embroidered pillowcases, and the lace curtains at the window, everything smelled fresh and new.

The gleaming floors were of the same polished wood as the door, windowsill, and corner table that held the basin. Floral paper in shades of blue and green adorned the walls, and a rag rug beside the bed cushioned her feet.

Noise from the street below drew her to the window. A light rain still fell, but clustered strangers milled about the boardwalk again. She shook her head. A far cry from the days when she recognized every face in town. She feared the discovery of oil would cause Humble to become as bustling and sprawling as nearby Houston. Why couldn't the confounded oil companies pack it in and leave for good? She wished they'd all hop the first train out and go back to where they came from.

All. . .except Buddy Pierce.

Charity fell onto the bed and stared at the ceiling. Just who was he anyway, this bull of a man who met her at every turn, the handsome stranger who rescued her and knew all of her secrets? Remembering his teasing and spirited laughter, she hugged herself and smiled.

Had she ever seen such eyes? Green as a bitter apple and rimmed in brown, they looked right through her. And the size of him! When Buddy pulled her to his chest, she felt small and safe. His arms wrapped around her stirred a peculiar sensation in her middle, pleasant and unpleasant in equal measure. Warm butterflies tumbled in her stomach now just thinking of him.

She lurched upright. How could she possibly entertain such scandalous musings when only days ago Daniel had stood at her side, Daniel had held her?

Perched on the edge of the bed, staring at her troubled reflection in the frosty windowpane, she admitted that it hadn't been the same. She'd never once thrilled to Daniel's touch or come to life in his presence the way she had with Buddy.

How can that be? I almost married Daniel Clark.

Yet she hadn't once grieved for him the way she had for Emmy. Hadn't they both betrayed her?

Charity remembered Emmy's mournful face turned to the light, pining for Daniel while she grieved over shattered trust. She pictured Daniel emerging from the shadows, saw Emmy embracing him in the moonlight.

How could I have ever loved that wicked girl?

Yet her heart was her undoing. Whatever the cost, whatever the fool her devotion made her, she loved Emily Dane more than herself. The faithless girl was the sister she'd never had, and one never stopped loving a sister.

"Oh drat!" In her angst, Charity had twisted her dress until the thin fabric ripped. Fingering the ragged edges, she wondered if she could fix it. She had only one other outfit not too worn or frayed to wear. Juggling between three dresses made her weary.

Washing them every week became a challenge. Scrubbing wore down the nap more each time. Every washday there were buttons to replace and tears to mend. If only Mama could afford more material. They had tucked away money for that purpose, but the infernal wedding gown had sapped every penny and then some. She toyed with converting the gown into something suitable, but the idea wasn't practical. The fabric proved too fine for everyday use.

Amy Jane Pike's offer to buy the dress struck Charity's mind like a thunderclap. She could afford material for three, maybe four dresses with that kind of money.

As fast as she remembered Amy Jane, she realized something else. She was on her own now. In order to survive, she would need every penny that fell into her hands for necessities. Nothing more. The thought filled her with regret. . .and fear.

"Young Mr. Pierce said you and Bertha may come by some money." Mother Dane's words came to her unbidden.

If oil truly lay under their land, buying clothes would never be a problem again. She could buy a trunk full. And Mama would never need to scrub another floor. She could replace her straggly teeth with a store-bought pair and afford fancy combs like Mother Dane's for her hair. Charity imagined her mama gussied up like Mother Dane, and the picture made her laugh out loud.

Having money could do all those things and more, but she pushed the temptation from her mind. Such thoughts opposed how she felt about the oil boom in her town, not to mention her convictions about the evils of too much wealth.

A moan from deep within Charity's stomach reminded her she hadn't had breakfast, though the hour was well past noon. Her immediate fortune lay in selling her wedding gown. She would go see Amy Jane and then find some food. . .as soon as she warmed up a bit.

She lay back and snuggled deeper into the feather mattress. Drawing the soft blue blanket against her face, she breathed in the fresh, new smell. Clouds darkened the sky outside the window, casting the small room into shadows, while overhead the light patter of rain on the roof pounded out a muted lullaby.

CHAPTER 8

Two minutes of high wind and scattered hail and the tempest was spent. Thunder and lightning in a pitch-black sky had been the worst of it. One of those storms that make empty threats.

By the time Buddy drew near the stable, he had made up his mind. A light drizzle still fell, but what of it? He was already wet, and Charity's mama would be worried sick if he didn't set her mind at ease.

The horse had the smell of the stall in his nostrils and showed reluctance when Buddy made him turn.

"Giddap, you lazy beast. You ain't worth your weight in sour oats. Cut dirt, or I'll trade you for a gasoline engine."

The horse laid back his ears but plodded past the livery door. In no hurry to part with his feed bag, he shivered with irritation while Buddy shivered from the cold. A damp chill had penetrated his bones, and he ached all over. Scraping his knuckles and picking up a splinter on the jagged wood, he groped beneath the seat and found a spare saddle blanket. The stale covering would cause him to smell like the stockyard but might save him from the grippe.

The trail to the Danes' house felt farther than it actually was, even after the horse accepted his plight and picked up the pace. With tremendous relief, Buddy finally pulled up to the house and climbed down. The rain had stopped completely. He shrugged off the blanket and headed up the walk.

The door opened before he reached it, and Charity's mama blew out of it raving. "Where's my girl? Was it you hauled her away from here?"

He held up his hands. "Your daughter's fine, Mrs. Bloom." The feral gleam in her eyes brought to mind the liveryman's estimation. She looked like Crazy Bertha.

"I said where is she? Why'd you take her, and what've you done to her?"

Flustered, Buddy glanced at Mrs. Dane, who had come to stand behind her friend. The big woman took one look at his face and came to his aid.

"Bert, let the boy get a word in. It appears he has something to say. Let's hear him."

"Talk fast, stranger. Magda, fetch me your shotgun for if'n I don't like what he has to say."

The cold left Buddy, driven away by fear of the tiny, wild-eyed woman. "Ma'am, on my honor, Charity's safe. I got her in out of the rain, and I'm sure she's warm and dry by now. Don't worry, I left her in good hands."

"Where at?"

"In town. I put her up at the Lone Star Hotel."

A shrill scream exploded from Mrs. Bloom's tight lips, and she charged him, head down, like a bull. He caught hold of her forehead before she could ram him and held her off. She swatted at him with both hands, connecting only with the air.

"Bertha!" Mrs. Dane caught her around the waist and hauled her back. "Let the boy explain."

Bertha thrashed against her friend's grip. "You heard him. He's done took her to the hotel and tarnished her."

Buddy rocked back on his heels. He'd never heard such talk from a lady before, and her words stunned him. Then he got mad. Being accused of the same thing twice in one day was quite enough.

"No, ma'am, I did no such thing." He had to shout over her screams. "I wouldn't do anything to hurt your daughter. Last I saw, she was standing in the hotel lobby where I left her, soaking wet and exhausted–a condition she came to be in through no fault of mine."

Mrs. Bloom ceased her struggling and stared up at him, no longer Crazy Bertha, just a guilt-ridden, heartbroken mother. She dropped her gaze before his accusation. "Why didn't you bring her here, then?"

"She refused to come back. No disrespect intended, ma'am, but you have a stubborn daughter."

From behind Bertha Bloom, arms still locked around her waist, Mrs. Dane nodded. "An inherited trait."

His fiery indignation cooled, Buddy pushed back his hat and stepped closer. "I only did what I thought best for Charity."

Mrs. Dane chimed in again. "He got her off the streets, Bert. You should be grateful for that, anyway."

Mrs. Bloom pursed her lips in thought, pressing her finger against them. The conclusion she came to smoothed her furrowed brow. She nodded then looked over her shoulder at Mrs. Dane. "Turn me loose, Magda. I got my right mind now."

"You sure?"

"I'm sure. Now let me go."

Mrs. Dane cautiously complied but held her arms at the ready, just in case.

Mrs. Bloom looked up at Buddy. "You swear on all things holy that you ain't hurt my daughter?"

"I don't hold with swearing on holy things, ma'am, but you have my word as a Christian gentleman. I'd cut off my arm before I'd hurt her."

Bertha Bloom folded her arms, stock-still except for her tongue, which slowly traced circles in her cheek. She tilted her head. "You mean that, don't you, son?"

"Ma'am, I sure do."

"Will you help me bring her home?"

He chewed over his next words then decided to take the risk. "I don't mean to interfere in your business, Mrs. Bloom, but don't you think you're asking a lot of Charity? To stay here, I mean?"

She weighed and measured him with a glance. "You know a few things about us, don't you, boy?"

"I know enough. I believe your daughter feels she doesn't have a home. Provide her one, and she'll come."

She jutted her chin. "Fine—then help me."

Buddy cocked his head and frowned. "Me, ma'am?"

"Who else? You're the only one that can."

"How so?"

She looked into the distance and drew a long, ragged breath. "I never trusted no oilman before. I've hated and shunned the lot of you. But something about you rang true from the beginning."

She fixed him with a stern gaze. "You're the one who talked me into leasing my house and half my property to pay for this well. Now get yourself over to my place and find oil. Else clear off so I can take my daughter home." Mrs. Bloom's direct stare was a challenge.

Buddy answered it with a nod. "There's oil beneath your land, all right. A lot of it. I'd stake my reputation as an oilman on that."

"Then go coax it out of the ground so I can buy my daughter a place to live. I'll give you two months to look. If you don't find anything by then, you clear out and I reclaim my property."

Despite the fire of his enthusiasm, the cold had begun to creep back into Buddy's limbs. He couldn't control the shivers that took him. "I'll g-get on over there f-first thing."

Mrs. Dane latched onto his sleeve. "Not so fast, young man." She held him at arm's length and looked him over. "Soaking wet and chilled to the bone. You won't be able to do anything if you catch your death."

Her grip tightened and she started for the house. He had no choice but to follow. "You need to get into some dry clothes. My husband's about your size, only shorter. 'Course, he's fleshy around the middle, not muscled up like you. I guess some of his things will have to do."

She paused and wrinkled her nose at him. "If you don't mind my saying, you need a good washing. You smell worse than a buffalo herd."

In one last desperate attempt, Buddy pulled free of her grasp. "Yes, ma'am. I reckon that's true, so I'd best get on back to town."

Mrs. Dane linked arms with him, but not in the delicate, genteel manner of a lady. In fact, she nearly wrestled him to the ground. "Don't make me take you by the ear, young man. Dry clothes and a warm tub is what you need, and I'll be taking no sass on the subject."

She dragged him past the front door and into the parlor. "You might as well save yourself the twenty-five cents. That's what a soak in hot water costs in town, you know, plus fifteen cents for a shave." She winked over at Mrs. Bloom. "I'm offering fifty cents worth of scrubbing, two dollars worth of duds, and a plate of vittles if you're hungry. . .and it won't cost you a plug nickel." She chuckled. "And, Mr. Pierce, 'free' is a bargain you can't afford to pass up."

Satisfied with the angle of her hat in the vanity mirror, Charity pulled on clean gloves and stepped into the hall. Two rooms down, a man stooped next to the keyhole struggling to fit his key into the lock. After a closer look, she realized it was Buddy, though something about him seemed different. She closed her door hard to get his attention.

He leaped and whirled as if she'd shot him, then spun without a word and went at the lock with a vengeance.

Planting her hands on her hips, she feigned anger. "So there you are. First you help a lady and then you run out on her."

Buddy's frantic fingers stilled. He straightened slowly and turned, one chestnut brow arched to the sky. "You know, a man can run into a heap of trouble in this town for that very thing."

Stunned by his angry face, Charity clasped her hands at her chest. "What very thing?"

He abandoned the stubborn key and charged like a bantam hen with chicks. "Trying to help a lady, that's what. Do you have any idea the humiliation I've suffered?"

For the first time she noticed his manner of dress. He wore a white shirt, suitable for Sunday service but made for smaller shoulders and a wider waist. Gathered folds allowed the sleeves to fit his big arms, but they ended far shy of his wrists. A woman's sash of robin's egg blue held up black trousers six inches too short and miles too big around the middle.

She stared, trying to take it all in. "Oh, Buddy! What in the world?"

"See what I mean?" He held his arms out to his sides. "This is my reward for the good deed of the day."

Charity ached to laugh, but the look on his face warned her not to. She pointed at his waist. "Is that. . . ? Why, Mother Dane has a sash exactly like that."

"Not anymore, she doesn't."

"Oh no!"

His gaze jerked to her handbag and his scowl quenched her grin. "Where do you think you're going? I've just wrestled a bobcat over putting you up in that room, and now you're leaving?"

The breath caught in her throat. "Mama."

"As bad as she was, your mama wasn't the worst of it. I'd sooner face Custer's Indians than deal with that Dane woman again. She had me shucked and in a tub before I could say Jack Sprat. Then she trussed me in this getup and left me no choice but to ride into town looking as queer as a pig in a parlor."

Charity jerked a hand to her mouth, glad he couldn't see behind it, and tried to look appalled. "How scandalous! They're a couple of ruffians, those two. Oh, Buddy, I should've warned you. Would have, too, if you'd bothered to tell me where you were going."

An elderly couple appeared at the head of the stairs, saw Buddy, and openly stared. Charity guessed they'd caught sight of him downstairs and were still in a stir. As they passed by, the grinning old man pointed at Buddy's bare ankles and whispered something about floodwater. In front of their door, they looked back with amused eyes, collapsed into giggles, and scrambled inside.

Buddy slouched and hung his head. "I'll have to fight every man in Humble before I live this down."

"Why on earth did you go to the Danes'?"

"Why do you think? You ran off without a thought for anyone. In a storm yet. For all they knew, a twister had you in a Louisiana swamp by now."

She stared into his eyes and knew his claim to be true. Ashamed, she dropped her gaze and leaned on the wall. "If not for you, it might've."

Buddy drew a deep breath then released it along with his air of indignation. He leaned against the wall beside her—too close—and lifted her chin with his finger. "Hardly accurate, since there was no twister. And stop changing the subject. Where are you off to?"

"I have business outside town."

He shook his head. "Whatever it is, it'll keep until tomorrow when I can go with you."

She raised her brows. "I'm grateful for the offer, but I've conducted business on my own for some time now. I think I can manage."

"And I gave my word to your mama that I'd watch out for you. I don't need you getting into mischief that I'll have to answer for later. Besides, you won't make it back before nightfall. I get the feeling Humble isn't the same safe town it was before."

Buddy was right. The streets grew wilder every day. She could count on one hand the times she'd been in town after dark, even before the boom. She stood upright and faced him. "Fine, you win. But why can't we go right now?"

"I'm exhausted and hungry, that's why. As soon as I change out of this silly garb, I'm finding myself something to eat and going to bed."

Her heart sank. At the mention of food, the rumble in her stomach picked up something fierce, but she wouldn't be eating until she sold her dress. Planting her feet, she got ready to take him head-on, though she felt dwarfed by his looming size. "I'm sorry, but I must go now. If you can't go with me, I'll be forced to go by myself."

"Why? What could be so all-fired important?"

She wilted a bit. "I can't say. It's personal."

"You have to give me more than that if you expect me to jump to your bidding."

Reluctance to answer his question knocked the air right out of her bluff. She gave a careless toss of her head. "Very well, then. Will you take me first thing tomorrow?"

"I have business of my own in the morning."

Her hungry stomach lurched. "I see."

"I should be finished sometime after lunch. We'll go then."

She burned with curiosity but wouldn't ask. She didn't hide it well, though, and he volunteered the information.

"I happen to be headed out to your place."

Her head jerked up. "Whatever for?"

"I promised your mama I'd get things moving along out there. First thing tomorrow I'll be riding out to see if I can't speed up those drills." He ambled over to the door and set to work struggling with the lock again. "Blast it all. What's wrong with this infernal thing?"

"Buddy?"

He turned.

"Take me with you."

"That's not a good idea."

"Why not?" She pouted, irked that he returned to the lock, dismissing her.

"It's no place for you. The yard is crawling with roughnecks and buried under equipment. Besides, I'm not taking the rig."

"I'll walk with you."

"Too muddy to walk. I'm going by horseback."

"I can ride."

He exhaled and shifted his weight to the other foot. "Why do you want to go out there anyway?"

Was he irritated at the lock or with her? "Just do. I'm curious."

"Well, the answer's no."

She crossed her arms and leaned against the door. He still fought with the key. After a bit she eased over to him. "You know, I think that must be the wrong one."

He straightened and frowned as though the thought hadn't occurred to him. "You think so?"

She watched him figure it out. He'd have to go downstairs, and he'd sooner be poached and pickled.

"Charity, could you. . . ?"

"Exchange it for you? Of course." She took the long brass key from his hand and dangled it between them. "In exchange for a favor."

His hopeful eyes narrowed. "You wouldn't bushwhack me like that."

She smiled her sweetest smile. "Such a harsh word."

He threw up his hands. "Who spawned the hardheaded women in this town? Go on, then. Get my key. But you'd best be ready to head out first thing in the morning."

"I'll be ready. I promise." She rushed to the head of the stairs and then turned. Blast pride—she was desperate. "Buddy?"

"Now what?"

"I haven't eaten all day, and I'm faint from hunger."

"Lucky for you, I am, too. We'll rustle up a bite downstairs before we turn in."

"Wonderful idea." She lifted the hem of her skirt and started down the stairs.

"I just hope you can keep up tomorrow," he called after her. "Because I won't be coddling you."

The fiery red and gold horizon, visible between fat, knotted trunks, belied the cold of the morning as Charity followed Buddy out of town. The horses' steady footfalls were quiet on the pine straw blanket, and the creak of leather and occasional snort of a horse were the only sounds to break the stillness. In the chill air, their breath, and that of their mounts, came out in smoky billows of mist. Charity shivered and drew her shawl closer, her attention on Buddy's back.

His spine as rigid as a tomato stake, he sat tall in the saddle on the big bay. As for his vow not to coddle her, so far he'd failed to keep his threat. While she couldn't claim Buddy had pampered her, he had certainly tended to her needs.

After staring hard at her denim britches, he wouldn't allow her to go with him to the livery, insisting she wait inside the hotel instead. In no time he returned with a gentle horse for her, shortening the stirrups before taking her elbow and helping her aboard. Then he led her through the swampy streets, guiding the little mare past the mud holes and deepest ruts before handing over the reins.

Charity blushed remembering how Buddy looked at her when she opened the door dressed in men's pants. She guessed the women in St. Louis wore split skirts or riding habits, but Humble afforded no such luxuries. Women here made their own by cutting worn-out frocks up the middle and sewing them into flared legs, or they borrowed jeans from a man. Thankfully, she'd packed an old pair handed down from her slip of an Irish grandfather.

She stared down at her legs. A mite snug and hardly the latest fashion, but the pants served her well for sitting a horse. "It's mighty cold, isn't it?" she asked then cringed, waiting for Buddy to order her to return to her room. She needn't have worried.

The quarrelsome man hadn't said ten words to her all morning. He'd had even less to say at dinner the night before.

She itched to get him talking again and searched her mind for something to draw him out. "Hey, what's that over there?"

Buddy looked over his shoulder, and she pointed near the edge of the trail. "Are those coyote droppings?" She winced at her choice of topic but forged ahead anyway. "You know, I think they are. He left some tracks, too. See? In front of the droppings. One paw in front of the other, as clear as day."

He acknowledged her findings with a grunt and turned away again.

"Coyotes don't usually come in this close to town. Wonder what drew him?"

Buddy shrugged. It seemed the most he would give, so Charity gave up. They rode the rest of the way in silence.

A quarter mile from her property, a commotion the likes of which she'd never heard reached Charity's ears. The sound grew louder as they neared the house, yet Buddy seemed unconcerned. She longed to ask about the source of the racket, but her offended pride wouldn't allow her.

As they rode up even with the yard, the hullabaloo frightened the horses. Buddy's mount sidestepped, prancing and bobbing his head until Buddy dug in his heels and coaxed him forward. Charity's skittish little mare fell in behind. They picked their way to the rear of the house and reined in at the edge of chaos.

Sludge-covered men darted to and fro, dodging wagons, equipment, and each other. Oxen strained against carts filled with pipe, their massive hooves slinging mud as they pawed the rain-soaked ground. Rigs loaded with timber sat off to one side. She recognized these as belonging to Bender's Mill. More stacks of lumber lined the bog in staggered piles. At least Charity thought it was the bog. Everything looked so different she found it hard to get her bearings.

A clearing stretched in a wide circle from the edge of the dense woods beyond the bog all the way to the scrub bushes behind the house, creating an open area that hadn't been there before. Heavy black boots had trampled the yard to mush, leaving very little grass—only a few tufts along the fence line.

Charity's stomach tightened. How odd to see strangers pouring in and out at the back entrance. Someone had tied the screen door open with a rope, an invitation to swarms of flies and mosquitoes. Muddy tracks crisscrossed the steps and porch. She shuddered to think what the floor inside must look like. Mama would be fit to bury!

Well, so be it. It was justice served. When all the nonsense was over and they returned to this mess, Charity wouldn't lift a finger to help clean.

"Morning, Miss Charity!"

She turned in her saddle to see who shouted the greeting.

Stubby Morgan grinned up at her, his copper hair and matching freckles stark against his pale complexion.

"Why, good morning. What are you doing way out here this time of day?" She glanced toward the mill wagons. "They got you making deliveries now?"

"No, ma'am. Don't work out at Bender's no more." He pointed over his shoulder with a grimy thumb. "I signed on with this outfit."

Stunned, Charity gaped at him. Stubby had gone to work for Bender's Mill the year his papa died. He was only fourteen at the time. Charity, barely ten when it happened, felt sad when he never returned to school.

His dappled face flinched under her searching gaze, and he shuffled his oversized feet. "The pay's good, Miss Charity." He brightened. "Three dollars a day! More'n twice what I brought home from the mill. In my family, that's too good to pass up."

She found her voice. "But don't you see? It won't last. I can't believe you quit your steady job to work for a company that'll be long gone in a matter of weeks."

A puzzled look lit briefly on his upturned face before he flashed an angelic smile. "Why, sure it'll last, ma'am. Humble's a boomer town now." He gestured over his head at a group of men standing nearby. "Just ask them fellers over yonder. Zeke there helped me land the job. He put in a good word for me with the drillers."

Charity followed his nod. Ezekiel Young and his son Isaac, her nearest neighbors to the north, stood in a long line of men passing boards from the wagon to the clearing. Charity understood their presence. The Young family had lost their cotton crop to boll weevils, and with Isaac set to wed Amy Jane Pike in three months, there'd be another mouth to feed.

Shamus Pike himself huddled with another group of men shouting to be heard over the ruckus. Despite Elsa's fancy airs, Shamus always worked extra jobs between crops. He had no choice. His wife and daughter scooped up money as fast as he raked it in. If the oil company paid so handsomely, Elsa would see to it that Shamus was first in line.

Charity leaned over in the saddle so Stubby could hear. "You've worked that mill for ten years." She frowned and nodded at the melee behind him. "Don't throw it away for this. I'll bet they'd let you change your mind if you asked."

Stubby shrugged his narrow shoulders. "Why would I change my mind? Like I said, Miss Charity, the pay's real good." He peered up at her, shading his eyes from the sun. "Don't worry none about your mail. I can still run out and fetch it for you every Saturday."

She shook her head at the kind-faced young man. "I won't have you go out of your way like that for me. I'm grateful for the offer, but don't trouble yourself about it anymore."

"You sure?"

She smiled. "Real sure."

A man near the house called Stubby's name. He grinned at Charity, tipped his battered hat, and ran off. Her gaze drifted past him and over the scope of her land, taking in every violation, every unspeakable change, every heavy-footed stranger tromping through her yard.

Her room sat tucked behind those mud-spattered walls. She pictured the quilt on her bed, a gift from Grandma Leona Bloom in Jefferson, covered in sludge. Remembered her diary with its too flimsy lock, left out on her desk. Nausea settled in the pit of her stomach, coupled with something akin to rage.

These men rode into Humble like a gang of roughs and thieves, turning everything upside down with their silly oil. They had disrupted her life and defiled her home. Hiring her friends and neighbors to take part in it dealt Charity a staggering blow.

She felt Buddy's gaze on her and glanced his way. He watched her from astride his horse with the same puzzled look she'd seen two days before. What must he be thinking?

Who cares what he thinks? This is his fault. All of it.

"I'm going," she spat. "I've seen enough." She whirled the mare and dug her heels into its flank, leaving Buddy in a spray of mud.

Charity hoped the horse knew the way back. She was too upset to think about where she was going. Clinging to the saddle horn, she let the mare take her where it would, while the trees on both sides of the trail passed in a blur.

Her life was a fine mess. In a week's time she'd lost her fiancé, her best friend, her home, and her mama, in that order. The only good had come to her at the hands of a stranger, a man at whom she'd just flung dirt.

Guilt niggled at her conscience. How could she be cruel to Buddy Pierce? He'd offered her nothing but kindness since the day they first met. If not for him, she would be homeless.

Forgive me, God. I've acted shamelessly. I should turn around and apologize.

Before Charity could act on her decision, a pause in the mare's stride broke the monotony of her plodding and a shudder coursed through her body. Her ears fell back, and she cantered to the side.

"Easy, girl. What's your trouble?"

The horse's breath came quicker and her head shot up. Eyes wild with fear and nostrils flared, she edged away from the right side of the trail, and it was all Charity could do to hold her. A low growl came from the bushes just before the mare reared, her legs pawing the air. Charity hit the ground hard and rolled in the mud, away from the flailing hooves. She fought to draw breath into her lungs but couldn't. This scared her almost as much as the scraggly beast crouching at the edge of the path.

The wolf, no longer interested in the fleeing horse, stalked Charity in short, quick bursts. His body lay low to the ground, his hollow haunches trembling from the effort. He bared his teeth in a wide, feral grin, and stringy spittle ran in rivulets from his mouth.

She struggled to get up, to breathe. Twenty more feet and he'd be on her. She groped the ground for a weapon. Desperate, scrambling fingers closed around a clump of muddy grass, and she tensed to hurl it at him.

Fifteen feet.

Ten.

Leering, taunting her, the wolf rose for the last advance. Sure of his kill, he swayed closer.

Charity met his eyes and saw evil. She dug her heels into the ground and scrambled away. Willing air into her lungs, she hurled the fistful of mud at his face. He wouldn't take her without a fight.

Still, he came. Almost upon her, he snarled and gnashed his teeth—the promise of things to come.

God, help me!

The wolf took two more steps then froze midstride. He crouched again, his attention drawn to an approaching rider.

Buddy reined in between them. "Don't move." His voice was grave with warning. "He's rabid."

Buddy's horse trembled, no happier than the mare to be so close to the snarling creature, but Buddy held him steady.

Charity struggled to her feet. Her lungs had somewhat eased, and she sucked in short, gasping breaths. She longed to leap for the horse but knew if she did, he might bolt.

The wolf held his ground, too blind-insane to be afraid.

A shot rang out from a nearby wooded grove. The wolf yelped and lunged, straight for the legs of Buddy's mount. The big bay reared, but Buddy held the saddle. The wolf died midleap and fell on the muddy trail with glazed eyes, teeth still bared. His tongue lolled to the side, and bloody foam rimmed his muzzle.

Charity shuddered at the sight. Buddy rode his frantic horse a few feet away, leaped off, and ran to Charity. Oblivious to her mud-covered clothes, she threw her arms around his neck and hid her face against his chest.

He held her and rubbed her back with both hands. "Are you all right?"

"My legs won't hold me."

"Don't worry, I've got you."

She nuzzled closer and shuddered. "I was so scared."

"Me, too," he whispered, "but it's over now."

She raised her head and sought his eyes. "I'm sorry for being mad at you, Buddy."

He cupped her chin with his finger and laughed down at her. "Were you mad at me? Funny, I thought I was mad at you."

She smiled and pressed her cheek against the rough fabric of his shirt, for the first time aware of the clean, woodsy smell of him. He held her tighter.

"You know," he said, his breath warm against her hair, "next time you get peeved at me, you might want to let me in on it. Seems a shameful waste of anger if I don't know."

She rose up and nodded at the wolf. "What happened? Who shot it?"

He tilted his chin toward something behind her. "I think there's your answer."

Charity looked over her shoulder. Three riders emerged from the trees, one of them Daniel Clark. He came alongside them, a rifle balanced across his saddle.

"You all right, Charity?" His blue eyes moved over her, dark with an emotion she'd never seen there before.

Aware that Buddy still held her, she drew a breath and moved away from him. "I will be."

Sidney Anderson spoke up. "We been trailing that wolf all day. Rabid, you know."

Buddy moved toward them, planting his feet carefully to give wide berth to the dead animal. "Yep, we figured that out."

Daniel motioned at the ground with his chin. "Sid, take a shovel and bury that critter. Put him deep. Cover the blood, too. Last thing we need around here is an outbreak of rabies. And, Jack"—he pointed down the trail—"follow Miss Charity's horse and make sure it gets back to the livery."

Buddy nodded at Daniel. "Much obliged. I'm grateful you

showed up when you did."

Daniel flashed a broad smile. "Oh, I reckon you could've handled the situation. We just came along at the right time. We've tracked that thing for miles."

Buddy grinned. "So you said."

Daniel leaned in the saddle to offer his hand. "I don't believe we've met. I'm Daniel Clark." He seemed to chew on the next part but said it anyway. "A friend of Miss Bloom's." His eyes shifted to her when he said it.

She could tell he wanted to catch her reaction. She forced herself not to have one.

Buddy seemed not to notice. He reached up and shook Daniel's hand. "Buddy Pierce. I work for an oil company here in town."

"Glad to know you, Mr. Pierce." Though he spoke to Buddy, Daniel stared at Charity. "Can I give you a ride into town, honey? You could use some cleaning up, and I'm headed that way."

The endearment stiffened Charity's spine. Daniel Clark was cockier than a man had a right to be. No matter how black his hair or broad his shoulders, there were some things you just didn't do. Besides, how did he know she was staying in town?

She took a step closer to Buddy. "No, thank you. Mr. Pierce will take me."

Daniel's dark eyebrows rose; then his gaze swept to Buddy. "I'll leave you in his capable hands then." He tipped his wide-brimmed hat and turned his horse.

"Daniel. . . ?"

Leather creaked as he shifted his weight to look at her.

She swallowed the ache in her throat and met his eyes. "Thank you. For shooting the wolf, I mean."

He held her gaze until her cheeks grew warm. Mischief teased the corners of his mouth. He glanced at Buddy. "I'd shoot a wolf for you any old time, sugar." He winked then spurred his horse and rode away.

Sidney fetched a shovel from his pack and bent to scoop up the carcass. Charity spun away from the gruesome sight. She doubted she'd ever forget the big animal standing over her, its trembling legs coiled and ready to spring.

Buddy's hands gripped her shoulders from behind. "I'm sorry you had to go through that, Charity. I feel responsible."

She reached to touch his fingers. "You? Nonsense. How could it be your fault?"

He stepped around to face her. "If I hadn't pouted like a schoolboy this morning, I would've taken a closer look at those tracks you found." He glanced over at the wolf. "I expect they belonged to our friend there."

Charity shook her head. "It's nobody's fault. And like you said, it's over now."

He smiled, mostly with his eyes, and nodded. "Let's get you back to town, then." His arm went across her shoulders, his grip firm.

Tucked against him, she felt safe. She allowed him to guide her to where the bay stood pawing the ground. On the way, she saw his hat, saved from the mud by a thatch of tall grass. She bent and picked it up, brushing it off before handing to him, but his curious gaze followed Daniel up the trail.

"That your Daniel?"

She halted, nearly tripping him, and dashed his hat to the ground. "He's not my Daniel! Why does everyone keep saying that?"

Buddy's forehead crumpled. "Ease up, little lady. I didn't mean to pry." He leaned for his hat, wiped the fresh mud from the brim onto his jeans, and walked on ahead.

Charity cringed and pressed her knuckles to her eyes. "Buddy, please wait."

Whatever she meant to say next, the words were lost when he stopped short and turned. Embarrassed, she spit out the first thing that came to mind. "Goodness, but you're a cantankerous man. You keep me in a constant state of gratitude or regret. I never know whether to thank you or say I'm sorry."

He lifted a brow. "Which one you offering this time?"

She winced. "Definitely the latter. I'm sorry. I truly am. I'm not the least bit mad at you. It's that insufferable Daniel Clark." She glared up the trail. "Have you ever witnessed such arrogance? Why, the nerve of him."

"He did seem mighty friendly, considering."

A blush crept up her cheeks.

Buddy brought the horse around and motioned for her to climb on. When she lifted her foot to the stirrup, he frowned at her mud-covered pants. "Reckon it's too late to whistle for old Daniel? I'm not sure I care to cozy up behind those all the way into town."

She swung into the saddle. "Don't tease. It's not funny."

He climbed up behind her and leaned to take the reins, so close his breath tickled her cheek. "It's none of my business, but if you ask me, Daniel Clark is a man having some regrets."

She squirmed around to glare at him. "Whatever do you mean?"

Buddy flicked the reins. "Like I said, Miss Bloom, it's none of my business."

CHAPTER 10

Emily Dane sprawled in her four-poster bed, idly gnawing a drumstick. Barefoot and still in her nightdress, she lay propped against goose-down pillows, one long leg crossed over the other. With her free hand, she twirled one of the blond ringlets framing her face while admiring the smooth, bare skin of her knees.

"You're downright scandalous in your impropriety, Emily Dane."

Mama's stern voice in her head made her giggle. That's what she'd say, all right, but what of it? According to Mama, she was forever downright scandalous in one silly thing or the other.

Emmy froze midbite and stared down at the greasy poultry until her eyes crossed. *Gracious! If I keep this up, I'll be prime pork and ready for the slaughter.* She extended her leg and stared, examining it from every angle before she smiled. *Then my thighs won't be quite so fetching, now, will they?*

Deliberately, and with great satisfaction, she flicked her wrist, tossing the half-eaten chicken leg through the open window. "There you go, Mama. Another pretty rose for your garden."

Emmy wiped her fingers on the lace napkin in her lap then gaped at the dark oily spots left behind. She had smuggled the fried chicken to her room wrapped in one of Mama's best linens. Holding the square of delicate cloth aloft, she surveyed the mess. "Oh bother! They'll hear her clear to Montgomery County if she gets wind of this."

She rolled onto her stomach and slid to the edge of the bed, peering into the dark recess between the floor and her lumpy mattress. Fighting to keep her balance, she leaned further in and worked at a tear by the nearest slat until she had removed a handful of fluff. Then she tucked the soiled cloth deep inside the hole. After stuffing the cotton in after it, she pushed upright and lay back with a satisfied smile.

There. Now she won't need to fret.

A thought flitted past, changing her smile to a frown. It was Mama's own fault, after all, for opening the door to Charity and Aunt Bert. She left Emmy no choice but to rummage like a thief in her own kitchen, so she'd have to live with the occasional missing napkin, now, wouldn't she?

She flopped on her side and stared at the floral wallpaper. During her confinement, she had memorized the line of every petal and every shade of pink. She knew how many blooms adorned each wall, as well as the numbers facing left and right. She had stared at the big ugly roses for days now, and they'd stared right back, silent witnesses to her frustration.

In truth, her history with the flowers started more than mere days ago. The horrid walls had been her constant companions for the past eight years, since Papa hired her room remodeled the summer she turned twelve. No one had touched it since. For Emmy, the youthful decor had long since lost its charm.

No matter. Soon she'd be mistress of her own big house, filled with brand-new rooms to look at, to decorate however she saw fit. Daniel had built it for Charity, but Charity would never live there. Emmy would marry Daniel, and the pretty, brick-fronted structure with its wide columns and a porch that wrapped all the way around would be hers. And there wouldn't be a pink rose in sight.

Hugging her pillow, she rolled to the other side of the bed where her vanity table beckoned. She knew she should dress and freshen up, but why go to all the trouble? Why wash her face, pin up her hair, get all gussied up for these four walls?

Hooves pounded up the drive. She leaped from the bed and rushed to her second-floor window, arriving just as the horse and rider passed from sight, hidden by the tangled branches of the oak outside her window. She peered out, using the lace curtain for cover, and caught a quick glimpse of muddy boots as the caller moved under the portico.

Next came the strident, angry voice of Auntie Bert. "You got a lot of nerve coming around here, Daniel Clark."

Emmy gasped. *Daniel? What in the world. . . ?*

"There ain't no need for that shotgun, ma'am."

Shotgun! Emmy's heart pounded so hard she feared they'd hear it downstairs.

Daniel's familiar voice rumbled, but she couldn't make out his words. Desperate to see, she leaned over as far as possible, but the front porch roof hid all but their feet.

Aunt Bert's voice became shrill. "Did you say wolf?"

"Mad with rabies, Mrs. Bloom. I shot it dead."

"Is my girl all right?"

"She's safe enough—from any four-legged threat, at least."

"What do you mean by that?" This from Emmy's mama.

"Mrs. Dane, there are prowling wolves of the two-legged sort that can be just as dangerous."

Aunt Bert's voice took a hard edge. "You can say that again. I'm looking at one."

Mama shushed her.

After an edgy silence, Aunt Bert piped up again. "What is it you're trying to say to us, boy?"

"If you're really aiming to know, I'll tell you."

"Get on with it, then."

Emmy strained to hear, but Daniel's next words escaped her. She considered shimmying down the trellis and listening from behind the hedge but feared they'd catch her. She leaned so far out she had to tangle the fingers of both hands in the ancient vines to keep from toppling headfirst out of the window.

"Mrs. Bloom, you don't even know where Charity is, do you?"

"Not that it's any of your business, but I know exactly where she is. She's over at the Lone Star Hotel under the watchful eye of a friend."

Daniel cleared his throat. "I suppose by *friend* you mean Buddy Pierce?"

"Yep. I got that nice boy looking out for my Charity. If it weren't for the likes of you and her so-called best friend, she'd be here with me where she belongs."

Emmy cringed, but Daniel let it pass. "Well, ma'am, that nice boy you speak of is a stranger around these parts, ain't he? Just how much do you know about him?"

Aunt Bert was quiet for so long Emmy wondered if she'd heard Daniel's question.

"I've had about enough out of you!"

She heard, all right. Fury boiled from Aunt Bert's mouth, so fierce it singed the fuzz on Emmy's ears.

"I ain't answering no more questions from a polecat. I trusted you with my girl once, but you turned out to be a fizzle. Don't come around here now telling me who to trust with my own daughter."

"Pour it into him, Bert. He ain't good for nothing but telling lies and shaming young girls."

Emmy's grip tightened on the vines. *Oh, Mama! How could you?*

Daniel's raised voice echoed beneath the vaulted roof. "What you think of me don't change the facts, Bertha Bloom. You ought to know I just parted company with Charity and Mr. Pierce. Your nice boy there had his hands all over Charity, right out in the open in the bright of day."

Tension charged the air, like the second before lightning strikes.

Emmy felt the hair on her scalp lift.

"I don't believe you." Aunt Bert's voice crashed the answering thunder.

"Ask Sidney Anderson and Jack Mayhew. They'll tell you it's true."

"No! I'm saying I don't believe you had the brash to march up here and spout something like this about my Charity, after what all you done to her." Aunt Bert's pitch might've shattered glass.

Another weighty hush.

Daniel shuffled his feet. "I didn't come here to fret nobody," he finally said. "I just thought you'd want to know."

"All I want to know is you in your saddle, riding away from here."

More silence. Emmy imagined them staring each other down.

Then Daniel's parting words floated up, as chipper as if they'd gathered for a Sunday social. "I'll take my leave then, ladies. You two have a pleasant day now, you hear?" Emmy pictured him tipping his hat, turning a rigid spine to the old biddies and walking away.

She withdrew a bit when Daniel stepped down off the porch and headed for his horse. He mounted up then rode out from under the oak tree and down the drive, slinging mud in his wake.

The women were still on the porch muttering dark curses at his back. Emmy leaned out again to better hear what Aunt Bert was saying.

"Why, if I weren't a lady, I'd kick him into a pulp."

"I'd tie him up and hold him for you. What you think he's up to, Bert?"

"No good, I'd say. Seems to be pulling some kind of a bluff."

Her mama paused for a bit before asking the question plaguing Emmy's mind. "You don't think there's any truth to what he said, do you?"

Aunt Bert's tone chilled Emmy's spine. "Magda. . .there'd better not be."

More shuffling feet, and then the door closed behind them.

Emmy pulled her head inside and made a mad dash for her clothes, dressing as if the house was on fire. On the way to climb out the window, she cast a glance at her image in the mirror over the dresser.

Drat! Her hair needed pinning, but there was no time to do it right. She had to catch Daniel.

He would take the trail out. She could catch him if she cut across the fields on Rebel. She wouldn't dare try it if Papa was home. Oh, there'd be trouble if she got caught. Terrible trouble. But she could outrun Mama.

In the barn, she paused before saddling old Rebel. Papa prized the palomino, still the fastest horse on the place, over most things in life, sometimes even her and Mama. Only there was no time to weigh the consequences. Daniel was riding away.

Five minutes later, Emmy raced across the field. She urged the horse through a tight thicket then over a marshy low spot to Jordan Gully. Despite her wishes, he slowed to pick his way across a deep ditch on the row of planks fashioned into a makeshift bridge. At the trail, she saw Daniel and laid a switch to Rebel's flank.

"Daniel! Oh, Daniel, wait."

He turned in the saddle and reined up his horse. As she approached, he drew alongside, and the press of his leg against her thigh took her breath.

"Emmy, what in blazes are you doing out here?"

The sound of her name in Daniel's long drawl raised gooseflesh on her arms. "I came to talk to you."

"Where'd you come from? I was just at your place."

"I know. I heard everything. Wasn't it dreadful?"

Daniel nudged his hat up and checked the trail behind her. "Come on. We'd best get you out of sight." He took the reins from her hand and led her horse into the cover of trees and thick underbrush.

They dismounted, and Emmy threw herself against him. "I had to come, sugar. I just had to. Please don't be cross." She pulled away to look at him. "I'm appalled by the hateful way Mama spoke to you. It made me feel sick to my stomach."

Daniel squirmed in her arms and didn't return her embrace. "If she catches us together, she'll have my hide and yours, too. I'm hardly in her good graces just now—or Bertha Bloom's, for that matter."

"Who cares? It's not fair. How dare those cackling crones treat you so shamefully! Would they rather you'd married Charity when you love me? What sort of life would that be for either of you? I say it's a blessing you woke up in time."

Her arms were tight around his neck, her body pressed close, but Daniel stood stiff as a plank with his arms to his sides.

She wiggled impatiently. "Hold me, sweetheart, and don't you fret. Things will turn out right in the end. We'll make them understand it was for the best. You'll see. Mama will finally come around to our way of thinking. Charity, too, for that matter."

At the mention of Charity's name, Daniel's body tensed, and he pushed her away. "I just don't know anymore, Emmy."

The tone of his voice, his gruff manner, even the sick-cow look on his face were all new to Emmy, and they frightened her. "What, sugar?" She tried to get a look at his eyes, but his head was lowered. "What don't you know?"

"It won't be that easy now. There's more to consider."

She drew back a step. "More to consider? Like what?"

Daniel took off his hat and used his arm to wipe the sweat from his brow. Then he propped the toe of his boot on a fallen tree and leaned into it, staring off into the woods.

Emmy watched and waited.

He cut his eyes around to her. "It's Mama."

Emmy knew they'd have her own mama's ruffled feathers to contend with, and Aunt Bert's, too. The mention of Mrs. Clark came straight out of nowhere. "Your mama? What about her?"

Daniel's foot slid off the tree and hit the dry leaves with a crash. He straightened and faced her, and his piercing blue eyes sliced her to the bone. "Emmy, she don't feel the same about you. She don't want us together."

Emmy's jaw dropped. Icy fingers of fear gripped the nape of her neck. She recovered and tried to smile, but her mouth quivered. "Don't be silly! She likes me. You've told me so a dozen times." She clutched her skirt in bunches to still her trembling hands. "Of course, you didn't need to tell me. I could see it for myself, whenever I was with her." She swallowed, trying to force the shrillness from her voice. "It's Charity she don't approve of, not me. She said I'm a much better catch than Bertha Bloom's daughter. You said so yourself."

Belligerence set Daniel's lips in a hard line. "That was before we shamed her in front of the whole town and tarnished her precious reputation. She's singing a different tune now, and it ain't a lullaby." He dashed his hat against his leg so hard it made her jump. "All because you chased me from the church house like a lovesick heifer. Why didn't you just keep your behind on that pew, Emmy? Couldn't you act like a lady for once?"

Emmy closed her gaping mouth and swiped her hand across it. "You'll take up for me, won't you? With your mama, I mean?"

He lowered his eyes and turned his back on her.

She rushed him and wrapped her arms around his waist. "You'll take a stand for me—for us—won't you?"

Daniel's body went rigid again. Even his voice came out stilted.

"Maybe we need to let things cool down some. Give folks time to forget."

She released him and withdrew. "The other night under that oak tree you didn't say anything about cooling down."

"Don't talk like a trollop. Besides, it ain't like that."

"What's it like, then?" Emmy felt like a shrew. She heard the harsh, strident tone of her voice but couldn't stop. "You can't even look at me, Daniel? I've risked everything to be with you. What will you risk for me?"

He didn't answer, didn't turn to face her.

She nodded at his obstinate shoulders. "All right, then. I don't need a pine knot to fall on my head. I guess this is good-bye."

Daniel whirled and caught her by the arm. "Come here now. Where do you think you're going?" He jerked her against him and tightened his grip on her waist. "I'm sorry, sweetness. Don't pay me no mind. I'm just confused by all the voices in my head—yours, Mama's, Charity's—all telling me different things. I can't think straight no more, that's all."

Emmy stiffened. "Charity's? You got Charity's voice in your head?"

Daniel looked like a hound caught in the coop. "Aw, now, not like you're thinking. I'm just mighty worried about her, that's all. She's been carrying on, all giggly and loose, with some stranger in town. It ain't like her."

"Stranger? Oh, you mean Buddy Pierce."

His eyes darkened again. "You know about him?"

"Well, I saw him. He was out at the house last night. Those two old guineas dragged him inside and gave him a bath."

Daniel blinked his disbelief. "A bath? I get the loud end of a shotgun, and that outsider gets a bath?" He glared as if she'd drawn the water herself. "Is there anyplace in town he ain't horned in on?"

Wary, she watched his angry face. "I can't tell why you're letting him get so far under your skin."

Daniel seemed to remember himself, but the dark storm remained on his face. "Ain't nobody under my skin. I just feel responsible for Charity, what with it being so soon after. . .well, you know. I feel like we drove her to act that way."

Emmy walked off from him a ways, hands on her hips, one side of her body angled toward him, the other side in retreat. She raised her head and sought his eyes. "And you're sure that's all that's bothering you?"

He gathered the ends of the reins and led the horses to where she stood. "Let me help you mount up. You'd best be getting back before they miss you. I got all the trouble I want right now. I don't need the sheriff down my neck."

Emmy snorted. "Those two wouldn't call the sheriff. They'd load up and hunt you down themselves."

Daniel made a stirrup for her with his hands and swung her up onto Rebel. "Then get home quick. I'd sooner face the sheriff than Crazy Bertha with a loaded gun."

He took to his own saddle, then eased past her and rode out to scout the trail before whistling the all-clear.

She followed and found him studying the sky. "It's getting on to the noon meal. They'll be looking for you."

"And they'll find me."

They measured each other with guarded looks. Daniel broke the silence. "Give me some time, Emmy. I'll set things to right."

She bit her bottom lip. "You know I'm not the patient sort."

He nodded.

Emmy nudged Rebel and they trotted away a bit. Then she yanked on the reins and pulled him around. "Daniel?"

He sat in the same spot, watching her. His lifted chin bade her speak.

Pulling one foot close to the saddle, she fiddled with her bootstrap. "Is she all right?" Her gaze flickered to his face then returned to her boot. "Charity, I mean? Did that wolf hurt her any?"

"Never touched her. Charity's fine."

Emmy nodded, still not meeting his eyes. "That's good."

"Go on, girl. Get home."

She found her stirrup again. "I'm going."

Emmy dug her heels into Rebel's side. He responded by breaking into a gallop and then a run. She rode hard and didn't look back, fleeing the bitter truth before it surfaced and ruined everything.

The big horse tried to slow before the gully, hesitant to cross the plank bridge. She laid the switch to his side and he leapt for it. They landed with a jarring thud and his hooves beat against the boards, sending vibrations through her body. The wind whistled past her ears as they flew over the marsh. Rebel stumbled, bogging down and tripping over roots. She urged him faster. He risked falling, breaking a leg, but still she pushed him.

On the far side of the swamp, she sent him barreling headlong into the brush. Tangled branches tore at her skirt, exposing her bare legs to deep scratches. Rebel threatened to buck, so she pulled him out again and sent him crashing into a grove of young trees instead. Somehow he made it through, and she drove him toward the house as if the hounds of hell chased them.

Inside the dark, cool barn, she worked feverishly to unsaddle the old horse. Rebel heaved and blew, his body lathered with foamy sweat that ran red from deep scratches. Blood matted his long white mane, now a tangle of sticks and twigs.

Emmy dropped the saddle on the ground and stared at the terrible sight. "Oh, Rebel. What have I done?" Guilt consumed her. She had punished Papa's horse for Daniel's sins.

Her tingling legs began to throb and sting. She pulled up her dress and gasped at the state of her torn and bleeding flesh. Her thighs weren't so comely now. Unlike Rebel, she knew she deserved it.

As if confirming her thoughts, a shadow loomed from behind, blocking the warmth of the sun. Startled, she whirled. Mama stood at the barn door, glaring at Emmy's bare skin.

"You wicked girl." She spoke quietly, matter-of-factly.

Emmy dropped her skirt. "I'm sorry, Mama."

"Where have you been, Emily? What have you been up to that put your legs in that condition?"

"It's not what you think."

"So it has nothing to do with Daniel Clark? That's what you're telling me?"

Emmy couldn't summon the right answer.

Mama shook her head. "Just as I thought." She caught sight of the horse and rushed inside the barn. "For heaven's sake! What happened?" She ran her hands over the bloody cuts. Rebel flinched, and tears sprang to her eyes. She spoke without looking at Emmy, her voice jagged iron. "Find Nash and have him come tend to this animal. Then get upstairs to your room. This time I say when you come out."

"Yes, ma'am." Emmy hurried toward the barn door, but Mama called her back. She turned slowly, dreading what she might hear.

"There won't be no hiding this from your Papa. No telling what he'll do to you, but I won't lie to him on your account."

Emmy forced herself to look at her mama's face. "No, ma'am," she whispered.

Mama nodded. "As long as we understand each other. Now git."

Even more than having Papa find out, Emmy dreaded telling Nash. She could already imagine the look on his face. He had tended Rebel since the horse was a colt.

She found him and delivered the message, careful to avoid his eyes. Then she trudged to the house, feeling like she'd sooner face a noose. Not that she minded going back inside her rose-covered prison. Her actions merited worse. The part she couldn't bear was being shut in with the memory of what had just happened between her and Daniel.

CHAPTER 11

The morning dawned clear and milder than days past. The sun, bright and hot outside the window of the Lone Star Hotel, arched warm, hazy rays through the open shade, chasing the chill from the room.

Not ready to leave the soft cotton mattress, Charity lay on the bed and watched the sky, enjoying the heat of the sunshine on her feet. A pleasant day in the middle of January was common for Texas and a welcome change from the one before.

Buddy never took her to see Amy Jane like he'd promised. After the wolf encounter, he hustled her to town instead and delivered her straight to her room. Then he ordered a bath brought up and made her promise to take to her bed right after. She found the special treatment downright silly, since she'd only sustained a few bruises and muddy knees, but he insisted. She didn't argue long. Buddy's determination and size made him a formidable opponent. Satisfied he had her settled in for the night, he headed back out to her place, and she hadn't seen him since.

Wide awake now, Charity stretched then winced at the pain.

I guess we can add rattled bones to bruises and muddy knees.

It seemed Buddy was right after all. She had hit the ground harder than she thought. With great care, she rolled to the side of the bed and sat up.

Patting her hollow stomach, she felt more than heard the

familiar growl. Buddy had paid for her breakfast the day before. She wouldn't allow him to do it again. Today she became mistress of her own fate.

Amy Jane Pike had expressed interest in her wedding dress. Charity intended to find her first thing and speak to her about buying it. If things went the way she hoped, she could soon afford to pay for her own breakfast.

Aware of every sore muscle, she stood and hobbled to the basin of water. Cold, but it would have to do; she couldn't wait for more. She tended to her toiletries, pinned up her hair, and pulled on a faded day dress. The comfortable jeans had beckoned, but they were a mess. Besides, she wouldn't be traveling on horseback today. She'd have to rely on her feet instead.

When all was in order, Charity limped into the hall. On impulse, she knocked at Buddy's door. He didn't answer. Up and gone before daylight most likely.

She shuffled past his room and made her way to the stairs. Halfway down, she noted that each step came easier than the last. Moving and using her taut muscles warmed and relaxed them, bringing some relief.

Sam looked up as she tottered past the front desk. "Miss Bloom, will you come here, please?"

Too late, she realized Buddy had likely set the old clerk to watch out for her. If so, she might never get out the door.

Balderdash! Let him try to stop me.

She steeled herself and turned on her brightest smile. "Morning, Sam. Lovely day, is it not?"

He glanced toward the window. "Yes, I reckon it is."

She approached the desk, determined to move with grace. It wouldn't do for him to notice her stiffness. "Did you wish to speak to me?"

"Surely you're not going out?" He posed it as a question. Implied it as a fact.

"But I am." She raised her brows. "Is that a problem?"

He gestured toward the dining hall with a palsied hand. "You haven't had breakfast, miss. Mr. Buddy says I'm to make sure you eat. Said to put it on his tab."

Mr. . . .who?

She focused on Sam's face. If she allowed her gaze to follow where he pointed, she'd be undone. Her nose would take over and chase the wafting aroma of biscuits and crisp bacon down the hall to the dining room.

"I'm not"—to say she wasn't hungry would be false—"ready to eat just yet." A contradiction rumbled in her inward parts, but at least she'd spoken the truth. She would be ready to eat when her own money lay in her hand.

Sam grew agitated. "Mr. Buddy will be cross with me if you don't eat something."

There. He'd said it again. Her brows rose higher than before. "Mr. Buddy?"

"Yes, miss. That nice Mr. Pierce."

"Two days ago you were ready to string him up. Now he's *nice Mr. Buddy?*"

Sam grinned so wide his mustache fanned out above his mouth. "Well, you see, that was before."

"Before what?"

"Before I came to know what a fine young man he is. He's taken right good care of you during your"—he cleared his throat—"financial inconvenience."

That much was true. Buddy had tended to everything out of his own pocket, all for a woman he'd met only days before. It reminded Charity of a Bible story, the tale of the Good Samaritan. Except this battered traveler was all better now and ready to make her own way.

"Mr. Pierce has been more than kind." She leaned in and furrowed her brow. "I'm grateful. Don't think I'm not. I just can't let him do it any longer. It's not fitting. I won't eat another meal I haven't provided for myself."

"But, Miss Charity, breakfast is included in the cost of your lodging."

"And thereby you've made my point, Sam. I'm not exactly paying for my lodging, am I?"

His wide eyes challenged her over the top of wire-rimmed glasses. "Mr. Buddy won't like it."

"Then don't tell him." She pressed a gloved finger to his mouth. "Sam, I mean it. Now if you'll excuse me, I have to be about looking after my own needs for a change." She left him there, still scowling his disapproval, and sauntered outside to the boardwalk.

The sun seemed bent on drying up the mud. Except for a few shaded puddles, only the deepest holes still held water. Charity gathered her shawl about her, ducked into the noisy, milling crowd, and allowed herself to be swept eastward in the general direction of Moonshine Hill. Where the walkway ended just past the hardware store, she took the two steps down to the ground and set out for the Pikes' place. She breathed a sigh of relief when the drier streets and thinning crowd made her walk to the edge of town easier than she'd anticipated.

Moonshine Hill, a thriving community two miles east of Humble, sprang up overnight amid the clamor for oil and the clatter of drilling rigs. It had fast become bigger than Humble, the town that spawned it. Shamus and Elsa Pike owned a fair-sized patch of land northwest of there. Not as far from town as her own place, but still a good long stretch.

The midmorning sun warmed Charity's face. If not for a brisk north wind, she could have removed her shawl. The day felt crisp and clean with no hint of the oppressive Gulf moisture that often saturated the air. She found herself enjoying the walk.

Where the path leveled out for a good distance, Charity lifted her face to the sky and closed her eyes. She followed the sun blindly, until the bright light turned the backs of her eyelids white. When she opened them again, for fear of veering off course, shadowy squiggles darted about in her field of vision. She smiled and blinked them away.

Turning north, she found the trail leading to the Pikes' house suitably dry as well, so long as she dodged the deeper ruts in the dark, crumbling clay. Overhead a woodpecker knocked on a tree trunk, while a frenzied crow swooped by with a meal in his beak, a contender for the prize hot on his tail. She stopped to watch, curious about the outcome.

A buck stepped into the clearing a mere thirty feet in front of her and checked the air for danger, his nose tossed to the sky.

Charity was still and stood downwind of him, so he took no notice of her. When he crouched and lunged from the brush then sprang into the forest on the opposite side of the trail, it had nothing to do with her. Something had startled him and sent him darting for cover—something already chasing him.

The thicket from where the buck had first emerged began to shudder and sway, pulling her attention from the quivering undergrowth that had swallowed him on the other side. With a jolt, she realized another creature had taken the deer's place. A piteous whine, unmistakably canine, arose from the scrub, followed by a mournful growl. Charity stared hard at the bushes, her heart hammering apace with the woodpecker's beak.

Don't be silly. The wolf is dead. Daniel shot it. You saw it yourself.

Charity reversed her steps, determined not to turn her back on the devil that lurked in the brush.

Then what? A second wolf? Something worse?

She cast around in her mind for a way to protect herself. Could she outrun it? Not likely in a dress. Should she climb a tree? The tall straight pines nearby afforded no low branches. Would the Pikes hear if she called out? She filled her lungs and opened her mouth to scream. By golly, she'd make sure they heard.

The bushes rustled then parted to reveal the long velvet ears and wrinkled snout of the Pikes' bloodhound. Red pushed onto the trail, still dragging his ears, his frantic nose snuffling and sweeping the ground. He sensed or smelled Charity and jerked up, eyes alert, body tense. When he recognized her, he wriggled from head to tail. Torn between tracking the deer and greeting his guest, he finally ambled in her direction, grinning up at her through droopy folds.

Charity released the breath burning in her lungs, and weakness flooded her limbs. "Red, you old scoundrel. You scared me half to death."

The big hound wagged his tail and pushed his muzzle into her hand. Red was one of Papa's, or had been. Six years ago when Doozy birthed nine pups, Shamus Pike set his cap for the pick of the litter. Or, as Mama liked to say, he downright coveted Red. But Papa loved the little whelp from the moment he was born and wouldn't turn him loose. A year later Papa died, and Mama couldn't afford to keep the dogs. She sold the rest but gave Red to Shamus in memory of their longstanding friendship. Shamus had cried openly.

Charity knelt on the trail and pulled Red's big head close to give him a good scratching behind the ears. "Truth be told, darlin', I've never been more glad to see you."

Red accompanied Charity the rest of the way. He marched her through the yard and delivered her to the house, circling and collapsing in a panting heap as soon as they stepped on the porch.

Charity raised the brass door knocker and let it fall. It struck her as odd, considering Shamus and Papa's close ties, that she had seldom visited the Pikes' home.

In fact, despite Papa's friendship with Shamus, Mrs. Pike had always regarded Charity and her mama with an upturned nose, due in part to Mama's scandalous behavior but mostly because she envied Mama's relationship with Mother Dane. Elsa considered Magdalena Dane's influence in Humble society to be a prized feather for her cap, so she had sought Mother Dane's favor for years. Mama she could do without, and she had never found Charity worthy either before her betrothal to Eunice Clark's son.

Biting her bottom lip, Charity knocked again. She hadn't considered that they might not be home, which would mean the long walk was for naught. . .and her stomach would remain empty.

While she waited, she looked around the place. Fronted by trees and bordered by acres of plowed ground, the house was smaller than Mother Dane's but somewhat larger than her own. The Pikes farmed cotton. Shamus, with the help of hired men, planted every spare inch of his ground and leased more from other landowners, including Charity's mama. If not for the money he paid to farm their best ten acres, they wouldn't have survived after Papa died.

In three directions, the fields were plowed under in preparation for spring planting, with the exception of a patch of winter vegetables behind the barn. The bare, harrowed ground butted up against the tree line, with no other homes in sight. It seemed a lonely existence.

She raised her fist and knocked again, sure now she'd come all the way to the Pikes' for nothing.

"One moment, please."

The muted voice behind the door would be Mrs. Pike, because in the distance Amy Jane stepped out of the barn and headed up the path leading to the back door. She carried a galvanized bucket and moseyed along like someone in no kind of hurry. The pail contained milk that sloshed with every careless step, soaking her dress and leaving frothy white puddles on the ground.

Her attention on Amy Jane, Charity jumped when the door jerked open with a flourish.

Elsa stood with both hands clasped to her chest and a huge smile on her face. "Charity, dear! How grand."

She suppressed a smile. One would think royalty had come to call. Quite curious that Elsa Pike, who claimed to be descended from nobility herself, still seemed to consider Charity of social importance, despite her breakup with Daniel. Perhaps she thought it wise to hedge her bets, in case they reconciled.

Charity gave in to the smile and extended her hand. "Good morning. I apologize for the early hour."

"Nonsense. We've been up since dawn." Elsa stepped back and widened the opening. "Come right in." She wrinkled her nose and cast a disparaging glance at the ever-optimistic Red. He had risen halfway when she appeared, his droopy eyes hopeful. She shooed him with the hem of her dress. "Scat! Scat, you filthy beast! Charity, don't let him near you, honey. He stinks to high heaven."

Charity had to admit an impressive stench emanated from Red. She sidestepped the fleeing dog and crossed the threshold. "You're very kind to receive me without notice."

"We're glad to have you. Right this way, dear."

Charity followed Mrs. Pike along a dim, narrow hall adorned on both sides with framed tintypes of Elsa's supposedly blue-blooded ancestors. Staid men trussed up in dark suits and sporting handlebar mustaches scowled at her from the wall. Demure women with upswept hair and high-buttoned collars censured her as she passed. Charity made faces at them before turning her attention to Elsa's back.

She had dressed in a gown fit for a party, yet it gaped where she'd left two buttons unfastened. It appeared the crooked sash at her waist, inside out and mismatched, had been snatched up and tied on at the last minute. The state of her explained why she'd left Charity standing so long on the stoop.

They came to an arched doorway on the left, and Elsa waved Charity inside. "Have a seat in the drawing room, dear. Make yourself easy while I pour you some tea."

"Please don't trouble yourself, Mrs. Pike. I can't stay long."

"No trouble at all. There's a pot left from our morning repast, along with fresh blueberry scones. Would you care for one with your tea?"

Charity's mouth watered. *A buttered scone!* Such a casual offer of so dear a morsel. The only thing better would be manna served by the hand of God.

She gave a slight nod. "I might nibble at one if you don't mind, while I wait for Amy Jane."

Elsa clasped her hands again. "You've come to see Amy Jane? She'll be so pleased." She pointed behind them. "She's just outside in the. . .in the garden resting, poor lamb. She didn't sleep well last night. As you know, my Amy's quite delicate. Her aristocratic bloodlines, you see. The slightest thing throws her right off kilter."

Charity couldn't judge her thrown-off kilter, but the six-foot tall, big-boned Amy Jane was anything but delicate. She covered her mouth and feigned a small cough to hide her laugh. Mrs. Pike seemed not to notice.

"Make yourself at home, dear. I'll run out and get her then fetch your tea." With that, she spun and scurried from the room, slamming the back door on her way out.

Still smiling, Charity stepped inside the parlor. The room hadn't changed a whit since the last time she'd been inside, and that was a couple of years before Papa died. The same long divan dominated the small space. Across from it, the same low table and high-backed chairs. Curtains of yellow lace, a wedding gift from the old country, still graced the windows. Behind the divan, the colorful braided rug in front of the stone fireplace gave the room a warm, cheery glow.

She bypassed the chairs and walked to the window. By her calculations, Amy Jane and her bucket could've made it to the house three times by now. Charity was curious about where she'd gotten off to. She lifted the edge of the heavy shade and took a peek.

Amy Jane stood near the garden fence, staring out across the field, the bucket of milk at her feet forgotten. Her body gently swayed, as if to music, while her long hair kept tempo behind her. Mrs. Pike came into sight, bearing down on her with a vengeance. The serenity on the girl's face changed to shocked annoyance as her mama descended.

Elsa plucked at her—untying her apron, straightening her skirts, fussing with her hair—as though she had ten hands, all the while chattering like a frenzied squirrel. Charity couldn't hear her words, but the bossy tone was clear. She heard perfectly, however, when Amy Jane shouted, "Stop it, Mama!" and slapped her hands away.

Elsa took up the pail and herded the girl through the gate. When they disappeared behind the house, Charity whirled and bolted for the divan, feeling guilty for having spied.

In her haste she upset a small worktable and overturned it. The drawer slid out, spilling folded papers and a writing set onto the rug. Charity righted the spindly-legged piece, shoving the items deep inside the dovetailed drawer. She returned Shamus's pipe stand and tobacco box to the bottom shelf, sending up a prayer of thanksgiving they weren't broken. Scrambling to the divan, she sat down just as the back door opened.

After a whispered squabble in the kitchen, mother and daughter appeared on the threshold. Amy Jane sported fresh-pinned hair and a bonnet. Elsa carried a tray laden with a silver tea service, a platter of deep-fried scones, and a collection of jams and spreads. Pushing Amy Jane into the room ahead of her, she placed the tray on the table in front of Charity. After surveying her bountiful spread, Elsa gave a contented sigh and settled into one of the ornately carved chairs. Amy Jane dropped without ceremony into the opposite chair.

The aroma of hot blueberries and fresh-churned butter made its way to Charity's nose, setting her stomach to growling. She pressed her arm against her middle, but too late. Both women glanced at her and then looked away.

Elsa bent over the tray. "Here, dear. Let me serve you a scone. Amy

Jane, pour our guest some tea. She's just had a very long walk."

Amy Jane slouched in the chair with her arms folded, her jiggling knees a sign of her impatience. She watched Charity with wary eyes and pretended not to hear her mama. "What brings you way out here anyways?"

Elsa fired a horrified look at Amy Jane. "Mind your manners, child. She's come to see you, of course."

Unconvinced, the girl watched Charity with one raised brow.

Charity took a large, somewhat indelicate bite of scone and chased it with a sip of tea before she answered. "Actually, I'm here on business."

"Business?" Elsa's brow shot higher than Amy Jane's. "I thought—"

The girl cast a smug look at her mama.

Elsa made a face then moved her seat closer to Charity. "What sort of business, dear?"

"I've come to offer my wedding dress for sale."

The daughter's mouth fell open. The mother choked on a sip of tea. While they recovered, Elsa sat and stared, and a smile stole over Amy's face.

With a rattle, the older woman put down her china cup. "Are you serious?"

Charity nodded. "Yes, ma'am. Quite."

"Dear girl, your mama made that gown for you with her own two hands."

Amy Jane scowled. "Hush, Mama. Charity wants to sell the dress. She don't need you reminding her who made it." Her greedy eyes swept the room. "Do you have it with you?"

"No, but if you're interested in buying, I can return with it today."

Amy's hands went to her flushed face, and her eyes brightened. "Mama, could we? You know how I love that dress. It's absolutely perfect and prettier than any we've seen in the catalogs. Oh, please buy it for me."

Rubbing her eyes in circles with her forefingers, Elsa slumped in her chair. "I don't know, Amy Jane. It would have to be altered a great deal. Even then it might not fit you."

"It will, Mama. You'll see. I've been eating less than the chickens."

Elsa gave her oversized daughter a doubtful glance and sighed. Then her eyes met Charity's. "It's settled, then. Come what may, we'll take the dress."

Charity beamed and reached for a second scone. "I just know you won't be sorry, Mrs. Pike."

Elsa picked up her crocheted napkin and shook it. With a glance down at her mistake, she used the toe of her shoe to brush the scattered crumbs beneath the table. "Dear, there is one last detail."

Charity pressed her fingers to her mouth and swallowed the big bite she'd taken with a self-conscious gulp. "And that is. . .?"

Crossing her hands over her chest, Elsa swiveled toward her. "While I'm reluctant to discuss business—it's a man's job and one I don't envy—we must come to terms on the worth of the garment. Do you. . .um. . .have a price in mind?"

"I do, in fact. After giving the matter careful consideration"—Charity sat up taller and cleared her throat—"I'm asking thirty dollars for it." Her hopeful heart faltered a bit when Elsa's face blanched. "I know it's a lot, Mrs. Pike, but the gown is worth every penny."

Elsa plucked the napkin from her lap to fan herself, oblivious this time to the resulting shower of crumbs. Looking like she'd swallowed a pincushion, she shook her head. "Oh, I don't know, dear. Thirty dollars? My, that's a lot of money for a single item of clothing. After all, it is just a dress."

Amy Jane looked anxious. "Not *just*, Mama. It's the perfect dress. And I'll get lots of wear from it."

Elsa whirled on her. "Just where do you intend to wear a thing like that, and you married to Isaac Young?" She gathered her napkin into a wad and flung it on the silver tray. "Every time I think of it, I get the vapors. I'll never approve of your marrying a dirt-poor farm boy. Mark my words, if not for your hardheaded papa, it wouldn't be happening. Why, I—"

After a mortified glance at Charity, Amy Jane shot her mama a pointed look.

Elsa caught the warning. She cleared her throat and turned with a plastered smile. "We'll buy your wedding gown, Charity. Against my better judgment, we'll buy it. However, I can't pay you everything at once. I'll give you some now, some later, until we've paid it off."

Amy Jane wrung her hands. "That'll take weeks. I need the dress right now." Tears gathered at the corners of her lashes. "You know alterations take time."

"Well, I'm sorry, Amy Jane! We don't have that kind of money!"

Elsa's raised voice echoed in the stillness that followed. A raspberry tinge flushing her cheeks, she settled deeper in the chair and fiddled with a thread on her sleeve. Seconds passed before she licked her lips and addressed Charity, speaking in measured tones. "I meant to say money's a mite scarce just now. My husband's varied investments take all our ready cash. The end return is worth it, of course. However, we're forced to scrimp some during the dry spells." She gave a self-conscious laugh. "So I have only a few silver dollars in my purse. Oh, and a jarful of commissary tokens from Bender's Mill."

Charity saw her sale slipping away and along with it her independence. She scooted to the edge of her seat. "I have an idea. Suppose you give me some of the money now, like you said."

Elsa's eyes flickered with interest.

"Whatever you can manage. And I don't mind commissary tokens. They're as good as cash."

The flicker ignited to a flame. "Go on."

"I'll give you the dress now and trust you to pay the balance."

Amy Jane gasped and bit her knuckles.

Elsa leaned toward Charity. "You would do that for us?"

"Of course I will." *I must do it. . .for me.*

Amy Jane bounced in her chair, squealing like a cornered hog.

Despite the quick glance at her furniture and the disapproving look she sent her daughter's way, Elsa's smile remained in place. "Shall we shake on it, then? That's what the men do."

Charity set down her cup and wiped her mouth with the napkin. The three women stood together and took turns exchanging hearty shakes and broad grins.

Outside on the porch, Charity felt somewhat better about what she'd done. She had a full belly plus five dollars in silver coins and commissary tokens in her pocket, with the promise of more to come. Amy Jane was a happy bride-to-be, looking forward to wearing the wedding dress of her dreams. Overall, it had gone quite well for Charity's first business transaction.

She was almost clear of the yard when Red appeared at the edge of the trees and loped across the field to meet her. Dodging just in time, she followed Elsa's example and shooed him with the hem of her skirt. "You can't come with me, boy. Go on, git."

The big dog ducked his head and slunk out of reach but seemed determined to follow. She stamped her foot. "You hear me, now? I said git. You can't go home with me." She laughed at herself. "I can't go home myself, come to think of it."

All the way into town, Red tracked her. Charity threw sticks and small stones at him, but he persisted. Even when she couldn't hear or see him, she knew he was there, stalking her from the brush. Papa always said the only thing bloodhounds were better at than deer-trailing was man-trailing. She decided there was nothing she could do about it, so she ignored him and trudged ahead.

Only part of her plan had succeeded. She still had to make the trek to Mother Dane's house to get the dress then take it to Amy Jane. She dreaded the thought of all that walking. Worse, she dreaded telling Mama she'd sold the dress. She'd sooner face another rabid wolf.

CHAPTER 12

Daniel Clark sat propped against the outer wall of Sterling's Feed Store in a rickety ladder-back chair, his booted feet crossed high atop piled bags of grain. In the company of several men, Daniel was in no mood for talking, so he kept to himself and pretended to sleep.

He would have slept, too, but for the stretched-out hole in the cane-bottom seat. Half his backside protruded through it already. If his body relaxed, he'd wind up in quite a pickle.

A stiff southern breeze blew up the rain-soaked street, whisking the chill from the mild winter morning. The warmth of the gentle wind swept over him, bringing with it the pungent aroma of horses and mud—animals and land, the smells he loved best. The fragrance of his heritage and his future.

True enough, timber had made his daddy rich. Not Daniel. He sought his fortune in ranching, and the effort had padded his pockets. Lately, he dreamed of a different sort of gold. Black gold, they called it. If he showed the same knack for finding oil that he had for raising livestock, he'd put this mud-sucking town on the map. Better yet, he might move his talents to a bigger city. Somewhere on the Gulf, Galveston maybe. He reckoned he wouldn't mind seeing the ocean.

The uncommon stillness of the men seated about him pulled Daniel from his thoughts. Their endless trite chatter about weather and crops had ceased. Sidney Anderson chuckled under his breath. Ezekiel Young laughed outright. When they began to hoot and catcall to someone, Daniel opened one eye and took a peek.

Charity stood in the street with one hand resting on her hip, scolding a big red dog with the other. The hound cowered beneath her wagging finger and rolled over, his long ears splayed and his legs tucked submissively. The second Charity turned, he was up chasing after her skirts. The men beside Daniel roared, pointing at the girl while slapping their legs and clutching their sides.

Daniel grinned, too, when Charity whirled on the hound again, shouting and stamping her feet. The dog ran a short distance away and sat down to watch, as if waiting for her next move. Charity cast a few more words of warning in his direction, punctuated by pointed finger jabs, before stalking away.

The persistent creature perked his ears at her departing back. He squirmed to his feet then paused, took a few steps, and froze. He stayed put until Charity passed Rogers & Grossman's Dry Goods Store, but as soon as she disappeared around the corner, he shot to his feet and loped after her.

Jack Mayhew pulled a dirty handkerchief from his overalls and wiped the tears from his eyes. "By golly, I ain't laughed that hard in years. That old dog sure knows what he wants."

"He sure does," Sidney agreed. "Beats all I ever did see."

Ezekiel Young, the oldest of the men, squared around to offer his opinion. "I got a feeling he'll keep tracking her, too. Ain't nothing bound to stop him. Weren't no give-up in that animal."

Daniel let Zeke's words sink in a bit before he leaned forward, dropping the chair's front legs with a bang. He stood up and hooked his thumbs in his suspenders, his gaze fixed on the spot where Charity and the bloodhound had disappeared. "Gentlemen, a man could take a lesson from that old dog."

Ezekiel turned questioning eyes to Daniel. "What you 'bout to do, son?"

Daniel didn't bother to answer. Taking the two steps down to the street, he strode across in long, purposeful strides.

"What do you mean I can't have it?"

Charity hadn't meant to raise her voice. Giving Mama sass

wouldn't go very far in persuading her. Besides, the last thing she wanted was for Emmy to hear and find out she was there.

Mama glared. "Don't take that tone with me, girl. What do you mean marching up here demanding things what ain't your'n?"

Mother Dane appeared at the door behind Mama. "Don't leave Charity on the stoop like a common peddler, Bert. Bring her in."

"I already asked her in. She ain't having it."

Mother Dane reached past Mama and took Charity's arm. "Well, sure she is. Come take a load off, honey. You look plumb tuckered. Let Mother Dane fix you some lunch. You must be starved."

No match for the strength in the sturdy woman's grip, Charity was over the threshold before she could gather her wits. Heart in her throat, she cast a quick look around for any sign of the enemy.

"Don't bother looking," Mother Dane said. "You'll not be seeing her today. She won't be leaving her room for quite a spell, I can promise you that."

While she spoke, she herded Charity to the parlor. "Go on now. Sit and talk with your mama. I'll go scare us up some grub, if Emmy spared us any, that is. I guess I could always pick a bouquet of drumsticks from her pretty leftover bush." She hooted at her own joke then headed for the kitchen door, still chuckling under her breath.

Charity stared after her. "Leftover bush?"

"Never you mind," Mama said. "We got our own fat to fry." She pointed Charity toward the divan then perched across from her in the big green chair, arms folded over her chest. "Now then. Get to telling me why you need a wedding dress in such an all-fired hurry."

Charity widened her eyes. "Heavens! I'm sure it's not what you're thinking."

Mama looked away. "I don't know what to think. Whether you care or not, I've got a new crop of gray in my hair—with your name on every strand. You disappeared for two whole days. I had to find out secondhand that you were set on by a crazed wolf."

The strain in her voice squeezed Charity's heart. "Oh, but

I'm fine, see? He didn't hurt me none. They told you that much, didn't they?"

Mama shrugged. "I reckon so."

"All right, then. None of the rest matters."

"It matters a heap to me."

Charity reached to pat her hand. "I'm sorry, Mama. I truly am."

Mama's sorrowful gaze locked on her. "Just what is it you're sorry for? That's what I really need to know."

Surprised by her intensity, Charity slid to the edge of her seat. "What sort of question is that? What are you asking me?"

The probing green eyes found hers again, and tears welled there. "I'm asking what you've been up to, child."

Stunned, Charity sank back against the cushions. "What do you think I've been up to?"

Mama chewed her bottom lip and watched, saying nothing.

"Mama? Tell me what you mean."

After drawing a deep breath and rolling her shoulders back, Mama squirmed forward until their knees touched. Her suspicious glare pinned Charity to the sofa. "The word I got has you flouncing about town acting pert and chipper with Mr. Pierce."

The last possible words Charity expected out of her mouth.

"Pert and chipper? I don't understand."

"Don't play thick, daughter. You was seen in public snuggled up to Buddy Pierce with his hands all over you."

Charity felt rage. Indignation. She shot to her feet, no longer worried about Emmy or anyone else hearing. "I never did that! Who said such a vile thing?"

Mama seemed not to hear. "How you think it made me feel to have a snake like him come telling dirty stories on you? He said you had your arms around that man right out in plain sight, in front of half the men in town."

"Who, Mama? Who told you that?" Charity spewed the words in white-hot fury.

Mama shouted right back. "That dirty scum ex-feeancee of yours!"

At first Charity couldn't breathe. She groped in her mind

for an anchor that would hold. Something to help make sense of Mama's words. "Daniel?" she finally whispered. "Daniel said those things?"

"Do you deny it?"

She had to sit down. . .or fall. "Yes, I deny it. You don't believe him, do you? I thought you knew me better."

"I thought I did, too, seeing as how I raised you right. Two days ago I would've swore you'd never run out on me. Yet you did." Mama's voice broke, and she slumped over, hiding her face in her hands.

Charity pushed off the couch and knelt at her feet. "I didn't run out on you. I had to go, don't you see?" She held her, rocking back and forth. "I couldn't stay in Emily Dane's house after what she did. I couldn't bear to face her."

Mama sat up and wiped her eyes on her dress. "I knowed it'd be hard on you to come here. It was hard on me, too." She sniffed. "I never done it to hurt you. If it was a wrong decision, I'm sorry. I didn't see no other way at the time." She gave Charity an accusing glance. "We would've made out all right if you hadn't gone and made everything worse by locking Emmy out of the house."

Charity sat back on her heels. "You know?"

"Let's just say I guessed before. Now I know. What'd you do it for?"

Charity pointed toward the front of the house, her voice grim. "She was in the garden with Daniel. They were. . .together. I saw them through the window." The memory of the offense stirred righteous ire to the surface. She pointed again, as if they were still there, all of her wrath boiling from the tip of her trembling finger. "Let me tell you, those two make pert and chipper look like a spinster soiree."

Mama nodded. "Calm down now. I suspected as much. And Magda's no fool either." She pulled Charity close for an embrace. "Still, that don't justify what you done. Vengeance belongs to the Lord, sugar. He don't need our help in settling accounts."

Charity rested her head on her mama's thin shoulder. It felt so good she wanted to cry. "You're right. I don't know what came over me."

"It weren't like you to do such a mean-spirited thing."

Charity leaned back and searched her mama's face. "You don't believe that tommyrot Daniel said about me, do you?"

"If you're denying it, I don't." She cleared her throat. "Only he did name two other men who could back up his story. Said they seen it, too."

"Just two?" Charity smiled. "A minute ago half the men in Humble were witnesses."

Mama shrugged one shoulder. "Might as well have been. The whole town's heard by now."

Charity shook her head. "Then they've heard lies. You know I'd never—" The anchor Charity sought dropped with rattling chains and a heavy thud, dragging her words to a halt. She saw it now, clear and bright, as if the sun had just come up.

"Wait a second." She pulled herself to her feet and sat on the table in front of Mama's chair. "I know exactly what Daniel Clark saw. When the wolf attacked me, he was there, along with Sidney Anderson and Jack Mayhew."

"Yep, he mentioned them fellers."

"They rode up after Daniel shot the wolf. Buddy Pierce had just helped me up off the ground."

"Go on. I'm starting to get the picture."

"Buddy held me, all right, and I clung to him, too shaken to stand on my own. That's what they saw. Daniel made it ugly out of spite."

Mama leaned against the chair and closed her eyes. "It makes perfect sense. I believe you, daughter."

Charity picked up her mama's hands and squeezed them. "You do? Oh, I'm glad. Does that mean you're done scolding me?"

"No, just resting a bit. Give me a second to catch my breath."

Laughing, Charity kissed the backs of her hands. "Oh, you! What am I to do with you?"

Mother Dane swept into the room, carrying a tray piled high with food. "I heard laughter, so I figured it was safe to come in."

"It's safe enough, Magda, but we ain't talked everything out yet. We still need to have us a powwow about a certain wedding dress. You can stay here and referee."

For her part, Charity preferred to eat before any more discussions. The offerings on Mother Dane's tray looked downright tantalizing, and Mrs. Pike's blueberry scones had worn off halfway to town. The long walk, not to mention shooing Red every few feet, had worked her up a man-sized appetite. Not that she ever succeeded in chasing off the stubborn mutt. Most likely when she left, she'd find him waiting outside the front door.

No matter how hard she tried to pull her gaze away, the plate of piled-up sandwiches held her in a trance.

Gratefully, Mother Dane noticed and intervened. "Now, Bert, surely that skirmish can wait until after we eat a bite."

Charity jumped up to clear a place on the table. Her mouth watered at the sight of thick slabs of smoky ham wedged between chunky slices of bread, fresh-baked if her nose knew its business. Not to mention a platter of cold fried chicken, a bowl of potato salad, and a whole buttermilk pie.

Scrunching in beside Mother Dane on the divan, Charity ate until her eyes glazed over. She tried to make polite conversation but failed because her mouth stayed too full to speak.

When she reached for a second sandwich, Mama spoke up. "Charity, tell me you're not shoveling food like a field hand because you're starved. Buddy Pierce swore he'd look out for you."

Charity swallowed her bite and lowered the sandwich. "He has, Mama. Buddy's bought my every meal with money from his own pocket until today."

"What makes this day any different? Looks to me like you needed to eat today, too. Why wouldn't he feed you?"

She steeled herself. "I won't let him do it anymore, that's why."

Mama glared. "And he put up with that?"

"He doesn't know."

Mama lowered her sandwich to her plate. "What do you mean he don't know?"

"He's been buying my meals on his hotel tab, through Sam. I told Sam I won't eat any more meals Buddy pays for."

Mama sat back, considering her words. Then she raised one eyebrow. "You two have a falling out?"

"Of course not. I want to make my own way, that's all. I can't let Mr. Pierce continue to do for me." While she talked, she worked on getting a huge slice of buttermilk pie onto her plate without spilling a morsel. "To be honest, I don't know why you allowed it in the first place."

Mother Dane cleared her throat and shot a warning glance. Charity softened her tone. "I mean. . .we're beholden to a complete stranger, aren't we? Mr. Pierce is a very nice man, but he's not family. Not even an old friend. Yet he's shelling out a dollar per day for my room and board." She balled her fist and brought it down on the couch. "A dollar a day, Mama. How will we ever repay that kind of money?"

Mama stiffened. "I'm good for it. I'll give him back every penny."

"Oh, really? How?"

She sniffed and raised her chin. "When my well comes in."

Charity tried not to roll her eyes. "That well is just speculation, not a sure thing. Suppose it never comes in. Then what?" Before Mama could answer, she forged ahead. "Besides, how you reimburse Mr. Pierce is not the point. We just met him a few days ago, yet you've totally entrusted him with my care." She held up a creamy forkful of pie, poised to take a bite. "If you want to give this town something to talk about, let them get wind of that."

Mama lowered her brows and shifted her lips to the side. "I never looked at it that way. 'Course they're bound to talk anyways, what with a young girl living alone in a hotel when she has kinfolk alive to care for her. It just ain't done, daughter."

"It'll seem a lot more respectable if I'm paying my own way instead of living off a stranger. Besides, I'm hardly his responsibility."

"You're right about that. You're mine." She pushed up from her chair and came to sit beside Charity on the divan, resting the plate of food she'd barely touched on her lap. "Come back and stay with me, sugar. I'll set things straight before long. Buddy said that oil in the bog holds the promise of a future for us—of a day when I can put you in a big, fine house and take care of you myself. Living here might be hard for a spell, but—"

Charity slapped her hands over her ears. "Please don't."

Mama gulped, swallowing the rest of her words. "Don't what?"

"Spout one of those senseless things you always say."

Mama set her plate on the table then gave Charity a long look. "Well, for heaven's sake, what things?"

"Things like, 'It's never easy to blaze a new trail.' Or 'We gotta wrestle it through to the end.' "

Her mama heaved a sigh and slumped back on the divan.

Ashamed, Charity took her hands from her ears. "Oh, go on, then. Spout away since you're busting to."

Huffy, Mama leaned to retrieve her plate. "Well, I cain't now. You done took all my good 'uns." Eyes narrow and sulky, she picked up her sandwich and took a bite.

Laughing, Mother Dane slid one arm around Charity's shoulder and squeezed. "Your mama's right, though, darlin'. You need to come stay where you belong. I know it'll be hard to face Emmy, but you'll have to someday. You girls can't stay at odds forever. We're family."

Charity hugged Mother Dane. "I appreciate the offer; I really do. Right now I have a place to stay. All I need is this one bit of help so I can make my own way for a while longer."

Mother Dane looked puzzled. "What bit of help is that, sugar?"

Charity twisted to face her mama. "Permission to sell my wedding dress."

Mama's eyes flew as wide as the dish on her knees. "You want to sell the dress I made?"

Charity talked fast. "Lord knows I don't want to, but I got a real good price. Mrs. Pike agreed to pay me thirty dollars. Can you believe it? That's all the money I need to get myself out of this fix and to hold me until things get straight. Don't you see? It's the only way."

Mama slung her sandwich, missing the table and scattering greasy bread and chunks of ham over the rug. She stood to her feet. "If it's the only way, then you're sunk, little miss. You ain't about to sell that dress." That said, she swept past them to the landing and stomped upstairs, tackling each step as if it were a bitter enemy.

Charity started after her. "Mama, wait!"

Mother Dane grabbed her arm and lowered her to the divan. "Let her go, honey. She ain't mad. She's hurt. Bertha's dangerous when she's hurt."

Charity's mouth went dry as dirt. Fear tickled her insides like a swarm of scurrying spiders. "I have to talk to her."

"If you don't give her time to cool down, she'll say things she don't mean. Once said, they'll hang between you."

"You don't understand. I need that dress."

If a look could bare the soul, Charity's lay stripped to the bone before Mother Dane's probing eyes. "I'm afraid to ask, honey. Why so desperate?"

"Because. . .I've already sold it."

Mother Dane's jaw fell slack. "Oh, honey, you didn't."

Charity turned out the pocket on her skirt, displaying the bright silver coins. "Mrs. Pike gave partial payment. We shook hands."

Mother Dane stared at the money cupped in Charity's palms. Instead of offering a glimmer of hope, the expression on her face made Charity's insides hurt. She released the pocket, and the coins slid out of sight with a lighthearted jingle, an outlandish sound in the midst of such gloom. "I guess I should've known better, I know how mulish Mama can be. Now what am I to do?"

Mother Dane pulled her close and gave her a little shake. "Don't take on so. This will require a bit more time to figure, but we'll think of something. Go on and finish your lunch. Afterwards, we'll sort it out together."

Charity squinted at her plate. The slice of pie, so appealing a moment ago, caused her stomach to lurch. She passed the food to Mother Dane, stood, and picked up her shawl. "I have to go."

"Honey, don't leave. That'll just make matters worse. Her Irish temper will cool in a bit."

Charity pulled on her gloves with such force the seam of one finger busted. "I don't have time to wait for that cantankerous old woman to cool. If I'm to fend for myself in this world, then I need to be about it, don't I? Thank you for lunch, Mother Dane. If you'll excuse me, I have to go find a way out of this mess Mama's landed me in."

She rushed to the door. Red lay curled on the porch sound

asleep, his eyes hidden under saggy bags of skin. When Charity moaned at the sight of him, he jerked alert, his tail thumping a rhythm on the smooth stones. She was not so pleased to see him.

Mother Dane hustled up behind her. "Where are you going? What will you do?"

Charity stared at her in silence. Where would she go? "I don't know yet. I need time to think. Good-bye, Mother Dane."

There was no way around the big dog panting up at her, as persistent and immovable as the cut of ancient rock on which he lay. So Charity tiptoed over him, stepping wide to clear his bulk. Instead of making her way to the path, she jumped off the side of the porch and made a beeline for the front garden. Shaking all over, and still drained by the squabble with her mama, she stumbled into Mother Dane's shaded arbor and sat down in front of the fountain. She needed time to ponder, to get her bearings before starting the long trip back to the Pikes'.

Red had followed, and he promptly laid his nose to snuffling the soft clay around the trees and shrubs. Leaving him to his own devices, she leaned against the cold iron bench to think.

It would be easier to send Red home than to get that obstinate old woman to change her mind. In fact, if it came to a match between the two, Mama was more dog-stubborn than the dog.

A sound reached her ears over the whining and snorting of the big hound—a relentless tapping that penetrated the whirlwind in her head and plucked her from the pit of dismal thought. Annoyed, she looked around to find the source.

The rapping grew louder, followed by the rattle of a windowpane. Red lifted his head and growled deep in his throat. Thinking it had to be Mother Dane, Charity looked at the house, but a quick check of the lower windows proved her wrong.

Mama perhaps?

Expecting to see the crabby old grouse, she followed the noise to the upper floor. . .and came face-to-face with Emmy, peering down from her bedroom. Charity tried to look away, but the girl's wide-eyed stare held her fast.

Red trotted over and nudged her with his nose, demanding attention.

Her willful, disloyal gaze still fixed on the tortured blue eyes above, Charity's fingers found and caressed the dog's soft, bristly muzzle. The irony of the moment struck her. They had changed places, she and Emmy. Now Emmy watched from above while Charity embraced a mongrel in the garden.

With a start, she realized Emmy still wore her nightdress. Her flaxen curls, always pinned and perfect, fell past her shoulders, dull and matted. The lovely pale face Charity knew so well gazed down without expression, her breath misting frosty puffs on the glass. Without warning, she raised one hand, pressing her palm to the window. Leaning in, her face crumpled with grief.

Charity spun and bolted from the garden. With Red on her heels, she lifted her skirt and sprinted for the thick woods that lined the property. When she reached the cover of the trees, she dove in as fast as she could, dodging bog holes and saplings until she came to the trailhead. A good way up the path she stopped, completely spent. Bent over at the waist, one hand at her throbbing side, she gasped for air and fought the sobs crowding her throat.

Red left her side and trotted ahead a few paces to greet someone emerging from a thicket just off the path.

Startled, Charity jerked upright. "What are you doing here?"

"Waiting for you," Daniel said. "We need to talk."

CHAPTER 13

Her hand still pressed to the window, Emmy watched Charity reach the edge of the yard and dart into a sparse crop of seedlings. Plowing through their spindly branches, she fought her way to the mouth of the trail then ducked behind thick brushwood. Emmy caught only glimpses after that, until Charity finally disappeared into the trees.

Emmy knew what she must do. Even to her fevered mind the act seemed foolish, but there was no time to think it through. She opened the window and crawled over the ledge, deftly gaining a foothold on the rickety trellis. Hanging there, suspended between right and wrong, she wondered if her rose-infested tomb had driven her quite mad.

Dressed only in her gown in the bold light of day, she scrambled to the ground. When her bare feet touched the cold red clay, her mind went to Nash, the only person on the place besides Mama and Aunt Bert. No matter. She trusted him. Even if Nash saw her streak across the grounds in her nightdress, he'd sooner cut off his arm than snitch on her.

She gathered the hem of the cotton garment and lit out, feeling Mama's eyes on her back from every window in the house. She knew exactly at what point the trees would hide her from sight—the same place where they'd swallowed Charity—and she didn't breathe until she reached that spot.

Daniel had followed Charity down the trail then hung back when he saw where she was headed. He had a feeling she wouldn't be staying long, so rather than face the two clamorous shrews crouched on the back side of Mrs. Dane's door, he'd hunkered down behind a juniper tree to wait. The sight of Charity through spiny branches told him his hunch had paid off.

He couldn't wait to speak to her, to tell her he still loved her. He imagined the look on her face when he said it. Her dark brows would lift in surprise and the corners of her full, red lips would twitch with pleasure. Maybe she'd toss her head and laugh the way she had that day in the hotel.

Heart thumping, he moved closer. "Did you hear what I said, honey? We need to talk."

Her hat in her hands, her long black hair disheveled and freed from its pins, she looked wild and beautiful. . .and furious. She lifted her chin and her eyes flashed. "Oh, you're right about that, Daniel Clark. We need to talk, and that's for sure."

He took another step forward.

Charity matched it with one step back. "What are you doing out here anyway, skulking behind bushes, waiting to spring out on lone women?"

Daniel ignored the last part and reckoned the answer to the first should be obvious. He summoned the patience to respond. "Like I already said, I was waiting for you. I followed you all the way from town."

"Is that a fact?" She watched him from beneath her dark lashes.

Daniel's hands began to sweat. Things weren't going well. Her look remained guarded, not at all what he'd expected.

She held her unyielding stance and raked him with glaring eyes. "Maybe you weren't waiting for me at all. Maybe you were lurking out here until I left Mother Dane's house so you could slither up and spread more lies." She glanced around at the bushes and tall grass. "I don't see Sidney and Jack. Won't you need your two deceitful witnesses?"

So that was the burr in her britches. Well, it explained her fury.

"Now, honey, don't be mad. I didn't go to hurt you none. I was only trying to protect you from that oil company fellow."

His heartfelt words brought a curious reaction from Charity. Her eyes flew open, and her body recoiled like he'd struck her. Daniel realized afresh that he'd never understand women.

Scorn blazed in her eyes. She spoke, her tone low and mean. "Tell me something, Daniel. Why do I need the likes of you to protect me from anything?"

He rested his hands on his hips and stared at the ground. "I guess you don't. Looks like I had this figured all wrong. Turns out it might be me who's needing you."

Daniel held his breath, waiting for her reaction. When it seemed he could reach out and touch her silence, he glanced up and found her staring. Some other emotion had replaced the anger, one he didn't recognize. Whatever its source, it left Charity's face as blank as a new slate.

"Why would you say something like that to me?" she finally asked. "After all that's happened."

He edged closer, longing to touch her. Charity's body tensed, and the hound beside her stood up and growled. Daniel glanced at the dog but held his ground. "I said it because it's true. I love you, sugar. I know it now. I'd wrestle a bull to win you back."

Astonishment replaced her empty expression. Daniel bit off a smile and watched, waiting for it to turn to pleasure. "Please, Charity. Let me come close. I need to hold you. Let me soothe away the pain I've caused."

Her lips curled. She tilted her head and laughed, but not the way he remembered. "You think you can smooth things over just by holding me?" Her dark brows lifted–in contempt, not happy surprise. "I guess I should be grateful you got my name right. It must get rather confusing dangling two women on the same line." One brow rose higher. "Assuming there are just two of us."

"Now, honey, you know better."

"Do I?"

He dashed his hat against his leg. "Yes! I ain't never loved nobody but you."

"What about Emmy, Daniel? Can't you make up your mind

which one of us you want?"

This was all wrong. She should be in his arms by now. Angry at himself, frustrated with Charity, Daniel raised his voice. "Can't you see I made a mistake? I don't care nothing about Emmy. It's you I want. Emmy don't even matter no more."

Charity cringed and covered her face. "How can you say such a cruel thing?" She hurled the question, the accusation, at him in a low moan. "Emmy does, too, matter. She matters to me."

It was his turn to raise a brow. "Why? Lord knows she don't deserve it. That girl's not fit to kiss your feet. Shoot, she's not fit to pour out your chamber pot."

Charity lifted her face, her features set in stone. "Get out of my way."

"Just wait a minute. We're not done talking."

"Yes, we are." She tried to shove past, but he grabbed her shoulders.

"No, now! Please listen. I can't eat. Can't sleep. You're all I think about. All I care about. Don't go like this."

The dog advanced, hackles raised. The warning growl he gave was no bluff, so Daniel turned her loose. She lurched away from him and called off the dog.

Daniel gripped his head with his arms. He had to think, had to find the right thing to say. At the sound of hurried footsteps, he looked up to find that Charity had run up the trail, well away from him.

He cupped his hands over his mouth and shouted after her. "You just need time to ponder what I said. You'll come around, and when you do, I'll be waiting."

She didn't answer or even look behind her. Instead, she picked up her pace, stumbling along the rutted trail as if he were chasing her. Daniel followed, but not too closely, because every so often the old dog stopped and checked over his shoulder, making sure he kept his distance.

Emmy knelt in the brush, watching Daniel's broad back until he reached the far end of the trail. When he made the turn toward town, she gave in to trembling legs and dropped to the ground on her behind.

A large dung beetle attached to the side of her knee and walked the length of her bare leg, coming to rest at her thigh.

Emmy stared down at it, smiling at the irony, and accepted the reproach. She shivered at the feel of its barbed legs against her flesh but couldn't summon the will to brush it away.

She wished the numbness she felt extended to knees pressed too long against the cold, hard ground. She noted the indention of a pinecone etched into one, leaving a blue-black imprint in her flesh. It hurt, but not like the ache crowding her chest. An intolerable throbbing had started down deep and pushed up her throat in waves that kept time with her heartbeat.

"Emmy don't even matter no more."

"Emmy does too matter. She matters to me."

Emmy fell against the hard ground and surrendered to the pain. She lay in a hollow, a spot wallowed out in the tall brush by hogs. Certain she deserved the sharp sticks and knobby roots biting into her flesh, and the stale, fetid stink left by the last pig to sleep on the dead grass, she started to cry. As she stared up at the cloudless blue sky through a canopy of soaring pine and a blur of hot tears, something Aunt Bert had said years before echoed in her mind—words that had come to her more than once of late, but she'd pushed them away.

"Don't live your life for the devil, Emmy. Old Slue Foot plies his wares like they're treasures. Then when you least expect it, he trips you up and leaves you flat on your back."

She'd laughed when she heard it. The words had conjured a picture of the vendor carts at the St. Louis World's Fair, only Aunt Bert's peddler hawked his goods wearing horns and a forked tail.

"Don't live your life for the devil."

She mulled the words over again, feeling as if God Himself had bent to whisper in her ear.

Yet how unlikely that a holy God would stoop to where she'd fallen or speak to someone sprawled on the ground, laid worthless and bare.

Would You, God?

The swaying branches overhead swam into a cluster. Emmy felt, more than heard, a low moan starting in her throat, becoming a high-pitched wail as she cried out her shame. Clutching her face, she rolled over, drawn into a tight ball of misery.

The sensation that someone knelt beside her persisted. Emmy didn't understand one thing about it, but she knew in her heart that she wasn't alone. Something powerful swept over her, carrying her high above the rebuke of pain and the stench of swine, leaving ease and sweet release in its wake.

When she sat up, she couldn't tell how much time had passed. She thought she must've slept a bit. What else but sleep, though she'd never slept so well or found such peace at rest.

The sound of an approaching wagon roused her, striking fear in her fragile heart. It had to be coming from home. Theirs was the only house this far down the trail. Maybe only Nash, headed into town on an errand.

"Emily Bertha Dane! Where are you?"

Mama!

Emmy pressed close to the ground and willed herself small. The rig had pulled alongside her now, and she prayed the brush was thick enough to conceal her white nightgown.

"Where could she be, Bertha? I've seen that girl pull some high jinks in her day, but even I can't believe this one."

"That makes two of us. You sure he said she was in a nightdress?"

Nash, you no-'count scoundrel.

"Yes, and in broad daylight! I'm going to put her in a convent, Bert, I swear it."

"You ain't Catholic, honey."

The rig rattled past, drawing the voices out of earshot. Keeping low, Emmy rolled to her sore knees and parted the high grass to peer out. Well beyond her now, they headed in the direction of town. Nash wasn't with them, so Mama held the reins, and Aunt Bertha rode beside her. The women sat tall on the seat, the motion of the wheels on the rutted trail tossing them to and fro.

Emmy watched them, Mama's head turned to the left, Aunt Bert's to the right, searching the woods on both sides of the trail.

Low in the distance she heard Mama call out to her again. "Emmy? Emily Dane! Land sakes, child, answer me!"

Her eyes fixed on the distant wagon, Emmy backed out of her hiding place and slipped into the woods. She would have to make it home through the trees without being seen, even by that traitor Nash. Once safely there, she'd figure a story to tell them they'd believe.

At the edge of the clearing, she crouched behind an overgrowth of honeysuckle vine and watched for Nash. Seeing no sign of him, she dashed across the field to the yard. Reaching the trellis, she scrambled up like a hounded cat and tumbled over the windowsill, landing on the floor with a crash.

"Why you ain't jus' took the door, little miss?"

Whirling, she came face-to-face with a haughty, indignant Nash.

"No call to sneak no mo'. They's onto you."

She struggled to her feet and grabbed a quilt from the bed to wrap herself. "What are you doing in my room?"

Nash, who towered over tall men and loomed over her, filled the room with his presence. His bulk intimidated most people, but Emmy knew him to be as meek as a lamb. He jabbed his chest with his thumb. "What am I doing in here? What I'm s'posed to be doing. Waiting for you, like I's told." He gestured at the quilt. "Ain't no sense hiding what you done showed the whole world. That'd be like tying up the gunnysack after the kittens crawl out."

"Why'd you tell on me?"

He lowered his gaze. "Didn't want to. Didn't when I first seen you shimmy down that trellis in your altogethers. I jus' shook my head and mind my own business. I guess I be used to your shenanigans by now. But then I heard you squealing like you being skint."

Emmy gasped. "Did you tell that to Mama?"

"No, missy. Didn't want to scare her no more than I had to. But I was beholden to tell her something in case you was in trouble."

She flung herself back on the bed. "Oh, Nash! I am in trouble now. Mama will skin me herself."

He nodded. "Yep. When she find out you ain't dead, she jus'

might kill you. That be a murdering even old Nash can't spare you."

Emmy bolted upright, her fingers clasped under her chin. "But you *can* spare me. In fact, you're the only person who can."

Eyes wary, Nash eased toward the door. "Naw, now. Uh-uh. Don't you start in on me. I tol' you if you didn't quit flying out that window, you'd lose some of them fancy tail feathers. Now your behind's showing, and jus' like always, you expect me to help you cover it." He held up a restraining hand. "You may as well turn aside them bewitchin' blue eyes. They ain't doin' you no good this time."

"I wasn't doing anything bad, Nash. You believe me. I know you do. Help me think of something to tell Mama."

His brown eyes widened. "Miss Emmy, I loves you like one of my own. You know I do. Only I got to make myself scarce on this one."

"You can't! Not this time. Please, I need your help."

Doubt flickered in his eyes. He wagged his head, but his voice wavered. "You gon' lose me my job, Miss Emmy. I got mouths to feed."

She had him. Lowering her long lashes, she let her shoulders slump and her arms go slack. "Of course. I understand. Don't you worry about me none. I'll be fine." Trudging to the side of her bed, she plopped back down on the mattress. "I've grown accustomed to living in this room."

Like a convicted man offered a reprieve, Nash jerked open the door and started out. . .then paused on the threshold and sighed. "I reckon if you was to tell your mama she heard me wrong 'bout you running for the woods. . .if you was to tell her I found you in the barn tending old Rebel. . .I wouldn't say you was lying."

Emmy wanted to run and wrap her arms around him but remembered her state of undress and stayed put. She tried to convey the depth of her gratitude in the fervor of her quiet response. "Thank you, Nash."

He glanced at her with hooded eyes. "I'm plain weary of breaking commandments for you, girl. You've kept me sorrowful before the Almighty till my drawers be worn at the knees. Try and behave yourself for a spell."

She gave a dutiful nod. "I will. I promise."

He waved a bony finger in her face. "If you really want to thank me, stay on this side of that window from now on, leastwise while wearing your scanties." Looking around, he added one last thought. "If your mama don't nail it shut, that is." His scowl disappeared, replaced by a wide grin. He closed the door behind him, still chuckling as he made his way down the hall.

Emmy dropped the quilt and spun in a circle, then fell across her bed. She'd done it again–worked Nash with the skill of a puppeteer and had him prancing to her will. With the aid of her reluctant marionette, Mama would believe her. Oh, she'd call Emmy reckless, lecture her on modesty, and that would be that.

As she lay staring at the ceiling, an unfamiliar sensation wormed its way into her chest, not unlike the feel of the dung beetle on her thigh. The usually sweet victory bittered in her mouth like an underripe persimmon. She wasn't herself somehow and wondered if it showed. Curious, she scooted to the edge of the bed and leaned to stare hard at the mirror.

Her familiar image peered back at her, just the same as before, save a few sticks and leaves in her matted hair. Exactly the same. . . except for the eyes. Eyes that gazed back, guilty and troubled, in a way they'd never done before.

"Oh, pooh!" she told her reflection. "I'm being silly. Nothing has changed." She'd plied her tricks like always and managed to save her hide.

She picked up her brush and worked it through her tousled hair, pushing aside the scattered emotions that made this time feel different. Because the difference was, if Emmy admitted the truth, her game had lost its pleasure. . .and made her feel like she'd wallowed with the hogs.

CHAPTER 14

Charity didn't slow down until the trail opened out onto town. With a frightened glance at Daniel, still following in the distance, she dashed through a rain-soaked clearing, slip-sliding through the mud in her haste.

Sensitive to her fear, Red trotted stiff-legged beside her, the hair along the ridge of his back flared like porcupine quills.

Her dread of Daniel seemed unreasonable. Yet the chill she'd felt while staring into his brown, soulless eyes had oozed around her, encasing her in fright the way sap envelops a bug. His effect on Red didn't help.

Before they made the turn alongside Rogers & Grossman's Dry Goods Store, Red stopped for one last throaty growl aimed in their pursuer's direction.

In her heart, Charity knew it wasn't the first time she'd noticed Daniel's callous behavior toward others. The confusion came from his ability to turn it off in an instant while his winsome ways and aching good looks lulled her into believing she'd imagined the whole thing. Indiscretions too blatant to overlook, she'd explained away as a onetime occurrence, a momentary weakness. Until today.

"Charity, wait. What's got into you, girl?"

Her heart lurched. Daniel's long-legged stride had nearly closed the distance between them.

Red's growl deepened to a vicious snarl. Charity tapped his

head and sped up. "Let's go, boy." Wheeling too sharply around the corner of Rogers & Grossman's, she drove straight into the middle of Jerry Ritter, one of Buddy's men.

The poor man shouted, "Whoa!" then grabbed her and spun around to keep her from falling.

Buddy stood behind him on the boardwalk wearing a surprised grin.

Mr. Ritter beamed down, aglow with delighted surprise. "Well, shucks. Hello there, Miss Bloom. Are you all right?" He held her wrist and helped her gain her footing. "Best be more careful, ma'am. You're liable to get yourself hurt."

Buddy took the two steps down to the ground. "I thought you reserved that manner of greeting for me. Looks like running folks down in the street is just your little way of saying howdy." He chuckled. "I have to admit, I'm a mite disappointed." He sobered, his brows knitting together. "Say, aren't you supposed to be resting?"

She shot an anxious glance behind her. "I'm sorry, gentlemen. I'm in a terrible hurry."

Buddy drew near and pulled her close, his gaze following hers to the corner. "What's wrong? You look like the devil's chasing you."

Daniel rounded the building. Red whipped in front of her and crouched, baring his teeth. He cut loose with frenzied barking, his deep bray piercing Charity's ears. Daniel froze, but the dog didn't seem to be the thing holding him this time. In fact, despite the fuss Red was making, Daniel appeared not to notice him. His gaze seemed fixed on Buddy's hands resting on Charity's shoulders.

A curse spilled from his sneering mouth and he spun in the opposite direction, his frantic gait from earlier slowed to a cocky swagger.

Charity released her breath. The muscles in her legs, tensed so long in flight, relaxed in a rush of warmth. It left them trembling so hard Buddy's hands, still on her arms, were the only things holding her up.

Lee Allen, whom she hadn't noticed before, bounded down to stand beside Jerry, his attention on Daniel's back. "Was that fellow giving you trouble, ma'am?"

Embarrassed to admit how much, she shook her head.

Bristling as much as Red, Jerry puffed like rising dough and glowered after Daniel. "If he does, we'll sort him out for you." He sniffed and hitched up his britches. "Shouldn't take but a minute."

"It's nothing I can't handle myself," she protested, not sure whether she told the truth.

Buddy pinned her with a no-nonsense look. "Did he hurt you?"

She glanced away. "Of course not."

"Threaten you in some way?"

Squirming, she raised pleading eyes to Buddy's.

He gave an answering nod. "You boys go ahead without me. I'll catch up later."

Mr. Allen hooked his finger in Jerry's suspenders and hauled him around. "Let's go, Jim Jeffries. You retired from the ring this year, remember?"

A blank expression wiped the scowl from Jerry's forehead. "The champ's retired? Who told you so?" Meek as a baby bird, he followed Mr. Allen up to the boardwalk, still pecking for information. "Huh, Lee? Jim Jeffries quit boxing? Why didn't anybody tell me?"

Buddy stared over Charity's shoulder until their banter and heavy footsteps faded. His chin hovered so near, she noted wisps of whiskers too fine to shave at the edges of his mouth. They were golden brown like the hair curling from under his hat, only several shades lighter. The longer ones curved around his top lip, and she wondered if they tickled.

His gaze swept back and caught her looking, his soft green eyes turning her heart to pudding pie. He smiled. "Want to talk about it now?"

The compassion in his voice made mush of her insides.

Oh no! I'm going to cry.

She covered her face. . .too late. Buddy sheltered her under his arm and gently guided her. . .somewhere. When they stopped, he turned her against the front of his shirt and let her weep.

Though it felt so nice to be there, Charity composed herself as fast as possible and pushed free from his tender embrace. Wiping her eyes on the handkerchief he offered, she stole a quick glance at him. "I can't imagine what you must think of me. All I do is pout and squall." She blew her nose, mortified that it honked like a prodded goose. "I hope you'll believe me when I tell you this is the most I've cried since Papa died. Things are so awful now, no matter which way I turn." She sighed. "I guess I'm finding it hard to cope."

Rocking back on his heels, Buddy shot her a piercing look. "You didn't lock your friend outside again, did you?"

She gasped. "Absolutely not! Don't talk foolish."

He grinned. "Sorry. Just trying to make you smile. I've decided I don't like seeing you cry."

Charity returned his smile. "I've given you plenty of chances to come to that conclusion, haven't I? You must be sick of me."

Buddy cupped her chin in his double-portioned palm and pulled her head up, snaring her with the intensity in his eyes. "Sick of you? Oh no, ma'am. Not by a long shot."

A peculiar weakness, accompanied by the same warm sensation that afflicted her whenever she thought of him lately, nearly buckled her knees. Except this time the power of her feelings nearly swept her away. When the sky tilted, she refocused to find that the world consisted of little beyond the brim of Buddy's hat. Shocked by a bold urge to caress the fuzz on his lip, she lowered her eyes and backed away.

Determined to shake off his spell, Charity raised her head and looked around. He had led her around by the rear door of the dry goods store behind a mountainous pile of empty crates. The stack formed a half circle that butted up against the woods, creating a private, cozy den of sorts. The pine boxes held the mixed odor of whatever wares they'd last held. Some smelled strongly of coffee, some tobacco, and a few reeked with the pungent, clingy tang of onion. Red worked his way along the line, busily sniffing out any odors she had missed.

By the look of the cigar butts and empty liquor bottles littering the ground, they weren't the first inhabitants, but the secluded nook was nice.

Buddy pulled down several crates, testing them with his weight until he found two he trusted. He placed them next to the stack, facing each other, then bowed at the waist and motioned for her to sit. "Milady?"

Laughing despite her unease, she gingerly sat, straightening her skirt around her legs. Red trotted over and curled up at her feet, while Buddy pulled his seat a little closer and perched on the edge, watching her without saying a word.

Just as the silence grew heavy, he spoke. "I think the reason you get teary-eyed so often is because you haven't let it out."

Charity jerked her gaze to his earnest face.

He blushed, but his eyes held steady. "I'm serious. Maybe you just need to have yourself a good cry. A stomp-your-feet, pound-on-something, bawl-for-all-you're-worth sort of cry."

"Very well, if you insist."

He held up both hands. "Whoa, now. I didn't mean right here and now."

His panic amused her, and she grinned. A twinkle lit his eyes as a slow smile replaced the fear. She started to laugh, and he laughed with her.

When they were quiet again, she gave him a shy glance. "I suppose you want to know about Daniel."

He eased back a bit. "It's none of my business really."

She scooted forward, bothered by the distance he'd put between them. "That's not so. After all, you have quite a stake in me by now. One I'm bound to repay."

His head swung from side to side. "Nonsense. You don't owe me a thing. I only hope I've earned your friendship."

She tilted her chin. "Oh, Buddy, you've earned more than that. You have my eternal gratitude."

Brows drawn in concentration, he mulled over her words. As if he'd made up his mind, he suddenly leaned across the dog and took hold of her hand. "If that's so, I hope I've gained your trust as well."

Surprised at the direction he'd taken, she squeezed his hand. "You know you have."

He squeezed back, sending a jolt along her spine. "Will you answer one question for me, then? I've no right to ask, but it concerns a matter that's hounded me since we met."

Hesitant, because she had no idea what he might be about to say, she steeled herself and nodded. "Go ahead and ask."

"Why were you so angry the day we found oil on your land? It wasn't just about leaving your house, was it?"

He had noticed. She knew it that day. Scattered emotions crowded to the surface, all struggling for release.

What's wrong with me? I will not cry again!

She swallowed hard. "I don't want the oil."

He scrunched his brow and lifted his chin.

"Well, not the oil itself," she hurriedly explained. "I mean the money, I guess."

From the deeper scowl lines on his face, she reckoned Buddy was truly puzzled now.

He cleared his throat. "Most folks are right happy to get their hands on more dough. Especially that much."

She drew up her shoulders and pulled her hand free. "No amount is worth what it's doing to our town. I detest the sight of those derricks. Especially Mr. Beatty's number two well—the way it stretches to the sky, belching smoke and steam. It's an ugly old eyesore."

Doing a poor job of stifling a grin, Buddy slumped over and braced his arms on his knees. "Ma'am, that well pumps over eight thousand barrels a day from a depth of seven hundred feet. I hate to contradict, but she's considered quite a beauty around these parts."

"I don't care. I hate her." With a forceful swipe of her arm, Charity brushed at her skirt as if dashing Mr. Beatty and his well to the ground. If only she could so easily rid her lap of all the problems clustered there lately—all caused, directly or indirectly, by the oil boom.

Buddy angled his head. "That's a harsh tone from such a pretty little mouth."

"It's true. I hate her. And let's not insult my gender—that hulking stack of iron is no lady. I don't want to add to the unsightly display in Humble by erecting one like it in my own backyard."

Buddy patted her clenched fists. "Dear girl, don't you understand yet? The boom is here. There will be oil derricks stretched across this land as far as the eye can see. In a year or less, they'll be so thick you can jump from one to the other and make it clear across town without ever touching the ground. What's one more going to hurt?"

She stared at him a moment then pressed her knuckles against her temples. "Oh, Buddy, I hope not. And I sure don't want Mama to have any part in it."

He curled his finger under her chin and lifted her face. "It's going to happen, Charity. With or without your mama's well. You can't stop it, so you may as well reap something from it to make a better life for the two of you."

She pulled away. "Why do people keep saying that? We've always been poor. It's all we've ever known. But we were happy with the life we shared, at least before Papa–" She cut off a ragged sob just in time. Only an odd little hiccup escaped to give her away.

Buddy stood, pulling her up with him. He nudged Red's flank with his boot, startling him awake and sending him scurrying aside. Then his arms went around her again, and she melted against him.

"You miss him, don't you?"

She nodded against his chest. "He was a wonderful man," she said when she could speak. "I don't say that because time has sweetened the memories. He really was special."

"Why don't you tell me about him?"

She searched his eyes. "Really?"

"Yes, I'd like to hear."

Before she realized it might not be proper, she traced circles around the top button on his shirt with her index finger while memories flooded to the surface. Suddenly self-conscious, she jerked her finger away. "Papa was funny. Always teasing. When he came into a room, he brought life through the door. Back then our house seemed fit to burst at the seams with love, joy, and laughter"–she grinned up at him–"and long-eared dogs. Papa bred the finest bloodhounds in the state. They were his passion." She tipped her head toward Red, falling asleep again beside her crate. "He was one of them. Papa's favorite. He belongs to Shamus Pike now."

"How'd you wind up with him?"

She grimaced. "It's a story you don't have time for. Suffice it to say, I can't get shed of the old rascal."

Buddy grinned. "He's a fine specimen, all right. I heard about him in town. A lot of folks still boast about Thaddeus Bloom's prized hunting dogs. What happened to the rest?"

Her finger wandered to the button again. "Mama sold them. Every last one." Aware she sounded like a resentful child, she softened her tone. "I told her I would take care of them, but she said we could barely afford to feed ourselves, much less a pack of hungry hounds."

"And you were sorry to see them go."

She sighed. "It felt like losing Papa all over again."

"It may have been for the best, though, don't you think? It would've been a lot of hard work for a–"

Her hand came up. "Don't dare finish that sentence. I'll have you know I stood toe to toe with Papa from the time I could walk. There was nothing girlie about me growing up."

He gave her a skeptical look.

"It's true! Papa always wanted a son. When he wound up with me instead, he taught me to hunt, fish, and tend the hounds. I was a scandalous tomboy." She smiled, remembering. "He even called me Charlie."

"Charlie?"

"Sort of a play on Charity, I guess. But he did have a best friend named Charlie back home in Jefferson, so who knows."

"I think I like it. It suits you."

Her cheeks warmed, so she changed the subject. "Papa loved to fish most of all, and no man in the county was better at it. He always took me with him. . .except on that last day."

Buddy cleared his throat. "The day he died?"

She nodded. "He didn't wake me that morning. I've always wondered why. If I'd been with him, I could've done something."

"Weren't you still just a child?"

"Almost fifteen. Hardly a child."

Gentle fingers caressed the base of her neck, smoothing circles of comfort into her skin. "There was nothing you could do. You know that, right? If you'd gone with him that day, you'd likely be lost to us, too. Sounds to me like God intervened because it wasn't your time."

His words tumbled into her head and ricocheted. When they

settled, a light flickered somewhere in her mind. Charity had never considered such a possibility. It held the promise of absolution but conflicted with the guilt she'd carried since Papa's death. She'd need more time to sort it out. "I just know that the day he died, everything changed, and it's never stopped changing since." She ground tears from her eye with the heel of her hand. "I feel like I can't catch my breath."

Buddy lifted his head and stared over her shoulder into the woods behind them. "As an eagle stirs up her nest, flutters over her young, bears them on her wings. . ."

Her gaze jerked to his. "Excuse me?"

He took her arm and helped her to settle down on the crate. "I've felt the way you describe. I didn't quote it right just now, but I didn't find peace until I found that scripture."

"What does it mean?"

"I didn't understand either until someone taught me about eagles." He puffed his cheeks and released a long breath. "Let me see if I can explain." He pressed closer and played with her fingertips while he talked. "You see, a mother eagle works hard to build a good nest for her young. She makes it nice and thick, pads it real good. It's so comfortable, in fact, that her young would never venture out of it without her help."

Charity made a face. "Don't tell me. She pushes them."

"She doesn't have to." He grinned. "Old mama eagle's smarter than that. She flaps her big wings over that nice cozy nest, stirring up all the soft padding until the sticks and straw are exposed. Before long, sticks and straw is all that's left of the nest, and it doesn't take much convincing to coax those little fellows over the edge."

"Why would she do such a cruel thing to her own children?"

Buddy quit playing with her cold fingers and enveloped them in his warm hands. "Well, because"—he lifted tender, caring eyes—"it's the only way they'll ever learn to fly."

Unsettled by his comparison, she stood to her feet. "It's getting late, and I still have a long walk ahead. I have a pressing errand east of town."

He stood, too, bouncing the heel of his hand off his forehead. "That's right, your errand. I promised to help, remember?"

"Don't fret. I can manage."

"How will you get there?"

"The same way I got here—on foot."

"Now, Charity, there's no need for that. Let me take you, or hire you a buggy at least."

"Don't you think you've done enough? I appreciate the offer, but there's still plenty of daylight and. . ." She paused then continued. "Like I told you before, my errand is of a personal nature, so if you don't mind. . ."

He blushed and took a step back. "Of course."

As she brushed past him, Red came up from a sound sleep and loped toward her.

Buddy reached for her arm. "Charity, wait. About the drilling. . . you're not angry with me, are you?"

"Angry?" She gave him a warm smile. "No, not anymore."

He took off his hat and gave her a wry look. "But you were."

She dropped her gaze. "How did you know?"

"Wasn't hard to figure. That first day out at your place you were cross about something. Then after that old wolf got after you, you apologized for being mad at me. Didn't know why at the time and never dared to ask. Knowing how you feel about the well, I'm just putting two and two together."

Took you long enough.

"All right, I confess. I blamed you at first. You know. . .because you found the oil in the bog."

"Fair enough. How about now? Do you blame me still?"

Charity shook her head and gave him a warm smile. "Not very much." Laughing at his grimace, she placed her hand on his arm. "I don't blame you at all. And I could never be mad at you again."

He gave the top of his head an absentminded scratch. "Well, at the risk of changing that, I have one last question."

She groaned inside. Buddy Pierce was one truly exasperating man. "Which is?"

"Don't you want to see your mama's financial burden lifted? Wouldn't your papa want that, too?"

The air between them crackled.

Charity sucked in a breath through her nose and held it, but it didn't seem to meet her need to breathe. She'd have to be more careful in the future what she claimed she could never do again. "I really must be going. I'll see you back in town."

"I'm sorry, Charity. I didn't mean. . ."

After a few paces she turned, nearly tripping over Red. "To answer your question, I wish more than anything I could ease my mama's burden. I hate watching how hard she works, and I intend to help her just as soon as I find a way to earn some money. However, there's simply nothing I can do for her now, considering I'm left to provide for myself without a penny to polish."

She whirled to leave. As she passed the pile of crates, the corner of her pocket caught on a nail and tore away. Coins and commissary tokens tumbled in a sparkling shower, spilling over the ground. Charity spun, clutching at her ripped dress and staring at her secret scattered in plain sight between them.

Confusion masked Buddy's face. He bent to pick up a bright silver piece and held it out to her. "I think I see your point, Miss Bloom. Why fritter away time polishing pennies when your pockets are filled with these nice, shiny dollars?"

CHAPTER 15

The coin in Buddy's outstretched hand glinted in the sun like a circle of quartz. Beyond it, Charity stood like the statue of St. Louis of France—only pretty.

"It's not mine," she finally said, her wide eyes shifting like she'd been caught at something. "At least, not anymore." She flapped both hands in frustration. "I mean, it never really was." She pointed behind her. "In fact, that's my pressing errand. I'm going to return that money to its rightful owner."

Buddy didn't speak. She made so little sense he didn't know how to respond. Even worse, his eyebrows hovered somewhere in the vicinity of his hairline, and he couldn't coax them down.

She balled her fists and jammed them onto her hips. "Don't look at me like that, Buddy Pierce. I can assure you I didn't steal it."

When he couldn't answer, she stalked past and perched once more on her recently vacated seat. "I may as well tell you. You know every other humiliation I've endured—why not this?" She leaned to pat the opposite wooden box. "What are you waiting for? Sit down. I don't have all day."

Wordlessly, he pointed behind him at the coins on the ground.

She waved her gloved hand. "Leave them. They're not going anywhere."

He forced his brows to relax then sidestepped the dog, who sat with his head tilted toward Charity, looking as confused as

Buddy felt. Squeezing between her full skirt and his crate, Buddy sat down. Red trotted over and settled at Charity's feet with a groan of resignation.

She drew a breath and dove in. "The money belongs to Elsa Pike."

Buddy frowned and rubbed his chin. "Now where have I heard that name before?" Before she could answer, he held up his finger. "Oh, right. The duchess."

This earned him a smile. "She's not really a duchess. Folks call her that in jest. She claims she descended from royalty."

"And she really didn't?"

Charity shrugged. "No one knows for sure. Her husband acts embarrassed when anyone mentions it. Mama thinks Elsa made it up."

Buddy chuckled at the mention of Charity's feisty mama. "She could be right."

"So anyway, about the money. . ." She began to fidget. "I arranged a little business transaction with Mrs. Pike that fell through." Her tiny frown became a scowl. "Actually, it was run through by Mama's sharp tongue. That ornery woman can't abide to see me happy."

He laughed. Her head jerked up, so he traded his tickled grin for a sympathetic smile. "Sorry. You were saying?"

"It's my dress, after all. Oh, she made it, true enough, but she made it for me. I should have the right to do with it whatever I please." She glanced up and sought his eyes. "Don't you agree?"

He shook his head. "I'm sorry, I don't follow. You sold a dress?"

"My wedding dress. Haven't you heard a thing I've said?"

"I'm trying, sweetheart." The unexpected endearment slipped from his mouth, as natural as drawing a breath. Still, he blushed when he realized what he'd said.

So did Charity.

He tried again. "Let me see if I have this right. You sold your wedding dress to Elsa Pike, but your mama didn't approve so you're on your way to fix it."

She did a jaunty point with her finger. "Exactly."

He grinned. "See, I was listening. What if Elsa won't give it up?"

"We never got that far. I still have the dress, or rather Mama does. She's buried her talons and refuses to part with it. So I have to return Mrs. Pike's money and somehow. . ." She sighed. "Somehow break the news to Amy Jane."

Grateful she could so easily explain the money, Buddy felt the tension ease from his shoulders. "Is that all?"

Charity stiffened. "What do you mean, 'Is that all?' "

"I mean I don't see what's so scandalous about selling a frock."

She looked at him as if toadstools had sprouted from his ears. "Not just any frock, Buddy. My wedding gown. The one I wore for the hour it took to ruin my good name in this town."

He shot forward, startling Red, and wagged his finger. "Now you see? There's your problem. If you ask me, you set too much stock by what folks around here think. About you *and* your mama." He slouched back and pushed his hat off his forehead. "I thought you were about to bare your soul again, maybe tell a story as lively as your last confession. I have to say, I'm a little disappointed."

Charity's lips parted; then she swelled like a colicky horse. "Well, forgive me for letting you down. Hopefully my next calamity will provide you with more entertainment." She turned a frosty shoulder in his direction. "Perhaps the severity of my problem escapes you. When I hand this money over to Mrs. Pike, it means I won't be eating supper tonight."

Buddy bristled. "You know full well I'm not about to see you miss a meal. It's only when you're headstrong that you wind up with a hollow belly, not to mention a heap of trouble." He bent to give her the eye. "Now ain't that so?"

Charity stood. "I won't bother to answer such a ridiculous question." She leveled a withering glare at his outstretched legs. "If you'll be so kind as to move aside, I'll be going now."

Buddy lifted one pointy-toed boot to her crate, totally blocking the way. "No, ma'am, I won't excuse you. Not until you promise I can take you to the Pikes' in my rig."

The startled look in her bright eyes became a hooded challenge. "I've asked you kindly to remove your feet."

He took off his hat and fiddled with the band. "I'll be happy to. As soon as you agree."

With a swish of her skirts, Charity pivoted to face the rickety stack behind them. Chin held high, she seemed to weigh the danger of squeezing through the tight space. Obviously finding it too risky, she turned around and crossed her arms over her chest, so stiff she appeared to grow six inches in stature. "Why, Mr. Pierce, did I mistake you for a gentleman?"

He tucked his hat back on his head then pushed it up to see her face. "That's an impressive show of indignation from the same *lady* who bamboozled me a couple nights back. I consider this an act of justifiable recompense."

"Bamboozled? Why, I never–"

"You don't recall the matter involving me in a monkey-suit and you with a certain room key?"

Charity's scandalized expression disappeared, and her defiant chin lowered to her chest. She laced her hands behind her back and traced circles in the dirt with her shoe. "I didn't bamboozle you, Buddy. I wouldn't." She bit her bottom lip, but a tiny smile fluttered at the corners. "Besides, I believe the word you used then was 'bushwhacked.' " The smile widened into a grin. "And I've since decided your estimation of my actions was entirely too harsh."

The girl enchanted him. Before he could stop himself, he was on his feet with his arms around her, laughing like a man with no sense. He knew he didn't imagine it when she returned the enthusiasm of his embrace. When he could, he held her away from him and gazed at her beaming face. "Pardon my zeal, Miss Bloom, but has anyone ever told you how endearing you are?"

She affected a coy look. "Oh yes. Every day."

"I'd tell you every day if I could." Heat warmed his face, matched by a rosy flush on her cheeks. With her eyes cast down, all he saw were dark, sweeping lashes curled up at the ends. He longed to kiss each one but knew he'd gone too far already.

She lifted her gaze. "If you're sure you don't mind, I suppose you can give me a ride. If you still have the time. . ."

Buddy stepped aside. "After you, ma'am." He sighed. "That is, if you can hurdle that overgrown hound."

Charity smiled. "It wouldn't be the first time I've had to jump him, though I'd rather not." She nudged the dog with her toe. "Get up, Red."

He reluctantly stirred then followed them sleepy-eyed to the rig.

Buddy handed Charity aboard then scuttled back to pick up her assorted loot before swinging up onto the driver's side. One brow raised, he handed the money and tokens to Charity. Without a word, she snatched them then opened her one good pocket and let them tumble inside.

They rode quietly at first. Charity, whether staring off in the distance or watching Red trot alongside, seemed lost in thought.

Probably rehearsing her speech to Mrs. Pike.

Buddy was busy rehearsing a speech of his own. He noisily cleared his throat.

As he'd hoped, Charity's head swung around. "You have something you wish to say to me, Buddy?"

"I don't want to intrude on your musings."

She made a face. "Believe me, they bear intrusion."

"I just wanted you to know, although your situation appears bleak at the moment, I believe things will work out in the end."

A slight frown creased her forehead. "On what do you base such confidence?"

He grinned. "The Bible does say, 'Charity never faileth.' "

She didn't actually return his smile, but the slight deepening of her dimples gave her away. "I know you're probably right. It's just that things seem so hopeless."

"Hopeless? I haven't turned you out in the street yet, have I?"

She patted his hand. "That's because you're a wonderful man. Except I can't in good conscience allow you to continue what you've been doing. It's outlandish."

"I really don't mind." How could he admit that not only didn't he mind taking care of her, but he wanted to? How could he tell her that tending her needs just felt right somehow?

"I'm sorry–it's out of the question. If I can't pay my own way, I'll be forced to check out of the hotel in the morning."

Surprised, he spun on the seat. "And go where? To the Danes'?"

"Never!"

"Then where, I'd like to know?"

The dejected slump of her shoulders told him she couldn't answer his question.

They continued the ride in silence. Buddy's mind roamed in circles until he had crossed off every possibility and exhausted his imagination. He turned to prayer, where he should've started in the first place.

As they rattled down the road leading to the Pikes' farm, the solution darted up and hit him squarely between the eyes. He reined up and faced her on the seat. "I know what we can do."

Her eyes brightened. "There's a remedy to this predicament?"

"Indeed there is. It's simple really. The oil company owes your mama a fair sum for the lease of your house, isn't that so?"

She nodded, but the mention of the oil company dampened the expectant light in her eyes.

"Just listen now. If Bertha agrees, I believe I can arrange to charge off whatever money I've spent on you against her check. They'll deduct my portion and hold it for me. When she gets the balance, she can take over from there. Then you won't be taking anything from me."

Charity clasped her hands. "Oh, Buddy. Will the check be enough for all that?"

He nodded. "With money left over to hold you through the month. They're fairly free with their purse."

She sneered. "They can afford to be, can't they?"

Buddy picked up her hands. "Listen, I'll be the first to admit that drilling oil—like anything else involving fast money—attracts a bad bunch of men. Sure, there are depraved, greedy souls who take advantage of good folks to make a dollar, but we're not all bad."

She cringed and pulled one hand free to cover her mouth. "Oh, Buddy, I didn't mean. . .that is. . .well, you're not, of course."

"Not just me, Charity. If you took the time to get to know a few more of us, you'd find that the majority of men in the oil business are decent, hardworking, and honest." He gave her other hand a firm squeeze. "I intend to hang around long enough to prove that to you. I'll have you trusting oilmen again if it's the last thing I do."

She offered a brave smile and turned away, but not before he saw the flicker of doubt in her eyes.

CHAPTER 16

After more than two months, waking up at the Lone Star Hotel still felt peculiar even after Mama moved in. Rather, especially after Mama moved in. The feisty rascal refused to share the room until she could pay her own way, but the minute she got the first oil company check, she turned up at Charity's door with a bag of clothes and a stubborn mind-set. "Ain't no daughter of mine living in a hotel by herself as long as I can help it," she'd insisted. "Thaddeus Bloom would spin in his grave if he knew."

Living with her in their spacious, high-ceilinged home had been challenge enough. Sharing a space no bigger than Rebel's stall proved downright trying. Mama alternated between talking nonstop when awake and snoring down the rafters while she slept, so peace and rest became scarce in Charity's life. For that reason, when an uncommon stillness settled over the room, she rolled over in bed to look around.

Her rowdy companion was gone, though a sleepy glance at the window told Charity the sun had barely risen. She yawned and stretched then swung her feet to the cold floor. Usually by the end of March the weather was warm, but a recent cool snap had penetrated the smooth boards, turning them to ice beneath her toes.

At home she kept a pair of Papa's thick woolen socks in a dresser drawer for chilly mornings, but only heaven knew where they were now. Wearing them never failed to warm her heart right along with her feet, so she considered the lack of them one more casualty in a string of losses. She shuddered, picturing them mud-soaked and stretched over the big, smelly feet of a roughneck.

Not yet committed to rising, Charity reached behind her and pulled the warm blanket around her shoulders. She sighed, aware she'd awakened with the same confused feelings she'd taken to bed. Elation and despair, a miserable mix, fought for vantage in the pit of her stomach.

Last night, from out of nowhere, Mama announced they were going home. "Those men have searched for the bottom of that hole for nine weeks now," she'd said. "If they ain't found it yet, I expect they ain't likely to. We'll head out there first thing in the morning and tell them to clear out."

The unexpected words had pierced Charity's heart, unleashing a flood of forgiveness, relief, and joy. They were going home, to the house where she'd been born, to the only life she'd known before the specter of oil had curled sticky black fingers around Humble.

There was only one problem. The marauding invader employed a most agreeable representative in the person of Buddy Pierce.

During her stay at the hotel, Buddy had made a point to see Charity every day. Most evenings he made it back to town in time to clean up and take supper with her and Mama. If his work at the house detained him past their meal, he'd find some reason to knock on their door. For propriety's sake, he and Charity would stand in the hallway and whisper or sit in a secluded corner of the lobby and talk until bedtime. Mama noticed his attention and delighted in teasing her.

As if summoned by her thoughts, Mama jerked open the door and swept in like a gusty wind. "Get up, little gal, and shake that floor," she crowed. "Your old mama's running circles around you already." She came and perched on the side of the bed. "I've done been down to the livery and back. Hired us a rig for the trip out to the house. Ain't nothing fancy, but it'll get us there. The old man was hitching it up when I left. Said he'd deliver it to the hotel himself." She gave Charity a sharp slap on the leg. "What do you think about that?"

Her boisterous mood at the early hour rattled Charity's nerves.

She winced but offered a sleepy smile. "Morning, Mama," she mumbled, rubbing her eyes. "Gracious, but you're lively. How long have you been up?"

"Long enough to see your beau and his men leave for work before the cock ever crowed. He looked about as spry as you do. You two might want to consider trading some of that late-night talking for sleeping."

The wound-up little woman crossed to the window and peered down to the street. "Wahoo! Come on, gal. The wagon's sitting out front right now." She spun around laughing. "Took me a spell to convince that old possum to let me take it, but when he saw the color of my money, he couldn't find his pocket quick enough."

She came back and stood over the bed, brandishing a bony finger. "And that there's what I've been saying all along. Money makes a difference in people's lives, even oil company money."

Unwilling to wade those precarious waters, Charity bit her lip and nodded.

Oblivious, Mama continued, "Shame our cash is about to run out just when I'm getting used to having it." She heaved a sigh. "Even more of a shame that boy couldn't make good on his promise. Now we'll never know what it's like to make ends meet without stretching the life out of a dollar."

Charity's heart lurched. Buddy's question about easing Mama's burden came to mind. She hadn't yet lifted a finger in that direction, and in fact had only created a heavier load. Not to mention the fact that her disastrous wedding had put a terrible strain on Mama's purse. . .with no well-heeled son-in-law to show for her trouble. "I'll pitch in soon. I promise. I hear Elsa's looking for help around the house after Amy Jane marries. If she'll have me, after all the hullabaloo, I can work for her."

Mama scrunched up her face. "I reckon I'd rather see you slave after Emmy the rest of your life than work for Elsa Pike." She sat beside Charity on the bed and gripped her shoulders. "We'll deal with all that later. Right now, the only thing holding us here is you, so don't just sit there under them covers. Hurry and dress so we can get packed and eat a bite before we head home."

"Does Buddy know?"

"What? That we're coming? I started to tell him our plans this morning, but I don't need him trying to talk me out of what I know is right. I reckon the sight of us on the porch with our belongings should show him we mean business."

Pulling her chilly feet beneath her, Charity sat cross-legged in the bed. "But where will they go? The men, I mean."

"That ain't our concern now. We had a deal. Two months and no more. Their time is up."

Charity pictured the house and shuddered. She remembered the mud, tracked so thick on the porch she couldn't see the boards, with heavy-footed men traipsing in and out all the time. The kitchen had to be fly-spotted from leaving the screen tied back. No telling in what condition they'd find their beds. "Mama, the whole place is a in a muddle. How will we ever set it right again?"

Mama waved her hand. "Never mind about that. We'll just wrestle it through to the end."

Charity groaned and scratched her nose with the blanket. "That's fine for you to say. You haven't seen it."

"Don't worry, honey. The two of us will find a way. We always have, ain't we?" She cocked her head and stared dreamily. "Almost hate to leave here though. I think I might miss seeing that Lee feller around. He sure is nice. Makes me wish I was ten years younger."

"So it's *Lee* now, is it?"

Mama bristled, her face crimson. "Don't look so surprised. I ain't buried yet."

"I'm only surprised by what you said. You're not ten years older than Mr. Allen. A couple of years, at most."

Mama gazed at her, weighing her words. "Just two? You reckon so?"

Beaming, Charity swung her feet to the floor. "So you are sweet on him."

Dimples deeper than her own creased Mama's cheeks. "Hush up. We got no time for silly talk. Dress yourself, daughter, unless you've acquired Emmy's fondness for parading outside in your nightdress."

Charity laughed and pushed off the bed. Standing in front of the tall pine wardrobe, she picked through her clothes, studying them one by one. Besides her three old dresses and the bridal gown pushed to the back, two brand-new frocks hung there, one green and one blue. Not handmade like most things she owned but ordered straight from the catalog. Another good thing to come out of the oil company money, she grudgingly had to admit.

She held them up. "Can I wear one of these?"

Mama stood by the bed, shoving her clothes into a bag, not bothering to notice whether they were clean or dirty. She glanced back. "Out to that filthy place? Whatever for?"

"I want to, that's all. I'll change out of it before we start to clean." She tilted her head and pouted her lips. "Please?"

Mama gave her a knowing look. "Go on, then. Look nice for Buddy. But you'd better be careful. There won't be no more big checks to buy dresses once we take the house back."

Charity twirled and squealed. "Thank you, Mama! I promise not to muss it." She chose between the two outfits and returned the other one to its peg. Reaching to the back, she ran her fingers down the sequined bodice of the wedding gown. "Do you suppose Mrs. Pike and Amy Jane will ever forgive me for going back on our deal?"

"Sure they will. Time takes care of such things."

"They won't even speak to me, and they avoid me on the street."

Mama snorted. "Count your blessings."

Charity caressed the silky sleeve once more before gently tucking it back in place. "I must say, I'm glad it wound up this way. It's such a beautiful gown. I just hope I get to wear it before it yellows with age."

"Don't be silly, child. The way things are going with you and Buddy, you'll wear it, and soon I'll wager. You two are as cozy as turtles on a warm rock." A smug look crossed her face. "If I play my cards right with Mr. Allen, maybe I'll get a chance to wear it first. 'Course I'd have to shorten the hem by six inches at least." She hooted at her own daring then held up Charity's shoes. "Sit down and I'll help you put these on."

Charity slipped on her stockings then pulled out the chair in front of the dressing table. Sobered, Mama stooped to help her with the laces. "How long you reckon it'll take them men to clear off our land?"

Charity shrugged. "A few hours at most."

Mama breathed a contented sigh. "Tonight I'll actually get to sleep in my own bed. Never thought I'd choose it over all this finery, but I do."

Charity bent to squeeze her hand. "Me, too."

"Reckon we'll get the house clean by bedtime?"

"Not like it was, I don't expect, but if I have to sleep there tonight, I'm eager to get started. Only. . ."

Mama peered up at her and waited.

Charity extended one leg and feigned an interest in her shoe, trying hard to sound casual. "Does this mean Buddy will leave?"

Mama shook her head and went back to the laces. "Don't borrow trouble, honey. There's plenty of oil business in Humble to keep him right here. Besides, I get the feeling he's not so eager to leave town just yet. You keep batting them pretty eyes and I expect he'll be around for a good long while."

It was just a tiny bit of hope, but she latched onto it. "You really think so?"

Mama dropped Charity's foot on the floor and stood. "I do. Now let's go scare us up some grub before I perish."

They followed the aroma of food to the dining hall, where Sam saw to it they started their journey with a good breakfast. After a hearty platter of bacon, fried eggs, biscuits, and grits, they climbed aboard the hired rig and set out, their hearts as full as their bellies. They barely cleared the hotel before Red bounded up and fell in beside them, tail high, ears alert, as if he counted himself their personal escort.

"Fool dog," Mama murmured, casting him a withering look.

Charity just laughed and shook her head.

The cool of the morning persisted, though the sun had come up bright, casting long shadows over the trail. The countryside only hinted of spring, but there were patches of early wildflowers and tender new growth on a few bare limbs.

Charity closed her eyes and thanked God for a beautiful new day. In her estimation, life couldn't be better. The two things for which she had fervently prayed seemed close enough to reach out and touch.

Not only were they going home, but her heart stirred with

the possibility that Buddy might care for her enough to stay on in Humble. Since the latter part was too important to trust to Mama's scattered observations, Charity determined to find out for herself. She would see him in another half mile. She decided to be bold and watch him closely. If he truly cared, she'd know. She'd see it in his eyes.

Charity hoped she looked as good as she felt. She had worn the green dress. It was the prettiest and matched the color of her eyes. After Mama helped to pin up her hair and fasten her bonnet, Charity pulled long strands free, winding them into dark curls around her face. A splash of lavender water at the crook of each arm finished her off.

"You smell nice, baby. Just like springtime."

Startled, Charity glanced up. It was uncanny how Mama picked up her thoughts. "What a nice thing to say. Thank you."

"You look right pretty in that new frock, too. I'm glad you wore it."

Smoothing the fabric against her lap, Charity smiled. "I do love it. I'm so glad you bought it for me."

Mama turned her head to the trail again, but not before Charity saw tears glistening in her eyes. "I wanted to buy you lots of new things."

Charity leaned close and hugged her. "Don't you dare fret. I know you're disappointed, but what you're giving me today is worth more than ten new dresses." She squeezed her tighter. "We're going home, Mama! That's all that matters. I'm content without all the rest–honest, I am."

Red barked, loud and unexpected beside them, causing them both to jump. Mama shouted an insult at him, a coarse offense she'd picked up from Mother Dane.

"Mama!"

"I'm sorry, daughter. He scared me."

The dog ducked and cowered in shame, but his sense of obligation overshadowed his disgrace. He trotted alongside them, big head swaying to and fro, alert eyes sweeping the brush-lined trail. Evidently, whatever he had barked at earlier wasn't important enough to pull him from his self-appointed duty.

Obviously eager to get home, Mama kept the horse moving at a brisk pace. Determined to keep up, though he drooled and panted profusely, Red kept apace with the horse. Charity figured she might feel sorry for him if he weren't so pigheaded.

"Why do you suppose that stubborn old hound persists on following me wherever I go?"

Mama glanced down at Red and smiled. "Oh, I reckon I know why."

Her words, spoken with quiet assurance, surprised Charity. "You do?"

"Don't you?"

"No, ma'am. Enlighten me, please. Then maybe I can put a stop to it."

"That ain't likely." She ducked low and leaned in like a little girl sharing a secret. "He senses your daddy in you."

Charity frowned. "Papa?"

Softness settled over her mama's face the way it always did when she spoke of him. Like a magic wand, it blurred the faint lines around her eyes and lit a dreamy glow within their depths. "Red worshipped the ground he trod. You have his same spirit, Charity. All the good residing in Thad he left here with you when he passed." She faltered and pressed a hand to still her quivering lips. "You're so much like him, daughter. Did you know when you sit with me in a darkened room I feel he's there instead?"

Charity's eyes stung. "I'm really that much like him?"

"The breath and soul of him. You even love the Almighty the same. Thad worshipped the Lord free and joyful, like King David himself."

How could such beautiful words hurt so much? Charity swallowed hard against the tight knot in her throat and nodded. "I can still hear Papa's voice in my head: 'Let God do His work, honey. Confess your sins and let 'em go. Don't cling to your guilt. Enjoy the gift of freedom Jesus gave you. After all, it cost Him all He had.' "

Mama nodded. "You took them words to heart."

The tears flowed then, running down Charity's face and splashing onto the crisp green fabric of her dress. "I did, Mama. I pinned all my hope on them."

They embraced again. Since he barked the last time they hugged, Charity remembered Red. He wasn't on either side of the wagon, so she turned in her seat to look. He still followed, straggling a good way behind them. His panting had worsened, to boot.

"Stop the wagon, Mama."

"Why?"

"I want to put Red in the back."

"What for?"

Mama sounded doubtful, but she pulled on the reins nonetheless. Charity jumped to the ground and waited for Red to catch up. When he did, she lowered the tailgate and ordered him inside. Too tired to jump, he only managed to plant his two front paws on the rig. She stooped and wrapped her arms around the dog's body to give him a boost. Red scrambled inside, squirming with pleasure.

Mama threw up her hands. "Charity Bloom! Now you'll smell like that old rascal, and after you promised not to soil that new dress."

To show his gratitude, the drooling dog licked Charity from chin to eyebrows before she ever saw it coming.

"Heavens!" Mama shrieked. "Now you'll stink of dog breath, too. What on earth were you thinking?"

Charity closed the tailgate and dusted her hands. "I'm thinking a creature with Red's brand of devotion deserves to ride."

Mama cast a warning glance. "Don't lose sight of the facts, honey. That ain't our dog no more."

Scratching Red's wrinkled snout, Charity smiled. "Try telling that to him." She sauntered to the front of the wagon, the swish of new petticoats adding to her pleasure. Seated beside Mama once more, she nodded toward the horse. "Let's go. I'm anxious to get this over and done."

"That makes two of us."

Red groaned and fell to his side before stretching the length of the wagon bed and closing his eyes. Mama laughed and nodded. "I stand corrected, dog. I guess that makes three."

She shook the reins and clucked at the horse, setting him in motion. Pulling her foot up to rest the sole of her boot on the rail, she looked about her with a big smile. "The good Lord sure gave us a fine day for it, didn't He?"

"That He did."

"I reckon your sweetheart will be right disappointed in us when we get there."

Charity hadn't considered that possibility. She flashed her mama a worried look. "You think so?"

Mama nodded. "He sure wanted to find oil on our land. I expect he'd drill clear to China if we didn't stop him."

"You don't think he'll be mad at us, do you?"

Mama opened her mouth to answer, but if she said anything, Charity never heard it. A deafening explosion rocked the area, sending shock waves through the ground so violent they rattled the wagon. The horse reared and got set to bolt, but Mama held the reins, shouting at him to hold steady.

Over the treetops a column of mud blasted to the sky and then spewed in every direction. There followed a greenish-black surge that rushed into the air for eighty feet before raining down over the surrounding pine. Black ooze fell straight down, pelting them and bombarding the trail in giant globs, spooking the crazed horse even more. He threw himself back on his haunches again, his front legs pawing the air.

"Get off, Charity!" Mama cried. "I cain't hold him!"

Charity's feet hit the side rail, and she was on the ground, running for the horse's head. She clutched his harness, holding on for all she was worth. "Get down, Mama! Jump!"

Mama dropped the reins and shot to her feet. One leap and she was clear. . .and just in time. A wet wad of mud landed on the horse's back, and no power on earth could have held him. With glazed eyes and foaming mouth, he bucked just as Charity fell back and turned him loose. Then he burned up the trail, blindly running in the direction of the very thing he feared. As the wagon thundered by, Red, stiff-legged with fright, stood staring at them from behind the tailgate.

Mama lay on the ground where she'd landed then rolled. Propped on both elbows, she stared at the roaring apparition overhead.

Charity rushed to her side. "Are you all right?"

She lay slack-jawed with dread. "What's happening, Charity? What is that thing?"

Before Charity could answer, a lone horseman cut around the runaway rig, elbows high and flailing as he urged his mount. He didn't bother to stop the wagon but headed straight for them, riding hard.

Her mama still gazed at the sky. "Is it Armageddon, daughter?"

Charity pointed at the rider. "I don't know, but look."

Mama gaped as the man bore down on them whooping and hollering, covered head to toe in muck. He reined in his horse so fast the animal spun to the side, kicking up a cloud of dust.

Mama looked him over then turned to Charity. "Is that a man?"

She nodded. "I think so."

"Who is it, then?"

Charity leaned down and pulled her to her feet. "I'm not sure, but I think it's Buddy."

The dark figure leapt to the ground and came at them, laughing so hard he ran in a crooked line. "We did it!" He grabbed Mama in a bear hug and whirled her off her feet. "We got us a gusher!"

Charity gaped at the mess he'd made of her mama's clothes and backed away. He set Mama on the ground and smeared a sloppy kiss on her cheek. "No more cooking and scrubbing floors, little Bertha. You can hire your own help now."

Catching his mood, Mama started to laugh. She turned and pointed at the sky. "So that's what that thing is? Oil?"

"Oil, Mrs. Bloom, and plenty of it. Enough so you'll rest easy all your days. Charity, too, and her children's children."

At the mention of her name, he came at Charity, ready to grab her, too, but she screamed and darted away.

"Buddy Pierce, don't you dare touch me!"

He halted in his tracks, his arms still reaching for her. "And why not?"

She pointed. "Look at what you've done to Mama. She's covered in that stuff."

"Covered in gold, sugar. Come and get you some." He leered jokingly and came at her again.

She screeched and lit out for the trees, finding a big one to put between them.

He chased her around it laughing like a madman while Mama hooted from the trail.

"You stop right now—I mean it. This is my new dress, and I promised Mama I'd stay clean."

He paused long enough to nod at her arm, his grin crazy-white against the sludge on his face. "I hate to be the one to tell you, Miss Bloom, but it's too late for that now."

Charity followed his gaze to the greasy spatter on her sleeve, made worse every second by the shower of oil falling around them. "Oh no! Just look at that. It's ruined."

No longer smiling, Buddy stared at her around the tree trunk. She clutched the cool, rough bark and stared back.

"You still don't get it, do you, sweetheart? You're rich, Charity. You can buy a new dress every day of the week if you want. The whole shop, if you've a mind to."

And there it was. The thing in his eyes she had set out to find. Love offered up from the deep green depths, there for the whole world to see. Her knees grew weak. She had no choice but to allow Buddy to catch her before she hit the ground. With both arms clutching his neck, she watched over his shoulder with wide eyes as the roaring black spout rocked the sky.

CHAPTER 17

"Which one are you looking at now?"

Charity sat at the dressing table, pinning her hair and watching her mama through the big looking glass. Mama sat cross-legged in the middle of the bed, bent low over the catalog in her lap. At the question, her head came up, one finger held steady on the page to mark her place. Her eyes met Charity's in the mirror.

"It's the Henke-Pillot."

Charity pointed to the toppling stack wedged against her side. "And those?"

Mama picked up the topmost book. "This here's the Sears Roebuck." She pointed down at the pile. "That one's John Deere. The rest are old Harper's Weeklies. I'm studying on the adverts."

"John Deere? I thought you were set on raising cattle, not crops."

Her attention divided between her daughter and the catalog, she turned another page. "Ain't looking for me. Widow Sheffield's plow is held together by prayer and a wad of spit. I reckoned I might fetch her a new one when our money comes in."

Charity smiled at Mama's reflection. "I might've guessed. You haven't a greedy bone in your body."

Mama shook her head. "It ain't that. If God intends to bless me when I don't deserve it, how can I do less than bless others? I've always said money in the right hands does more good than harm. Now I aim to prove it."

Instead of returning to her browsing, Mama watched while Charity fussed with her hair, peering so intently that Charity started to squirm. She put down the brush and squinted back at the brooding image. "What now? You're staring."

Mama frowned. "You're mighty flushed, sugar. You ain't taking sick, are you?" Tossing the catalog aside, she wiggled to the edge of the bed and hurried over to press her palm against Charity's forehead. "Gracious, I reckon you're a mite warm, too."

Cheeks flaming, Charity caught the groping hand and pulled it away from her face. "I'm fine. It's a warm day, that's all."

Mama slid both arms around Charity's neck, resting her chin on top of her head. Their gazes locked in the glass. "Don't you get sick on me, you hear? Not now, when everything's about to change for the better."

Charity patted her hand. "I won't. I promise."

Relieved when her mama crawled to the center of the bed and took up her books again, Charity returned to taming her hair. She dared not confess the little meddler had caught her mooning over Buddy, an activity that warmed her cheeks quite often lately. He'd been gone for two whole days now, and Charity missed him something fierce.

They'd never made it home that day. Charity had begun making peace with the possibility they never would. Back in the hotel, Mama overflowed with plans to build a new house every bit as grand as Mother Dane's, with a stove like hers and a balcony attached to each of their bedrooms.

Buddy's lesson on the eagle had come to Charity on wings of mercy. She'd spent a lot of time pondering her death grip on the past and decided not to let it steal her future. Papa had been an immovable rock in her young life. When the floodwaters washed him downriver, they'd swept her sense of security along with him. Thanks to Buddy, she understood she'd been clinging to all the wrong things. The only constant in anyone's life was God. As long as He hovered nearby, she could soar above a few sticks and straws.

After the gusher blew in, Buddy commandeered every available freighter then hired men eager for work to drive wagons loaded with oil to Port Arthur. He said a refinery there would pay top dollar for every barrel they could haul.

The morning the makeshift caravan departed, Buddy had leaned down and pressed his lips to the corner of her mouth before swinging up on the lead wagon. That quick, stolen kiss consumed her thoughts far more than his parting words—the promise to return with so much money Mama couldn't spend it in a year.

Mama had spent the last few days trying. She haunted Rogers & Grossman's Dry Goods Store, bent on seeing, touching, and smelling every item for sale. Back in their room, she pored over catalogs for hours, making endless lists. Charity teased her about it but had to admit she'd jotted down a few notes of her own.

Buddy planned to take them to Houston when he got back, to the Kennedy Trading Post and Market Square. Mama had journeyed to Houston once when Papa was alive, but not by rail. Charity had never left Humble, much less set foot on a train. She and Mama awaited Buddy's return like children counting down to Christmas.

It amazed Charity to realize she'd known him for only a short time, yet it seemed she'd soon perish without him. His absence caused an ache deep inside that grew worse every day. Thinking of him was like scratching an itch—to do so made the problem worse, but she couldn't stop.

She glanced at the mirror to find her face bright red again. She looked away and struggled to compose herself before Mama noticed. Thankfully, a loud knock jarred them both, jerking Mama's attention to the door.

Charity's heart pitched. Had Buddy returned early?

Evidently the same thought had come to Mama. She cleared the bed in half the time it took her to root off of it before and crossed the room a split second ahead of Charity. She yanked at the door and slung it wide, her giddy grin saying she expected Buddy to be on the other side.

Shamus Pike stood in the hall clutching a scruffy hat. His hesitant smile revealed he hadn't expected the elaborate reception. "Afternoon, Bertha. Miss Charity."

"What in tarnation are you doing here?" Mama had never perfected the fine art of polite banter and wasn't one for beating around the bush.

Shamus's smile disappeared. "I come to discuss important business, Bert." He nodded into the room. "Can I come in?"

Mama waved him through but surprisingly left the door propped open. Concerning herself with the rules of respectability was not her usual behavior.

"This about the land lease money? It ain't due for two weeks yet, but I'll take it if you insist." She held out her hand and chuckled at her own wit.

Shamus shook his head, and color flooded his face. He wouldn't meet Mama's eyes, and his Adam's apple bobbed several times. Finally, he cleared his throat and got to the point of his visit. "Now, Bertha, don't think what I come to tell you means you won't be taken care of, you and Charity. I owe a debt of friendship to old Thad, God rest him, so I wouldn't have it any other way."

Mama dropped her head to the side the way Red cocked his and stared while getting scolded.

Charity didn't understand Shamus's words either, but the anxious way he blurted them flipped her stomach.

Mama motioned to the chair in front of the dressing table. "I reckon you're trying to tell me something, but I guess you'd better sit down and start over, because I ain't understood a word so far."

Hat still wadded in both hands, Shamus sidestepped to the chair and sat. A thick-middled, broad-shouldered man, he looked out of place seated on the delicate furniture. Mama and Charity perched together at the edge of the bed and waited for him to continue.

"What I come to say is hard for me." Shamus stared at the bare stretch of floor between them while he talked, his big hands working the old hat like dough. "I got no wish to hurt you, wouldn't do that for the world, but sometimes the dealings between men bring pain to their families. It's the way life is."

Mama scooted closer to Charity and took hold of her hand. "I'll thank you kindly to get to the point, then."

Shamus squirmed in the chair until Charity feared it would collapse. Finally, he looked up and rushed ahead as if he needed to get it said. "It's about your land, Bertha. Fact is, it ain't your land no more. At least it won't be soon enough."

Mama sat up straighter and stared him down. "What are you saying to me, Shamus Pike?"

He dropped his gaze again but kept on talking. "You know yourself old Thaddeus had a gambling problem once. A right reckless problem."

Mama tensed. "I ain't denying it, but that was a long time ago."

Charity's head jerked around.

Her mama shrank five inches under her searching gaze. "Sorry you had to hear it like this, baby. I'm afraid it's true. Games of chance always had a strong pull on your poor papa. He kept his weakness in check by teaching me and Magda how to play poker for fun. 'Course, we never bet nothing serious. Just harmless things like buttons, matches, hard candies sometimes."

Charity had always wondered how their weekly poker game came to be.

"After you was born, he changed," she continued. "Promised he'd never place another bet—a promise he kept as far as I know."

Shamus snorted. "He made one last wager. Thad gambled away your property before he died. To me."

Mama's fingernails dug into Charity's hand. "How so?"

Shamus leaned over and considered her with probing eyes. "You want the details?"

"I sure do."

He sat up again, watching them. "All right, then." He rubbed his palms down his trouser legs and swallowed hard. "Six months before he passed, Thad and me was in town together of a night, both feeling our oats, me liquored up and him just feeling spry. The bet was Thad's idea." His bloodshot eyes fixed on Charity. "Somehow it come to him to gamble on whose daughter would marry first, Amy Jane or Charity there. The stakes we put up were our homesteads."

Charity couldn't tell if the trembling in their clasped hands was Mama's or her own.

"Thad wouldn't do a thing like that. He told me he was finished with gambling." Though her voice quivered, Mama's words were forceful.

Shamus glared her way. "He not only done it; he goaded me

into it whilst I was drunk!"

His expression softened when Mama drew back. He ducked his head and cleared his throat then continued in a quieter voice. "Later on Thad's conscience got the best of him. He tried to get out of it, but I wouldn't allow him to welsh on a bet. I'd sobered up by then and had some time to think. Old Thad thought he had a sure thing, what with Amy Jane so big and plain and Charity so fetching. But I reckoned I might be able to turn things around on him. I figured I had a fair enough chance, considering men around these parts need a good sturdy woman–one who can bear lots of babies and help shoulder the load. As pretty as Charity is, I figured Amy Jane stacked up better in that respect."

He glanced Charity's way again. "No insult intended."

She nodded, speechless.

"When Daniel Clark started up courting Charity, I got real nervous. Took a gun to my head when he proposed." He sat back and exhaled. "Good thing I didn't pull the trigger."

Mama grunted. "Good for who?"

His eyebrow spiked. "Say again?"

She waved him off. "I wouldn't have come after your land even if Charity had got married to Daniel. First off, I never heard any of this before now." She lifted her chin at him. "And second, only a heartless reprobate would snatch a person's home right out from under them."

Shamus sputtered. His ears turned purple, and his chest heaved. "That's because you're a woman, and women are weak. You can't understand the ways of a man. Sometimes we got to do things we don't like to make our way in this life. That includes taking risks."

He opened his mouth to say more, but Mama stopped him. "No, sir. That don't apply to Thad. He was a good man. Better than most. I can boast about him in this company, because we all know it's true." She shifted toward him, prepared to do battle. "You'll never convince me he risked our home. He wouldn't do that to us."

Shamus leaned forward and met her charge. "He would on a sure bet."

Charity couldn't stay still. "If such a bet existed, Papa's death canceled it out."

Shamus wagged his graying head. " 'Taint so, Charity. In the weeks leading up to your wedding, I figured I'd lost it all and I was bound to give it. When Amy Jane steps to the altar, I'll accept no less from you." He slouched in the chair and folded his arms, his eyes hard on Mama's face. "Bertha Bloom, I expect you to honor your dead husband's word."

Charity didn't wait for Mama's answer. She pointed at Shamus. "That's why you pushed Amy Jane's marriage to Isaac Young, even against Elsa's wishes." She knew it was true, but it felt odd to say it. In other circumstances, she'd never speak so boldly.

Shamus glared at her finger through narrowing eyes. "I'll thank you to pull in that claw and mind your tongue, little cat. This here's betwixt me and your ma."

Mama stared at Shamus like he'd turned green. "You're telling me if Charity had married Daniel, I'd own your whole place right now? Shamus, that's crazy talk."

"It might be crazy, but in a few days I'll hold your deed."

Mama jumped to her feet. "I don't believe it! You got no proof."

"Oh yes, ma'am, I do." Shamus stood. As if he'd been waiting for the chance to do so, he reached into the hip pocket of his overalls. Producing a square of paper, he waved it in her face. "The proof is right here." He undid the folds and crossed the small room to stand before Mama, his thumb pressed to the bottom of the page. "Ain't that your Thad's writing?" He looked from Mama to the paper then to Charity, his eyes bulging, his voice shrill with emotion. "And that's his very own John Hancock signed in ink right there at the bottom. Now you can't deny that."

Mama trembled as she took the paper. She handled the scrawled signature with a reverent touch, and tears sprang to her eyes. "Them's his marks, all right. I'd know them anywhere." She handed the paper to Charity and slumped back onto the bed. "Read it to me, daughter. Real slow."

The tears in Charity's own eyes blurred the page. She swiped at them with the back of her hand and tried to focus on the words. "It says, 'I, Thaddeus Horatio Bloom, square of mind and in possession of my good sense, do hereby enter into a bound agreement with one Shamus P. Pike–' "

"No, Thad!"

Charity jumped at the tortured cry that tore from her mama's throat, her plea directed at Papa as if he were right in the room uttering the terrible words himself. Mama fell onto the bed with her hands over her ears and wailed. "Don't read me no more. I cain't stand to hear it!" She reached for a pillow and buried her face in it. "Read it to yourself, daughter; then tell me it's not true. Please say my Thad didn't do this to me."

Charity read on, searching for some shred of hope. She read clear to the bottom without finding it. The room swirled and seemed to inhale sharply, sucking the air from her lungs. Shamus still hovered just above her face, and though she couldn't bring him into focus, she became acutely aware of the smell of him–manure, the open field, burnt oil.

Oil!

She pushed to her feet, forcing Shamus to stumble away. Glaring at him, she shook the paper in his face. "I understand it all now. I know why you're doing this."

His determined gaze grew wary.

"You don't want our land," Charity spat. "You're after what they drilled on it."

At the mention of their gusher, Mama moaned and wailed louder.

Shamus set his jaw. "It's a fair bet between me and your pa, Charity. Neither of us knew the future when we made it."

He snatched the document from her hand, blotting at the tear-smudged ink with a filthy rag before cramming it into his pocket. "This paper will hold up under the law, too. I already checked. So consider this official notice. I'll be taking possession of your place directly after Amy Jane's wedding. Make sure you're cleared out by then."

He shoved his hat down on his head and marched to the door, pausing on the threshold as if something had just occurred to him. "You should count yourself lucky that well came in before the wedding. At least you'll get something out of it before you lose it."

He left, leaving the door standing open behind him. Charity jumped up to slam it, desperate to shut him out along with the terrible news he'd brought in with him, but it was too late. One look at Mama told her the damage was done.

She had scrambled to the middle of the bed and pulled her knees close to her body. Deep, heartrending sobs ripped from her throat, loud enough to disturb the other guests. Charity crawled onto the bed behind her and shielded the tiny body with her own.

"Don't you cry, Mama. Don't you fret now, you hear?" Charity cradled her, rocking and stroking her hair. "Hush now. Everything will be fine. You'll see. Everything will be just fine. I promise."

Too angry to pray, she rocked until Mama slept while her mind whirled with a plan that would help her to keep her promise.

CHAPTER 18

With a grunt, Daniel heaved a feed sack onto the growing stack he'd raised in the corner of the barn then propped his arms against the burlap bag and leaned his head to rest. The pungent odor of jute mingled with grain assailed his nostrils, reviving him a bit. Up since dawn, he'd tackled and finished a long list of chores, though it wasn't yet ten in the morning. For a man to be bone-weary two hours shy of midday was just plain no good.

He'd found little rest the night before. The minute his body grew still enough for sleep, his head kicked up, filling his thoughts with long black curls and a wide, laughing mouth. He fared no better with the morning. Charity had come to him in his waking hours, just as she had throughout the night, teasing, taunting, hovering just out of reach.

Longing for her one minute and cursing her the next, the weight of conflicted emotions had bruised his insides. Whether he felt more anger toward Charity, Emmy, Buddy Pierce, or himself he couldn't tell and grew weary from trying to sort it out.

Daniel jerked up from the feed and forced Charity out of his mind. He'd have to work harder, stay too busy to think. Better worn out and sore than tormented by his own thoughts.

He rubbed the stiffness from his aching shoulders and headed out to fetch another bag from the wagon beside the barn. When he stepped outside, the Dunmans' dogs across the road were barking, so he glanced up to see what had caused the commotion. Not that their braying was uncommon. Those two set up a ruckus with very little goading, but he could tell from their excitement something unusual was afoot.

He shaded his eyes and peered closer. What he saw set his heart to racing, though good sense told him his bleary eyes were seeing things. He rubbed them with the heels of his grimy palms and took another look. . .and there she was. The phantom that robbed his sleep at night and plagued his soul by day stood just outside the gate.

Down off her horse, Charity hovered near its flank, bent over with her back to Daniel.

Hesitant, he crossed the yard. He couldn't think what to say to her when he got there, couldn't imagine her answer. Still, he walked.

She jerked around when he opened the gate. "Goodness, Daniel! You gave me a start."

He smiled and nodded. "Sorry. Didn't mean to."

Reaching down, she cradled the horse's hind foot and ran her hand around the shoe, her long fingers moving gently over the soft inner flesh. Daniel waited for her to speak. When she didn't, he latched the gate behind him and eased closer. "What you got there? A rock?"

Charity answered without looking up. "She was favoring one side a bit. I thought I'd better check." She let go of the mare's hoof and dusted off her hands. "Whatever it was seems to be gone now."

"What brings you out this way?" Even with hope frolicking inside his chest, he hated himself for asking.

She stared across the street at his neighbors' shuttered windows. "Mama sent me to the Dunmans' on an errand, but from here, it looks like no one's home."

He shook his head. "Took the train to Houston to visit kinfolk. I've tended their dogs all week."

Charity glanced at him. "Is that so? Well, that's odd. Mother Dane usually gets wind of such things before anyone else."

He nodded toward the house. "They left in a rush. Sickness in the family, I heard."

Daniel didn't quite know what to do with his hands. He finally rested them on his hips, but then, feeling like an old woman, he let them drop to his sides. "I see you got shed of that old red hound." He winced and cursed himself for reminding her of that day.

Charity glanced around her legs, as if she might find the dog there. "It seems I have. For now, at least."

She smiled slightly and Daniel returned the expression, ashamed of the joy it stirred in his heart. His mind reeled. Why were they discussing horses and neighbors and dogs with all that lay between them?

"I guess I'd better head on home." She took the horse's reins in her hands and prepared to mount.

Daniel surged forward and clutched her wrist. "Charity, wait. I know why you're here."

Her body stiffened. "Whatever do you mean?"

"I mean I've thought of you night and day since I saw you last. Now fate has set you right outside my gate. It's meant to be, sugar. Can't you see it, too?"

She relaxed her shoulders and faced him. Was that a smile tugging the corners of her mouth? He felt sure of it, and the sight quickened his heartbeat.

"Fate, Daniel?" It was all she said, but the way she said it, and the fact that she seemed not the least bit eager to mount the horse, told him volumes. . .and gave him courage.

He stepped closer. "You've missed me, too. Don't deny it, Charity–I can feel it."

She stood between him and the horse, staring at the ground by his feet, her big eyes veiled by long, dark lashes. She had on a blue dress he'd never seen before and wore her hair pinned up in back, though several dark curls had escaped, teasing her delicate face. He was near enough to smell her, and it made him dizzy.

When she didn't retreat from his advance or react to his nearness, he let eager arms encircle her waist. She tensed up a bit but didn't pull away. Too far gone to control himself, he buried his face in her hair and drew in her scent while he had the chance. When his lips brushed the soft skin of her neck, she withdrew, alarm in her eyes.

"I'm sorry, honey." He took an unsteady breath. "I've just missed you so. I've gone mad thinking of you."

She nodded then looked around his shoulder toward the house.

He followed her gaze. "Don't fret about Mama. She's not at home. Besides, I don't care anymore what she thinks."

Charity closed her eyes and reached trembling fingers to his face. "You really mean that?"

He clutched her hand and drew it to his lips. "I never meant anything more in my life. I want you for my wife, Charity. I want to be with you forever."

She sagged against the horse, but Daniel caught her and pulled her close, laughing as he held her. "Oh, sugar, I know. You're as relieved as I am. We're together again now, and I promise to do everything in my power to make it up to you."

"Anything, Daniel?"

With her face pressed so tightly against his chest, Daniel barely heard the muffled question. He rested his cheek against her head, thanking his lucky stars for such good fortune.

"Anything, sugar. Anything at all."

Charity rode away from Daniel's house with shattered emotions. It amazed her how easily she had deceived him, how effortlessly she'd slipped into the role of a jezebel. At the same time, it frightened her how natural it felt. Mother Dane's long-held hope that Charity's behavior would rub off on Emmy may have worked in reverse. Emily Dane herself couldn't have carried out what Charity had just accomplished.

It was settled. She and Daniel would marry in three days' time.

"The sooner the better," he had said.

Yet how hard it had been to embrace him, to let him hold her. She'd had to close her eyes and imagine Buddy standing there, Buddy's arms around her, Buddy's cheek beneath her fingers. A brazen device, still it would get her through the coming days. After the wedding, she'd have to put such faithless thoughts out of her mind, and Buddy out of her heart forever.

Daniel had balked when Charity asked him to keep their plans a secret, insisting no one could know there was a wedding afoot until they were officially husband and wife. He believed she feared his mama would stop the marriage. She let him think what he wanted, so long as he complied with her wishes.

I did it, Mama. Now everything will be fine. Just like I promised.

She knew her mama wouldn't be happy at first. It would require some fancy talking to get her to go along with the scheme. Charity would just have to convince her there was no other way. In the end, she'd come around to Charity's way of thinking. She had no choice.

"You done what!" Mama slammed the brush on the dressing table and whirled on Charity, her face so red with rage that Charity expected fire to blast from her nostrils.

"Mama, just listen for a minute."

"I ain't having it, Charity. Do you hear me? I'll go to my grave poor and homeless before I'll see you married to that uppity, no-account scalawag."

Charity tried to stay calm, but hysteria crept into her voice. "Surely you see this is the only way?"

"To have you marry a lying, cheating fool? The only way for what? To ruin your life? I won't let you do that for me."

"After all you've done for me? It would be an honor to ruin my life for you, but that's not what I'm doing. I'm saving us."

Mama's eyes flashed. "I already got me a Savior, daughter. He don't need no help from you."

"You know what I mean. It'll save our home. Besides, Daniel loves me. He really does. I can feel it."

Mama's eyes became slits, and she grunted. "Then what was that foolishness with Emmy?"

Charity flicked her hand, as if the gesture or her next words could ever take the sting out of what those two had done. "Emmy turned his head for a bit, that's all. You know Emmy can do that to a man. But Daniel's in his right mind now. He knows what he wants, and it's me."

"You don't say? And what do you want?"

She averted her eyes. "I almost married him once, with your blessing. It must be my fate." Daniel had used the same word. Now it rang hollow in her ears.

"A fate worse than death." Mama spat the bitter epitaph and scowled like she could taste it.

"My goodness. Straighten that terrible face." Charity wrapped her arms around her mama's waist and whirled her around the room. "Come on now. Just think of it. I'll be all set. A proper married lady. Plus it will keep Shamus Pike's conniving hands off of our land. It's a perfect plan, and you know it."

Mama broke free and backed away. "I asked you a question, Charity."

Busying herself at the dressing table, she shrugged. "What question?"

"I asked what you want, except I reckon I already know the answer. There's a bigger, better man in your thoughts than that dirty scum of a Clark boy. A real man, one worthy of you."

Charity turned her face away, but Mama took hold of her arms and shook her. "I'm dead right," she cried. "I can see it right there in the mirror. You're in love with Buddy Pierce. How can you think of marrying anyone else?"

She fought the tears. That would be all it took to have Mama forbid her. Forcing a smile instead, she measured her words. "Like I said, it's my fate to marry Daniel."

"Honey, no! Why not just marry the man you love?"

Charity turned from the mirror and pulled her mama close. "Because he's never asked me, that's why." She bit her lip hard to hold back a sob. "Anyway," she said, staring across the top of Mama's head through brimming eyes. "Buddy's not here right now, is he?"

CHAPTER 19

Emmy paused to wipe her feet on the tattered rug at the back door. Mama said it would stop Nash from tracking in half the barnyard, and it worked when he remembered to use it. Emmy had a good share of the outdoors on her own shoes, so she took care to wipe them well.

Easing the door open, she slipped through to the kitchen, ears alert. She didn't relish another confrontation with her mama and avoided her whenever she could. Things hadn't gone well between them since the day Emmy climbed out of the window in her nightdress.

Mama had listened to her claim that she'd been in the barn tending Rebel. She even sat quietly through Nash's version, but it was clear she wasn't convinced. She'd cast long, suspicious looks at the conspirators before sending Nash outside to work and Emmy to her room. And for the first time in her life, Emmy felt bad about telling a lie.

The events of that day had strained their relationship more than ever, to say the least. It vexed Emmy to no end and caused an ache in the pit of her stomach. The only bright spot of late had come in the form of a telegram from Papa. Urgent business held him up north for six more months at least. So he never needed to see what she'd done to his horse, and Mama wouldn't tell. Despite her reprieve, Emmy faithfully took care of Rebel, though it was Nash's job. She felt it was the least she could do, and the old horse seemed pleased by the arrangement.

Commotion from the parlor caused her to pause midstride. She recognized Auntie Bert's voice, and she sounded upset, so Emmy tiptoed to the door and listened.

"What am I to do, Magda? I cain't let her throw her life away on that boy. It just ain't right. Especially now that she loves someone else."

Emmy's heartbeat quickened. Were they discussing Charity? Charity in love with someone besides Daniel? Impossible! If so, on what boy was she about to throw away her life?

The way she saw things, this could only work to her advantage. She eased closer and pressed her ear to the door.

"When did all this come about, honey?" Her mama's voice was low and soothing, in that tone she only used with Aunt Bert.

"This morning. Charity broke it to me over at the hotel not an hour ago. Poor little thing, acting so cheerful for my sake when I know her heart is breaking."

Was Aunt Bertha crying? Emmy's pounding heart lurched. She'd never heard her cry before. Mama said she cried buckets when Uncle Thad passed, but Emmy never saw it.

She suddenly wailed from behind the door, dispelling any doubts and sending a chill through Emmy's veins. "I had to get out of there. I couldn't stay in that room another second and watch her put on a brave face. I know she's doing it for me, and I cain't stand it."

"Don't let her do it, Bert."

"I don't want her to. You know that. I tried my best to sway her, but that stubborn girl's mind is set like flint. She says after Shamus takes our place, we'll lose the oil company money, too, and then we won't be able to afford the hotel. We'll have nowhere to go."

"You and Charity ain't at the mercy of Shamus Pike. You can live with me. You know I would take care of you both 'til the day I died."

After a lengthy silence and a sniff, Aunt Bert finally answered. "I know you would, honey, but that ain't right, neither. And with things turned inside out between our girls, it won't work. Charity's not about to stay here, and this time I won't stay without her."

"So what, then?"

Aunt Bert sighed before she answered. "I guess I can see it clear now as bad as it tastes in my mouth. We got no choice. I pray the good Lord will show us another way, but meanwhile we got us a wedding to plan."

"What about Buddy?"

"I'd wager he feels the same about my girl as she does for him, but he ain't here to ask. By the time he comes around again, it won't make no difference. She'll be married to someone else."

So Charity was in love with Buddy Pierce. It answered the first part of Emmy's question. A twister spun into her chest. If Charity loved Mr. Pierce, exactly whom did she plan to marry?

"It makes me see red, though," Aunt Bert continued. "That other one ain't nothing but a cheating scoundrel. I'd sooner see him dead than married to Charity. Daniel Clark don't deserve my little girl."

Emmy reeled from the door, hoping they hadn't heard her gasp. She reached for the table to steady herself and fell into the nearest chair. Lowering her head, she clutched her face so tightly her fingernails bit into her flesh.

Daniel was going to marry Charity. After all they'd meant to each other, after what she'd sacrificed. She could no longer tell herself he hadn't meant what he'd said that day on the trail. He meant it, all right. She didn't matter to him and never had. He loved Charity instead, and she would be his bride.

"Emily Bertha Dane, how much did you hear?"

She shot upright, wiping her eyes on her sleeves. Mama and Aunt Bert loomed over her, their faces tight with rage.

"Why, she heard it all, Magda. You can tell that by looking at her."

Her mama took her by the wrist and jerked her to her feet, causing the chair to tip over and hit the wall with a bang. Strong hands dragged her away from the table, and her anklebone took a sharp rap against the carved wooden leg. She howled in pain to no avail. Mama hauled her into the parlor and forced her to sit on the divan, then stood over her with Aunt Bertha.

Emmy stared up at them, more afraid than she'd ever been in her life. She didn't recognize the squint-eyed women crouched above her like bobcats on a rabbit.

"Emily, I asked you a question. How much did you hear?"

She drew back, desperate to put distance between herself and Mama's red face. "I didn't hear anything. Honest!"

"Don't you dare lie!"

"Why?" Emmy shrieked. "Why does it matter so much what I heard?"

Aunt Bertha beat Mama to the answer. "Oh, it matters all right, little gal. It matters a heap."

Emmy's wide eyes shifted to her mama. "Won't somebody please tell me what's going on?"

"Emmy, I'll sit on you for three days if I have to, to make sure you don't ruin this for Aunt Bert and Charity. You've dealt them enough pain as it is. Come to think of it, you're the cause of all this trouble."

The weight of the words struck them dumb as the truth hung heavy in the room. Then Emmy started to cry. Deep, wracking sobs rolled up and out from her middle, breaking the painful silence.

Her mama eased down beside her and pulled her close. "There, there, now. I didn't mean to hurt you, baby. I just can't understand why you insist on doing what you know is wrong. Listening behind doors, for instance. How many times have I warned you about it? I told you it would catch up to you someday."

Still rigid with emotion, Aunt Bert sat down on the other side. "This here's that day. Emmy, I need you to tell me what you heard us talking about. It's important."

"And no more lies," Mama added.

Emmy wiped her eyes and sat up. Whatever was going on, she'd never seen the two of them act so strangely. She took courage from Mama's arms around her and decided to try the truth for a change.

"I heard you say Charity's in love with Buddy Pierce, but she's fixing to marry Daniel."

Mama and Aunt Bert shared a grim expression.

"And I heard something about Shamus Pike taking your land."

Aunt Bert leaned forward and slapped her legs with both

hands. "Well, that's it, then. Our goose is cooked."

Mama released Emmy and scooted around to glare at her with one raised brow. "No, it ain't, because she won't tell. Will you, Emmy?"

"Tell what? Land sakes, you two are talking in riddles."

The older women sat in tense silence, obviously deciding whether to enlighten her or not.

Emmy gathered her nerve and dared to ask the only question she wanted answered. "Why is Charity marrying Daniel if she's in love with Buddy Pierce?" She looked back and forth between them, waiting for one of them to speak.

Aunt Bert fixed her with a piercing stare. "Emmy, do you love your Aunt Bertha?"

"Yes. Of course I do."

"Do you have any feelings left for Charity?"

"You know I do!"

"Then sit up and listen good, because I'm about to trust you with our very lives. What I'm going to tell you ain't ever to leave this room."

Aunt Bert gave her a look so intense the force of it pressed Emmy against the couch. "I won't tell a soul, Auntie Bertha. I promise."

CHAPTER 20

Buddy stepped out of the stable, tired but elated after leaving his horse strapped to a feed bag in the liveryman's care. Hungry himself, he intended to belly up to breakfast just as quick as the dining hall of the Lone Star opened for business.

He stood on the already bustling boardwalk in the cold gray dawn and tried to work the miles out of his backside. It had been a long, tough pull, but he made the ride from Port Arthur in record time. And no town ever looked so good to a man as Humble looked to Buddy that morning.

He shifted the weight of the saddlebag on his shoulder and patted its bulging pockets. Bertha Bloom would be mighty happy to see the contents, but not nearly as glad as he would be to see her beautiful daughter.

Thoughts of Charity pushed aside the empty gnawing in his stomach and replaced it with the now familiar ache he got whenever she came to mind. The only remedy was to have her near—medicine he planned to swallow in large doses as soon as the sun rose a bit higher.

He smiled, imagining the look on her face when she saw him back ahead of schedule. To accomplish it, he'd left it up to Lee and Jerry to return with the wagons and bought himself a horse. An irresponsible move, no doubt, but he couldn't wait another week to see Charity.

If things went according to plan, if she accepted the ring in his vest pocket, no matter where his work took him next, they wouldn't be split up again. She could go along wherever he went, at least until they started a family. Then he'd find a way to spend as much time as possible at home. He imagined Charity in the family way, her round belly ripe with his child, and his face glowed with pleasure at the bold thought.

Mind still fixed on the future, Buddy drew in deep of the clear morning air and stepped off the boardwalk into the path of a big black horse pulling a loaded wagon. The wild-eyed creature reared, and the driver cursed, jerking the reins to the side. Buddy scrambled out of the way just before the front wheel ran him over.

The rig lumbered to a stop, and the man leaped down. Buddy saw right away it was Daniel Clark. Daniel, who didn't seem to recognize him, closed the distance between them in quick, angry strides. A scowl as black as a thunderhead darkened his face. "By golly, I almost hit you, mister. Didn't you hear me coming? What in tarnation were you thinking?"

Buddy took off his hat and offered his hand. "Accept my apologies, sir. My mind is elsewhere this morning."

Daniel wiped his palm on his trouser leg before taking Buddy's in a firm grip. "Whatever has your mind, I hope it's worth your life. It almost got you killed." He leaned in for a closer look. "Well, if it ain't Mr. Pierce. I didn't recognize you under all that dirt and facial hair. Can't tell if you've had a hard ride or been rode hard."

Giddy with fatigue and pure joy, Buddy ignored the sarcasm. "If you said both, you wouldn't miss it by much. Truth is, I'm at the easy side of a long, hard ride, but it was worth every mile considering what's waiting for me on this end."

Daniel raised one brow. "Do tell? Sounds like a woman to me. Got a little gal waiting for you?"

Buddy felt reckless. "Not just any gal. The prettiest in Texas." He knew he sounded cocky, but he wasn't in a mood to consider Daniel's feelings. After all, the foolish man had trifled with Charity's heart.

Unaffected, Daniel returned his smile. "Well, I don't see how that could be, partner, since I'm about to marry the prettiest girl in Texas."

Daniel getting married? Buddy felt like scratching his head. Could he mean Emily Dane? Charity claimed he was done with her. One thing was for sure—the man's swagger got more annoying by the second.

"That's right, Buddy, old boy. You need to check your facts and try again. The sweetest prize in the county fair is spoken for, and the blue ribbon goes to me."

Something about the way he said it brought heat to Buddy's neck. Clark was enjoying himself too much. He offered another handshake, determined to hide his fear. "I guess congratulations are in order, then. Who might the lovely lady be?"

Daniel gripped his hand, too tightly to be mistaken for goodwill. His eyes burned with anticipation like a cat ready to pounce. "Oh, you know her quite well."

Buddy fought to control his breathing. He wouldn't let the man see him rattled. "That's not likely. I don't know that many women in Humble."

"I reckon you're well acquainted with this one." Daniel stepped so near that Buddy smelled barber soap on his face. "Charity and I have reconciled. She's consented to be my wife. In a few days, Charity Bloom will be Charity Clark." He lowered his voice and affected a conspiratorial tone. "I'll thank you kindly to stick that under your hat though. We've decided to keep it quiet for a spell."

Buddy jerked his hand free and glared at him. "I don't believe you."

Daniel smirked, blatantly enjoying Buddy's pain. He whirled away with a laugh and ran both hands through his hair, preening. The cat cleaning his paws after the kill. When he faced Buddy again, his smile had turned cold. "I can see how you might not want to believe it, seeing as how you've gone sweet on her, but it's true. What say we ramble on down to the hotel, and you can ask her for yourself?"

Buddy longed to knock the sneer off Daniel's face. There wasn't much doubt he was telling the truth. He didn't seem the type who could pull off a bluff. He was too shallow and easy to read. If he intended to walk Buddy straight to Charity, he couldn't be lying.

Daniel interrupted his thoughts. "I don't mind waiting for you to make up your mind. Just don't take all day. You see, I have a house to make ready for my new bride." He took two deliberate steps forward and looked Buddy dead in the eye, his leer leaving no doubt of the intent behind his boast. "And when I carry her over that threshold. . .no one can stop me. . .from making her mine."

Buddy didn't remember what Daniel said next. He barely recalled passing him the saddlebag with instructions to give it to Bertha. He didn't think about anything until he found himself on the boardwalk in front of the depot. Pausing briefly at the door, he crossed the threshold and approached the counter to book passage on a southbound train. Plenty of work awaited him in Houston. Lee and Jerry could handle things here. He would wire instructions and word of his whereabouts when he arrived at Union Station.

Bertha's trusting face drifted before him, but he pushed it aside. Unlike him, she'd be fine. He had left her in the capable hands of two men he trusted. As for Charity, he couldn't allow even the thought of her into his mind for fear of bawling like a boy in knickers.

He paid for his ticket and stepped outside just in time. The Houston, East & West Texas engine roared into the station, wheels churning, stack belching. It barely stopped before passengers boiled out in a great wave, jockeying for position on the platform. Those waiting to board pressed against the tide of people trying to get off.

He hoisted his bag to one shoulder and stormed into the flood, grateful for the distracting noise and clamor. Pushing his way to the door, he handed his ticket to the conductor and swung his bag on board. He followed it without a backward glance at the accursed town of Humble, the black hole that had swallowed his heart.

Daniel burned with satisfaction as he watched the big engine roar to life with short bursts of smoke. The wheels began to turn, picking up speed as the train pulled out of the station. . .hauling Buddy Pierce out of Charity's life. His gamble had paid off. Daniel's future with Charity was wrapped up and tied with a big red bow. She would be his, all legal and proper, with nothing to stand in his way.

The HE&WT disappeared down the tracks in a shimmering cloud of dust.

Daniel smiled slow and easy and tipped his hat. *You have a nice trip now. You hear?*

He turned on his heel, ready to strut up the boardwalk to his rig. The tune he whistled died on his lips when he saw who stood blocking his way. "Well, hello, Emmy."

"What did you say to him?" Her eyes were hard, her lips white-rimmed and tight.

"Good morning to you, too. You're up and about early, ain't you, sugar?"

She bristled. "Come now, Daniel. It's utterly boorish to pretend things are right between us after all this time."

Daniel held up his hands in surrender. "Fine. If that's how you want it." He had dreaded this confrontation for weeks and needed to get it done, but why this morning, when things were going so well?

Emmy edged closer. "I asked you a question. What did you say to that man?"

He held his arms out to his sides, making a show of looking around at the crowd. "Which man? As you can see, there's no shortage of men in Humble this morning. No proper place for an unescorted lady, I might add."

He glanced past her shoulder. "And you are without escort again, I see. Question is, are you a lady?" He leaned into her angry face. "Tell me, *Miss Dane*, does your mama know you're following me around again?"

Something flickered in her eyes besides fury. Whether pain or shame he couldn't tell, but he had waded too deep to stop now. "Ah, well, probably not. She don't always know where you are—or what you're up to—now, does she?"

Emmy pointed up the track behind him. "I just saw Buddy Pierce get on that train bound for Houston, and I get the feeling it was an unscheduled trip. You said something to make him leave, didn't you? And I know what it was. You're not so good at keeping secrets, are you?"

Daniel grabbed her arm. "Maybe you don't know as much as you think you do, sugar."

Her eyes went to the saddlebag slung over his shoulder and darkened. "I saw him hand you that bag. Would you like for me to deliver it to Aunt Bertha?"

He tightened his grip, causing her to wince. "You won't mention Buddy Pierce *or* this bag to anyone. You hear me?"

"Let go, Daniel. That hurts."

Daniel checked the jostling crowd for witnesses before he jerked Emmy close and breathed a threat against her startled face. "Just know this. If you do one thing to spoil things between me and Charity, I'll kill you with my bare hands."

She stared up at him, disbelief in her eyes, but he knew his threat had found its mark. He shook her once for emphasis. "You messed it up for us before, flaunting yourself, pressing against me until I couldn't think straight. I won't let you do it again, Emmy. You hear me? Be warned. I won't let you ruin this for me." He turned loose of her arm, despising the feel of her flesh.

"Don't you dare talk that way to me." The words were an angry snarl, but he saw fear in her eyes.

"Like I said, Emmy–be warned."

Emmy backed away, rubbing her arm. She ignored the curses and complaints of those she bumped into, her eyes never leaving his face. Not until she'd put considerable distance between them did she lift the hem of her skirt, lunge for the less-crowded street, and run. She dashed across, dodging mud holes, horses, and a team of oxen. Racing along in front of the far boardwalk, she scurried to the first side street and disappeared from sight.

Daniel sucked in deep through flared nostrils and realized he'd been holding his breath. He looked down at his clenched fists and willed them to relax. Emmy flashed through his mind–cowering in fear, rubbing her mottled arm.

"Let go, Daniel. That hurts."

Flushed with shame, he covered his face with trembling hands.

"You all right, mister?"

The gentle hand on his shoulder, the sudden voice in his ear, hurled Daniel's heart to his throat. He spun and clutched the stranger's wrist in a cruel grip.

Startled by Daniel's reaction, the old man lost his balance. Skinny arms flailing like disjointed sticks, he fought to gain purchase with his cane. "Let go, mister!" he cried. "I meant you no harm!"

Daniel eased his hold and the man pulled free, teetering a bit before leaning hard on his walking stick. With his other hand on the cane, he had no way to rub his wrist, so he rolled it against his vest. Pain etched deeper lines in his weathered face.

"I thought you might need a doctor or something, but hang you if'n you do. You're no better'n a mad dog." He staggered away, giving Daniel wide berth, and limped down the boardwalk muttering to himself.

A mad dog? Is that what he'd become? Perhaps, but he saw no cure except in marrying Charity—and, by golly, that's what he aimed to do. Maybe then he could return to his right mind.

No one, be it Emily Dane, Buddy Pierce, or Charity herself, had better try to stop him.

He squinted as the sun's first rays cleared the rooftops and hit him square in the eyes. Morning had hardly begun, yet he'd had a week's worth of trouble already. Well, so be it. But let any trouble that lurked in the remaining hours find and fall on someone else. He'd had more than his fair share for the day.

Bertha stood on Magdalena's front porch, hesitant for the first time ever to open the big oak door and step inside. She sorely needed to jaw a spell with Magda but reckoned she wasn't up yet and didn't have the heart to rouse her. The big house loomed dark, with no light behind the drawn shades, and Bertha couldn't bear the thought of sitting inside alone.

Mopping beads of sweat from her top lip with her sleeve, she gazed around the yard. In their part of Texas, a body couldn't always tell the difference between spring and summer, and the hazy morning foretold a sultry day. Just a few days before, they had awakened to downright cold mornings. Thad always said if a fella didn't cotton to

Texas weather, all he had to do was wait a minute.

Despite the heat, Nash was already hard at work in the side yard, bent low over a wagon wheel. If he wasn't the biggest man Bertha had ever seen, he sure was in the running. As if he heard her thoughts, he stood upright and stretched, like a bear rising to full height. Shading his eyes with his arm, he balanced a wrench in his other hand and absently scanned the horizon. When his gaze passed over the house, he took a backward glance and squinted Bertha's way, until his eyes lit on her there in the shadows.

She waved.

He grinned and waved back with the rust-colored tool before crouching down by the wheel.

She stifled a yawn. Thanks to Charity she'd been awake for hours, long before first light. The girl had kept her up half the night, moaning and panting as if something chased her. When Bertha gave up on sleep and got up, Charity kept to her bed, but just barely. The way she pitched and rolled, it wouldn't be long before she threw herself to the floor.

It hurt Bertha so fiercely to watch, she had to get plumb out of the room. She'd left Charity a note saying where she'd be and struck out on foot before sunup, headed for Magda's place.

Now that she was here, she felt a mite silly. There was no sense in bothering Magda again. No matter how many times they hashed it over, they came up with the same answer.

The die was cast. The milk spilt. Tomorrow her only child would become one in the sight of God with a man not fit to touch her. Bertha didn't reckon she could bear it.

Careful to steer clear of the rosebush, she stepped on a crate and pulled herself up to sit on the rail. The haunting smell of the red blossoms wafted up, wrapping her in scent as heavy as her sorrow. She leaned her head against the post and settled in for a good cry, but the sudden sense of another presence raised the hairs on her arms. She took a slow, careful look behind her.

"Squeeze that rail any harder and you'll snap it in two."

She shrieked and leaped to her feet, nearly twisting her ankle.

Magda stood on the threshold in a blush-colored dressing gown, her hair let down to her waist.

Bertha fell against the rail, one hand over her pounding heart. "Land sakes, Magda, you scared me right out of my bloomers."

Unruffled, her friend regarded her with doubtful eyes. "Honey, Humble ain't ready for that one."

"You ought not to sneak up on a body. With your hair all loose and flowing, I thought you was a spirit."

Magda grinned. "A ghost in a pink sheet? Get in here out of the dew, honey. I reckon it's soaked your brain." She made a sweeping motion toward the door. "Well? What are you waiting for? This calls for scrambled eggs."

Bertha held up her hand. Long scratches dotted with tiny drops of blood ran the length of her forearm. "You ain't getting no eggs out of me. Look, you made me brush up agin' those blasted thorns."

Magda dismissed her wounds with a glance. "Well, we can summon the doctor if you like, but I believe I can patch that up myself." She held the door wider. "But not with you on the porch. Get yourself inside."

Bertha allowed herself to be herded into the house. Just before Magda closed the door, she leaned out and searched the yard for Nash. When she spotted him, she shouted orders in his direction, loud enough to be heard in town. "Nash! Leave what you're doing and fetch us some eggs. Get a whole mess, and we'll scramble some for you."

Nash laid the wrench aside and stood up smiling. Remembering how damp grass rusted out a tool, he stooped to pick it up again, wiping it on his trousers before laying it in the wagon bed.

Fetch some cackleberries, you say? Yes, ma'am! I'm gon' fetch plenty, and right this minute.

He headed for the chicken yard, stomach rumbling under his belt. Wasn't much he liked better than those two cooking up something in the kitchen. He'd never say it to Ophelia, didn't dare, but Miz Bloom stirred up the best pan of biscuits he ever tasted. When she drizzled on bacon-fat gravy and paired them with eggs, there wasn't no better eating this side of the river.

At the coop, he shut the gate behind him and hurried up the slanted ramp into the henhouse. Right off he sensed the birds were restless. All around in the dim, dank-smelling house they shuffled and squirmed, making the low, throaty babble that always brought to mind the foolish chatter of women. "What be wrong with you old gals?" he cooed. "Has something done crawled in this here house?"

His mind went to a chicken snake, making him think twice about poking his hand in the nests. He loathed the slithery beasts and didn't care to run across one today. "If an old snake was in here, you'd be stirring up more of a squawk, now, wouldn't you? Maybe we got us a rat instead."

Nash cocked his head and stared about, willing his eyes to adjust. "Mistah Rat, is that you? Come on now, don't tease old Nash. Who be in this henhouse besides these tetchy hens?"

He waited. Not that he expected Mr. Rat to answer. In fact, that'd be the last thing he'd want to hear. He only hoped the sound of his voice would drive the intruder away. Hearing nothing except more chatter and babble, he smiled around at the small, dark space. "Look like it just be us chickens. Now, ladies, if you don't mind, I need to borrow me some breakfast."

He shifted the basket down his arm and eased his other hand under the first hen. His fingers closed around two warm eggs, and he pulled them out, testing their weight to see if he'd picked up the laying egg. Before he got them to the basket, a quiet sniffle drifted from the corner behind him.

Nash spun toward the sound, dropping his prize. The real one landed at his feet with a splat. The marble laying egg hit the floor with a thud then wobbled away. "Who that now! Who be in here with me?"

A loud wail was his answer. One he'd heard before.

"Miss Emmy!" He tossed the basket aside and took a step in her direction. "That's you, all right."

The rightful dwellers of the house set up a squawk to match the girl's mournful caterwauling. Some ran in wild circles, getting nowhere fast in the closed-up space. Others sailed past his head, beating their wings in his ears like giant hummingbirds.

"Come on now. Stop that howling–else these hens ain't never gon' lay another egg. They'll all wind up in a pot of dumplin's, and it'll be all yo' fault. Here, let Nash help you up off that nasty floor."

He lifted Emmy to her feet, but when he turned her loose, she fell again. He caught her and held her upright. "What's ailing you, Miss Emmy? What you doing hiding in the henhouse?"

She clung to him, still bawling like a lost heifer, and Nash could feel her trembling.

This gal's jus' a child, he thought as he held her. *A wayward child, and that's for sure, but a child no less.* He wondered what she'd gotten herself into now.

"Talk to me, girl. Did some fool hurt you? If they did, they's gon' answer to Nash."

He realized she wore her town clothes and knew in his soul that her mama reckoned her still in bed. "Where you been, Miss Emmy?" he asked in a low voice. "What done happen to you?"

"Oh, Nash!" She was crying so hard he scarcely understood. "It was awful. Just awful."

CHAPTER 21

Bertha sat in the big green chair, pinned between the padded arm and her padded friend. Wedged in beside her, Magda brandished a sewing needle, determined to tease the dark tip of a thorn from Bertha's hand. Bertha struggled to get free, but Magda hoisted a leg over both of hers, ending all hope of escape.

"Stop your wiggling and let me get it."

"Not yet, I told you. It's too fresh. Let the bleeding stop first."

"I never saw a body take on so over a tiny bit of blood. Hush now. I've almost got it."

Bertha squirmed again. "Get up, Magda. This chair won't hold us both. The legs are bound to cave."

"Then you'd best let me get this done."

"Let me up," she shouted. "I cain't feel my legs no more. You got 'em wadded in a knot."

"Bertha, hold still!"

The front door burst open. Emmy tottered on the threshold, fully dressed this time, but covered in feathery tufts from head to toe, her indigo day dress dotted with splotches of white. Red face swollen from crying, she seemed past caring what they thought.

The sight of her struck Bertha dumb. She reckoned Magda, still holding the needle aloft and staring at Emmy, suffered the same. Without a word, Emmy flew past them and up the stairs. The stench that lingered in her wake left no doubt about the nature of the white splotches. They had come from the same place as the feathers.

The two women gawked until Emmy passed out of sight and her bedroom door slammed shut. After a brief silence, the sound of hysterical crying reached their ears.

Magda broke the spell. "Well, if that don't beat all. Where the devil has she been this time of the morning?"

Bertha's disbelieving gaze swung her friend's way. Magda couldn't be that dumb. "Where you think she's been?"

Poor Magda aimed vacant eyes at her. "She looked like she just came from tending the chickens, but why would she get all gussied up for that?"

Maybe she was that dumb. "Honey, Emmy ain't been tending chickens–she's been wallowing with them. She ain't just come *in* from the henhouse. She came home *through* the henhouse. There's the difference. She's been hiding."

Magda blinked once, twice. "From what?"

"From us. She seen us on the porch and tried to wait us out in the coop."

To Bertha's great relief, despite the crushing and pinching of her body it caused, Magda struggled up from the chair. She faced Bertha with her hands on her hips. "What are you telling me?"

Bertha stretched to work the kinks from her side and lowered her tingling legs to the floor. "She's been with Daniel."

After a stunned silence, tiny wrinkles formed between Magda's brows. "Come now. You don't really think that, do you?"

"Think it? I know it."

Fire blazed in Magda's eyes. "Bert, I'll skin her. I mean it."

Bertha shook her head. "Leave her be. What's done is done. By the look of her, I'd guess Daniel didn't say what she wanted to hear, though I almost wish he had. Whatever passed betwixt them two, I reckon come tomorrow we'll still be having us a wedding."

Magda spun and glared up the stairs. "I can't believe the unmitigated brash of that girl. And after we warned her. . ." She looked back at Bertha and shook her head. "No, sir. I've had all I can take. I'm going up there to reckon with my wayward child. By the time I finish with Emmy, she'll swear she's seen the wrath of God."

"You'll do no such thing."

"She gave us her word!"

Bertha curled her legs into the cushioned seat and patted the space in front of her. "Get over here now. I need you to pluck out this here thorn. After all, it's your fault I got it."

Magda pressed the heels of her hands to her forehead. "What am I to do with my daughter, Bertha? Lord knows I can't control her no more. Should I send her up north to stay with her pa?"

"It ain't too late to turn Catholic."

"This ain't funny, Bert. I've reached my wit's end."

Bertha smiled. "And that was a trip hardly worth packing for." She patted the chair again. "Come sit, honey, and let's talk. That's right. Come on now."

Magda ambled over and slumped beside her so heavily Bertha feared her prediction about broken legs would come to pass. She bit back her fear and wrapped her arms around Magda instead. "Give her some time, honey. We been so het up about Charity's happiness that we plumb forgot about Emmy's. That girl's in love, whether she has the right to be or not. Right now she's hurting."

Magda sighed. "It's hard to feel sorry for her. Her own willful nature got her into this mess. What will become of her, Bert?"

"Oh, she'll be fine."

"What do you base that on?"

"She's your daughter, ain't she? Besides, we gave our girls to God a long time ago. Don't go taking Emmy out of His hands just when she needs Him the most. Leave God room to work."

Magda released her breath in a ragged sigh. "I pray for her, Bert. All the time. I actually thought I saw her beginning to change. She's been different lately. I can't explain how exactly, but it seemed a change for the good. Did I imagine it?"

Bertha shook her head. "No, I seen it, too."

Magda's eyes filled with tears. "I felt so good when she broke down and cried over what she'd done to you and Charity. Before that day, I wondered if the girl had a conscience."

Bertha nodded and rocked her gently. "Do you recollect how pretty Emmy was as a baby? I never seen a more beautiful child, before or since."

Magda smiled, a faraway look in her eyes. "She was a delightful child. So precocious." She shook her head and the smile left. "I reckon we encouraged that for our own amusement. . .and look where it got us."

Bertha leaned to hug her tight. "Oh, honey, she's still that same sweet little gal. Under that vinegar and sass, she's still our very own Emmy. We just need to find some way to coax her back to the surface."

Magda let slip the slightest of grins. "How do you propose to do that? With a bull whip?"

Bertha roared with laughter. "I wouldn't tote no bull whip into that room tonight! Not with Emmy in need of some way to ease her frustrations."

Magda laughed along with her then sobered straightaway, her gaze fixed on the landing. "Do you think I should go to her?"

"I wouldn't. If she don't come down by suppertime, maybe you could duck in. You'll just upset each other now."

Magda nodded.

A commotion in the kitchen caught their attention.

Bertha pushed against Magda with her feet. "Let me up. That's Nash coming in the back door. I reckon he's got me some eggs to scramble. I'm so hungry I could eat a bushel."

As they struggled to rise, the truth crept up on Bertha. A tickle in the back of her mind at first, then clear in a sudden rush. Magda stilled, too. From the look on her face, the same thought had dawned on her. Emmy had been hiding in the chicken house—and Nash had just come from there.

"Reckon he knows anything?"

Magda set her jaw. "If he did, he wouldn't tell. Them two are in cahoots. That blasted disloyal Nash takes her side over mine every time. I should fire him and be done with it."

"Fine. Then Emmy would have nobody. You leave Nash to me. If there's something to be pulled out of that man, I can do it with my cooking."

Magda grinned. "That might do it. Nash goes weak in the knees at the mention of your biscuits."

"Go on, then. Move your mountain so I can get up. After I get us fed, Nash can take me back to town. I need to see how Charity's faring."

Halfway to the kitchen with Magda close on her heels, she stopped midstride and almost fell when Magda bumped into her from behind. She spun and gripped her friend's arms, peering up into her eyes. "Magda, you know what I just realized?"

"What's that, sugar?"

"This is my last day to look after Charity."

Magda gave her a tender smile and pulled her close. "I doubt that. You'll be trying to look after Charity for the rest of your life whether she's married or not."

Though Bertha suspected the words were true, they brought her no comfort. "Oh, Magda, hurry. Help me get breakfast over and done. I want to spend time with my baby whilst she's still mine."

The swinging door opened behind them. When Nash saw them embracing, he lowered his head and started back out again, but Magda's deep voice stopped him cold. "Get that wheel finished while we cook breakfast. After we eat, I need you to drive us into town."

Nash's head whipped around. He stared like Magda had spoken Chinese, then shuffled his feet and worried his shirttail before he answered. "Um. . .yes'm, Miz Dane. Only that old wheel be plumb shot. I was about to ask could I run it on in to the blacksmith. It needs a good patchin'."

"You saying it won't take us into town?"

He took a step forward, avoiding their eyes. "No, ma'am, that ain't what I'm saying. It'll get us to town, all right. But whilst we there, I s'pose I needs to haul it over to the smithy. See if he can do something to make it las' longer." He brightened a bit, as if he liked what he'd just said. "Yes'm, that's right. It jus' need to las' longer this time."

With one glance, Bertha saw he didn't fool Magda either. They followed him into the kitchen, Magda eyeballing him all the way. She stopped him before he got to the back door.

"Nash?"

He turned, his smile too bright. "Yes'm, Miz Dane?"

"You feeling all right?"

"Oh yes, ma'am. Fine and dandy. Be a sight better when I'm chomping on Miz Bertha's biscuits and gravy."

Magda cocked her head, watching him.

His smile floundered and died. "All right, then. I'll go see to that busted wheel now."

"You do that, Nash."

"Yes'm. I'll do that right now."

When the door banged shut behind him, Magda hiked her brows at Bertha. "He's up to something."

Bertha pulled the heavy iron skillet off a hook on the wall. The weight of it pulled her close to the floor before she hefted it up onto the stove. "That he is."

"What you reckon?"

She lit the gas burner and poured bacon fat into the skillet from an earthen jar. "He's a man, ain't he? No telling what he's up to. And don't waste your time trying to find out. It'll come to light soon enough. It always does. Men ain't worth spit at covering their tracks."

Daniel sat tall on the buckboard seat, his gaze sweeping the wide expanse of open field in front of him. So much land. His land. He had bought the property, cleared it, even built the house himself with the help of a few hired hands. The knowledge warmed his insides.

He paid cash for it, every cent his own, earned with sunbaked flesh and a busted back. Raising cattle wasn't the easiest way to earn a dollar. He refused to let the old man put a nickel toward building the house and was mighty glad of it now. He'd never bucked his folks before, so he couldn't predict their reaction. One thing was sure as sunrise–marrying Charity without his mama's blessing spelled trouble. But even if they disowned him, stripped him of his inheritance, they could never take his ranch.

Daniel turned his attention to the house. He took particular pride in the tall structure, two stories high and fronted with brick shipped from up north. Whitewashed columns graced the front entrance, beams as thick as a man's waist, supporting a gabled overhang. The portico extended to a wraparound porch, which led to an attached gazebo in the rear garden.

He had cleared the surrounding pine, leaving the house nestled in an oak grove. Crafted big and fine, the dwelling bore enough modern trappings to make any woman happy, yet he'd furnished it with the simple things Charity grew up with, things to please a country girl's heart.

Daniel had built the house for Charity, and tomorrow she would live here. A thrill shot through him at the thought. Followed by a chill at how close he'd come to losing her.

And for what?

He leaned and spat on the ground then wiped his chin on his sleeve. What on earth attracted him to Emmy Dane in the first place? He'd never chased her in school, fawning over her, panting for her attention like the other boys. Oh, she was pretty, all right. Always had been, but only on the outside. Unlike Charity, Emmy's insides stank like rotting flesh.

Despite Charity's pure heart, he'd seen another side of her lately, a fiery depth she'd never revealed before. Now that he'd noticed, her innocence coupled with this smoldering fire had nearly driven him mad. He wondered at the source of the mysterious flame. Had it always been there? How had he missed it before now? He pushed from his mind the fact that he'd only glimpsed it while she was in the company of that spineless Buddy Pierce.

Well, no matter. Fate had granted him a second chance. Tomorrow Charity would be his. He'd have a lifetime to find out all there was to know about her.

He heaved a sigh of relief and looked back at the contents of the wagon. He had hauled in the furniture weeks ago; it was time now to lay in supplies. Tools for her garden, staples for her pantry, sheets for her bed. All the things necessary to turn Charity's house into a home.

Charity reached deep into the wardrobe and pulled out her wedding gown. Stepping in front of the mirror, she held it against her body and turned from side to side in order to see it from every angle. Such a lovely dress, the prettiest she'd ever seen. Even more precious given the sweet hands that made it.

She clutched the fabric to her face and breathed in the smell. A mixture of sweet magnolia, infused there from spending so much time in Mama's room, mingled with the scent of pine picked up from weeks of hanging in her closet at home.

Home. The word conjured a picture of the big house she loved, fronted by the very magnolias she smelled on the dress and flanked by the towering pine from which Papa had cut wood for the closet. But it was her home no longer and would never be again. Even if she and Mama moved in today, Charity couldn't stay long enough to take off her shoes.

Tomorrow she would go to live with Daniel, and the thought made her feel lost. His was a lovely house, built just for her. She'd walked through it with him, laughing and planning the day they would share it. There'd been a time she thought that day would never come.

When she understood about Daniel and Emmy, she had grieved for the house, mourned the fact that it would be Emmy's things adorning the rooms, her clothes in the closets, her children playing in the yard.

Now the fickle house had changed mistresses again, only this time Charity couldn't imagine herself living there. Her vision of blue-eyed children running over those grounds had gone, replaced by a ruddy-cheeked, sandy-haired brood that scampered among sweet magnolia and pine, gazing up at her through smoky green eyes. Her mind couldn't conceive of any other way.

She groaned and lifted her face to God. *I've never asked You for anything this important before. Can You? Will You?*

A shrill voice in the hall interrupted her tortured prayer. "Charity! Where are you, baby?" Mama burst through the door and flew at her, her breath coming in labored gasps. She wrapped Charity, dress and all, in her arms and squeezed her so tightly it hurt.

"Mama, for heaven's sake! I'm right here where you left me. What on earth?"

Mama didn't answer, just held her, rocking back and forth.

Mother Dane lumbered in, more breathless than Mama, and shut the door behind her. "Pay her no mind, sugar. She's just being Bertha."

Charity smiled over the little woman's head. "Well, that explains a lot, but not nearly enough. Why is she breathing like this? Has she been running?"

"Up the stairs. I tried to stop her, but I couldn't catch her."

Mama, her swollen eyes squeezed shut, still grasped at her, straining to get a better hold.

Charity pulled her loose and held her at arm's length. "Stop it now. What's ailing you?"

Mother Dane sprawled on the bed, her chest heaving. "When I catch my breath, I'll give you the long version. The short of it is, it finally dawned on her that you're getting married tomorrow."

"Oh, mercy. Come here." Charity pulled her weeping mama close and held her while she cried, fighting hard to push aside her own bitter tears.

CHAPTER 22

Charity stretched out on a knotted rag rug across from her mama and Mother Dane. Mama sat cross-legged on the floor in front of the bed chattering like a schoolgirl while Mother Dane wound her long mane into a proper bun. Charity smiled each time Mama mindlessly held up a hairpin when Mother Dane wiggled her fingers, never missing a beat in her story. Yet Charity's mind was on anything but hair and idle babble.

Every footstep on the stairs was Buddy, every word in the hall his voice. She watched the door until her eyes hurt, ears straining for the sound of a knock that never came.

"That reminds me, Magda," Mama said, "did you check on Emmy before we left?"

Mother Dane scrunched her lips and sniffed. "A lot of good it did me. She just curled up and moaned. Didn't even bother to answer."

Charity sat up straight. Their conversation had taken an interesting turn. "What's ailing Emmy?"

It took too long for them to answer. Mama caught Mother Dane's finger and pinched it before she let go of the next hairpin. Mother Dane gave an answering tug on her hair.

Mama winced then smiled up at Charity. "She ain't herself today, baby. That's all."

"What's the matter? Is she sick?"

"No, not sick, really. More like a bit out of sorts."

Charity crossed her arms and looked from one to the other. "What are you two keeping from me?"

Mama's shoulders drooped. "All right, then. Emmy found it out, and she's grieving."

"Found what out?"

"That you're marrying up with Daniel." Mama's eyes widened. "We didn't tell her though. She snookered us."

The words sent Charity's mind reeling. *Emmy grieving? Over Daniel?*

"She loves him, then?" It eased her heart to know it. It meant Emmy hadn't toyed with their lives just to ease her boredom.

Mother Dane turned kind eyes her way. "Don't you fret over Emmy, pet. The Good Book says we reap what we sow. If Emmy's heart is heavy today, it's because it's harvesttime and she's finding her crop hard to swallow." She went back to pinning Mama's hair. "You have enough grief to bear, Charity. Don't throw Emmy's weight on your shoulders." She heaved a deep sigh. "Anyway, I reckon she's my load to carry. Speaking of which, I need to head on back and see about her. What time of the day is it getting to be?"

Charity pushed off the floor and opened the shade. "The boardwalk's thinned out and it sounds like the dining crowd has waned. That would make it well past one."

"Could it be that late? No wonder I'm hungry. We plumb missed lunch."

Mama handed up another pin. "Now there's a first, you missing a meal. You ate enough this morning to hold you past noontime tomorrow."

Mother Dane pulled Mama's hair again. "Did not. You rushed us through breakfast so fast that Nash stuffed biscuits in his pockets on his way out of the house." She glanced toward the window. "Where is that ornery man anyway? He said he'd have the rig downstairs in three hours. It's been more like five."

"But, Mother Dane," Charity said, looking over her shoulder then back at the street, "the rig *is* downstairs."

Mother Dane's head jerked up. "It is?"

"Yes, ma'am." Charity pointed. "It's right there. Parked just below us."

Throwing one leg over Mama's head, Mother Dane pushed off the bed. She joined Charity at the window and aimed her gaze along Charity's finger. "Oh, for heaven's sake. That's my wagon, all right. Now why didn't Nash send someone up for us?"

Mama twisted around to all fours and pushed up, rear end first. Shoving her way between them, she craned her neck left and right then looked up at Mother Dane. "He ain't down there, that's why."

Mother Dane strained to see as far up and down the street as possible. "Now where do you suppose that man's gone off to?"

Mama tugged on her sleeve. "Remember how he acted this morning?"

"You think this has something to do with that?"

"Why not? Maybe he's chasing some fast woman."

Mother Dane shook her head. "Nash ain't like that. He's a Christian man, with a family."

"Any man who ain't careful can be snared by easy trash."

"Not any man, Mama," Charity said, "just Clark men." She gasped and put a hand to her mouth, her round eyes fixed on Mother Dane's face. "I'm so sorry. I didn't mean. . ."

Mother Dane patted her shoulder. "I know what you meant, honey. I just pray for your sake Daniel's not such easy prey next time."

Mama sneered. "There'd best not be a next time if he values all his parts." She started for the door. "Let's get down there and find Nash. I'm getting a mite hungry myself. Are you planning to feed us, Magda? I expect they're done serving downstairs."

"If there's any cooking to be done, you'll do it. Otherwise it's finger food."

Mama turned at the door. "Charity, get your things. We'll stay the night at Magda's and get ready for the wedding there." She held up her hand before Charity could protest. "No arguments. You can do this for me. It's only one night. You can stand on your head for one night." She frowned and nodded at the sequined gown hanging on the wardrobe door. "Don't forget that thing. It's not how we planned it, but I expect it'll finally be put to some use."

Downstairs on the street, a jubilant Red leapt up and barked a greeting, dancing around them on his long hind legs. The stubborn dog survived his runaway-wagon ride intact, turning up the day after looking no worse for wear. He'd kept a vigil outside the hotel ever since, lying in constant wait for Charity.

There was no sign of Nash. He had strapped the horse to a feed bag and tied it to a post, as if he planned to be gone a good long while.

Mother Dane stood on the boardwalk, hands on her hips, staring at the rig. "When that man turns up, I should fire him on the spot."

"Let's leave him here," Mama said. "Let him walk back. It'll serve him right."

Mother Dane unfastened the feed bag and tossed it into the wagon bed. "Bertha, that's mean-spirited enough to make me feel better. Hop on, girls. This here conveyance is homeward bound."

Whooping like a raiding war party, Mama clambered onto the seat. "That's telling him, Magda."

Mother Dane pulled herself up beside her. "It ain't telling him half what I plan to when he finally shows himself. That man's due a good tongue-lashing."

Charity looked around to make sure no one was watching before she gathered her skirts and climbed on back. Whining piteously, Red planted his big paws on the tailgate and jumped like an oversized jackrabbit, trying his best to scramble aboard.

"No, boy," Charity scolded. "Not this time. Git now! Shoo! Go over yonder and lay down."

Mother Dane turned the horse's nose toward home. The wagon bounced along the rutted street until they reached the trail, where Charity braced for a rough ride home. Red heeded her commands no better than usual and followed them all the way. When the wagon came to rest in the yard, he stared at her from the ground, his long dappled tongue lolled to the side and a wide grin on his face.

She shook her finger at him. "You're a bad dog, Red Pike. Or is it Mr. Bloom these days?"

He wagged his tail.

"So that's what you think, is it? That you've wormed your way in? Well, get such thoughts out of your head, old man. Despite your noble beginnings, you're numbered with the enemy now. They'll make you slink home to join their ranks one day soon, and don't you forget it."

The dog wriggled so violently he was bound to get dizzy. Charity hopped down and cupped his big head in her hands. "You haven't heeded a word I've said, have you? Be still now. Keep that up and you won't be able to walk a straight line."

While Mother Dane unhitched the horse, Charity took the dog by his baggy scruff and led him to the house. At the door, she ordered him to lie down. He dropped and curled at her feet.

Mama chuckled as she stepped over his long legs to get into the house. "I ain't seen him pay you no mind before. I guess you scared him with that talk about sending him home. Get him some water, sugar. His tongue's dragging. We'll have to rustle him something to eat in a bit."

By the time Charity tended Red and joined Mama in the kitchen, Mother Dane was coming in at the back door. "Get to shaking that skillet, Bert," she called. "I've worked me up a raging hunger. This is the longest I've ever waited for lunch."

"I'm moving as fast as I can. Pull out the ham and slice it. That coffee we made this morning's strong enough to stand up and holler by now. Thought I'd use it to stir up some redeye gravy. Charity, hand me the coffeepot, sugar."

Mother Dane rubbed her hands together. "Now you're talking."

While Charity fetched the pot, Mother Dane hurried for the covered charger that held the smoked ham. Balancing it on one hip, she carried it to the table.

"Emmy must be faint from hunger," Mama said from the stove. "When I get everything ready, you can carry her up a plate."

From behind them came a gasp. Charity and Mama turned in unison to look.

Mother Dane stood over the pan with the lid in her hand, staring down at the meat. "That won't be necessary," she announced. "Believe me, that girl ain't hungry."

"What is it, Magda?"

"Just Emmy up to her old tricks."

Mama set down the coffeepot and joined Mother Dane at the table. "What are you going on about?"

"As you can see, Emmy's already eaten, and eaten good by the look of it. This ham's been whittled to the bone."

Mama whistled. "There's enough meat cut from that shank to feed her for a week, and Nash to boot." Mama shook her head and headed back to the stove. "And here I was worried about her empty stomach. Magda, if there's anything left, whack it off and lay it on a platter. We'll eat it with bread. That'll stretch it."

CHAPTER 23

Bertha lounged on Magda's green-striped sofa and watched her lumber down the stairs. She could've tracked her progress with her eyes closed by the groaning of the old floorboards. Never a small woman, Magda had fattened up considerably over the years. Fretting over her daughter drove the poor woman to eat. In the place of corn liquor, Magda drowned her sorrow in corn pone, corn pudding, and corn on the cob.

Bertha had battled her own bouts of distress since Thad died. She wondered if her scattered emotions during the year of bone-numbing grief that followed had hastened all the vexing maladies plaguing her these days. If so, she wouldn't mind trading places with Magda. She'd rather contend with a wider girth than droopy skin and whiskers.

She glanced at the tray Magda had carried in earlier from the kitchen. "Are you still planning to eat this sandwich? It's your third, you know."

Magda trudged the last few steps and plopped down on the divan. "I didn't bring it out here to look at it. And I can count, thank you. Where's Charity?"

Pain echoed through Bertha's chest. "She went to lay out her wedding dress. How's Emmy?"

Magda reached for her food. From the look in her eyes, she nursed the same heartache. "I poked my head in, but she wouldn't answer. Just laid there with the quilt pulled over her face. I let her be. I only hope she's asleep and not pouting. At least her belly's full and she's not bawling."

Bertha nodded. "Her belly should be full. I never seen a body eat so much food, except you, when you were carrying her."

Magda choked on her bite of sandwich. When she recovered, she stared at Bertha with bulging eyes.

Bertha shook her head. "Honey, don't even think it. That would be a tragedy worthy of Shakespeare's quill. Emmy put in the family way by Charity's husband?" She shuddered. "None of us could bear it."

Magda blotted her glistening neck with the napkin in her lap. "How can we be certain? After all, she's acting so desperate."

"I give Emmy credit for having more sense than that. She's willful, not stupid."

"I'm glad you think so. I'm not so sure anymore. Judging by the stunts she's pulled lately, you wouldn't know Emmy had any sense at all."

Compassion tugged at Bertha's heart. "She's suffering for it now, though, poor little thing. Despite all she's done, a body can't help but pity her."

"Pity?" Magda's lips took a dubious turn. "I'm not sure she deserves it."

"Listen to you!" A small shred of ham rested in the hollow of Magda's chin. Bertha snatched the napkin from her hand and plucked it off with a lacy corner. "And after you told me I dealt too harsh with Charity."

"I don't mean to sound harsh, Bertha. I love Emmy. Trouble is, my bullheaded daughter thinks if she wants something, then everyone should just understand and get out of her way. If she gets moon-eyed over her best friend's fiancé, why, that's reason enough to set her cap for him. After all, hasn't she always got whatever she wanted?"

Bertha smiled. "And whose fault is that?"

Returning her food to the plate, Magda wiped her fingertips. "I already admitted we spoiled her. Don't forget, you had a hand in it, too. But what she done to Charity she never learned from me.

I had a spell of mooning over Thad years back, but it never once entered my mind to try the stunt Emmy pulled."

Bertha fell against the button-tucked cushion and stared. "Magdalena Dane, are you telling me you was swimmy-headed over my Thad?"

Magda's cheeks flushed a bright pink. "For about one minute. Then Willem came along and that was the end of it."

Bertha scooted to the edge of her seat. " 'Til Willem came along? Honey, that was a year before we had our babies. You'd known Thad seven years by then. That's a heap more'n a minute."

Magda sat mute, studying her hands.

"All this time and you never told me?"

"Didn't see no reason to."

Bertha couldn't get past it. Magda sweet on Thad for that long but never once letting on. It explained a couple of things—why Magda was an old maid before she finally married, and why Thad's death hit her so hard.

"You and Thad. Honey, if I'd only known. . ."

Magda shook her head. "If you'd known, things would be just as they are. It was never me and Thad. The two of you belonged together from the start, just like Willem and me. I've had no room in my head for anyone but him from the first day we met." She winked. "Despite Thaddeus Bloom's winning ways and powerful good looks."

Bertha gazed at the ceiling, remembering. "He sure was a fine figure of a man."

Magda grinned. "*Ein hübscher Mann*, as my mama used to say. As handsome as you were pretty. You two made a lovely couple."

Bertha returned her grin and nodded. "I had good teeth back then and nice skin." She traced her fingers over her cheek and frowned. "Hard work and old age be hanged!"

Magda hoisted her glass of milk. "Hear, hear!"

"I don't think Thad would know me if he come back now."

"Balderdash. He'd still cut you out of a herd."

Bertha tilted her head. "You reckon?"

"I do."

She leaned to pinch off a corner of Magda's ham sandwich and poked it into her mouth. "I never was as pretty as Charity," she said, her mouth full. "And nowhere near the likes of Emmy."

Magda sighed. "I only wish Emmy acted pretty." She pointed her finger at Bertha. "Besides, you're mistaken. You were more fetching than the two of them put together. Don't you recall being chased about town by Moses Pharr and the rest? Every boy in Jefferson, Texas, wanted to court you." She chuckled. "You led them a merry chase. . .at least until Thad come along."

Nudging a greasy piece of ham deeper between the two thick slices of bread, she picked up her sandwich. "Are you forgetting you were twice the rascal that Emmy can be? Never made no sense how I wound up with my girl and you with yours. If I hadn't watched you deliver a month before I birthed Emmy, I'd vow those two got switched."

Bertha slapped her legs, laughter bubbling up from her belly. "Weren't no mixing them babies, what with Charity's black hair and Emmy's crop of white curls."

"Still as white as the day she was born. I blame Willem's seed for that curse. A curse it's been, too, since men are bound to make fools of themselves over fair-haired women. And Emmy's too weak in character to resist the attention."

Bertha shook her head. "Don't sell her short. That girl's strong-willed and smart. She's just learned to use what she's got to get what she wants."

Magda snorted. "Trouble is, most times what she wants belongs to someone else. That brings sorrow to everyone concerned."

Bertha patted her friend's knee. "The Lord uses our mistakes to guide us." She nodded toward the top of the stairs. "Emmy's feeling the sting of her own actions, but she'll be the better for it. It'll teach her to count the cost before she jumps next time."

"Sugar, I hope you're right. If Emmy learned to love others half as much as she loves herself, it sure would save me some grief."

Bertha offered a sympathetic grin. "I don't think she sets out to cause you pain. Do you?"

Magda took a big bite and waved one hand absently at Bertha. "Not really," she said with bulging jaws. "She just gets in over her head sometimes."

Emmy took another bite of her sandwich and waved one hand absently at Nash. "This ham is divine. Packing a lunch was the best idea you ever had."

Nash seemed not to hear. He sat hunched in the seat across from her with his face pressed against the passenger car window while the countryside scrolled past. Emmy could see his reflection in the glass. His wide eyes danced back and forth, trying to take in everything at once.

She held out a sandwich wrapped in paper. "Here. Eat some before it goes bad."

He shook his head and answered without turning. "Got no time for to be eating. Ain't never rode me no train before, and I don't aim to miss it."

Emmy grinned. "So you like it, do you?"

"It's jus' like I reckoned."

Emmy giggled at the wonder in his voice. "And you were scared to come. I knew you'd love it. Didn't I say you wouldn't be sorry?"

He faced her then. "Love it, I do. Sorry is what I'll be when your mama finds out. Sorry, no 'count, and out of work–if I ain't lynched first."

"Oh, Nash."

"Don't you 'Oh, Nash' me. How long you reckon before Miz Dane jerk back that quilt and see them pillows sleeping in yo' bed instead of you? Probably already did see. I bet all my wages she's got the sheriff dogging us now. Most likely a posse on horseback chasing this train."

Emmy wiped a greasy thumb on the paper around her sandwich. "Don't be silly. I don't want to hear that foolish talk."

Eyes bulging, he gawked at her. "You ain't gon' be saying silly when he catch up to us. Jus' how silly you gon' feel watching me swing from a rope? I still cain't figure how you got me into this mess." He shook his head. "Mm, mm, mm. No, sir. I sho' can't figure it."

Emmy cast a nervous glance at the surrounding passengers. Raising her nose a bit higher, she ignored their angry glares. She had obtained permission for Nash to ride up front by insisting she needed her *boy* for protection and to carry her bags. It made Emmy's stomach ache to say such a hurtful thing, and even more so when Nash lowered his head, but there was no help for it.

She frowned across the aisle at him. "Shush now, before someone hears. You'd be in worse trouble if you'd have let me come alone. You know it yourself."

He glowered. "There now, you see? Hanged if I do and shot if I don't. You done hauled me into a full-sized mess."

"Oh, pooh. Quit your squawking. We had to come, didn't we, if we want to save Charity?"

The memory of Daniel's threat made her shudder. "I still can't believe how he fooled me. . .fooled us both." She rubbed her wrist, still feeling his cruel grip on her arm. "Of course, he wouldn't dare lay a hand on Charity until after they're married, but by then it'll be too late. You want to help me prevent that, don't you?"

Nash didn't answer. He perched across from her, too busy wading through deep indignation to answer, sullen to the point of pouting. He spared her a look. "What good you reckon finding Mistah Pierce gon' do?"

"Gracious. Don't you ever listen when I speak?"

He shook his head. "Not so much. Generally gets me in too much trouble."

Emmy wadded her sandwich wrapper and shoved it inside the sack. "It may not help at all. But if there's any truth to what I heard. . ." She leaned close and lowered her voice. "If Mr. Pierce feels one spark of affection for Charity, then he's our only hope. It's a gamble, but a gamble we must take."

Nash's tense hands worried the tattered hat on his lap. "You reckon they know we's gone by now?"

"Maybe." Emmy considered her answer for a minute and then nodded. "Most likely, in fact." She shook her head to dislodge the thought and handed Nash a sandwich. "Eat this and don't talk about it. What's done is done. There's no going back."

Nash took the wrapped offering in one hand, shooing her words like pesky flies with the other. "Naw, missy. Ain't nothing done yet. I could go back, all right. I could get off this contraption and walk home. Tell Miz Dane I ain't seen hide nor hair of her wayward child."

Burying his face in the paper, he took a huge bite of the sandwich and proceeded to talk around it. "That's right, I sho' could. In fact, I jus' might."

Emmy shrugged. "Suit yourself, but you're in for a mighty long walk, considering we're pulling into the station. We're here, Nash! We're in Houston!"

He narrowed his eyes at her. "Miss Emmy, don't you try to fool old Nash."

She pointed out her side window. "See for yourself."

He squirmed in his seat, trying to see through every glass at once. "No, we ain't! That fast?" A grin spread over his face, wider than the grease on his cheeks. "Now don't that jus' beat all?"

Emmy stood, fighting to keep her balance as the big engine rolled to a jerky stop. She grabbed her reticule and handed Nash her leather bag. "Stop that gawking and follow me."

She moved into the aisle and started for the exit, helped along by the surging crush of people. When she looked back and found herself alone, she stepped aside before the disorderly stampede pushed her right out the door.

Nash still hovered over her seat, trying to gather the remaining sandwiches with one hand while juggling their bags with the other.

"Leave that, Nash. It's trash now. It won't last in this heat. We'll find something to eat later on."

Nash dropped the bundle with some reluctance and pushed his hat down on his head. He pressed into the aisle and came toward her, glancing back several times at the food.

"Stop dawdling over that trifling ham," she shouted past the scrambling passengers. "Don't worry, I won't let you starve."

"But, Miss Emmy, we ain't got us no money."

The rush swept Emmy along. She had no choice but to step down off the train into bedlam. Gentility and manners had vanished with the coming of the oil boom, along with every trace of decency and order. Those waiting to board merged with those departing, becoming a blur of frantic people. Emmy broke free and shoved her way to the side, adjusting her hat and smoothing her rumpled skirt while she waited for Nash. He appeared on the threshold at last, holding their bags aloft.

"There's no need to fret about money or food," she called up to him. "I have my ways."

A burly man pushed past Emmy in his rush to board, jostling her so rudely she would've toppled and been trampled underfoot had Nash not leaped to the platform to offer a steady hand. He cast a dark look at the surrounding horde. "I ain't so sure even your wily ways gon' help in this place."

Emmy followed his gaze. A most curious assortment of people milled about on the boardwalk. Not even in Humble, where the boom had brought thousands of strangers to her town, had Emmy seen the likes of this lot. Work-roughened, sin-coarsened men loomed on every side. Whatever lured them, whether the promise of excitement or unbridled greed, they allowed themselves to be driven like cattle toward the train.

Three women elbowed past, shouting and laughing, holding their own with the men. By the look of them, they were headed to find work in the saloon at Moonshine Hill, or perhaps to ply a different trade on the outskirts of Tent City. The stale odor of toilet water, whiskey, and bad breath hung in the air behind them. Emmy's stomach lurched. Sudden panic washed over her, and she groped for Nash's arm.

Next to her, a drunken man in a cleric's collar clung possessively to the sort of woman Aunt Bert called a "painted lady." The woman stared at them in a brazen way, her bloodshot eyes going to Emmy's hand on Nash's sleeve. Then she leered, as if they shared a secret, her loose crimson mouth vulgar against her yellow teeth. Emmy shuddered and turned away.

"Come along, Miss Emmy," Nash said. "Let me take you out of this mess."

He tucked her behind his back, using his body as a shield as he pushed through the rush of people. Along the tracks, men heaved burlap bags of feed, crates filled with sacks of pinto beans, and boxed canned goods onto the cars, supplies bound for Humble. These days everything from heavy equipment to sewing needles found its way there by train. Provision for the boomers.

Rail bosses hurled orders laced with vile curses in loud, angry voices. Emmy covered her ears as Nash guided her past the men. Those who noticed her with him cast angry glares at Nash or looked her over in such a way that she yearned for her quilt from home to wrap up in.

Nash pulled her along in zigzag fashion until they reached the far end of the platform. Here the mob thinned out a bit, though the laughter and cries of the jostling crowd, mingling with the din near the railcar, stirred a rush in Emmy's chest that made her head spin. She found it unsettling but exhilarating at the same time.

She guessed Nash felt it, too. Despite his nervous darting eyes, a smile stretched over his face. "Whoo-ee!" he cried. "These the most folks I ever seen in one place."

"In one place? Oh, Nash, it's the most I've seen in my life."

He flashed his grin her way. "Me, too. Reckon they all live in Houston?"

Emmy barely heard. Near the spot they'd just left, a man on the swarming platform caught her attention.

"Nash, look!"

"Look where?"

She pointed. "Right there. There's something familiar about that gentleman. I know him from somewhere."

Nash shaded his eyes and stared. "Which one? There's a whole mess of gentlemen over there."

Emmy's head bobbed as she strained to get a better look at the long-legged fellow.

Behind her Nash grunted. "Miss Emmy, you got me looking for a boll weevil in tall cotton. I don't see nothing but a whole mess of bodies."

For the space of two seconds, she had an unobstructed view of a handsome young face. Her mind scrambled to place him. "Oh my! I think. . ."

Emmy gripped Nash's arm. "Yes, by golly, it's him!" She pointed a trembling finger. "That man works with Mr. Pierce." She craned her neck to search the milling throng. "That means he must be here somewhere." Joy filled her heart, so full she could taste the sweetness. "See the goodness of God? He's led us straight to Buddy Pierce."

Glancing up, Emmy found Nash watching her. She squirmed under his searching gaze but steeled herself and met his eyes. "What are you gawking at?"

He shoved his hat aside and scratched his curly head. "If I didn't know different, I'd think I's gawking at Miss Charity. Them words sound like they come right out of her mouth."

Feeling petulant, Emmy raised her brows. "Stop your meddling and get yourself over there before Mr. Pierce gets away. Now hurry! Find him and bring him back here."

Nash squinted hard, shaking his head. "I can't bring what ain't there. I reckon you seeing things. You said yourself Mistah Pierce was alone when he left on that train."

Emmy longed to thrash him. "That man over there knows where he is now. And look! He's leaving!"

"Miss Emmy, stop all that bouncing. Ain't ladylike. Show me what face you know in all them faces, and I'll fetch him for you."

She aimed her finger again, so excited she barely held it straight. "There. The tall, thin man with bushy hair. Hurry, he's getting away."

Mumbling under his breath, Nash scurried in the general direction she'd pointed. Emmy gathered her skirts and lit out after him. She lagged a few steps behind when he reached the young man's side.

"Suh? Excuse me, suh. I don't mean to trouble you none, but the little lady over there. . ." He turned to point at Emmy, then frowned and adjusted his words when he found her on his heels. "This young lady right here sho' hankering to have a word with you."

The gentleman took off his hat and turned a shy smile her way. Confusion mingled with admiration in his warm brown eyes. He bowed slightly. "Yes, ma'am? What can I do for you?"

Emmy turned on her brightest smile. She knew the power wielded by her full lips and deep dimples. She'd learned at an early age how to use them to gain advantage over men. "Good afternoon, sir." She tilted her chin up at him. "Forgive my boldness, but I need your help."

Confusion won over admiration. "My help? I'm afraid I–"

"Don't trouble yourself trying to remember. We haven't been introduced. Still, I know who you are. You work with Buddy Pierce, isn't that so?" She expected the mention of Buddy's name to reassure him. He stiffened instead.

"Yes, ma'am, I sure do, but–"

In her excitement, Emmy cut him off again. "I need to speak to Mr. Pierce right away. Will you take me to him?"

A glimmer of suspicion crept into his eyes.

Emmy pressed closer and turned up her smile. "Heavens, where are my manners?" She extended a gloved hand. "I'm Emily Dane, daughter of Willem and Magdalena Dane of Humble. This is our man, Nash."

The young man offered a hesitant smile and accepted her hand. She watched him try to work it out in his mind. "Name's Jerry Ritter. It's a pleasure to meet you, miss."

"Mr. Ritter, you were a guest in my home awhile back. You came there with Mr. Pierce."

His frown deepened.

Emmy felt her smile fade a bit. "We didn't meet that day. I was. . .feeling poorly, so I never joined you. But I saw you from the landing. You were there on behalf of Bertha and Charity Bloom."

A flicker of recognition shimmered in his eyes. When he smiled, she rushed ahead. "Mr. Ritter, I must find Buddy Pierce. It's a matter of extreme urgency."

His young face grew serious. "Well now, it looks like we've got that much in common. I'm trying to locate him myself."

Emmy's heart lurched. "You mean he's not traveling with you?"

"Well, he was. Then he took off for Humble on his own, carrying a saddlebag stuffed with money. Me and Lee–that's our partner–we got worried about Buddy traveling alone with so much currency, so I lit out after him. Never did catch him though. When I got to Humble, Buddy had already come and gone. One of our roughnecks claimed he saw him leaving town, so I hopped the first train bound for Houston, and here I am."

Understanding dawned on Emmy. "You were on the same train we rode in on, weren't you?"

"If you pulled in just now, then I guess I was."

Desperation weighted Emmy's heart. "Do you know where in Houston Mr. Pierce might go?"

"Not exactly. I just know it ain't like him to be so unpredictable." He looked away, but not before concern flickered in his brown eyes. "That man's as honest and God-fearing as the day is long, but there was an awful lot of money in that bag. It's got me right anxious."

Emmy decided to show her cards. "Mr. Ritter, I know exactly why your friend took an unscheduled trip to Houston, and it had nothing whatever to do with money."

He shifted his weight toward her. "Keep talking."

"Mr. Pierce found out Charity Bloom is set to get married tomorrow, to Daniel Clark."

He winced and nodded. "That explains a lot. Buddy was carrying a ring in his pocket that he hoped to slip on her finger."

Emmy felt a rush of excitement. "That can still happen. Charity doesn't love Daniel. The truth is, she's in love with Mr. Pierce. It's him she wants to wed."

His eyes widened. "Then why is she getting hitched to someone else?"

"There's no time to explain right now. Just know Charity's being forced to marry in haste for her mama's sake. She's tried to wait for your Mr. Pierce, but she's running out of time."

Mr. Ritter's eyes twinkled and his cheeks flushed red. He'd caught her enthusiasm. "Miss Dane, are you sure about all of this?"

"Yes, that's why we're here. We have to find Buddy before it's too late for both of them. Oh, please! Can't you help us?"

He pressed a finger to his chin and nodded. "Maybe I can."

"Then you know where Buddy is?"

"I have a few ideas. Grab your bags and follow me."

CHAPTER 24

Charity stood before Mother Dane's stove pouring hot water into a skillet of golden-brown flour. When the liquid hit the smoking pan, it sizzled and steam rose to the ceiling. Elbows waving, Charity clutched the heavy black handle and went at the mixture in a stirring frenzy. Still, the bubbling gravy inched toward the top, until Mama stepped beside her and lowered the gas.

Waving her hand to dissipate the billowing moisture, Charity glanced over her shoulder. "Thanks, Mama. I'm not used to this newfangled cooker. I'm beginning to appreciate Mother Dane's attitude toward it."

"Keep your eyes on that fire, or you'll see another side to her attitude. If'n that blue flame turns red and yellow, this whole place will fill up with smoke." She wrinkled her nose in distaste. "Leaves a black mess on everything it touches."

Charity regarded the stove with newfound respect, her eyes trained on the dancing blue blaze. The cast-iron behemoth stood a foot taller than her and took up one whole corner of the kitchen. She still marveled that it was fueled by gas, the first such contraption of its kind in Humble. Uncle Willem had borne it home along with a good supply of fuel after a trip to the Midwest. He claimed he had a close call somewhere in Kansas, where he averted a mishap just in time to avoid blasting a hole in the earth the size of the Grand Canyon, sending him on an untimely journey to meet his Maker.

He bought the stove as a birthday surprise for Mother Dane, who despised the thing. She cursed it often, using words that burned Charity's ears. She lamented her old box stove with the same fervor and swore to make Uncle Willem's life wretched until he brought it home.

Charity gave the gravy another stir and lowered the burner still more, easing the heavy lid onto the skillet. "Mercy, all they do around this house is eat. It's a wonder you stay so slim."

Mama scraped a pot of buttered mashed potatoes into a serving bowl before she answered. "The Danes do love their vittles, daughter. When they ain't eating, they're talking about it. I reckon when folks can hire their work done, there ain't much left to do but sit about and eat. Besides, Magda always did like her grub. Even as a girl, they had to shoo her away from the table."

Charity peered out the window over the sink. "Speaking of Mother Dane, where do you suppose she's gone off to? It's getting dark out there."

Heavy boots hit the porch with a thud, and Mother Dane muttered to herself while she scraped them on the rug. When she opened the door, her ashen face gave Charity such a start that she dropped her ladle on the stove with a clatter and rushed to her aid. "Oh my! You're pale as paste. Are you all right?"

Winded, Mother Dane leaned against the doorpost, wiping her glistening face with her apron. "I'll be fine, sugar. Just need to rest a spell. Tending that horse sure takes it out of me." She drew a deep, shaky breath and took Charity's arm for help over the threshold. "I guess this old body's seen better days."

Mama turned from mixing salt into the potatoes. "You need to shed that weight, Magda, and you know it. You cain't carry it like when you was young."

Mother Dane gave her the eye. "Now I'm fat *and* old. Thank you, Bert."

Chuckling, Mama went on stirring. "Did you tend them squawking chickens?"

Mother Dane shook her head. "I fed Rebel and that's about it. The rest of those critters can fend for themselves for one night. I got no tending left in me."

Handing off the bowl to Charity, Mama led her friend to the table. "Come take a load off them feet. Me and Charity can ramble out and finish up later. Still no sign of Nash?"

Moaning, Mother Dane sank into a kitchen chair. "Not a peep. I guess he's gone for good this time, though I can't imagine why. We treated that man like family." She sniffed, and her bottom lip trembled. "He let me down bad this time. With Willem gone and Emmy too frail to help out, I'm left with the whole thing in my lap. He sure picked a bad time to skedaddle."

Charity hurried over to set the gravy boat on the table then rested a silver spoon at its side. "Nash isn't gone for good. He'll be back. You can count on it."

Mama turned from the stove. "You reckon so, baby?"

"Yes, ma'am, I do."

"Then where's he at?"

"I couldn't venture to guess. I'm certain he'll have a lively excuse when he shows up."

Mother Dane drew herself up in the chair. "This time he'll tell it to the wind whilst I sweep his sorry hide off the porch."

Charity smiled at Mama, and Mama winked. The Dane household would soon founder without strong, capable Nash, and they all knew it.

From the cupboard as familiar as her own, Charity pulled down a heavy mason jar filled with the green beans she'd helped Emmy put up last summer—not that Emmy had weighed in on the task. She spent most of the morning sitting cross-legged on the table singing silly ditties and telling stories. In short, trying to do all she could to keep Charity too entertained to notice she hadn't lifted a finger to help with the canning.

Charity wrapped a cup towel around the mouth of the jar and pried the lid off with a satisfying pop, then drained the beans and poured them into a warming pan. She tossed in a strip of salted fat and put on the lid. Mama took up the golden-brown pork chops that Charity had just fried and layered them on a cloth-covered platter to soak up the grease. Snuffing the fire under the skillet, Charity turned to the table to take inventory.

Still slumped in her chair, Mother Dane pressed a hand to her back and groaned, her face a tight grimace. "I'm bushed, girls. Let's eat quick so I can turn in and get an early start on tomorrow."

Mama crossed to the table, her arms loaded with the platter of breaded chops. "You cain't turn in yet, Magda. I had my heart set on a round of cards."

Mother Dane frowned her disapproval. "At this hour? Honey, it's too late."

Concern pinched Mama's face. "Since when did you ever think it was too late to play cards? Are you feeling all right?"

"No, I'm not. I'm right fizzled out, if you really care to know."

"Aw, come on," Mama wheedled. "You got enough steam left for one or two hands."

Mother Dane picked up a piece of meat, then winced and tossed it at her plate.

"Careful, they're hot," Charity called from the stove.

Shoving her finger and thumb inside her mouth, Mother Dane spoke around them. "Blast it, Bert, I'm tired. Why do you suddenly want to play cards so all-fired bad?"

Mama cut mournful eyes at Charity before she answered. "I ain't in any hurry to get to bed, that's why. Tomorrow will come soon enough as it is."

Watching Mama's face, Mother Dane nodded. "Sure thing, sugar. I guess I can make it for a hand or two."

"You'll join us, won't you, daughter?"

Charity looked at them through a blur of tears. "Of course I will. I'm not all that anxious myself to see this day end."

Mama wiped her hands on her apron. "It's settled, then. What say we serve up this food and get it ate?"

Charity joined them at the table, her eyes still damp. "Won't Emmy be starved by now, Mother Dane? I can fix a nice plate for her, and you can take it up before we sit down."

Mother Dane and Mama stared until Charity's cheeks began to warm. She didn't know how to explain it, but the idea that Emmy loved Daniel had patched her wounded heart and replaced her anger with pity. After all, she found herself in much the same state—devoted to a man she couldn't have.

Mother Dane motioned her closer for a hug. "The Creator ran

short on love after making you, Charity. Your mama named you right, that's for certain." She patted Charity's hand. "Don't trouble yourself. I'll take something up in a while."

Mama slumped into a chair, piled her plate high with mashed potatoes, and passed the bowl. "That child ain't sat down to a decent meal in days. Don't that worry you none?"

Mother Dane's eyes bulged. "Are you forgetting the ham, Bert? She's been eating better than we have. Didn't even throw food in the yard this time."

Mama chuckled. "She could've thrown something out, Magda. Don't forget, Red's out there somewhere. He'd make quick work of ham scraps."

Charity gasped and laid down her fork. "I forgot to feed that worrisome old dog." She looked around at the scraps on their plates and brightened. "I'll toss him these pork chop bones after dinner. He'll be glad to see them."

"Tomorrow early, I'll tie him in the wagon and cart him home," Mother Dane said. "Shamus may have to pen him for a spell to keep him there."

Mama grinned and nodded. "If they don't pen or tie him, he'll be waiting for you on the porch when you get back."

They finished the meal amid laughter and light chatter. Afterward, they rose together to clear the table. Even Mother Dane stayed in the kitchen to help, as if reluctant to leave their company. With everything covered and put away, the big stove scrubbed clean of greasy splatters, and Red offered his feast of bones, Charity followed the older women into the parlor.

While Mother Dane set up the game table, Charity and Mama brought in three chairs from the dining room. Charity pushed hers into place then took a step back and squinted. "What happened to this one?"

Mama winked at Mother Dane as if Charity wasn't looking right at her. "Something wrong with that chair, you say?" She perused the item in question with one hand on her hip and the other rubbing her chin. "I don't know. It appears just fine to me. Don't you think so, Magda?"

"It sure does."

Charity frowned and held one hand over the backrest of each seat to gauge the height. "No, look. This one's much shorter than the rest."

Mother Dane chimed in. "Are you trying to convince us that chair shrunk?"

"Don't be daft, Magda. Furniture don't shrink. Maybe Charity growed instead." Mama lifted the chair and studied it, her glee scarcely contained. "Wait, I see what you've done, daughter. You've hauled in the milking stool."

"Oh, Mama!"

"Hush and behave yourself, Bertha," Mother Dane called from the sideboard. "Old dependable Nash leveled that chair for me, Charity. I'm just glad he didn't fix them all, or we'd be sitting with our knees around our ears." She opened the door to the shelf where she kept her parlor games. "Now then, ladies, name your poison."

Still grinning, Mama slung her arm around Charity's waist. "How 'bout dominoes, girls?"

Mother Dane raised an eyebrow at Charity. "Did she say dominoes?"

Shrugging one shoulder, Mama sat down and made a show of dusting the table. "If Emmy felt better, we could play euchre. Takes four to make a good game of euchre." She tapped a finger against her lips while she pondered then held it up in the air. "Wait, I know. We'll take turns at cooncan. There, it's settled. Bring out the cards, Magda."

Mother Dane nodded at Charity. "Go over and feel her forehead. I believe she's come down with the fever."

Mama glared. "Leave off me, woman." She jabbed her chest with her thumb. "This here's the new Bertha. No more gambling. You might as well get used to it."

Mother Dane, her eyes as wide as Charity's felt, joined her beside the table. Speechless, they stared down at Mama, who sat rigidly in her chair.

"Pick up your jaws. It's true," she affirmed in a sullen voice. "I don't know why I ever gambled in the first place. It's brought us nothing but heartache and loss. Charity wouldn't be in this mess if Thad hadn't made that silly bet. I don't know how he could do such a sorrowful thing, but at least it's opened my eyes. I vow on his grave I'll never lay another wager as long as I live."

Charity dropped a kiss on the top of her head. "Don't swear, Mama. You're not supposed to."

"I promise, then. I promise you won't see me gamble no more. I know it always grieved your tender conscience, and I'm sorry."

Across the table, Mother Dane cleared her throat. When Mama's wet-rimmed eyes swung toward her, she glanced away and pulled out her chair. She kept her head down and her attention on the table while she dealt the cards, but mirth teased the corners of her mouth.

Mama gave her an angry glare. "Don't think I didn't see you rolling those eyes, Magda. And wipe that grin off your face. Whether you believe it or not, I'm dead serious."

"Don't be silly, sugar. I never doubted you for a minute."

Muttering under her breath, Mama directed her attention to the game. She picked up her cards, studied them, and then gave a low whistle. "I'll be hanged if these wouldn't make a right fine hand of poker."

Charity met Mother Dane's astonished eyes across the table before they both collapsed into laughter. Charity howled until she cried, wiping her eyes on the sleeve of her cotton dress. Mother Dane's deep belly laugh all but rattled the windows. Mama watched them, furious at first, until a huge grin lit her face and she fell over in a fit of giggles.

After several more outbursts, laced with Mother Dane's side-clutching and her mama's moans, they settled into a companionable silence. Charity couldn't stop smiling until Mama broke the spell.

"If you don't mind my saying so, daughter, I never expected to attend so many weddings in your honor." She looked up from her cards and gave Charity a sweet smile. "I always reckoned one day to lose you to some addlepated upstart, and that would be bad enough." She shrugged her shoulders. "But I never, ever expected things to turn out like this."

Mother Dane frowned a warning. "You talk like tomorrow is Charity's last day on earth. She's not dying, for pity's sake. She's getting married."

Mama bristled. "To Daniel Clark! Dying would be more tolerable, in my opinion."

"Bertha!"

"Well?"

Charity sighed. "That's all right, Mother Dane. I know what she means. It would be different if we were planning a real wedding."

Mama nodded. "Like if you was set to marry Buddy, you mean."

His name conjured the dear face Charity had pushed from her mind all day. Crushing pain struck deep in her chest like she hadn't endured since Papa died. Mama was right. This wedding felt like a funeral.

She laid down her cards and scooted her chair back. "I think I'll go on up now. I'm feeling tired."

Before Charity could stand, her mama dropped to her knees beside her chair. "Baby, I'm sorry. I never meant to hurt you. I don't know why I spew such blether. I just don't think."

"You didn't–"

"Yes, I did. I made you sad. I know you're grieving over Buddy. I know how much you love him." She clutched Charity's hands. "Daughter, you don't have to go through with this wedding. Your feller will be back soon. He'll come riding into town looking for you. Don't let him find you in Daniel's house."

Charity's heart leapt at the words, but she pushed it back down and pulled free. "Hush now. It's all decided."

"But I changed my mind. I don't want you doing this fool thing." She swatted the air. "I don't care about the house. We'll get by without it. Ain't nothing more important to me than your happiness."

Charity took the familiar little face in her hands. "You listen to me. I'm going up those stairs to bed. I need my rest because tomorrow is my wedding day. I'm marrying Daniel, just like we planned, and you're going to be there, happy and smiling, to give us your blessing."

Mama seemed struck dumb by Charity's calm, forceful words, a favor for which Charity felt grateful. She had no confidence in her own strength and didn't know how long she could hold out.

She gave Mama's tearstained cheek a tender kiss. "Move now.

Let me out of this chair so I can go to bed. I suggest you two do the same. The hour is late."

Mother Dane came around the table and helped lift Mama from the floor.

Charity couldn't bear to see her mama's stricken look, so she averted her gaze and brushed another kiss on her forehead as she passed. One foot on the bottom step, she forced a bright smile and turned. "Good night now. Get some rest. I need you fresh tomorrow."

Mother Dane wrapped Mama in a bear hug from behind, laying her cheek against the top of her head. "Too late for that, child. This old thing ain't been fresh for many a year."

Though her heart was shattered, Charity couldn't help but laugh.

The awful pain returned as she made her way up the stairs. She wanted to get to her room before she broke down and cried, but on impulse she paused near the top landing.

The two of them, still hugging, still staring up at her, hadn't budged.

"There is one more thing."

Mama leaned forward. "What's that, baby?"

"Where's Papa's Bible? I thought I'd read a bit before I turn in."

Mama's eyes melted into dark pools of sorrow, as her heart swelled up and broke there.

Charity despised her own weakness. She shouldn't have asked for the Bible. It only served to reveal the depth of her pain.

"It's in Magda's room. On the table by the bed. You want me to fetch it for you?"

The anguish in Mama's voice matched the agony in her eyes. Charity longed to rush down and hug her again but knew it would only make matters worse. Instead, she turned and took the last two steps up the staircase. "Don't trouble yourself. I'll get it. Good night, Mama. Good night, Mother Dane."

"Sleep tight, sugar," they called in unison.

The worn leather book lay open beside the bed in Mother Dane's room, just as Mama had said. Charity closed it gently and tucked it under her arm.

In the hallway, she turned to stare at Emmy's door. A force she couldn't understand pulled her toward it. Perhaps it was the desire to escape the present, to go back in time to simpler days, when she and Emmy were young, carefree girls. Perhaps her battered heart sought comfort from the person who knew her best, a person whose own heart was wracked with grief. Whatever the reason, Charity found herself standing outside Emmy's room, her trembling hand clutching the knob.

The pounding in her chest seemed audible as she opened the door. The gaslight in the hall poured a shaft of light across the floor in front of her. Charity held her breath and ducked inside. Shadows etched the room. She could just make out Emmy in the center of the high, four-poster bed, the covers drawn over her face.

In that moment, everything in Charity's life seemed caught in a ludicrous dream. Tomorrow she would marry a man on whom she'd set her cap for years, yet she'd rather be drawn and quartered. Marrying him would bring heartache to a person she loved with all her heart, a person who lay a mere six feet away, yet she dared not call her name.

It was more than Charity could bear. She clutched the Bible to her chest and fled, taking no care to be quiet. She ran down the hall with her hand pressed against her mouth to suppress a wail, knowing once she gave in to it, she'd bawl like a motherless calf.

CHAPTER 25

Buddy leaned against the bar, tracing ever-widening circles with the base of a tall, sweaty mug. He gripped the handle and took another drink, wondering again why he'd stormed into a place like this only to embarrass himself at the last minute.

Under the scrutiny of every man in the place, he had turned up the glass and taken a long, deliberate swig, as if the sticky-sweet sarsaparilla was his intention all along. He had no taste for strong liquor and wanted no part of it, despite how bad he felt.

Something about the dank, smoke-filled saloon brought Buddy a measure of comfort, even a sense of camaraderie with the men. Perhaps due to the feeling of shared hopelessness or the sight of his own pain reflected back from their hollow eyes.

None of the long faces seemed interested in conversation; Buddy reckoned the other patrons swirled in pits of their own trouble. He felt isolated and anonymous but at the same time accepted into a curious brotherhood of suffering.

A wizened old man strengthened this notion when he stopped to pat Buddy's back on the way out the door. Buddy had never felt such misery. It seemed fitting to hole up in the most miserable place he'd ever been.

He had walked in on impulse a couple of hours past noon. Driven from his room by hunger, he left the hotel to scout out a bite to eat. Instead, he barged into the saloon. He wasn't sure how long he'd nursed his wounds in the dimly lit room. Long enough to watch the bright square of light above the swinging doors fade to orange and then darken.

Having never been inside a saloon in his life, Buddy couldn't believe he'd passed so much time there. He spent much of it comparing Charity to every woman he'd ever known and had been forced to admit her attributes were not his imagination. She was in fact the most wonderful woman he'd ever met, a conclusion that only added to his misery.

The rest of his confinement passed in a blur of strange faces, cigar smoke, the stench of stale liquor and unwashed bodies, and more sarsaparilla than he'd consumed in a lifetime.

"What in blue blazes. . . ?"

The familiar voice pulled Buddy's attention to the mirror behind the bar. Lit by the gaslight on the wall, in sharp relief against the dark opening, the reflection of a familiar face topped by an unruly shock of hair stared back at him from the door.

Buddy spun around grinning, confused but immensely glad to see Jerry Ritter. "Well, lookie here! You're a welcome sight, Tumbleweed. When'd you blow in?"

Jerry reluctantly left his place at the door and pushed into the room, leading a curious and unlikely parade. One of the prettiest women Buddy had ever seen followed him in like she belonged there, though she clearly didn't. On her heels, his posture afraid and defiant at the same time, came big Nash, Magdalena Dane's oversized handyman.

Buddy's head reeled at the sight of them strolling in together. He couldn't have guessed the reason for it if he'd tried.

"What's he doing in here?" The barkeep glared hard at Nash. "Can't y'all read?" He pointed at a sign nailed over the door. "That boy can't come in here. No darkies allowed."

Stepping in front of Nash with a swish of her skirts, the tiny woman tilted her chin and faced the bartender. "This man is with me, sir. We'll only be a minute, and I'll see he does no harm. You have my word. You can do a lady one small favor, can't you?"

The slightest movement of her head caught the glow from the gaslight, causing pinpoints of fire to ricochet through her hair.

She reached a finger to twirl one glittering curl, and the effect was mesmerizing. Every eye in the room held an answering light, and Buddy found himself falling under her spell. He stared at the lovely face, convinced her smile would sweeten day-old coffee.

The allure of plump lips and bottomless dimples weakened the barkeep's will. It was obvious women like her seldom graced his establishment. Looking like he'd swallowed the pickle barrel, the poor man managed a nod.

By the scowl on Jerry's face, he might've swallowed one himself. "Well, if this ain't the last place I expected to find you. . ." His narrowed gaze fixed on Buddy's glass.

Buddy raised the mug. "Don't worry, partner. I'm still a teetotaler."

Jerry leaned to smell the offending drink, his face set in a grimace. When he rose up, his countenance had brightened considerably. "Why, that's sarsaparilla!"

Buddy set the mug down and shoved it away with one finger. "That's what it is, all right. I should know. I've swallowed buckets of it. I don't reckon I'll drink another for the rest of my natural life." He shuddered and turned from the bar. "How did you find me?"

"We weren't planning to look in here, I can tell you that." Jerry flashed his teeth and nodded. "Though it's a good thing we did. We were headed to the hotel next door. I remembered staying there the last time we came to town."

The lady elbowed past Jerry. "Gentlemen, please. We have no time for idle chatter." She held out her hand. "Mr. Pierce, my name is Emily Dane. I can't tell you how glad I am to meet you."

He nodded and returned the gesture. "So you're Emily. I might've guessed." While he couldn't imagine a man letting go of a woman like Charity Bloom, the sight of the pretty little thing before him answered a few hard questions about Daniel Clark.

Buddy's gaze traveled from Emily to Jerry then to Nash. He leaned to rest his elbows on the bar, amused by the improbable grouping. "So what's going on here? Where did you three meet up, and what in tarnation are you doing in Houston?"

Emily's expression was grave. "We came to find you, Mr. Pierce. I have a matter of utmost importance to discuss."

Buddy smiled and winked at Jerry. "In that case, you'd best call me Buddy."

She held his gaze. "All right, then. . .Buddy."

His grin widened. "Well, go ahead. Say what you traveled all this way to tell me. You have my undivided attention."

She wasted no time getting to the point. "Charity's in trouble and you're the only one who can help her."

Buddy bolted upright. His head reeled, his stomach churned, and it had nothing to do with the sarsaparilla. At least he didn't think so. "What kind of trouble?"

Emily's sober expression revealed little emotion, but her bright eyes blazed. "She's about to marry Daniel Clark."

His heart eased and he slumped on the bar stool, wholly defeated. "Miss Dane, I'm afraid you came all this way to tell me what I already know. Forgive my boldness, but you and I are the only poor souls who find that news disquieting." He spun on his heel. "Now if you'll excuse me. . ."

She clutched his arm. "That's where you're wrong, Mr. Pierce. Charity's plenty disquieted. She may be set to marry Daniel, but she's in love with you."

Buddy twisted to look over his shoulder. "What did you say?"

"It's true. Trust me. I heard it from a reliable source."

"Then why?"

"I'll cut straight through the fat. Charity has to be married by day's end tomorrow or Bertha loses her home to Shamus Pike. She felt she had no choice but to marry whoever was handy, so she hoodwinked Daniel and got him to propose. You weren't there, and she feared you wouldn't make it back in time."

"But I was there."

"I know. I watched Daniel drive you out of town."

Buddy flushed at her rebuke. "Didn't you tell her?"

Emily lowered her eyes. "She's not exactly speaking to me just now." Then she raised her head, her expression fierce. "I figured it would mean more to her if I show up with you by my side."

"You don't think Daniel said anything?"

Emily sneered. "What do you think?"

"But I gave him a saddlebag full of money for Bertha. Didn't he give it to her?"

"No, and he won't until after the wedding or they'll know you came back. That's information he'll play close to his chest until Charity says, 'I will,' tomorrow."

Tomorrow! The word caused a jolt to his middle. He stood, tall and determined. "Charity won't be saying, 'I will,' to Daniel ever, if I have anything to say about it." He turned and counted out money onto the bar then strode past Emily toward the door.

Jerry called to him, but it didn't slow him down. Outside on the boardwalk, Jerry burst out of the saloon behind him, his voice frantic. "Buddy, wait up. Where do you think you're going?"

"I have a train to catch."

"Not tonight, you don't."

Something in the way he said it made Buddy stop and turn. Jerry ran into him. Emily and Nash weren't far behind.

"Why don't I?"

"We came in on the last run from Humble, that's why. There won't be another one out until tomorrow morning."

Buddy glanced around at their faces. When Emily nodded, he continued down the boardwalk with the three of them fast on his heels.

Jerry ran to catch up. "Slow up a mite, big fella. What do you aim to do?"

"I aim to hire me a horse and ride to Humble."

"Aw, Buddy! Now you have me wondering if sarsaparilla is all you've had to drink. Riding to Humble is a foolhardy idea. By the time you can get there, the whole town will be rolled up for the night."

He whipped around. "I have to see Charity."

"What for? To wake her up?"

"Then I'll go see Clark first and set him straight."

Nash's eyes widened. "No, suh. That'll just land you in irons."

"I don't care. I'll do what I need to if it'll stop that marriage."

Emily tugged on Buddy's shirt. "The wedding's not until noon tomorrow, if that helps."

Buddy knew she meant to comfort him, but the words caused

a band to tighten around his head. "Miss Dane, if you'll take a closer look at our situation, you'll realize that's not much time." He freed his shirtsleeve from her fingertips and hastened down the boardwalk.

The livery was shut up tight and padlocked when they arrived. Buddy grasped his head and moaned then pounded on the doors until the proprietor stepped out of a side entrance with a large key ring dangling from his hand.

"Sorry, folks. We're closed. You'll have to come back tomorrow."

Buddy hustled his direction with Jerry and Nash on his heels. "Sir, this won't take much of your time. I need a horse right away."

Emily crowded in between them. "He means four horses."

Keys jingling, the pale, scrawny man scratched his armpit. "Yep. You and half of Houston. I ain't got none available. Might have a couple in the morning though."

Buddy shifted his weight to peer between the cracks in the boards. "I can't wait that long. You must have something in there I could ride."

"Something *we* could ride," Emily corrected, bobbing and weaving beside him, trying to see inside the stable.

The liveryman sniffed, wiping his nose on the back of his hand. He regarded Emily as if trying to guess her weight. "I got one broken-down nag. She's along in years and swaybacked. Couldn't handle anyone heavier than this little gal here."

All eyes swung to Emily. Her throat worked up and down, but she took a bold step forward. "We'll take her."

Buddy held up his hand. "What good will that do?"

She frowned her opinion of his question. "I could ride ahead and tell Charity you're coming."

Nash chuckled. "That old mare gon' wind up riding you into town."

Jerry grinned. "We'll wave at you in the morning as our train passes you by."

Buddy steeled his jaw. "It's out of the question, Miss Dane. Too dangerous."

Nash sobered. "He's right, Miss Emmy. I cain't let you do it."

The liveryman finished locking the side door then leaned

against the wall. "Sure wish I could help."

"Thank you kindly, sir," Buddy said. "Maybe you still can. Do you know anyone who might be willing to sell me a horse? I'm willing to pay handsomely."

The old fellow's eyes lit. He pointed behind him. "Like I said, I got this mare–" After a glance at Buddy's scowl, he shrugged. "Sorry, mister."

"That's the best you can do?"

"Haven't you looked around? This town's gone mad since they struck oil in Humble. Makes a man wish he had a hundred horses. Even then, I don't guess I'd have any for you folks tonight."

Buddy had heard of men keeling over from grievous frustration. Thankfully, they were much older, or the rate of his heartbeat would concern him. He hit the wall with a balled-up fist, rattling the doors and arousing a muffled whinny from the lone horse inside. "Blast it! Now what?"

They all stared at him with startled faces. The liveryman took a broad step in the other direction.

Emily gripped his shoulder. "We'll think of something, Mr. Pierce."

Without waiting to hear what the pretty lady's *something* might be, Buddy tore off down the street.

Jerry rushed to get in front of him, walking backwards while he talked. "Listen, Buddy, the train pulls out at dawn tomorrow. You can rest tonight and still make it in plenty of time. That makes more sense than riding hard all night and arriving bushed. What do you say to that?"

Buddy slowed his stride, considering Jerry's suggestion. "I don't think so."

Emily nodded toward Jerry. "He's right, Mr. Pierce. Something could happen to you on the trail at night. You could be ambushed or your horse might break a leg. Then you'd never make it in time to save Charity."

He stopped walking. "That's the first thing anyone has said that makes sense."

"Besides," she continued, "you don't know what you'll be walking into when you get there. You'll want to be fresh and clear-minded."

Buddy's gaze traveled from Emily to Jerry then back to Emily. "None of it sits well with me, but it appears I have no choice."

Jerry slapped him on the back. "Now you're talking. Let's see the lady tucked in for the night and go get us some shut-eye."

Shut-eye was the last thing Buddy would get with every muscle twitching to get back to Charity. "I plan to be the first man on that train in the morning. You hear?"

Despite Jerry's smaller size and Buddy's dragging feet, Jerry hustled him down the boardwalk toward the hotel. Emily ran alongside, panting from the effort to keep up, and Nash lumbered along behind them. Inside, Buddy arranged rooms for the three of them and inquired about shelter for Nash.

At the door to Emily's room, she reached to touch Buddy's arm. "Mr. Pierce, you won't leave without me tomorrow, will you?"

Buddy met her haunting blue eyes. "I don't mind you stringing along, Miss Dane, but I won't wait for you. I suggest you arrive at the station on time if you plan on riding into Humble with me." He tipped his hat. "Good night now."

He left her staring after him and made his way down the hall to his room.

CHAPTER 26

A single moonbeam, slipping through a broken slat in the shade, bored behind Daniel's eyelids. He pitched and tossed on the wide bed, trying in vain to escape the pesky glow. Not that the amount of light in his room had changed. He'd lost his talent for sleeping through a hurricane. The air was heavy and hot, insufferably so, but he dozed at last, until sweat trickled past his ear, tickling him awake. Stirring, he cursed and punched the lumpy pillow into submission before flopping over onto his stomach.

Charity came to him then. She hovered over the bed and whispered through pouting red lips, so close her soft breath in his ear raised gooseflesh on his neck. He rolled onto his back and her long dark hair fell over him, caressing his face, his chest. He could smell her skin, taste her breath as she drew closer. Ecstatic, he reached to encircle her waist with his arms, convinced she was there.

His pounding heart jerked him awake and Charity was gone, her vivid presence replaced by deep loneliness, his faithful companion for much of the night.

Why had he excused himself and gone up to bed early? So far sleep had eluded him, and now, after the dream, there was no hope of rest.

He sat up on the side of the bed. When his bare toes hit the floor, it gave him a shock to realize the room he thought stifling hot was in fact quite nippy. Straining to reach it with his heel, he dragged a sock beneath his feet. Only his feet were cold. In the predawn chill, his stirring blood continued to warm his body and torture his mind.

He would have to get up. There was no help for it, though it made him frustrated and angry with himself. He needed sleep. The day that lay before him would be taxing enough with a rested body.

He had decided to tell his parents about the wedding, but only at the last minute on his way out the door. If they were willing to accept Charity, if they wanted to witness the marriage of their only son, they would be welcome to ride with him to the church. That prospect warmed his heart.

The other possibility scared him witless. His parents could very likely disown him today, shun him, and strip him of his inheritance. If so, it would be his mama's doing, but Papa would go along with her to keep the peace.

Daniel grimaced. If that's how things went, then blast them both! He didn't need them. He'd proven that. And Charity was worth it. He would lose anything to gain her. Why hadn't he realized that before? At any rate, he would face heaven and earth—worse, his mama's wrath—to take a stand for her today.

He shivered. Whether chilled by his thoughts or the icy floor he couldn't tell, but the cold had started to penetrate his body. He turned up the lamp in order to locate his other sock and smiled when he discovered he'd slept with it wadded among the covers. He reached for the one under his feet, pulled them both on, and then crossed the room to stand before the tall, mirrored wardrobe.

Peering closer, he rubbed his stubbled chin. "Funny, you don't look like a groom," he muttered to his rumpled reflection. "Look sharp, old boy. Today's your wedding day."

The words broke the spell. The bleak mood that had hovered through the night lifted, and Daniel had to laugh at the simpleton grinning at him from the mirror.

He would hurry and dress, then pack the rest of his clothes and hide them with the other belongings he'd stashed in the buckboard. After that, he would get started on his chores. It was too early yet to feed the stock, but there were things he could do, tasks done so many times he could manage them in the dark.

Stunned, Daniel realized it was the last time the responsibility would be his. Overseeing his father's property would fall to someone else tomorrow because Daniel would have chores of his own. From now on, the affairs of his house, his and Charity's, would occupy his time. The thought brought a thrill that shot right through him and roared in his ears.

He eased from his room, pausing to peer down the hall toward his parents' bedroom. No light shone from beneath the door and no sound came from within. He tiptoed past, mindful of the squeaky boards, and headed for the landing.

A hearty yawn watered his eyes as he descended the stairs, sleepy at last. Smiling, he shook it off. Too late now. Any rest he got would have to come later, after Charity became his bride.

"Come on, Miss Emmy, this ain't no Sunday stroll. You best hurry now or you gon' be chasing that train down the track."

"For pity's sake, Nash, I'm coming." Out of breath, Emmy strained to close the gap between them. "No one in God's creation can keep up with your gait, much less a body saddled with my short legs. I'm doing the best I can."

Despite the weight of both their bags, Nash breezed along ahead of her, still a good distance away until he stopped short to stare. "You best hush all that fussing and save your breath for running. That train's coming now. I can see it."

The sun glinted off a speck of metal in the distance, and a thin plume of smoke spiraled into the air. Emmy picked up her pace, turning her attention to the station platform. "Do you see Mr. Pierce and Mr. Ritter?"

"Not yet, I don't. Ain't likely to, neither, what with all these folks flocking around. I reckon we won't see them two men again 'til after we's boarded. Maybe not even 'til we get home."

Emmy's eyes lit on a rumpled head of brightly colored hair. "Oh, but you're wrong." She pointed toward the far edge of the platform. "There's Mr. Ritter now."

They pushed through to where the young man stood craning his neck at the crowd. When he saw them, he flushed with pleasure and waved frantically until they reached his side.

"Where's Buddy?" Emmy asked, only to hear her question parroted back. She stared up at him. "What do you mean where's Buddy? Isn't he with you?"

Mr. Ritter gaped at her, his face a picture of her own confusion. "I thought he was with you."

The first flicker of panic flashed in Emmy's chest. Heart racing, she studied the melee around them. "Well, he must be here somewhere."

Mr. Ritter shook his head. "I was one of the first men on the platform this morning. I've watched every person come and go since."

"You must be mistaken. He was so determined to catch this train."

The words were hardly free of her mouth when the big engine roared into the station, belching black smoke in rhythmic blasts. The mob surged toward it in one massive heave, bumping and jostling Emmy as they shoved past. She sought Buddy in the swirling sea of faces and then remembered Nash, who stood head and shoulders above the rest. She tugged at his sleeve. "Do you see him, Nash?"

"No, Miss Emmy. I don't see hide nor hair of Mistah Pierce."

"Oh, do look harder. He must be here. If he's not, then. . ."

"Something's wrong," Mr. Ritter finished for her. "Come on, let's go."

Emmy fell in behind the men as they raced down the near-empty boardwalk, headed for the hotel. Despite the early hour, Mr. Ritter paused to peer into the saloon. From what Emmy could see, there wasn't much going on in the shadows behind the swinging doors, and Buddy was nowhere in sight.

The long-legged rascals ran ahead of Emmy, leaving her trailing behind. Inside the shabby hotel lobby, she saw Mr. Ritter already on the stairs with Nash right behind him. She glanced at the clerk, prepared to hear him raise a fuss about Nash going upstairs, but some matter in the other direction held his attention. Emmy heaved a sigh of relief before raising the hem of her skirt and barreling after the two men. She caught up with them just outside Buddy's room.

"Why did you leave without him in the first place?" she demanded of Mr. Ritter, who stood pounding with the palm of his hand.

He gave another hard whack. "I knocked this morning, but he didn't answer. I figured he left without me."

"You really believed he wouldn't wait for you?"

Mr. Ritter glanced over his shoulder. "You heard him last night, same as I did. He wasn't planning to wait for nobody."

Nash doubled his massive fist and hit the door several times, so hard the frame rattled, then pressed his ear against the polished wood. Stepping back, he shook his head. "He ain't in this room, that's for sure. We could've raised the dead with all this ruckus."

Several occupants along the hall stuck out their heads and glared their way. Nash jumped behind Emmy and Mr. Ritter in a feeble attempt to hide his bulk. "We best get on out of here," he whispered. " 'Fore we winds up in a mess."

Emmy shook her head and rattled the doorknob. "I won't leave without Buddy. He's the reason we came. Help me get this open."

Mr. Ritter placed his hand over hers on the knob. Compassion had softened his gentle eyes. "Buddy's not here, ma'am. Come along now. Maybe he's made it to the station by now."

Nash shook his head. "If'n he did finally make it to the station, we'll never know it. He'll be somewhere on that big old train."

Emmy spun around to face him. "And we won't know whether to board or not!" She moaned, pressing her knuckles to her throbbing temples. "Oh my goodness, we're just too addlepated for words. One of us should've waited on the platform. Now what are we going to do?"

She cast around in her mind for a solution. There had to be something sensible. If she could just get one moment to catch her breath, she knew it would come to her. Trouble was, they were fresh out of moments. That train wouldn't wait.

Jerry started for the stairs, waving them on with his hand. "Let's go," he called. "There's nothing more to do here."

With some reluctance, Emmy moved to follow. Just as she gave in and turned away, just as her hand released the knob, she heard a sound from inside. It was a man's voice, weak and faint, yet desperate in tone. She whirled toward the stairs. "Mr. Ritter, come back! He's in there. Buddy's in this room."

Jerry stopped and stared at her. He hooked his long thumbs in the waistband of his trousers and let his shoulders slouch in defeat. "Ma'am, I understand your frustration–I really do. But I'm growing a mite impatient with you now."

Emmy stomped her foot. "I tell you he's in there and he's in trouble. Get over here right now. Both of you."

Like boys responding to their mama's no-nonsense voice, the men dashed to her side and pressed their ears to the door.

"You right, Miss Emmy," Nash whispered. "Somebody's in there."

Jerry nodded. "I hear it, too." He stood up and rapped hard twice, then placed his mouth next to the jamb. "Buddy, is that you? Open up."

Emmy felt her panic growing. "Nash, you're going to have to break it down."

Always ready to oblige, Nash backed up and prepared to charge. Before he could make his move, Jerry lunged in front of him.

"Now just hold on there. We can get inside without leveling the wall. I can't afford to replace it. You two wait here and don't move. I'm going after a key." He wagged a finger at Nash as he jogged by. "Don't get any more ideas about busting down doors."

Emmy pressed her face to the inlaid panel. "Hang on, Mr. Pierce. We're here to help you. Mr. Ritter's bringing the key."

She heard a loud groan in answer and thought to have Nash proceed with the original plan, but Mr. Ritter appeared at the top of the landing with a brass key dangling from his hand. He ran the last few steps toward them, and Emmy backed out of his way.

"I'm here, Buddy. Hang on," he called as he worked the key in the lock.

When the door swung open, the three of them burst inside the room. An unbearable stench met them first, and Emmy covered her nose with her sleeve. Buddy sprawled across the mattress, on top of the covers, dressed in the same clothes he'd worn the day before.

"What in the world? Why, he's not even made it to bed properly." Mr. Ritter approached his friend and peered down. "What's up, old man? What happened to you?"

Buddy's eyes were bloodshot and glazed, his face the same shade of green as the blanket on which he lay. Nash nodded at the gruesome washbasin on the floor beside the bed and backed toward the exit. "He sick, that's what. Powerful sick. Something done turned his stomach inside out."

Tears flooded Emmy's eyes. How could Buddy be sick? He was the one person in the world with any hope of saving Charity, but he had to be in Humble to do it.

Buddy raised a trembling hand toward Jerry. "Get me to the station," he whispered.

Jerry shook his head. "Sorry, my friend. You're in no condition for a train ride. You've taken ill."

He motioned Jerry closer. "Not ill. Just a little weak in my gut. Too much sarsaparilla on an empty stomach."

Jerry stared hard at him then doubled over and roared with laughter. "Are you telling me you got this way from drinking sarsaparilla?" He hooted and slapped his leg. "I never met a feller who couldn't hold his sarsaparilla before. Maybe you should've stuck with whiskey."

Grabbing the front of Jerry's shirt, Buddy pulled him down against his chest and ground out a threat. "Ritter, you'd best get me down to that station right now, or I'll. . ." He fell against his pillow, too weak to finish.

Jerry paled. Whether from Buddy's anger or his foul breath, Emmy couldn't tell, but the man had his attention.

"Have you lost your senses?" he wailed. "How am I supposed to get you anywhere when you can't even stand up?"

"Carry me," Buddy gasped. "Hog-tie me with a rope and drag me—I don't care. Do what you have to do to get me on that train."

Backing out of Buddy's reach, Jerry crossed his arms. "I won't do it. You're far too sick to be moved."

Buddy lunged at him. "Get me on that train, Jerry! I tell you I can make it."

"No, sir. I'm sorry. You can't."

"Oh yes, he can!"

Buddy's determination had lit a fire in Emmy. She pushed Jerry out of the way. "Nash, come over here and help Mr. Pierce out of this bed. Hurry. This man has a train to catch."

CHAPTER 27

Bertha lay in Magda's big bed with the covers pulled up to her chin. Awake for hours, she'd heard the creak of every settling board and the hoot of every barn owl. She was also privy to the snores, snorts, and sleepy ramblings coming from her roommate. Not to mention that Magda's every toss and turn wrought a symphony of rattles and groans from the makeshift bed in the corner.

Thankfully, Magda stirred at last and eased out of bed. Bertha knew she should be up, too, and already down in the kitchen with a good start on breakfast, but she couldn't convince her body to move.

When Magda tiptoed past for the third time, Bertha rolled onto her side and cleared her throat. "I ain't asleep, you know. You can stop all that creeping about and light the lamp."

In the dim room, Magda leaned to look at her from behind the wardrobe door. "Did I wake you, sugar? I tried real hard to be quiet."

Bertha propped up on one elbow. "I hate to hear that, because you made enough noise to wake Rebel clear out in the barn. You never could tread softly worth a hoot."

Magda came over and sat on the bed beside her. "I know. That's why I was leaving the room." She reached to touch Bertha's forehead. "Are you feeling all right? You never sleep this late."

Bertha took Magda's cool hand and held it to her cheek. "No,

I ain't feeling one bit all right."

"Are you taking sick?"

She nodded. "Heartsick, I guess."

Magda patted her face. "I know, sweetie."

"Charity's run out of time."

"I know," Magda cooed.

"I'm her mama. I should be able to save her, but I'm not smart enough. I don't know how to help her out of this one."

Magda squared around on the bed and faced her. "Maybe you're not supposed to. Did you ever consider that? Maybe Daniel's the man God intended for Charity all along. Remember, she wanted to marry him once and with your blessing. The thing that turned you against Daniel is his jilting her, which he's trying to make amends for."

Bertha sat up and shook her head. "I don't know, Magda. There's something about that boy that ain't quite right. I always sensed it."

Magda gave her a piercing look. "Is this one of those *feelings* you get?"

She crossed her arms. "Don't you go discounting my feelings again. They've served me well over the years. I believe they're from God." She jabbed Magda in the arm with her finger. "Anyway, look who's talking. It was you who said he weren't good for nothing but telling lies and shaming young girls."

Magda nodded. "He did those things and that's a fact—but, honey, people make mistakes. I do things every day that I regret. If Daniel really loves Charity, don't you think he deserves another chance?"

Bertha took Magda by the shoulders and stared into her eyes. "Let me ask you this: If Daniel really loves my girl, how could he hurt her by tossing her aside like trash in front of the whole town? If he respects her, why did he spread lies about her virtue?"

Magda shook her head.

"Thad never would've done that to me. Willem couldn't have treated you so shamefully either, and you know it. On my wedding day, I had no doubt Thad loved me, even cherished me. I want the same for my little girl."

Magda nodded. "I remember your wedding day like it happened yesterday. You were a beautiful bride. Thad was so proud." She got a faraway look in her eyes. "Honey, the way that man looked at you—" Picking up Bertha's hands, she squeezed them hard. "Oh, Bert, you're right. If we let Charity marry Daniel, it could ruin her life. What're we going to do?"

Bertha set her jaw. "I don't know just yet. One thing's for sure—we need to pray like we've never done before."

Charity came awake with a gasp. Her wide eyes sought something to ground her, to still her pounding heart. Recognition came slowly, one familiar sight at a time. First, the broad water stain on the ceiling in the shape of a woman's boot—or the country of Italy, depending on how you looked at it. Just below the boot were the tall spires of a four-poster bed with a backdrop of bright yellow wallpaper. Her eyes quickly swept the other furnishings, and she released her breath. She had awakened in the Danes' guestroom, in a bed as familiar as her own. Mother Dane and Mama were just down the hall.

So why did she feel so lost?

She moved to sit up and realized Papa's Bible lay open across her chest. It came to her then in a rush, as the rising sun flooded the room. Her gaze jerked to the window. It looked like a beautiful morning, hardly a fitting start for the darkest day of her life.

When that same sun rises tomorrow, I'll be married to Daniel Clark. Daniel. Not Buddy.

The thought of it crushed her, and she regretted waking. Rolling onto her side, she fought to return to unconscious oblivion, but sleep eluded her. The light was too bright, the truth too harsh to shut out. It didn't help that her wedding dress hung on a peg near the window, mocking her.

The day before she had clutched the dress to her face and asked God for help. The words of her prayer came back, and she whispered them aloud. "I've never asked You for anything this important before. Can You? Will You?"

He could, of course. God could do anything. It would be a small matter for Him, a tiny miracle in the great scheme of things. The problem was, He hadn't. For whatever reason, it appeared

God wanted her to marry Daniel.

Disturbed by the thought, she picked up Papa's Bible and sat upright in bed. Crossing her legs to cradle the worn book, she let it fall open in her lap. Then she closed her eyes and pressed her index finger to the page. Feeling foolish, yet afraid of what she might see, she opened her eyes and looked.

"Greater love hath no man than this, that a man lay down his life for his friends."

Her heart pounded. Was that the answer? Did God expect her to lay down her life, her future happiness, for her mama? Could she do it? Could she give up her dreams for love and contentment and never grow to resent it?

If God had truly called her to such an unselfish act, He would have to help her. It seemed beyond human strength, no task for mortal flesh. What sort of love was that anyway? And what was the source?

She remembered the passage in Corinthians from which Mama had taken her name. "Charity" in that text meant "love." Mama always said love was the only fitting name for a child born to her and Papa.

Charity knew the verses by heart. She'd heard them often enough. Still, she thumbed her way to the scripture.

"Charity suffereth long. . ."

Well, that part rang true. She had suffered every day since Emmy fled the church with Daniel.

"And is kind. . ."

She had tried to be.

"Charity envieth not; charity vaunteth not itself, is not puffed up, doth not behave itself unseemly. . ."

These might require more diligence on her part.

"Seeketh not her own. . ."

That part felt like divine direction, but she didn't like it much. She read on.

"Beareth all things, believeth all things, hopeth all things, endureth all things. Charity never faileth."

The last part gave her pause. Love never fails. That's what it really said.

She felt as if God had tossed her question back at her. "Can you? Will you?"

Charity closed the book, careful to tuck back all the mementos Mama kept inside. Scraps of paper, clippings and lists, pressed magnolia blossoms, and little notes from Papa, yellowed with age, were scattered throughout his Bible.

She wriggled one of the notes from between the delicate pages and smiled. Papa preferred lead to ink for writing and carried a pencil with him always. He once read that George Washington used a three-inch pencil when he surveyed the Ohio Territory in 1762 and that Thomas Edison kept one in his vest pocket to jot down notes. "Sugar," he liked to say, "what's good enough for George and Tom is plenty good for old Thad."

She held the page closer to the window and strained to read the faded words, barely visible now. She could make out only, "Love always, Thad," scratched at the end.

The words burned in her heart. Despite the fix they were in, despite evidence that Papa had caused it, she knew how much he had loved them. She knew he would sacrifice his happiness for Mama without a backward glance.

Charity fell against the bed and stared at the ceiling. The written words of both her earthly father and her heavenly Father conveyed the same message–a lesson on love–and she would do her best to listen.

Mother Dane and Mama were stirring down the hall.

Charity swung her legs over the side of the bed and stood up. It was high time to get started, to quit stewing over things she couldn't change. It was her wedding day.

CHAPTER 28

The whistle blew, followed by a shout for all to board. Emmy's body tensed, and she picked up the pace, ears strained for the chug of the engine or the screech of turning wheels. She couldn't see the platform for the row of buildings yet to pass, but she knew they were out of time.

She whirled to check the progress of her companions. The three struggled along several yards back, poor white-faced Buddy Pierce held up between Nash and a panting Jerry Ritter.

"Do hurry," she shouted. "The train is leaving."

"We is hurrying, Miss Emmy. It ain't easy toting a grown man, and this one is a mite overgrowed."

Emmy found it hard to feel compassion while saddled with a burden of her own. Thankfully, Nash had stowed Buddy's bag under his free arm, but the task of toting her own luggage and that of Mr. Ritter had fallen to her. Unaccustomed to carrying so much weight, she had to stop and shift the load a bit to ease her aching fingers. "Oh pooh. You could carry two more like him and you know it. Stop your bellyaching and come on."

They rounded the corner of the last building together. Emmy sighted her mark, an open passenger car, and bore down on it just as the car began to move. The bespectacled conductor leaned halfway out of the door and watched her.

"Wait, sir!" she called to him. "Stop the train."

The man shook his head. "Sorry, little lady. Can't do that."

"Oh please, you must!"

Emmy dropped the bags and ran. The man's mouth was moving, but the churning wheels carried him away too quickly for her to hear. She gathered her skirts and ran faster. Nash shouted something, but she couldn't make out his words either over the roar in her ears.

"Come on!" she screamed back at them. "Pick up your feet. We can still make it."

Nash caught up with her then, lifting her away just as the last car rumbled by shaking the ground at their feet. He carried her some distance from the tracks and set her down hard on the platform.

"Miss Emmy, that was the most foolhardy thing I ever seen. Is you trying to get killed?"

Emmy turned toward Jerry, who stood pale as death staring her way, and Buddy, who sprawled in the dust where Nash had dropped him.

"I'm sorry, I. . ."

"You what?" Nash shouted. "A lunatic? Yes, you is. Now get over there away from these tracks."

Without waiting to see if she complied, Nash headed for the scattered luggage. He retrieved the bags in short angry jerks, all the while rolling his eyes and muttering dark curses under his breath.

Emmy trudged to where Jerry stood and looked down at Buddy. "I'm very sorry, Mr. Pierce. Are you all right?"

Squinting against the rising sun, he peered up at her. "I reckon I will be. If I live."

She glanced over her shoulder at the silver speck wending its way in the distance. "We missed it. Now what?"

Jerry pivoted toward the depot. "When's the next one?"

She shrugged. "I don't know. They're never on time."

"Forget going by rail." Weakness strained Buddy's voice. Or maybe desperation. "The Rabbit is slower than cold honey. We'd never make Humble by noon."

Jerry nodded. "Makes you wonder why folks gave it that name."

Emmy laughed. "Certainly not because of its speed. The old-timers claim she used to make unscheduled stops along the tracks so passengers could shoot jackrabbits. Most believe she earned the name by how she jerks and hops."

Straightening his elbow, Buddy propped himself higher. "Thank you for the timely history lesson, Miss Dane."

She curled her top lip at him.

"Either way the train's out. I'm telling you, we need to hire some horses."

"You can barely sit upright. How would you ride clear to Humble?"

"I'll find a way, Jerry. I have to."

Nash returned and handed the bags to Emmy, all of them this time, then helped Jerry lift Buddy off the ground. "Let's get this poor ailing man a place to sit. After that we can figure what we gon' do."

They found a bench against the outer wall of the depot and lowered Buddy onto the paint-chipped slats. A more natural shade had replaced his alternating green and sickly white pallor.

Emmy hoped it was a good sign. "Mr. Ritter, I think a bite to eat would benefit your friend greatly. Why don't you go see what you can find for him while we try to solve this problem?"

A grin eased the worried frown from Jerry's face. He patted his stomach. "I could use a bite myself, ma'am. How about you?"

At the mention of food, Emmy realized she was famished. "I wouldn't mind it a bit." She nodded toward Nash. "Him, too. We took no time for breakfast."

Jerry nodded. "I'll fetch us all something, then."

Seated between them on the bench, Buddy's glare followed Jerry and then Emmy. "Hold up. Have you two forgotten why we're here? Charity's clock is ticking. We don't have time for a family picnic."

Emmy patted his shoulder. "Mr. Pierce, I'm anxious, too. But it won't take long to eat, and we'll gain strength for the journey."

Buddy scowled. "A journey that needs to get started." He yanked a small pouch from his vest pocket, pulled out money, and handed it to Jerry. "Get jerky and hardtack, and any other food we can eat on the road." He pointed at something behind them. "When you get back, you can hustle over there and get me a horse."

The livery stable perched directly across the tracks. The towering building with its wide facade looked different by morning light. The grounds teemed with animals and people, from the holding pens on each side of the slung-back doors to the trampled areas in front. By the look of it, the liveryman did all right by himself, and the railroad company wasn't the only venture in town to profit from the boom.

A wagon rumbled over the tracks beside them, the driver sharply reining his two-horse team into the muddy yard.

Emmy gripped Buddy's arm. "I have a better idea."

Buddy waved Jerry away to buy the food while his gaze remained fixed on her face. "I'm listening."

Emmy pointed at another passing rig. "What about one of those?"

"You want to buy a wagon?"

"Not buy. Hire. That way, you can rest in back until you're feeling better."

Nash rubbed his dark chin and nodded at Buddy. "That may not be a bad idea, Mistah Pierce."

Buddy's brow furrowed. "Good thinking. If they don't have a rig for hire, we can book passage on one bound for Humble. I'll pay the asking price to anyone who can get me there before noon."

Emmy stared down the boardwalk in the direction Jerry had gone, shading her eyes to see better. "Then it's settled. When Mr. Ritter comes back, he can make inquiries."

Buddy shook his head. "I say the two of you go now. I get the feeling you're just as capable, and there's no time to waste."

Emmy searched his earnest green eyes. "But you'll be left on your own."

"I'll be fine. Besides, Jerry will be back soon." He didn't give her time to argue but shooed her and Nash with a backward wave of his hand. "Go on now, and hurry."

Though reluctant to leave him alone, Emmy opened her parasol and motioned for Nash to lead the way. "You heard the man. Let's find us a ride home."

Nash led her past the depot and along the boardwalk to a well-traveled crossing. Her determination faded a bit as they approached the front of the livery. Up close, they found it even busier than it appeared from the station. Wagons of every size and description boiled out of the stables and onto the rutted road, some passing far too close to suit her.

It didn't take long to learn there were no rigs left for hire. Together they walked the grounds, asking questions and checking wagons. The majority of travelers headed for Humble seemed more than willing to help, but their conveyances were too full to accommodate a traveling band sitting upright, much less a man the size of Buddy lying flat of his back.

Fighting the urge to wring her hands, she looked up at Nash. "What do we do now?"

Nash drew a deep breath that lifted and filled his broad chest. "We don't give up, that's what we do." He cut his eyes down at her. "Don't fret now. We'll find something."

"You saw for yourself. Not one of these people has room for us." Emmy bit back tears and tried to still the tremor in her voice. "It can't be God's will for Charity to spend her life with someone like Daniel. Why are we having such a hard time trying to save her?"

Nash's roaming gaze came to rest on her face. "Whoa, now." His rumbling voice was a gentle rebuke. "Is that what we doing here? Saving Miss Charity? If so, you can count me out. I ain't fit to save myself, much less Miss Charity. Child, that be God's business."

Something behind her caught and held his attention. A smile lit his eyes. "And the Almighty might jus' have a little trick up His sleeve."

She followed his pointing finger in time to see a stocky young man toss a faded satchel into the bed of an otherwise empty wagon. He walked to the rear and closed the tailgate, then hurried around to help a tall, gray-haired woman onto the seat.

Emmy let out her breath in a rush and clutched his shirt. "What if they're not going to Humble?"

"Ain't but one way to find out."

"You're right. Let's go ask them."

She started forward, but Nash caught hold of her arm. "Where you going?"

"To negotiate a ride, of course."

"No, you ain't. You staying over here. Them's my people, Miss Emmy. We stand a much better chance if you let me do the talking."

"That's ridiculous."

"No, missy, it ain't. You jus' stay put this time. I'll be back directly."

In a casual, unhurried stride, Nash approached the wagon with his hat in his hands. The kind-faced woman smiled and nodded a greeting. The young man beamed and quickly extended his hand. Nash talked with low tones and quick gestures, lifting his chin toward the wagon and jabbing his finger back toward her. Emmy saw the man's wide grin fade just before he cast a frown her way. Nash stayed a few seconds more then turned and hurried across the yard.

"What'd they say?" Eager to know, she called out the question while Nash was yet halfway back.

He waited to answer until he reached her side. "Them be good folks, Miss Emmy. They headed for Humble, all right, and the boy, he say we can ride. Don't want no money for it neither. Only. . ."

Her excitement had soared higher with every word until the last. Something in the way he said it foretold bad news. "Only what? Speak up, Nash."

He cleared his throat and looked away. "He say he ain't about to put his old mama in the back of that wagon, not for you or nobody else. Not for no amount of money."

Emmy looked across to where the two strangers huddled close together. It appeared the woman gently scolded. The boy answered with a firm shake of his head before he jumped from the seat and walked away.

Emmy blinked up at Nash. "Of course he won't put her in back. Why, I don't blame him. Tell him we accept his terms, only we will indeed pay them for their trouble. Mr. Pierce said so."

"But, Miss Emmy. . ."

"Go ahead, tell them."

"Well, but. . ."

"What now?"

He pointed behind him. "That there rig ain't but a one-seater, which puts you riding in back." He lifted both dark brows. "With all us men."

Emmy saw his point. She had to swallow before she could answer but tried hard to sound nonchalant. "So?"

"So it won't look proper. 'Sides that, it's a long, bumpy ride, and that bed ain't made for comfort. Yo' mama gon' skin me good if'n I haul you through Humble throwed off in the bottom of a wagon like a sack of potatoes." He took a quick look over his shoulder and leaned closer. "Worse yet, whatever they been hauling in that thing be long past burying."

Emmy tried not to pause, tried not to ask. "Are you saying there's a bad smell?"

Nash shook his curly head. "You gon' wish it jus' bad. Truth is, that smell done took a turn toward evil." His expression was guarded, watchful.

She made up her mind. "It doesn't matter. What's a little odor to contend with for Charity's sake? You tell them yes. I'll let Buddy and Jerry know we have our ride."

Emmy turned to go. Nash reached to stay her, and she looked back at him with questioning eyes. The way he squinted down at her made her insides pitch. She glanced away. "What is it, Nash? Why are you peering a hole through me?"

"I'm wondering what done changed you, that's all."

She forced a laugh. "Don't be silly. I'm no different."

His hand on her elbow held her fast, but his voice was kind. "Yes'm, you different. Nothing I can point a finger to, but I see change all over you."

"Don't talk foolish."

"Ain't nothing foolish. Don't forget I've known you quite a spell. I watched you learn to toddle. In all this time, I ain't never seen you cross the road to help nobody, much less be willing to wallow in stink. Don't tell me you ain't different."

She met his stare, trying to maintain a steady gaze. "I don't know what you're talking about."

He laughed and wagged his head. "You can't fool old Nash that easy. You know jus' what I'm talking about. Them big blue eyes telling on you."

Emmy flinched and could've pinched herself for it. She pulled free and stalked away. "I know this—we don't have time to discuss it. Get on over there and tell those folks to wait for us. Inform them we'll be back with two more passengers. Then hightail it back to the depot so you can help with Mr. Pierce."

Five minutes later, Jerry Ritter, the young stranger, and Nash—mostly Nash—had Buddy loaded into the bed of the wagon. They propped him against the dilapidated tailgate of the old freighter, the wood so battered by time and pocked by beetles that Emmy feared he'd wind up riddled with splinters.

It seemed a fitting backdrop for a man so broken and battered himself. Too weak to sit up, Buddy sprawled over most of the rear, crowding Jerry into the far corner. Emmy perched at Buddy's feet on a cushion of feed sacks Nash had gathered for her, and Nash sat by her side.

Buddy insisted he felt some better, yet his green pallor had returned. Emmy wondered if she ought not secure a bucket for him, but thought better of it when she considered their traveling companions. She hadn't missed the look that passed between them when they learned Buddy was ill. In lieu of offering him a bucket in case his stomach resisted the jerky he had eaten, Emmy sent up a quick prayer that Buddy wouldn't need it, then cringed and prayed harder when she remembered Nash had predicted a long, bumpy ride.

CHAPTER 29

The odor Nash warned of rose like a specter from the wagon bed, becoming unbearable when the wind died down. Emmy began to lose faith in her prayer, convinced even divine intervention couldn't lessen the effect of that powerful stench on a sour stomach.

She leaned toward Buddy and stared. "Are you all right, Mr. Pierce?" Though she whispered, the woman riding up front glanced back with a troubled expression.

Buddy nodded grimly without opening his eyes. "I'll be fine."

The tremor in his voice belied his confident answer. Emmy settled down and prepared for a difficult ride.

Nash had introduced the young man as Benjamin, the woman as Miss Lucille. They seemed to be decent people, especially the mother, though her son rode stiffly on the seat and said little. Emmy wondered if he felt uncomfortable about his decision to put her in the rear.

While the right thing to do for Miss Lucille's sake, it took courage on Benjamin's part, especially when the locals stopped to glare as they made their way down the street. Emmy made a point to smile and wave as she passed. It served to take the edge off their collective indignation, but only a bit, and no one in the wagon relaxed until they were well out of town.

Emmy heard Miss Lucille let go of a deep sigh. Nash, too, exhaled loudly and grinned, and Jerry's good-natured smile returned.

Nash sat up straighter and broke the silence. "Whoo-ee! We going home, and I sure is glad. I seen the big city now and don't care much for it. Ain't no fit way to live, all that coming and going and everybody a stranger. I expect old Nash gon' stay put from now on."

He tilted his chin and looked up at Benjamin. "Son, you folks from around here?"

"No, suh," Benjamin answered without looking back.

Miss Lucille turned in the seat, her lovely face set in a serene smile. "We come to Houston by way of Louisiana, Mr. Nash. After Benjamin's papa, God rest him, went to be with the Lord."

Nash lifted his battered hat. "Sure sorry, ma'am."

She bit her bottom lip and nodded. "He's in a better place now, but thank you kindly. So anyways, when Benjamin heard them oil companies was hiring folks in Texas, he figured they'd be plenty of work for a man with a strong back." She patted her son's shoulder. "My Benny here is one of the strongest men around."

Emmy considered the empty wagon bed. "Where are your belongings, Miss Lucille?"

Nash cleared his throat and pressed his elbow against Emmy's ribs.

Miss Lucille gave him a tender glance. "That's all right, Mr. Nash. I don't mind."

When her dark eyes returned to Emmy, humiliation swam in their brown depths. Emmy felt like she'd been caught in the woman's underwear drawer. "Sorry, ma'am."

"Don't fret, child. You meant no harm. The truth is, we own the clothes on our backs, a few things in that bag under the seat, and little else. Took selling everything we had to buy us this wagon. Benny got a good deal on it, though, down at the stockyards."

Emmy and Nash exchanged knowing looks. Miss Lucille smiled and pulled a square of cloth from her waistband, handing it back to Emmy. "Here, baby. Hold this against your nose; it'll help some. It's what I do when there ain't no breeze to take the edge off." She laughed. "You wouldn't think so, but you get used to it after a while."

Emmy reached for the cloth, handing it down to Buddy instead. "Thank you, ma'am, but if you don't mind, I think he needs it more."

Buddy took the tattered fabric from Emmy's hand then nodded weakly toward the flask strapped to Nash's side. "You think I could have a sip of that water?"

Nash bent to hand it over. "Why sure, Mistah Pierce. Help yourself."

Buddy pushed himself to a sitting position. He drank deeply, wiping his mouth with the cloth when he was done. Passing the flask to Nash, he took in his surroundings as if aware of them for the first time. "What time you reckon it is?"

Nash dipped his head at the sun, still low in the sky. "It's early yet."

Buddy nodded. "I think we'll make it in plenty of time, don't you?"

"Don't know about plenty, but yes, suh, we gon' make it."

Buddy took one more look around, then pressed the rag to his face and hunkered down. The motion of the wagon soon lulled him to sleep. Whether from the cloth, the water, or fervent prayers on his behalf, Buddy did look some better. The color had returned to his face, and he looked peaceful at rest. Beside him Jerry dozed sitting upright, while his head lolled about in a comical fashion.

Emmy felt herself drifting off as well, until Miss Lucille began to hum a haunting melody. Her lovely warble didn't startle Emmy awake but rather the familiar hymn. She'd heard it many times, and not just at Sunday service. Aunt Bert, Charity, even Mama sang it often, though never with the depth of emotion she heard in Miss Lucille's rich voice.

Nash closed his eyes, nodding slowly up and down, and then leaned his head against the seat and took up the words.

" 'Amazing grace, how sweet the sound that saved a wretch like me.' "

His deep baritone rumbled in Emmy's chest, sending a chill through her body and raising the hairs at the nape of her neck. Miss Lucille harmonized with Nash in a high, clear voice, and even Benjamin joined in. Their blended voices became an angel chorus as their song swelled about her.

" 'I once was lost, but now am found, was blind, but now I see.' "

Emmy had never paid any mind to the lyrics before, despite the many times she'd heard them. She closed her eyes and listened, attuned to them for the first time. They rolled over her like the warm, salty surf on a Galveston beach, each wave heavy with import just for her, each word filled with meaning, like a precious gift discovered. They filled her with peace and an unfamiliar emotion that lifted and thrilled her in ways her trysts with Daniel never had. She raised her face to the sun, surrendering the whole of her being to the overwhelming feeling, allowing it to carry her away.

"Miss Emmy?"

She opened one eye. Nash stared down at her, and she smiled at his worried frown. Still warmed by the joy bubbling inside, she leaned toward him and lowered her voice to a whisper. "Do you believe in God?"

His eyes widened. "You know I do."

"No, I mean really believe that God exists. That He's not just something to say grace to or an excuse to pass the offering plate. Do you think He's actually out there somewhere. . .listening when we talk?"

Nash sat up straight and narrowed his eyes. "Girl, what's got you pondering such things? It ain't like you."

"Because I believe it, Nash. I really do." She cut her eyes up at him. "Don't you dare laugh."

He shook his head. "I ain't doing no laughing."

Benjamin and Miss Lucille still crooned just over Emmy's head. They had switched to a spiritual, singing now about crossing the Jordan, the two of them oblivious to anything else.

Emmy glanced to see if Buddy and Jerry were still asleep then scooted closer to Nash and lowered her voice even more. "Do you remember the day I crawled out the window in my nightdress?"

Nash rolled his eyes toward heaven. "How am I gon' forget that day?"

She placed a finger to his lips to shush him. Shifting around in front of him, she continued. "Something happened to me out there in those woods. Something so bad I wanted to die from the hurt and shame."

Suspicion erased the grin from Nash's face. "That Clark boy spoiled you, didn't he? Jus' like I figured." Murderous rage seethed in his eyes.

"No! Not that way. And keep your voice down." After a quick look around, she continued. "What Daniel did, he did to my heart, to my soul." The bitter taste of his name drained the joyful warmth from her heart.

"He spoiled me, all right, but with cruel words and callous indifference. The worst part is, I helped him do it. When I realized how he tricked me, used me, I was so ashamed. I hid out in the brush and prayed for the ground to swallow me whole and a fat oak tree to fall in behind me. I never wanted to draw another breath."

Nash averted his eyes. "You ain't got to tell me none of this."

"Yes, I do. Daniel made it look like I chased him, wooed him away from Charity. I promise you on Mama's life it was the other way around. Everywhere I turned, he was there. He made sport of it. He'd catch Charity not looking and wink at me or sidle up and whisper things he shouldn't. Once he caught me alone in the kitchen and kissed me full on the mouth. He worked me that way for weeks, until he had the blood boiling in my veins."

Nash frowned and shook his finger in her face. "Hush now. You don't s'posed be saying such things."

"It's just the truth. Everyone blamed me—Mama, Charity, Aunt Bert. Even Daniel acted like he never said he loved me. Oh, Nash, I hated him so!"

Nash shifted his gaze to something over her shoulder. He grimaced and his brows shot up. "You want to be lowering your voice. You got all these folks watching you."

Emmy realized with a start that Benjamin and Miss Lucille had stopped singing and were staring over their shoulders at her. She whirled to find Buddy raised up on one elbow and Jerry watching, bleary-eyed and openmouthed.

"Go ahead and look, all of you!" she shouted at their blurring faces. "See if I care. I've been gawked at all my life."

Buddy closed his eyes and settled down. Jerry cleared his throat and turned over.

Emmy burst into tears, and Nash drew her to his shoulder. She hid her face against the rough fabric of his shirt until Benjamin and Miss Lucille returned to their song. When she finally dared to peek, Buddy slept again and Jerry, his eyes squirming and lashes fluttering, pretended to.

Unable to rest until she knew Nash understood, she peered up at him. "I didn't want to die because of what Daniel did to me," she whispered. "It was because I saw the darkness of my own heart. Charity, who knew me best, somehow loved me most, yet I betrayed her. I shamed my folks and hurt my aunt Bert." She swiped her nose with the side of her hand. "Even you, Nash. I've treated you just awful."

Emmy watched his face for a reaction, any sign of ridicule. Instead, he pulled a discolored hankie from his pocket and pressed it into her hand, then waited for her to continue.

"I never wanted to listen when you all talked to me about sin. It made me feel funny inside, so I closed my ears to it. But that day I saw myself as a sinner. I talked to God for the first time in my life, and He heard me. I know it, because afterwards I didn't hurt so bad and I didn't want to die anymore." She shook her head. "Oh, I'm making a mess of telling this." She gripped his hand. "Something happened to me out in that thicket. Something real."

Nash sat taller and grinned all over. If he'd been a dog, his tail would've been wagging.

She wanted to stop and ask what he found so funny, but her words spilled out too fast. "When I got to the house, I was so blind-afraid of Mama, I put it out of my mind, but when I woke up the next morning, I felt different. About Daniel, about myself, about everything.

"And here's the strangest part," she said, poking his arm for emphasis. "A lie don't set easy with me at all now. When we told Mama I was in the barn with Rebel instead of in the woods, I barely got the words past my lips."

He laughed then, and she grinned along with him but quickly sobered. "The thing I did to Charity pressed me so hard I knew I had to see her, to beg her forgiveness. That's where I was headed the morning I ran into Daniel in town, and. . .well, you know the rest."

Nash still beamed. "That explains what's so different about you." He snapped his fingers. "I knowed it had to be something."

Annoyance tickled her brow. "I'm glad you understand it. Now explain it to me."

"Don't you see, child? You found religion. The real kind."

The simple words sounded so important. So final.

"I found what?"

"You found Jesus, Miss Emmy."

She shook her head a bit to let the words sink in. "I did? Are you sure?"

Nash laughed. "I reckon the truth is, you got still long enough for Him to find you."

Emmy fell against the splintered board behind the seat, her attention glued to his face. "If what you say is true, what does it mean?"

"It means God always gon' be your heavenly Father."

Papa's stern face came to mind, and Emmy had trouble imagining how that could be a good thing.

Nash tried again. "It means you been accepted into the family of God, and you gon' go live in heaven someday."

Heaven. That mysterious, illusive place Mama swore Emmy would never see if she didn't mend her ways. The prospect of missing it hadn't bothered her one fig. Mending her ways to live in a place she'd never understood required too much energy on her part, and she'd long ago abandoned all hope of ever seeing it. "What if I don't want to go? Why do I need to live somewhere else? If God really cares to make Emily Dane happy, he can let me live on in Humble, Texas, for all eternity."

Nash fell back and roared with laughter.

Emmy feigned a stern look but giggled despite herself. "Now look what you've gone and done. You woke Mr. Pierce again."

Nash slapped his leg and crowed louder. "I cain't help it. You something else, Miss Emmy, and that's the truth. How you gon' compare those rutted trails in Humble with streets of pure gold?"

She lifted her chin. "Unless I can bust them up and spend them, what good are they?"

Nash sobered and wiped his eyes on his shirtsleeve. "Jus'

what you gon' buy with your busted-up streets? Ain't nobody got nothing for sale to measure up with what's waiting for you in heaven. Someday you'll know that to be true."

A smile sweetened Buddy's face.

Emmy smiled in return, wondering how much he'd heard. "Go back to sleep, Mr. Pierce. There's a long ride ahead of us yet. I'll try harder to keep this thoughtless man quiet."

Buddy nodded and turned over. The still-groggy Jerry settled his head onto his arm.

Emmy closed her eyes and leaned against the backboard, trying to imagine Humble's trampled, muddy streets paved with gold. She decided it would be a shameful extravagance and sat up prepared to say so when the look on Nash's face stopped her cold. "Gracious, what's wrong?"

He had to swallow first, his jutting Adam's apple rising and falling just over her head. "Miss Emmy, we might be about to see heaven a mite sooner than we expected." He pointed, his terrified stare fixed on something behind them.

Dread of the unknown settled in the pit of Emmy's stomach. She tracked the line of his muscular arm to the tip of his trembling finger. At first she saw only a flurry of motion in a raised cloud of dust. As they drew nearer, she made out the silhouettes of what had to be men on horseback hastening their way, but they didn't look quite right somehow.

"What on earth, Nash? Are those men?"

"Miss Emmy, I got me a good hunch they's devils." He gripped the toe of Buddy's boot and gave it a shake. "Wake yourself, Mistah Pierce. We got company."

Buddy came up fast, turning to look behind them to where Nash pointed. "You think they're coming for us?"

Emmy took comfort from the strength in Buddy's voice, but his words made her chest ache with fear. The approaching men shouted and whooped like Indians on a raid. They were near enough now to count. Six. . .no, seven riders, closing fast.

Jerry, fully alert, gripped the edge of the tailgate. "We might have a delay in our trip."

Nash scrambled to his knees and leaned forward. He rubbed

his eyes hard, as if he couldn't believe what he saw, and then rubbed them again. "Naw, suh, Mistah Ritter. We got us worse than any delay. We got a mess of pure trouble." His voice came out strained, as if his throat had gone dry.

Buddy glanced at him. "Calm down, Nash. Probably just young bucks on a lark."

Emmy had never seen Nash's eyes so wide. Even the whites bulged from his face.

"Naw, Mistah Pierce, them ain't bucks on a lark. They got sheets on they heads. We all dead men."

Miss Lucille found her voice. Ice filled Emmy's veins at her words, shot through with fear. "Help us," she hissed. "Lord, help us all!"

CHAPTER 30

Lord, help us all!"

The tortured cry rang through the parlor like a pronouncement of doom. Charity's head jerked up. Mama hovered at the head of the stairs, the picture of overstated tragedy. Still barefoot, she had at least donned the pale blue dress Mother Dane had bought for her to wear to the wedding.

Mother Dane exchanged a quick smile with Charity before she crossed to the bottom landing. "What's the matter now, Bertha Maye?"

Charity drew up her shoulders. Mother Dane must be feeling exceptionally brave.

Mama scowled down at her. "What do you think is the matter? I declare, you must be sleepwalking half the time." She caught their smiles and descended the stairs in a huff, fussing and muttering the whole way.

She had never looked so nice. Charity knew Mother Dane had pinned her hair, because every strand lay perfectly in place. The lace-trimmed skirt of her new dress stood out, starched and crisp. Another of Mother Dane's interventions, since Mama never pressed her clothes.

Still frowning, she joined them in the parlor, her busy fingers pulling at her collar and plucking at her skirt. Mother Dane slapped her hands away when she reached for her hair.

CHASING CHARITY

"Stop fidgeting and leave that alone. You're determined to muss it before we get out the door. Can't you let yourself look nice for a change?"

"I cain't help it. I'm plain miserable trussed up like this."

"It's a special occasion, Bert. You can let yourself fall apart again as soon as it's over."

"Special?" Mama hissed. "A funeral's an occasion, too, but I wouldn't call it special."

Mother Dane ignored her comment, stepping in front of the hall mirror to primp. "Where's Emmy? I thought you said you could coax her down."

Mama patted her piled-up hair. "I tried. Didn't get very far. She's still curled up in bed, pouting, by the look of it. Wouldn't even speak to me."

"Is that a fact?" Mother Dane balled her fists and glared up the stairs. "Well, if you'll pardon me, ladies, by golly, I think I can persuade her out of that bed."

Mama grabbed her sleeve. "Don't do it, Magda."

The storm on Mother Dane's face blew with full fury. "This here's Charity's wedding day. Emmy ought to be there. Charity should mean more to her than some scalawag of a man."

"Go easy on her now. Daniel Clark is a scoundrel, but I guess our Emmy's in love with him. Don't you see what that means, honey? The man of her dreams is marrying her best friend today. It'd be right cruel to make her stand and watch."

Mother Dane faltered a bit. "Well, it don't seem right."

Mama took Charity's hand. "It is right, and Charity agrees. Don't you, honey?"

Fighting back tears, Charity nodded. "Leave her be. I understand. I really do."

But did she? She never imagined her best friend would be absent from her wedding. Who cared if Emmy found it hard to watch? It was a miserable day for everyone concerned.

Except Daniel, of course. Somehow he always got what he wanted. Right now he wanted Charity. She had to wonder how long it would last. The one thing she knew for certain, with Emmy present or not, she would get married today. Only a miracle could save her now, and no miracles were visible on the horizon.

She put her arms around Mother Dane and Mama, her gaze going from one dear face to the other. "So that's it, then. Let's get going, ladies. It's time."

Mama pulled her close. "Oh, daughter! I can hardly bear this. It feels like doomsday."

Charity rubbed her back and kissed her cheek. "It's the only way, Mama. It's God's will, I think."

Mama sniffled. "You don't sound too sure."

She made a wry face. "I'm afraid it's the best I can do."

Staring down at Mama's feet, Mother Dane sighed. "I thought I felt those long toes underfoot. You going to your daughter's wedding without shoes, Bertha?"

" 'Course not. What do you think I am, some loutish hick? My boots are on the back porch. I left them there last night after I fed the chickens."

"Bertha!"

"Well, I couldn't bring them in after I stomped around in the coop. They was covered in poo. I'll slip into them on the way out the door."

Mother Dane held her ground. "You'll do no such thing."

"Why? They're dry now. A little beating and scraping should take care of the droppings." She rubbed her chin. "Ain't much I can do about that smell though."

Mother Dane gaped at Mama, her jaw slack.

A giggle rippled in Charity's chest, exploding into a laugh. She doubled over and laughed so hard she couldn't tell if mirth or madness had taken her—and she didn't care. First Mama, then Mother Dane caught it and howled along with her. The three of them clung together in the middle of the parlor, gasping for breath and struggling to hold each other up.

Mama straightened first, her face a broad grin. "We'd better take care now. Last time this happened we ended up bawling."

Charity struggled to compose herself. She stood up, smiling and wiping her eyes. "Not this time, Mrs. Bloom. Only happy tears allowed on my wedding day."

At the stricken look on both their faces, she hurriedly explained.

"Listen, you two, my fate is in God's hands. I'm all right with that. If God doesn't want me to marry Daniel Clark, it won't happen. Can't you put your faith there, too?"

Mama gazed up at her and nodded, then whispered the words she had uttered from the top of the stairs, only this time they were more of a prayer. "God, help us. God, help us all."

Mother Dane snatched Mama's arm and turned her around. "You march up those stairs and put on the shoes I bought for you."

"They hurt my feet."

"Too bad. You're not wearing smelly boots to your daughter's wedding. Now go. We'll wait for you in the rig."

The mention of the wagon seemed to remind Mother Dane of another weighty cross she bore. "Blast that infernal hired man of mine. He should be here to drive us into town today. I can't help but wonder where he could be." She released a long, shuddering sigh. "After all these years. . .well, I just don't understand it, that's all. I guess I'll never forgive Nash for the way he's let me and Emmy down."

"Miss Emmy!" Nash shouted. "Get yourself up under that seat!"

For once the girl seemed too scared to argue. Nash would be sure to thank the good Lord just as soon as they were out of this mess. He only hoped he wouldn't be thanking Him in person. Miss Emmy scrambled under the buckboard seat, and Nash covered her in burlap bags.

"Benjamin, hand your mama back this way so's I can get her hid."

Mr. Ritter shot forward to help Miss Lucille swing her legs past her son. Together, he and Nash pushed her down to lie beside Emmy.

"Sorry, ma'am," Nash said softly before he spread a smelly bag over her face.

Mr. Pierce turned from watching the riders close the gap between them. He nodded toward the women. "I'm not sure how much good that'll do. They've seen them by now."

Ignoring him, Nash whirled toward young Benjamin "Son,

you best drive this rig like you ain't never drove before." Though he shouted, his voice echoed in his ears like it came from the bottom of a rain barrel. He skittered up behind the boy's tense back and yelled louder. "Don't you stop no matter what. You hear me now?"

Benjamin answered by laying his whip across the lead horse's flank. The animal leaped forward and strained at the harness, his hooves pounding the hard-packed trail. The other horse had no choice but to speed up, too.

They hit a rut that nearly tossed everyone over the sides, bringing a loud wail from one of the women. The next hole was worse, and the sharp crack of splitting wood came from under the bed.

"It's no good," Mr. Ritter hollered from where he sat. "If that was the axle, this thing won't hold together. We have to stop."

"He's right," Mr. Pierce called, his eyes fixed on Nash. "We can't outrun those riders. We'll have to face them sooner or later."

Fear clawed Nash's throat. He had to make these fool men understand. "Easy for you to say, Mistah Pierce. They ain't aimin' to hurt none of you white folk."

"I won't let them hurt you, Nash."

"Then they gon' hang you, too."

Mr. Pierce had the audacious brash to smile. "Those men won't be hanging anyone. They're just trying to scare us a little."

"You ain't from the South, is you, mistah? We already scared, and they know it. No, suh. If they catch us, they's gon' kill us."

A bullet whizzed through the back of the buckboard, narrowly missing Mr. Pierce and wiping the grin clean off his face.

Before Nash could recover from the shock, a hooded rider on a fast horse caught up and pulled alongside. Nash braced for a bullet, but the man passed them by without a glance. To his horror, the rider swung from his mount onto the back of the lead horse and struggled to rein him in.

Benjamin stood up and lashed at the intruder with his whip, showing courage Nash knew he didn't have—courage or the foolishness of youth. Nash had lived longer than young Benjamin, long enough to learn how harsh the penalty for such an act, and how cruelly delivered.

No matter how hard Benjamin struck, the man held on and eventually stopped the horse. The wagon pulled up with a shudder.

Amid the mad laughter and shouting of the veiled gang, Nash thought he heard Miss Lucille let go an agonized whimper. He wondered if the dread in her heart matched his own, wondered if Benjamin knew enough to be afraid.

Mr. Pierce lurched to his feet and faced the riders. "Whatever you men are looking for, you won't find it here."

One of them spurred his mount forward. "I ain't so sure about that, mister."

"You've made a mistake. We're carrying nothing of value."

Through holes cut in the makeshift hood, the man aimed a hard stare at Nash. Nash dropped from his knees to his backside and willed himself small, thinking it better to pose no threat.

"Ain't no mistake," the flinty-eyed devil sneered. "I'm looking at what we're after. But you're right about one thing. It ain't worth much."

The other men hooted and catcalled, and all of them edged closer to the wagon.

Mr. Ritter stood up beside Mr. Pierce and turned his pockets inside out. "We got no money. See?"

The man cocked his gun and leveled it at him. "You just keep those hands still."

Mr. Ritter frowned and answered boldly, but Nash heard the tremor in his voice. "We don't want any trouble. We're nothing but a band of travelers headed for Humble to look for work."

The stone-cold eyes swung to Nash again. "Well, you see, that there's your problem. Me and the boys don't much care for your choice of traveling companions."

The lone rider who had stopped them jumped down from Benjamin's horse and sauntered back to where Benjamin still stood with the whip in his hand. Violence and hatred marked his haughty stride. "That's right," he said. "We don't care for them at all. Especially this one."

"This" spewed out like a curse as his hands closed around the boy's leg and pulled, jerking him off his feet. Benjamin fell down hard, crying out in pain when his back struck the buckboard seat.

Miss Lucille screamed, a mix of fear and rage in her voice. The hateful man jerked off his hood and hopped onto the side of the wagon, a loathsome grin on his face. "Well now, what we got here?"

Nash saw he was no more than an overgrown boy, which explained his reckless manner.

The lead rider growled in frustration. "What are you doing, Jackie? Put that back on."

"Why? It don't matter none if they see me. They won't be around long enough to talk about it." He pushed dirty blond hair from his eyes and leered at Nash. "Ain't that right, boy?"

Nash hung his head and tried to come up with the answer they wanted. A hard kick against the side rails rattled the rig and brought him to quick attention. "Yes, suh, that's right."

"You best pay attention when I'm talking to you, boy."

Nash raised his head, but it was hard to bear the contempt on the smug young face.

The brash fool looked over his shoulder. "See there, fellers? He knows I'm right. I can see it in them big eyes of his. He knows he won't be around to tell any tales."

His cruel laugh chilled Nash on the inside. When he turned again, his face had changed, and Nash wished the hatred and cruelty would come back. In its place he saw dark mischief and the glint of evil desire.

His smile widened. "Now then, Big Eyes, let's see what you got stashed under that seat."

The boy swung aboard the wagon and pulled the burlap off the women in one quick jerk.

Miss Lucille screamed again. Dread whitewashed Miss Emmy's face.

"Well, I'll be!" he shouted then winked at Mr. Pierce. "And you said you weren't carrying nothing of value."

He grabbed Miss Emmy's arm, so hard she yelped, and dragged her from under the seat. As he pulled her past Miss Lucille, she glanced at Nash, her eyes pleading for help. It was the last thing he saw before his world faded into white-hot rage and swinging fists.

CHAPTER 31

Charity looked around the small chapel. The room hadn't changed, though it held less people than the last time she'd been there. Her gown was the same, but this time, instead of feeling like a bride, she could hardly stand to look at the dress–a sentiment that extended to the ecstatic groom at her side.

A smiling country preacher stood ready to sign the marriage license, the same diminutive man who had gazed at her with pity on that other wedding day. Charity knew by the way he beamed at her now, he considered the impending ceremony to be reconciliation, the righting of a terrible wrong. Well, it was true, wasn't it? Marrying Daniel would make things right, but in a way the preacher might never suspect.

He lowered his pen to the document with a flourish, oblivious to Charity's misery. Desperate, foolish thoughts filled her mind as she watched him sign her doom.

Why couldn't he sign in pencil the way Papa always had? Then I could erase the signature legalizing this union. . .and use the same eraser to rub the smile off Daniel's face and the misery from Mama's eyes. After that I would use it on my mind to obliterate all memory of this wretched day.

Maybe that's why Papa preferred a pencil. Ink was so final, so permanent. It left no room for changing your mind.

Daniel nudged her alert with his elbow. She struggled free of her musings to find both men gazing expectantly at her.

The preacher cleared his throat. "Would you like for me to repeat that?"

She warmed clear to her toes. "I guess you'd better."

He adjusted his glasses and glanced at his notes. "Very well, then. Charity Bloom, will you take this man to be your lawfully wedded husband, to have and to hold. . ."

Despite herself, she lost focus again. Something niggled at her from just beneath the surface. A matter of great importance, to be sure, but she couldn't quite get a bead on it.

This time Daniel buried his elbow with some force, hard enough to make her gasp. "Wake up, sugar. You're supposed to say something here."

She stared up at him but couldn't see his face for the vivid image that, until that moment, had lurked in the dark recesses of her mind. A picture that loomed before her now, bathed in white light.

"Daniel, I–"

"Just say, 'I will,' Charity. That's all you have to say, and then it'll be my turn." His eyes begged her to speak.

She spun on her heels instead and sought her mama's face.

Mama stood as if pulled by an overhead string.

Charity stepped off the platform and swept up the aisle, her eyes locked on her mama's as she passed. She had a second to wonder if the gaping mouth and raised brows signaled panic or relief.

When she bolted for the door, Daniel followed. He caught up with her there and latched onto her arm, pulling her up short. "Why are you doing this? You want to hurt me, is that it?" He whirled her around to face him. "That's it, right? You're taking your revenge for what I've done."

"That's not it at all. I just need some time."

His expression turned pleading. "Honey, please don't do this. I said I was sorry for hurting you. I'll do anything to make it up."

Charity narrowed her eyes. "If that's so, then turn me loose. There's something I have to do first. I'll be back within the hour. I promise."

Hope washed over his face. "And then you'll marry me?"

She lowered her voice and told the truth. "I don't know yet."

The words sharpened his tone and fanned a blaze in his eyes. "Hold up there, little girl." His fingers dug into her arm. "I gave up everything for you—my parents, my inheritance, my whole life. What do you mean you don't know?"

Charity winced and tried to pull away. "Stop it, Daniel. You're hurting me."

"Turn her loose, boy," Mama growled behind them, "if'n you value your life." Her tiny body trembled with rage, and her mottled face held a warning. Mother Dane stood with her, adding weight to the threat.

The preacher stepped around the women and glared at Daniel's grip on Charity's wrist. "I don't know what's going on here," he said in a low voice, "but, son, you'd be well advised to let go of her arm."

One by one, Daniel's fingers lifted, revealing white marks on Charity's skin.

She spun and raced for the chapel entrance. Before her hand fully closed around the knob, someone jerked the door open from the other side. She gasped and heard the sound repeated in unison behind her by Mama and Mother Dane.

Frantically swiping the tears that prevented a clear view of his dear face, Charity tried to say his name. It came out an incredulous whispered question. "Buddy?"

His eager eyes looked everywhere at once, taking in her dress, the chapel, and those gathered behind her. When they finally settled on her face, they held a mixture of panic and pain. "Tell me I'm not too late, Charity. Please tell me you didn't go through with it."

In two steps she met him on the threshold. Her gaze locked on his, and she touched his battered cheek. "What happened to your face?"

He pressed her hand to his bruised flesh then pulled her palm to his lips for a soft kiss. In his eyes blazed the same emotion she'd witnessed that day on the trail when the well blew in. This time fear mingled with his passion, so the fire raged even hotter.

Charity started to speak, but a shrill voice, as recognizable as her own, broke the spell. "Wait, Charity! Don't do it!"

From across the churchyard, a peculiar apparition staggered in their general direction, twice weaving off course before correcting itself. Charity watched in fascination as the figure stumbled up the steps and lunged for Buddy, using his body to prevent falling headlong through the door.

The creature clung to Buddy and peered around him from the threshold. It spoke again, Emmy's unmistakably familiar voice emanating from a decidedly unfamiliar form. "Don't tell me we're too late!"

Unable to believe her ears, Charity gasped. "Emmy?"

The pale, gaunt face, scratched and dirt-streaked, with one eye swollen shut, hardly resembled her. Bits of hay and woody debris tangled her hair, the blond locks half pinned, half flowing free. Her frock fared worse, the skirt so filthy it made the color uncertain, the bodice stained by a substance that resembled dried blood. The dress was torn in several places, and muddy water darkened six inches of the hem.

Full of questions, Charity drew a deep breath and opened her mouth. An unspeakable stench snaked around her like a fog, so dense it seemed tangible. With every breath it grew stronger, more caustic. Incredibly, it seemed to emanate from Emmy and Buddy, so awful Charity couldn't imagine the source. Whatever the cause, the horrid smell threatened to turn her stomach.

Mother Dane stepped forward and squinted. "Why, Emily Dane. It is you. Have you been tipping the bottle?"

Mama took a step back and pinched her nose shut with two fingers. "Pee-yew. What have you two wallowed in to take on a stink like that? Emmy, this rivals your recent trip to the henhouse."

Mother Dane rested her hands on her hips. "What have you been up to, little miss? And how did you get in this condition? When I left you an hour ago, you were still in bed."

Charity jerked her gaze to Emmy. It didn't seem possible to wind up in such a state between the Danes' house and the church. She recalled the night she had slipped into Emmy's room, ready to bare her soul to a carefully arranged pile of pillows.

You little trickster! You were never in your room. You weren't even in the house!

Her head reeled. Emmy had somehow gone after Buddy and brought him back.

"Pierce!" In the midst of Charity's revelation, a strident voice bellowed at her back. "I might've known you had something to do with this."

Daniel! Charity had forgotten him in the commotion. He stormed from the center aisle to stand at her elbow, his face a furious mask.

Buddy took a step forward. "You're right, Clark. I have everything to do with it." His blazing eyes swept toward Charity and instantly softened. He took her shoulders in his hands and pulled her close in a protective gesture. Unlike Daniel's harsh hands, Charity found Buddy's touch gentle, his fingers a light caress on her skin.

His earnest gaze searched her face. "Emmy told me everything, honey. You don't have to marry Daniel. I'll marry you right now, if you'll have me. And not just to save your land. I love you, Charity. More than I can say."

Daniel swelled like a blowfish and lunged, his fingers clamping down on Buddy's arm. "Get your filthy paws off my bride."

Buddy froze, his gaze locked on Daniel's hand. "Is that so, Charity? Are you this man's wife?"

The preacher stepped from behind Mama and Mother Dane and cleared his throat. "There have been no vows exchanged here today." He spoke the words with authority, in a tone that contradicted his small stature. The pronouncement made Charity's heart soar.

Daniel wailed like a wild thing. He whirled and jerked up a nearby chair, then rushed Buddy with it.

Distracted by Charity, Buddy never saw him coming. She screamed, but it came too late for him to move.

A shadow loomed behind them and a long arm shot out, catching hold of the chair just before it came down on Buddy's head. Jerked from Daniel's grasp, the makeshift weapon rose over their heads and sailed past Daniel, where it shattered to kindling against the wall.

Chest heaving, Nash jutted his chin at Daniel. "You jus' step on back now, Mistah Clark. I done walloped me one mess of fools today. I got no qualms 'bout adding you to the pile." Behind

Nash stood Jerry Ritter. Two people Charity had never seen before hovered just outside the door.

Charity marveled at the change in docile, mild-mannered Nash. He stood with fists clenched at his waist, his feet planted in a determined stance. His big hands were cut and swollen, but from the look in his eyes, that wouldn't deter him from using them again.

Daniel seemed to make the same assessment. His eyes traveled from Nash's hands to his somber face and back again. For all his bravado, it was clear Daniel wasn't ready to take on big Nash, but the ugly snarl and menacing look he shot him made Charity queasy.

"You'll live just long enough to regret this day, boy," was all he said before he shoved past them and out the door.

Nash watched him, his expression grave. "He prob'ly right about that," he whispered. "They gon' hang me now for sure."

"Nobody will hang you for defending a man," Buddy said. "That's all you were doing. I'll make sure no one lays a hand on you."

Mama elbowed her way closer. "You reckon we're finally shed of that varmint?"

Buddy glanced toward the door. "I doubt it, Mrs. Bloom. We'll face that trial when it comes." He held out his hand to Nash. "Meanwhile, sir, I owe you a debt of gratitude."

Nash grinned and stood taller. "Call us even, Mistah Pierce. I wouldn't be here now if'n you hadn't waded in and helped me back yonder." He nodded at Jerry and the younger man. "Same goes for you two."

A huge smile overcame Buddy's grave expression. He pulled Emmy to stand among them. "Don't leave out our Miss Dane, here. She darted in and delivered a fair lick or two of her own."

The little band of misfits exchanged wide, knowing grins. Charity burned with curiosity, but another more pressing matter consumed her. She touched Buddy's arm. "Though I would dearly love to stay and hear more of this adventure, I desperately need to get somewhere, and fast. Mother Dane, may I take your buggy?"

"Sure you can, sugar. It's right outside. Nash can drive you." She glowered at him with flashing eyes. "If he's still working for me, that is."

Nash looked like she'd caught him with an empty pie tin. His shoulders, so broad and proud just seconds ago, rounded to a slump. "Yes'm, if you'll have me."

"All right, then. Take Miss Charity where she needs to go. Mind you, I have a few things I need to say to you, but I guess they can simmer a mite longer." She aimed raised brows at Emmy, who wilted before her searching gaze. "And don't think you've gotten away with anything. There's too many unanswered questions to suit me. We'll have a set-to, the lot of us, when the smoke clears."

"Yes'm, Miz Dane," Nash said and backed out the door.

Charity smiled. Facing an angry fist, even a charging bull, was a whole different matter for a man than standing up to Magdalena Dane.

"Wait just a second now." Buddy touched Charity's shoulder. "I hate to be a pest, honey, but I just proposed marriage to you. You haven't said yes, though I don't recall you saying no, either." He gestured around him. "I mean, we are standing in a chapel." He nodded toward the reverend. "And this fine gentleman came ready to perform a ceremony. The way I see it, there's no sense wasting a perfect arrangement."

Charity's heart swelled. "Oh, Buddy. Yes, I want to marry you. More than anything. I will, too, but there's something I have to take care of first."

Mama had stood quietly long enough. "Charity, what on earth are you saying? You go on and marry this boy. Ain't it just what we wanted? It'll solve everything."

She shook her head. "Not everything, Mama. Let's go, Nash."

"I don't understand. Where are you going?" Buddy asked.

"To the Pikes' place."

Mama gasped and laid a hand to her heart. "Straight into the devil's jaws? Daughter, you cain't."

"I have to. If my hunch is right, it'll pull our bacon out of those jaws for good."

Mama took a determined step forward and locked arms with her. "If you're going to see that nasty, no-good Shamus Pike, I'm going with you."

Buddy latched onto her other arm. "Me, too."

Charity smiled down at Mama then up at Buddy. "I guess there's no talking you two out of it, so let's go."

As they passed Emmy, her burning stare caught and held Charity's attention. Charity never expected the tenderness she saw in Emmy's blue eyes or the grief etched on her battered face, and it pierced her heart. Pent-up tears welled, and Charity reached to take her hand, but her overeager companions herded her out the door.

Mother Dane and Mama crowded up front with Nash, while Charity and Buddy climbed onto the back of the wagon. Emmy, Mr. Ritter, and the two strangers piled into the other rig and struck out after them. Though warmed by Buddy's presence and thrilled by his hand clasped tightly over hers, she was too preoccupied to enjoy it fully. As hard as she tried to focus on Buddy or what lay ahead at the Pikes', she couldn't keep her mind off the mournful look on Emmy's face. The girl was busting to tell her something, but she didn't get the chance.

Behind them, Emmy sat tall in the bed of the old wagon, her back against the tailgate, arms draped casually over the rail as they bumped along the trail. The fact that Emmy climbed into the rear surprised Charity. The sight of her so comfortable there astonished her. She couldn't help but smile.

Charity never intended to arrive at the Pikes' in a caravan, but the situation had spun out of control. Given the gravity of the accusation she was about to make, a few more witnesses wouldn't be a bad idea. The closer they came to Shamus Pike's place, the better she felt about having some company. When they turned down the long drive and headed in the direction of the house, she was downright glad of it.

CHAPTER 32

"Goodness. What's all this?"

Elsa Pike, stationed at the entrance of her home like a dowdy sentry, stared past Charity, her gaze shifting from face to face. Evidently quite confused by the unlikely assembly, a frown replaced her customary smile.

Charity bit back a chuckle. Lo, the would-be queen of Humble society caught at her worst and too surprised to care.

She'd been baking again, her apron a testament to the different ingredients. Flour had somehow wound up on her head, perhaps while scratching an itch, and mixed with sweat to become tacky pearls of dough strung in her hair. The bejeweled strands hung in damp gray rings about her face, as limp as the dignity she fought to regain.

Charity held out her hand. "Good morning, Elsa. My apologies for barging in like this, but I'm here on urgent business."

Elsa took Charity's hand then cringed at the mess left by her fingers. She nodded at Mama and Mother Dane in turn while she offered Charity the end of her apron.

"Bertha. Magdalena. It's so good to see you."

Amy Jane appeared behind her mama, her customary frown intact, edging her thick brows even closer. Unlike Elsa, she seemed oblivious to everyone but Charity. She gasped and pointed an accusing finger. "Will you look at that! She's wearing my dress."

Her smile restored, Elsa reached around to swipe at Amy Jane. She missed. "Well, so she is. What's going on here, Charity, dear?"

Amy Jane pushed closer. "She's come to rub my nose in it, that's what."

Elsa whirled on her. "Amy Jane! Charity has not donned that silly dress and hauled all these people onto our front lawn just to get under your skin. Hush now, and let her explain herself."

She returned her attention to Charity. "Forgive my outburst, child. Go ahead, then."

Now that she actually stood on the Pikes' porch, Charity's confidence waned. She reached for Buddy's supportive hand. "I've come to see Shamus."

"Shamus?" Elsa failed to hide her disappointment.

"Yes, ma'am," Charity said. "My business is with him." She peered past them but detected no movement in the deep shadows of the house.

Elsa untied her apron and whisked it off. "I'm afraid he's not here at present, but I expect him back real soon. Would you care to wait?"

"If you don't mind."

Curiosity had crowded Elsa's manners aside. Her eyes strayed back to the odd assortment of people, mostly strangers, dotting her front lawn. Unable to contain herself, she asked one more eager, leading question.

"Isn't there something I can do for you in the meantime?"

Too anxious to stand on formality, Charity forged ahead. "Mrs. Pike, I know I'm taking disgraceful liberties, but I have no choice. Will you permit me to examine something in your parlor?"

Visibly relieved to be back in the center of things, Elsa swung wide the door. "Of course, dear. I have nothing to hide. Come in, all of you."

Charity's grip on Buddy's hand tightened, and they walked inside, Charity aware that a parade of people slipped in behind them. First Mama and Mother Dane. Mr. Ritter and Emmy came next. She imagined Elsa and Amy Jane brought up the rear. Elsa's invitation didn't likely extend to poor Nash and his friends, and they doubtless waited beside the rig. In the close confines of the narrow hallway, the smell that arose from Buddy and company grew so fierce that Charity feared Elsa might order them back outside as well.

How peculiar the stern expressions on the wall had seemed to Charity the last time she'd walked the dimly lit passage, and how comical Elsa in her unbuttoned, disheveled dress. Now the bedraggled characters who filed past the framed faces made all that seem proper by comparison.

Once inside the cheery parlor, Charity wasted no time. She headed straight for the mahogany working table and yanked out the bottom drawer.

Her mama gasped. "Charity Bloom, what on earth? I raised you better than that." She shot a nervous glance at the parlor door, but Elsa hadn't yet made it inside. "You can't go snooping through drawers without permission, whatever the reason."

"I know, Mama."

"Close it, then."

"Yes, ma'am, in a second." Charity stooped to better see inside, while her frantic fingers searched the contents.

Behind them Elsa cleared her throat, and Mama lost her patience. "Charity Bloom!"

Charity stood, careful to keep her back to the group clustered at the door. Her gaze swept the papers in her hand, taking in the information as fast as she could manage. Then she faced the assembled group, holding aloft the documents and Shamus's writing set.

"I knew it," she said and then drew a deep, cleansing breath. "I just knew it."

Mama's scorching gaze traveled from Charity's face to her upraised hands. "What is that you're holding?"

"Our freedom."

"Explain yourself."

"Mama, I stood beside Daniel and watched that preacher sign our marriage license, wishing he would sign in pencil the way Papa always did, so I could erase it. That's when these two documents came to mind as clear as day." She waved each one in turn. "One in pencil, one in pen, both in Papa's handwriting."

She watched the circle of familiar faces, waiting for them to catch on. "This one"—she passed it to her mama—"is the only one Papa actually wrote."

Mama took it from her and scanned it front and back. "Thad always did prefer a pencil for scratching on paper."

Charity held up the other. "This one, the document Shamus brought to our hotel room, was traced out in ink by someone else."

Buddy stepped up and took both papers. "What's the difference between them?"

Charity smiled. "A big difference." She faced Elsa. "Mrs. Pike, did you know about this?"

Elsa's cheeks had lost their rosy glow. "I must say I'm at a loss. I make it a rule not to plunder through my husband's things, so I haven't a clue what those"—she waved toward Buddy, who stood over the lamp studying the writings—"scribblings might be. Enlighten me, please. Just what is it you think you've pulled from my Shamus's drawer?"

Her eagerness dimmed by the fear she read on Elsa's face, Charity cleared her throat and started again. "Are you aware of a bet between Shamus and my father?"

"A bet?" Elsa frowned and shook her head. "Between Shamus and Thad? I don't know anything about that."

"Did you know Shamus had plans to take our home?"

Mama sputtered. "Take it? More like steal it right out from under us."

Elsa whirled on Mama. "Bertha Bloom, bite your tongue. My Shamus was Thad's closest friend. I'll thank you to remember that."

Mama glared back at her. "He's been no friend to me or my daughter, Elsa Pike. That's what I'll remember." She nodded at the documents in Buddy's hands, her eyes searching Charity's for understanding. "Do those papers mean what I think they mean? Your papa never made no bet at all?"

"He did, but not for our home. Papa only put up the ten acres Shamus leases from us. Nothing more."

"But why would Shamus put his whole place up against ten acres? That ain't sensible."

"He didn't. He only put up ten acres to match Papa's bet. Shamus lied about that, too."

Buddy held up the copy he had taken from Charity's hands. "Then where did this other one come from?"

Before she could answer, the back door slammed, followed by heavy footfalls in the hall. The already tense muscles in Charity's back contracted with dread, and her legs trembled so hard she feared falling. Afraid to turn, she heard him before she saw him.

"What's going on in here?" The booming voice gave them all a start. Shamus hulked in the doorway, hat in hand. His gaze swept Charity, from the hem of her dress to the flowers in her hair. His dark eyes narrowed to slits when they reached her face. "Well now, ain't you a sight."

He tilted a tight jaw toward Elsa, his gaze still locked on Charity. "What are these people doing here?"

Charity's throat constricted and all the moisture left her mouth, but she held her ground. She glanced at Buddy for strength before she took the papers from his hands and approached Shamus. "Mr. Pierce here just asked the origin of this forged document." The confident, steady tone of her own voice surprised Charity. She had expected it to match the way she trembled inside. "You can answer that question for him, can't you, Mr. Pike? I do believe you know."

One glance at the evidence Charity waved in his face stirred a flicker of fear in Shamus's eyes. He shook his head and brushed past her. "You're speaking in riddles, girl. I don't know anything about a forged document. Now tell me what you're doing here or clear out."

Mama squinted and jutted her hip. "Just look at him. Fidgety as a bag of cats. He's guilty, all right." She squared off in front of Shamus, blocking his way. He seemed to shrink before the tiny woman, and Charity knew Mama's size didn't hold the big man in check.

Mama took a bead on Shamus with her eyes. "To think I spent the last years guarding my land from crooked strangers, when all the time the knife was coming at me from behind. Shame on you, Shamus Pike. You've trod on Thad's memory and betrayed our long friendship. I curse the day that river swallowed him up, but at least he ain't here to see what you tried to do to his family."

Tears flooded Shamus's eyes, and he lifted one hand toward Mama. "Bertha, I can explain."

She drew back with a hiss. "Don't you bother. I wish the dead could come back so Thad could haunt you. As for me, I don't care to ever lay eyes on you again."

She glanced around the hushed room. "Well, that's it, then. We're done here." Her head swung in Charity's direction, her eyes bright with tears. "Come on, daughter, and bring them papers with you."

Charity fell in behind her as they filed out of the parlor, but she turned at the threshold to glance back at Shamus, who stood staring down at the floor. "We won't need to call the sheriff about this. That is, so long as you leave us be."

He nodded without looking up.

Buddy's hand at Charity's back urged her out the door. At the wagon, the little group huddled around her and her mama, and Buddy's hand became a firm, comforting arm encircling her waist. Admiration shone from his eyes. "How did you know?"

"Good question, boy," Mama chimed in. "How did you know about them papers, sugar? Or even where to find them?"

Charity gathered the silky folds of her wedding dress in both hands. "Would you believe it? I owe it all to this gown."

Lifting her thin shoulders, Mama peered vacantly at the frock. "To that thing? How so?"

"You see, the day I came out here to offer it for sale, I stumbled over that table and knocked it to the floor, along with the contents of the drawer. I shoved everything back so quickly I had no time to look them over. But I guess the sight of Papa's handwriting on those documents got stuck somewhere in my mind."

Mama nodded thoughtfully. "I never understood Thad's stubborn partiality to a pencil. Not sure he did either." Her eyes brightened. "I reckon God understood. It was for this day, so Shamus couldn't steal from us."

"It's a miracle. An answer to prayer." Emmy, standing just outside the circle of friends, had breathed the awestruck words.

Charity smiled and moved in her direction. "Yes, a miracle. One of many."

Emmy took the last few steps to meet her, a plea in her smoldering blue eyes. "I have something to say to you, Charity Bloom. Something you need to know."

The diminutive Emmy, though shorter than Charity, had never seemed childlike. Yet standing there wringing her hands, her upturned face streaked with dirt, she bore an innocence Charity had never seen in her before.

She nodded. "You'd best go ahead and say it."

"I know you think I lit out after Buddy and brought him back so I could have Daniel for myself, but it just isn't so."

"Then why would you do such a thing?"

"It was for you. I did it for you." Once started, something broke loose in Emmy, and a rush of words followed. "I discovered the truth about Daniel." She grasped Charity's fingers. "You don't really know him. Neither did I—that is, until a few days ago. He hoodwinked us both. Beneath all that charm and polish lies a cruel and vicious man. Please take my word for it. I've seen his dark side, and I love you too much to see you married to him. I set out to bring Buddy back no matter what the cost."

In tears now, she took hold of Charity's arms. "I know it won't earn your forgiveness. I mean, how could you forgive the things I've done? Even so, I had to save you from that mean, no-account scoundrel. I simply had to."

Emmy let go of Charity and fished a lace hankie from her bodice, likely the only clean piece of cloth left on her body, and wiped her eyes. "Of course, it must seem hypocritical of me to call Daniel cruel after the pain I dealt you. What I did was reprehensible."

"Yes, it was."

"Wicked."

"Quite."

"Completely selfish."

"You left out disloyal."

With each agreement, Emmy's tirade grew less impassioned. She glanced up at Charity with uncertain eyes before faltering ahead.

"So like I said, you could never be expected to forgive me."

Charity grinned. "Yes, I could."

"I'd walk over hot coals to make it possible, though I know you could never. . ."

"I can, Emmy. I already have."

Emmy looked as if she dared not hope. "What did you say?"

"I said I forgive you."

"After I betrayed you, humiliated you? No, you couldn't. I've ruined our friendship for good."

"Emily Dane, you've done no such thing. We'll be friends forever."

The words brought Emmy's wringing and squirming to a halt. She stared at Charity in wonder. "But how?"

Charity raised her hands out to her sides. "To be honest, I don't know! Maybe I love you too much, Emmy. Or maybe I discovered I'm capable of hurtful, spiteful things myself."

She pointed toward the house. "All I know is back there I looked at Shamus Pike and saw true regret. He let greed get the better of him, and now he's sorry. I expect he wishes more than anything to undo it, to make it right again." She placed her hands on Emmy's shoulders. "I see that same look in your eyes."

Emmy's fingers clenched into fists that she tucked under her trembling chin. "I am so ashamed. I would do anything to make it up to you."

Charity took Emmy's face in her hands. "Goodness, by the look of you, you already have." She laughed and wiped a smudge from Emmy's face. "Do you know you're an absolute mess?"

"Yes, and I always have been."

Charity laughed. "Honey, I didn't mean. . ."

"It's true, and you know it. I made a mess of my whole life then tried to ruin yours, too."

Charity lifted her chin. "Emmy, it's all right. Besides, if you think about it"—she cast a pointed glance at Buddy—"you did me quite a favor."

She opened her arms, and Emmy walked into them. They held each other in the midst of the damp-eyed circle of witnesses and wept.

Mother Dane and Mama stood arm in arm, sniffing and wiping their eyes, Mother Dane on her lace hankie, Mama on her sleeve.

A tearful Mother Dane motioned to Emmy. "Come over here, sugar pie, and let your mama hug you, too."

Emmy rushed over and fell against her ample bosom. "Does this mean you're not cross with me anymore?"

Mother Dane grunted. "I never said I wasn't cross, little girl. You still have some explaining to do. But we'll worry about that later." She made a face and held Emmy at arm's length. "Land sakes, what foul mischief have you rolled in?" She held up her hand. "Don't tell me. Just climb up on that wagon and let me get you home and in a washtub. You're wanting a good scrubbing."

Buddy's warm hands settled on Charity's shoulders and turned her around. "Can I talk you into that wedding now? I don't imagine that preacher has gotten too far away."

Smiling, she caressed his filthy, swollen face. "As handsome as you are today, how can I refuse?"

When he beamed, she patted his broad chest. "Yet I must."

His smile died and his chest deflated. "This is no time for jokes, Charity. Don't you love me?"

The hurt in his eyes struck deep. Charity took his hands in her own. "Buddy, I love you very much, but I don't want to remember my wedding as the day I was supposed to marry Daniel Clark. I think I'd rather plan our own, wouldn't you? And do it up right from start to finish?"

Buddy's arms went around her again, strong and secure. "You just set the date, ma'am. I'll be there." His brows gathered in a mock frown. "Don't make me wait too long now. You hear?"

From behind them, Charity's mama gave a huge sigh. "So be it," she said then crooked a finger at Nash. "Come on and get me home. If there ain't to be no more weddings today, I need to get shed of these boots. They're killing me."

Mother Dane spun around. "Tell me you didn't–" Without waiting for an answer, she bent and raised the hem of Mama's dress. "You did! Bert, how could you?"

"Magdalena Dane, take your hands off me before you're left

with a stub. I told you those shoes pinch my feet." She raised her foot up off the ground and waved it in the air. "I cleaned these up real nice. They don't even smell."

Mother Dane looked at Charity and shook her head. "Honey, I tried, but you can't dress up a mule's behind to look like anything else."

Mama spit and sputtered. "Least I ain't a mule's behind sashaying around in frilly hats and lace hankies. Don't forget, I knew you long before you married money."

Charity laughed and hugged her mama, her heart so light it seemed she could rise to her toes, lift off the ground, and soar over the treetops. "Don't you worry, Mother Dane. Have I mentioned the fact that my mama is oil-rich? She can afford to buy as many shoes as she pleases. We're bound to find her a comfortable pair to wear to my next wedding." She glanced over at Buddy and smiled. "My *last* wedding."

Mother Dane sniffed. "You might find a pair to suit her, but it'll take some time and likely every cent she's got."

Mama grinned at Charity. "I'd still have a good pair if that feller of yours had ever found the one I lost in the bog." She cocked her head and cackled. "It likely blasted to kingdom come and back when that well blew in. It's probably wedged in the top of a pine tree right now."

Mother Dane turned from giving Emmy a hand up onto her rig. "I can't think of a more fitting end to that old piece of leather. You've worn that pair since you married Thad. I was glad to see them go." She held out her hand to Mama. "Now come over here and let me help you up so we can go home. I wouldn't mind stepping out of my own shoes for a spell. I got a corn on my great toe that's ready to sprout ears."

CHAPTER 33

Charity stood on the top landing of Mother Dane's staircase, holding her breath. The steps spiraling down to the parlor and to the unavoidable confrontation with Mama seemed far too few. Heart pounding, she prepared to take the first one then paused to wait out a brief bout of vertigo. When it passed, she breathed a shaky laugh and steeled herself to try again.

You can do this, Charity. You can do this. . . .

"Charity!"

The strident voice startled her severely, and she almost lost her balance.

Mama stared up at her from the bottom step with horror-struck eyes. She pointed behind Charity. "Get back in there this minute and take that thing off."

Charity clutched at her bodice. "You scared me right out of my skin."

Mama's expression turned hard. And determined. "I mean to scare you right out of that dress. Go take it off. You can't wear that infernal thing again."

Charity lifted the hem of her wedding gown clear of her feet and started down the stairs. "Of course I can."

Mama, turning red now, watched her descend. "Daughter, go take it off like I said. Put on that store-bought one that we picked out."

Charity reached the bottom step and twirled. "What's wrong with this one?"

Shrinking away from her, Mama pointed a trembling finger. "You know what's wrong with that thing. It's hexed. You've worn it for two weddings now, but you still ain't married."

Charity jumped flat-footed to the floor. She felt lighthearted and somewhat daring, as young and carefree as a child. "That fact alone makes it a blessing in my book. Besides, how could something so lovely bring bad luck?" She picked up her mama's tiny hands and caressed the bent fingers. "Especially considering it was fashioned in hope by these dear hands, with love sewn in every stitch."

Mama tried to wriggle her hands free. "I thought we already decided you weren't to wear it."

"You decided. I just went along to save you from fussing. But now I've changed my mind." Charity kissed each of her mama's palms and drew her close for a hug. "The dress was made for this day," she whispered against her mama's hair. "We just didn't know it before now."

Mama raised her face, and Charity's heart caught at the measure of love that shone from her eyes. "This day is all I ever wanted for you, baby. God sent Buddy to us."

"I know, Mama. God is so good. He knows just what our hearts need."

Emmy stood up from the divan and crossed the parlor. "I was about to come up and help with your hair, but, oh my, I see you didn't need me." Her eyes brimmed, and a single tear tracked down her cheek. "You're a vision, Charity."

Charity laughed and pulled her into the hug. "Stop it now. You'll just get me started, and I don't want to cry today."

Mother Dane pushed herself up from the big green chair. "You do look exquisite in that gown, sugar, but I think your beauty has more to do with the joy on your face than how you're dressed. Right this minute you'd look good in a feed sack. There's nothing more beautiful than the glow of a bride in love."

Mama beamed. "The glow of a bride in love? Now that's something she ain't wore to a wedding before." Her bright smile faded. "I just wish your papa was here to see how pretty you are. He'd be so awful proud to strut you down the aisle."

Charity gently tugged a lock of Mama's hair. "We're not going to cry today, remember?"

"You're right, sugar," she said, wiping her eyes. "He wouldn't want us to."

Nash opened the kitchen door behind them. "The rig's out front, Miz Dane."

Mama spun to face him, her tears forgotten. "Well, get in it. You're coming to my daughter's wedding, ain't you?"

Nash looked aghast. "Miz Bloom, you know I cain't hardly do that."

"Oh pooh! Why not?"

He stepped into the room, fidgeting with his suspenders while he searched for something to say. "Miz Bloom, that's a white man's church. How could I do such a thing?"

"Because I asked you, that's how. I don't give two hoots what this town thinks of it, neither. It's the least they'd expect out of Crazy Bertha. We might as well give 'em something new to jaw about." She winked and jutted her chin. "Since Buddy reclaimed my money from that Clark rascal before he took off to Galveston, and since there's plenty more where that come from, I'm rich enough to do whatever I want."

She leveled her finger at Nash. "So you put on your Sunday best and come, you hear? Bring that nice Benjamin and Miss Lucille, too. Today's special. I want to share it with my friends."

"But, Miz Bloom–"

Mama jerked her finger up again. "No buts now. I'll expect to see you there."

Charity slid her arm around Mama's waist and smiled in his direction. "Please come, Nash. Buddy would be so pleased."

Nash looked from face to face, a desperate plea in his eyes. His gaze finally settled on Mother Dane, who offered him no help at all.

"You go on and do like she says, Nash. It'll be all right."

"Yes'm, Miz Dane," he whined. "I'll do like she say. But this family gon' get me hanged." He backed out the way he came in, muttering and shaking his head.

Mama lifted one foot high in the air, struggling to maintain her balance. "Look, Charity," she crowed. "I'm wearing my new shoes."

"I'm proud of you, Mama. They're stunning. How do they feel?"

She frowned and squirmed a bit. "Well, they do pinch my big toes."

Mother Dane donned her wide-brimmed hat, securing it with a long gilded pin, and then lifted her parasol. "Charity, make sure Bertha's hem is long enough to cover them toes. She'll be barefoot before you can say, 'I do.' " Smiling, she opened the front door with a flourish. "Let's us go to a wedding, ladies!"

Charity gazed around the little chapel and tried to commit the scene to memory. It would be the last time she stood among family and friends to say her vows.

Mama sat on the second row with Mother Dane and Emmy by her side. Jerry Ritter and Lee Allen were there for Buddy, sitting tall and beaming with pride.

Mr. Allen's presence presented quite a dilemma for Mama. Torn between staring at him or her daughter, she was bound to develop a crick in her swiveling neck. Even more surprising were the shy glances passing between Emmy and young Mr. Ritter.

Nash and Benjamin stood against the back wall near the door, whispering and twisting their hats. Miss Lucille sat on the last pew with a beautiful smile on her face, clearly at home in God's house, wherever she found it.

The preacher came to stand before Charity and Buddy, his hands clasped at his waist. He smiled at them, but Charity's cheeks still flamed. What must he think, presiding over three weddings in a row, all for the same bride?

He nodded at her and Buddy in turn then cleared his throat. "Before we begin, I'm going to need your full names for the marriage certificate." He paused and ducked his head. "Well, the groom's at least. I have the bride's name filled in."

Behind them Mama cackled. "I reckon you know it by heart by now." She grunted then nudged Mother Dane. "Keep them elbows to yourself, Magda."

Charity wondered how red her face must appear against the

white wedding gown. Buddy smiled in delight and squeezed her hand. Good thing he and Mama were having such a grand time.

The preacher nodded again at Buddy. "And the groom's name?"

"Buddy Pierce." Buddy's voice rang out clear and strong, but he squirmed when he said it and refused to meet the preacher's eyes.

The man frowned. "Buddy's a nickname, isn't it? What's your given name, son?"

"Well, sir, never you mind about that."

His words gave Charity a start. She had asked him the same question on the day they met. His answer then had been the same. She looked at him in disbelief. Was she about to marry a man whose name she didn't even know?

The preacher lifted the paper toward Buddy and jabbed at it with a long, bony finger. "This here's a legal document. I can't put a nickname on it. It won't be official."

Buddy released Charity's hand and stepped closer to the man. She watched in disbelief as he lowered his head and whispered something in his ear. At first, the man of God looked like he'd swallowed a pinecone. He gaped at Buddy until Buddy nodded; then he chuckled and shook his head before he wrote it down.

When Buddy returned to Charity's side, she stared up at him. "Buddy?"

He smiled at her. "Yes, Charity-from-the-Bible?"

So he remembers, too.

"We're about to be married. Don't you think I should know your name?"

"Buddy will do for now."

"When are you planning to tell me?"

"I can't see how you'd ever need to know."

Charity heard scattered laughter behind her and turned to look. The room had stilled, and every person watched.

"I see," she said, lifting her chin stubbornly. "And what shall I call our firstborn son?"

"What's wrong with Junior?"

The assembled guests erupted in delighted titters, Mama loudest of them all.

Charity was done tiptoeing. "For crying in a bucket! Just tell me." She crossed her arms and turned her back on him. "I refuse to marry you until I know your name."

Mama gasped and stood up. "What did she just say?"

Mother Dane groaned. "Surely she didn't."

Mama and Mother Dane pushed out into the aisle and stormed forward, with Emmy just behind them. With each step, the slap of Mama's bare feet on the smooth wooden floor echoed through the hushed chapel.

She clambered onto the podium and latched onto the reverend as if to prevent his getaway. "Don't listen to this foolish girl, Preacher. She'll marry this man or answer to me." She spun around to point at Benjamin and Nash. "Block the door, men. No one leaves this room." Then she gave the man of God a shake. "Stop messing about and get on with it."

"Wait a minute, Mama," Charity said. "I didn't say I would never marry him. Just not until he tells me his name." She whirled on Buddy. "I don't see one thing funny about it, either."

Buddy held up both hands. "All right, sugar, if you insist. Just remember, I tried to warn you. It's a heavy cross to bear. Don't blame me if you really do change your mind after hearing it." He whispered in her ear then stood back grinning.

Charity blinked up at him, sure she'd heard him wrong. "You didn't say Wigglesworth?"

He placed his hand over his heart. "On my honor, Miss Bloom, that's my handle."

She shook her head. "No one would burden a child with that name. Not with a straight face."

"Oh, I doubt my mother had one. Her sense of humor rivaled her passion for poetry, especially the works of Michael Wigglesworth, the seventeenth-century poet."

Mama gave Charity a grave look. "Buddy was right, baby. Some things is better kept quiet."

Lee Allen slapped Jerry Ritter on the back. "Wigglesworth, is it? After all these years, it took a woman to get it out of him. I'd say that's true love, wouldn't you, Jerry?"

Mr. Ritter grinned and nodded. "Can't say I much blame him for holding out."

When the laughter in the room died down, Charity peered into Buddy's eyes. "So you're telling me the truth?"

His expression never wavered.

She nodded and sighed. "Junior it is, then. We owe it to our son to spare him the pain."

The preacher stepped forward, containing his mirth with visible effort. "Shall we proceed? Or is this wedding called off, too?"

Still smiling, Buddy looked at Charity, his expressive brows raised in question. She latched onto his arm and squared around to the front. "Go ahead, sir. I'm ready now."

"Very good." He directed a look over his spectacles at Mama, Mother Dane, and Emmy. "Now, ladies, if you'll please take your seats, we'll commence to marrying these two young folks."

Mother Dane and Emmy filed back to their pew, but Mama held her ground. "If it's all the same to you, Reverend, I'll stay close by until they're hitched." She tilted her chin at Charity. "Just in case."

The preacher nodded and adjusted his glasses. "I guess that'll be all right, but I think it's safe for you to turn loose of my arm now."

Mama stepped back after a warning glance at Charity and a sheepish grin for the preacher. He cleared his throat and began.

"Dearly beloved, we are gathered here today, in the sight of God and man, to join this couple in the bonds of holy matrimony. . . ."

EPILOGUE

Shamus Pike stood on the road outside the church. Red strained at the tether in his hand, pawing the ground and whining to get free.

Before Charity could stop her, Mama stomped off the porch and across the chapel lawn. Charity tightened her grip on Buddy's hand and hurried down the steps with the others falling in behind.

"You're too late, Shamus," Mama spewed. "They're married now. Whatever you hoped to gain by coming here won't work. We're onto your tricks."

Shamus held up his hands in surrender. "No tricks, Bertha, I swear."

"That'd be a stretch to believe. What are you doing here?"

"I come to bring little Charity there a wedding present." The strain on his face turned his weak smile into a grimace. "Found this old dog here over to Magda's again yesterday morning and hauled him home."

The grimace grew wider, and he chuckled. "Weren't even lunchtime before he was right back over there. Ain't no rope will hold him, and I just can't see penning him up all the time."

Mama took a step forward, her fists clenched. "We ain't interested in your present or your story. Now clear out."

Charity gripped her arm. "Wait. Let him speak."

Shamus turned haunted eyes on Charity. "Red's always looking for you, gal. He's powerful spoilt to you of a sudden. I figure this hound has his heart set on where he wants to be, and I can't fight it no more." He held the rope out to her. "You'd be doing me a favor if you'd just go ahead and take him."

Thunderstruck, Charity fumbled to speak. Shamus parting with Red was unthinkable. "Are you sure?"

His expression looked more like a smile now. "Consider him a wedding gift from me and my girls. Please take him, Charity. I think it would've pleased Thad."

"Don't speak his name," Mama hissed. "You ain't worthy of it."

Charity pulled her back. "Mama, don't—"

Shamus held up his hand. "No, let her talk. It's the truth, and she's got every right to say it."

The anguish on his face made Charity's insides ache.

He turned to Mama. "Just let me explain a few things, Bertha; then I'll be on my way."

Charity slid her arm around her mama's waist. "Go ahead, Mr. Pike. Have your say."

Before he spoke, Shamus eyed Mama as if waiting for her to protest. "I don't know if you all know this, but my wife is descended from royal stock."

Mother Dane nodded. "I reckon Elsa's mentioned it once or twice."

Mama grunted. "Once or twice a day."

Shamus lowered his eyes. "Oh, she wallows in it, all right, but it's true enough. Her great-grandpappy was the ruler of some foreign country I can't even pronounce. A real blue blood who left behind plenty of money. 'Course the family pretty much disowned Elsa after she run off with a poor farmer like me."

He got a faraway look in his eyes. "I guess my Elsa loved me in the early days. Back then she made me feel like I was a king myself." He shook his head. "But I ain't never provided for her the way she was accustomed to. Not like she deserved." He sighed. "I told myself if I could just do more, work harder. . ." He faltered and looked away.

Charity met Mother Dane's eyes over Mama's head.

"Folks all around me were striking oil and getting rich, and not a drop to be found on my whole place. You have to understand, it made me feel doomed to failure."

Shamus dropped his shoulders and cried great, gulping sobs that tore from his throat and sent chills up Charity's spine. He cried so hard it forced him to his knees, and he knelt there and sobbed out the rest. "Bertha, I'm so ashamed. I told myself it was for Thad, that a woman alone couldn't manage the kind of money you'd come into, that I would still provide for you and Charity." He covered his ears with his hands as if he couldn't stand to hear his own words. "The truth is, I wanted it for my girls. I needed to see them proud of me again."

Peering at Mama with grief-stricken eyes, he began to plead. "I know it's no excuse for what I done to you and Charity, Bertie, but Lord knows, I'm sorry. Could you ever find it in your hearts to forgive me?"

When Charity started toward Shamus, Red surged forward, pulling free of Shamus's hand. He reached Charity and leaped, prancing around on his hind legs.

Buddy caught the rope just in time to keep the dog off her dress and handed him off to Nash. Then he helped Charity lift the sobbing man to his feet.

Charity wrapped her arms around Shamus. "There now. Please don't cry, Mr. Pike. Of course we forgive you."

Mama planted herself in glaring defiance. "Don't you dare speak for me, daughter. I do no such thing. I ain't forgave nothing."

Whipping around, Charity stared at her in disbelief. "Mama, look at him!"

"I don't care."

Motioning for Emmy to join her, Charity walked to where Mama stood, all tight fists and rigid back. She placed Emmy between them and pulled her into a tight embrace from behind. "Mama, you've always tried to live your life according to God's Word, and you taught me to do the same. Now isn't that true?"

She bit her bottom lip and nodded.

"Don't you remember the passage that says, 'Ye thought evil against me; but God meant it unto good'? Look around you. This day would be so different if Emmy hadn't done what she did. I'm not saying she did a good thing, but God turned it around and used it to bless us. If I hadn't forgiven her, if she wasn't here to share it with me, this day would hold far less meaning."

She gave Emmy one more squeeze then took hold of Mama's shoulders, pointing her to where Shamus cried unashamedly next to Buddy. "He made a terrible mistake, but Shamus was Papa's dearest friend. He came here today to ask for mercy."

Mama shrugged and swayed like a stubborn child. "Maybe someday I'll give it. Just not today. The hurt's too fresh."

"He's asking today."

"I want to," she whispered, slanting her eyes up at Charity. "I just cain't. What he done was too bad."

Charity gave her a pointed look. "And where is that written in scripture?"

Still sullen, Mama stared off down the road for a time before she answered. "I guess it ain't."

"And what is? You've said it to me a thousand times."

Mama dropped her shoulders and sighed. " 'If ye forgive not men their trespasses, neither will your Father forgive your trespasses.' "

Shamus staggered forward, a plea in his hollow eyes. "I can't live with myself no more, Bert. Please grant me pardon. I won't go home 'til you do. I'll hound you worse than Red's done Charity."

Charity slid her arm around her mama's waist. "I think your someday has come. Today is a perfect day for forgiveness."

Mama tensed in Charity's arms. She shuddered and sighed once more before her body relaxed. Pulling free, she turned to smile at each expectant face. "We've laid a feast for my daughter's wedding party over to the Danes' house. I expect to see all of you there."

She squared her shoulders and started across the yard. As she passed by Shamus, she paused, her eyes still aimed straight ahead. "Nash laid a wild hog and some backstrap on the pit. Seeing you're partial to smoked meat, why don't you fetch Elsa and Amy Jane and come on by the house."

Shamus reached as if to touch her arm but didn't. "Thank you, Bertha. I know right well I don't deserve it."

As if they were the words she needed to hear, Mama met his eyes at last. "None of us do, Shamus. None of us do."

She peered up at him for several minutes, one hand on her hip, the other shading her eyes from the sun, until she seemed to come to a decision. "Say, do you know anything about raising cattle?"

The man's shame-laden eyelids widened in surprise. "Cattle, you say? I reckon I know some."

"Tell you what," Mama said. "Let's you and me have us a little powwow on the subject after this shindig, all right?" She waved over her shoulder at Mother Dane. "Come along, Magda. Quit lolly-gagging about. We got us a feed to put on."

Buddy slipped up behind Charity. "We'd best get started, too, honey. It's a long way to St. Louis, and that's after your mama turns us loose."

Emmy took Charity's hand and squeezed it. "I'm going to miss you so much."

"I'll miss you, too, just dreadfully. But I have to meet my new in-laws, don't I?" She patted Emmy's fingers. "Don't worry, the month will go by fast and we'll be home again. We won't stay a day longer than we planned. Buddy has to get back and help Mama run the oil business."

Buddy shook his head. "We won't have that reason to hurry back, sugar." He put one arm around Lee's shoulder and the other around Jerry's. "We're leaving your mama in capable hands."

Charity considered their warm, open faces and decided Buddy was right. Not all oilmen were bad, after all.

Buddy nodded at Red. "Now I guess we'll need someone to keep your old dog in line. Nash, do you mind keeping an eye on that flop-eared critter until we get home?"

Nash grinned all over and tightened his hold on the rope. "Why sure, Mistah Pierce. I'll be more'n happy to."

Charity pressed against Buddy and let him take her in his arms. "So, dear husband, how does the idea of raising champion bloodhounds strike you?"

Buddy smiled. "Harder than raising a brood of kids, I'd wager."

"If they're all as stubborn as Red, you'll win that bet," she said, laughing. "He's just a big old baby himself."

At the mention of his name, the dog strained against the rope in Nash's hand and drew a slow, lazy tongue over Charity's fingers.

Emmy laughed and pointed. "Look at that. He kissed your hand."

Charity frowned and pulled a lace hankie from her bodice. "Goodness, he's forever doing that."

"Sure he does," Nash said, leaning to scratch Red between the ears. "This old boy's a true Southern gentleman. A gentleman gon' always kiss a lady's hand."

Red lowered himself to the ground and stretched his legs out in front. With a contented sigh, he rested his head, letting his big ears puddle in a wad, and closed his droopy eyes.

Nash chuckled. "Least he don't too much mind sharing Miss Charity. You're in luck there, Mistah Pierce."

Buddy frowned. "I guess it wouldn't matter if *I* minded some, now, would it?"

When the laughter died down, Charity feigned anger. "You all make me sound like some old bone to be fought over."

Buddy leaned to kiss her cheek. The way he cupped her head, tangling his fingers in the hair at the base of her neck, thrilled Charity to her toes.

"Not just any old bone, little wife," he whispered. " 'Bone of my bones, and flesh of my flesh,' which leaves old Red there out in the cold."

Charity blushed and pulled away. "Well, at least he's finally calmed down some. Look at him. Just lying there as meek as a lamb."

"That's because his heart be at rest," Nash said. "He finally caught up to what he been chasing."

Buddy pulled Charity close again and tilted her face to his, love so evident in his eyes. "I know how you feel, old boy." He directed his words at Red, but his gaze remained locked on Charity's face. "I know just how you feel."

A stiff breeze picked up, gusting over the church grounds, mussing Charity's hair and flapping her skirts. Unafraid, she raised her face to greet the sheltering wings and welcomed the changing wind.

Marcia Gruver

Marcia is a full-time writer who hails from southeast Texas. Inordinately enamored by the past, she delights in writing historical fiction. Marcia's deep south-central roots lend a southern comfort style and touch of humor to her writing. Recently awarded a three-book contract by Barbour Publishing, she's busy these days pounding on the keyboard and watching the deadline clock.

She and her husband, Lee, have one daughter and four sons. Collectively, this motley crew has graced them with ten grandchildren and one great-granddaughter—so far.

If you enjoyed

CHASING CHARITY

then be sure to read

DIAMOND DUO

available now and

EMMY'S EQUAL

Coming Fall 2009